GRAVE CONCERNS

With his Peaceful Repose Cemetery, Drew Slocombe is determined to make cheap, ecologically sound burials a popular choice. Unfortunately, Drew's gravedigger has just discovered that the body of an elderly woman has been occupying the field for months before Drew opened for business. The police seem to think that her body is that of a vagrant, but for Drew, things don't add up: even if the woman died a natural death, *someone* was responsible for burying her. Then Genevieve Slater turns up wanting Drew to prove the body is that of her missing mother – and Genevieve proves impossible to resist...

GRAVE CONCERNS

GRAVE CONCERNS

by

Rebecca Tope

Magna Large Print Books
Long Preston, North Yorkshire,
BD23 4ND, England.

British Library Cataloguing in Publication Data.

Tope, Rebecca
    Grave concerns.

    A catalogue record of this book is
    available from the British Library

    ISBN   0-7505-1696-8

First published in Great Britain in 2000 by
Judy Piatkus (Publishers) Ltd.

Cover illustration © Rob Flemming by arrangement with
Swift Imagery International Photo Library

The moral right of the author has been asserted

Published in Large Print 2001 by arrangement with
Judy Piatkus (Publishers) Ltd.

Magna Large Print is an imprint of Library Magna Books Ltd.

Printed and bound in Great Britain by
T.J. (International) Ltd., Cornwall, PL28 8RW

For
Adam, David, Esther and Gemma

PROLOGUE

Caroline Kennett was dozing uncomfortably, her head lolling against the train window, her mouth insistently flopping open. She'd rushed to catch the last train and the effort had been exhausting in the August heat. Listening to Aunt Hilda moaning on about how forgetful Uncle George was becoming, and telling endless stories about all her friends and neighbours, had been hard work too. All she wanted now was to get home and go to bed.

The train was sparsely occupied and seemed to be travelling at half speed. The lights had flickered on and off several times, giving the overall impression of a battery running down, a machine struggling to function. Outside it was dark, so she had no idea where they were. Somewhere between Taunton and Exeter was all she knew.

Shaken awake by an unusually sharp jolt that banged her head painfully against the glass, she opened her eyes to total darkness. The train's battery had obviously given up the ghost – or the line had leaves on it – or – or – the rail operators always had an inventive new excuse to hand. They juddered to a halt and a mechanical sigh of hopelessness was emitted from somewhere underneath Caroline's seat.

Outside, it turned out not to be so dark after all. They were in deep countryside, with hilly

9

fields etched by the deep shadows of hedges and trees. A flickering, darting light caught her attention.

Two figures were visible forty or fifty yards away in a field that sloped gently downhill from the railway line. Their pale featureless faces were turned towards the train; they seemed frozen into an unnatural immobility. One held a torch, the other some kind of implement. There were two darker patches on the ground nearby.

Caroline frowned, pressing her face to the window, trying to understand what she was seeing. Everything was monochrome, mere shapes in pale or dark grey. As her eyes adjusted and focused more clearly, the tableau began to make sense, to tell a story. One of the shapes on the ground was a mound of earth, presumably dug by the implement – no doubt a spade. The second shape, almost identical in size and configuration, was – well, it *could have been* – a body.

The lights came on again without warning. The train began to move, slowly and gently. The scene receded into the realm of dream, another reality so distant and separate that Caroline had no feeling of responsibility or connection with it.

She imagined, vaguely, how it would be to tell what she had seen. 'I saw a body being buried in a field. It was somewhere in East Devon. We went through a station soon afterwards, but I couldn't catch its name. Of course, it could have been a sheep or a large dog. Or...' She might say something to Jim, with a dismissive little laugh.

Or she might just forget the whole thing.

CHAPTER ONE

'Imagine a flower pushing up through a grave, fed by the organic matter below. This is a picture many of us cherish as a symbol of our own recycling – our bodies continuing in a different biological form.'

Drew paused and scanned the faces in front of him, letting the image gain favour and overcome any shivers of distaste. The East Caddling Women's Institute ladies were distinctly unsure about this whole subject, he could see. And indeed, his timing could certainly have been better. Two days earlier, a coach carrying twenty-three Bradbourne schoolchildren had crashed in flames, killing eight precious youngsters. A hurried consultation with the WI President had assured him there'd be no grieving grannies in his audience – but even so, it added to his nervousness.

One or two of the ladies were scowling at him; others were wide-eyed with agitation at his imprudent reference to dead bodies. He shook his head exaggeratedly, his face a picture of regret.

'Unfortunately, at the present time at least, the idea of our bodies as fertiliser is pure fantasy. Burials as they are now practised are entirely useless as far as recycling is concerned. They're too deep in the ground. The body is wrapped in

11

a sheet of plastic and often embalmed. The coffin takes too long to disintegrate. Cremation might be a wicked waste of energy and organic matter – but burial is almost as bad.'

Small intakes of breath warned him that he was in danger of going too far. His own youth worked against him at times like this. He squared his shoulders confidently. He'd done this before and knew where the limits were, knew he reminded them of their own sons and thus invited maternal affection. Despite ladylike protests to the contrary, he also knew only too well how fascinated his audience was with what he had to say. With an average age of at least seventy-five, they had considerable personal investment in the subject. And it was a rare individual who could honestly claim to have no interest in what happened to their mortal remains when the awful moment finally arrived.

'It's time we thought about changing this,' he told them earnestly. 'It's time to help that image of the blooming flower on the grave to live once again…'

A movement at the back caught his attention. It was Maggs, standing close to the door, one finger raised as if trying to make a bid at Sotheby's. She wagged it jerkily, the motion small but unmistakable. She wanted to speak to him, and urgently. She'd never have dared interrupt him otherwise. He cocked an eyebrow at her and carried on with his speech. Three more minutes could make no difference to anything, and there were important points he still needed to get across.

'Changes in the great rituals of life – and death – come slowly, and I am certainly not seeking to overturn any dearly-held notions. I'm simply suggesting that you give it some thought. Question your assumptions. For example, it isn't true that cremation is cheaper, or more environmentally benign. Some societies choose cremation for social, environmental or religious reasons, but I am here to make a case for a return to burial, for many very similar reasons. Now, if you'll excuse me, I'll take a short break, and return in five minutes for questions.'

Maggs was waiting for him at the back. He worked his way down one side of the crowded hall, smiling politely at anyone who caught his eye. When he reached his colleague, she took a pinch of his sleeve and led him into the small kitchen adjacent to the main hall. There she addressed him in a whisper.

'There's trouble at the field,' she hissed. 'You'll have to come. Jeffrey insists on calling the police. I told him you'd be there in half an hour. That was–' she glanced at her watch '–twenty minutes ago.'

'What sort of trouble?'

'He's found a body.'

Drew couldn't help it. He laughed: just one brief shout of amusement before taking control of himself. Maggs tightened her mouth. 'Sorry,' he said. 'But you must admit it has a funny side. A dead body in a burial ground.'

'It's not funny, Drew. It's disgusting. Jeffrey thinks it's been dead for months. He found it

13

with the metal detector.'

He glanced distractedly back towards the hall, aware of his unfinished presentation. 'I can't just leave,' he said. 'You know how important this is.'

'Then it's all right to call the police?'

'Why not? Of course we should. Did you say *metal* detector?'

'Yes – there's some sort of necklace. I really think you should be there. It's your field.' Her chubby face glared at him with the kind of reproach only found in girls of her age, when everything still seemed either entirely right or utterly wrong.

'I'll finish here in another twenty minutes. With any luck, the police won't have arrived by the time I catch up with you.'

'I'll wait for you,' she said. 'Jeffrey will have to manage without me.'

The audience's questions were impressively direct. 'Exactly how deep will your graves be?' 'What would a funeral cost, done your way?' 'Has anybody dear to you been buried in the way you advocate?' and 'Have you no respect for the dignity of death?' This last came from a bristling woman in a blue felt hat that had to be forty years old. Some people groaned and one said, 'Oh Marjorie!'

But Drew was delighted. He launched into an impassioned description of the awesomeness of death, how nobody could ever get used to it or properly understand it. He waxed lyrical about the serenity and beauty of a burial ground such as his would be. But Maggs would not allow him to go on. Her eyes remained fixed on him from

14

beside the door at the back, and reluctantly he called a halt, made his excuses and left.

The field was seven miles away. Maggs led the way on her motor scooter, Drew following in his van, the narrow country lanes keeping his pace as slow as hers. They arrived to find Jeffrey standing beside the road, his face pale, muddy boots performing an agitated jig apparently of their own accord. Drew finally allowed himself to believe that something serious was happening. He jumped out of the van and addressed his grave-digger-cum-handyman.

'What's all this, Jeff? Did you call the police?'

The man nodded. 'Should be here any moment. You took your time, didn't you?'

'I was busy,' Drew said shortly. 'You're obviously coping well enough without me. Have you told Karen what's going on?'

Jeffrey shook his head. 'She's not in.'

'So where is it – this body?' Drew peered into his field, where it sloped gently upwards from the road. Its acquisition had come about serendipitously, when a great-aunt had died a year before, leaving her village property to Drew's mother. The cottage and adjoining ten acres of land were only a few miles from Bradbourne, where Drew and Karen had been living. Encouraged by both Karen and his mother, Drew had wasted no time in putting into practice his ideas for a natural burial service. Increasingly uncomfortable working for a traditional undertaker, he had leapt at the chance to set up on his own.

15

Three months ago, they had opened for business. Planning permission had been less difficult to obtain than they'd expected, and media interest had been substantial. Drew had been interviewed on local television and national radio, and continued to be in demand as a speaker. The inhabitants of the hamlet of North Staverton, being on the whole no-nonsense rustic folk with few anxieties about death and its trappings, had adapted to the change of use of Little Barn Field with surprising equanimity. Tucked away between the river and the railway, clustered around the large and relatively modern North Staverton Farm, a handful of properties of the hamlet already lived alongside herds of cows, flocks of sheep and fleets of tractors and agricultural machines passing through their single narrow street. Makeshift hearses and curious sightseers, attracted to Drew's field from time to time, hardly bothered them.

The cottage had been adapted to comprise an office and 'cool room' with a separate entrance, as well as living quarters for Drew and his family. A parking area for funeral business had been created and a tasteful sign painted. *PEACEFUL REPOSE FUNERALS. Natural Burial Ground. Proprietor: A F Slocombe.*

Gazing over his acres now, with the five initial graves clearly visible in the lower right-hand corner, Drew pondered the idea that a previous unauthorised burial had already taken place there, unbeknown to him or his partners. It brought a mixture of feelings: curiosity, annoyance, and an undercurrent of gratification.

16

Somebody had sought out the much-publicised natural burial ground of their own accord; whatever the unpleasant truth of the matter turned out to be, it did at least show some sort of sensitivity in their choice of a place to hide their victim.

'How much have you uncovered?' he asked. 'Maggs seems to think it's still got flesh on it.'

'She's right,' grunted Jeffrey curtly. 'Not that it's sticking to the bones too well.'

Drew mentally dismissed the theory that had come to him in the van: that the body might be centuries old, something of historical rather than human interest. He made an inarticulate sound of disgust, tempered with professional acceptance. He'd seen many-months-dead bodies before, though only once or twice – they hadn't been very appealing.

Jeffrey pointed to a spot near the top of the slope where the ground was uneven and scattered with an early spring growth of nettles and thistles. Drew's field was far from being a smooth green pasture – when he first acquired it, it had been chest-high with weeds and riddled with rabbit holes. He could see where Jeffrey had been digging, the spade still sticking out of the dark loam.

'It's wearing a necklace – that's what set my metal detector off,' Jeffrey said. 'It's not down very deep – couple of feet at most. I unwrapped it down to the shoulders or thereabouts. Long white hair.' The two men, followed closely by Maggs, were walking quickly up to the spot. Drew's thoughts were fractured, skittering

17

randomly around his head. *Why? Who? When?* He tried to piece together the story behind the discovery. What possible reason could there be, other than murder, for such a burial?

'The police are going to want this like holes in their heads,' he commented. 'With all this school bus chaos. They've got eight post-mortems already – we'll be lucky if they get to this one before next week.'

'Trust you, Jeffrey,' said Maggs. 'Why'd you have to go and find it now?'

The gravedigger turned on her angrily. 'Shut up, you – you–'

Drew put out a hand. 'Stop it, you two. Well, this is it, then,' he continued, halting at the edge of Jeffrey's digging and gazing down at what lay at his feet. 'Looks like a woman,' he said.

'It is a woman,' said Maggs, with youthful eagerness. 'She's wearing a dress, see? Funny how a bit of material can last longer than a person's body. And that jewellery – I suppose that'd last forever.'

'Jewellery might, but material wouldn't,' Drew remarked. 'So it looks fairly recent. Pity it's been such a wet winter – makes it a lot harder to estimate how long she's been here.'

He was hardly aware of what he was saying, his gaze held by the uncovered head, revealing the uncompromising reality of what happens to human tissue when left under the ground for any length of time. Parts of the woman's face had come away when Jeffrey had pulled the wrapping off it; grey bones showed here and there. Hanks of white hair stood out starkly

18

against the red-brown soil.

'Not a lot of point in a post-mortem,' Drew went on. 'Unless she was poisoned and they find arsenic in the hair, or she's got broken bones, or she was shot and there's a bullet, I can't see them ever finding a cause of death. There's going to be a serious shortage of evidence on this one, you see if I'm not right.'

The police car was not sounding its siren, but they heard it approaching anyway. Very little road traffic passed Drew's field in the middle of the day. 'Here we go, then,' Drew said, taking a deep breath. 'Brace yourselves.'

The police were initially highly efficient. They erected barriers around the impromptu grave, and summoned the Police Surgeon and his entourage to supervise the slow and careful disinterment of the body. 'She's been well tucked in,' Drew heard him remark. 'Hands neatly folded. All laid out straight, too. Like a proper burial.' Flashbulbs popped and every detail was recorded on tape.

Drew watched the whole process, feeling a sense of obligation to the corpse that he couldn't have adequately explained. As the dead woman was lifted free, one of the men lost his footing in the damp soil and let go; a faint ripping sound gave Drew's guts a nasty twist. The material in which the body had been wrapped came loose, and the garment underneath was exposed. A knee-length dress, stained and shapeless: it rode up over the body's hips. The ripping sound had been that of decomposing skin and tissue separating at the sudden jolt. One leg dangled horribly, like that of a broken doll.

'Christ!' said the man who'd slipped, taking hold of the leg in gloved hands and trying to straighten it. 'This is a right game.'

'Better than those burnt kids,' said his partner, holding tightly to the body's shoulders.

'You won't forget this week in a hurry,' Drew said sympathetically. 'Why is it everything always happens at once?'

The police officer in charge consulted Drew about removing the body to the Pathology Lab. 'You're an undertaker,' he said dubiously. 'Maybe you could do it. Though we usually call Plant's for Coroner's removals.'

'Call them if you like,' said Drew. 'I'm not going to argue.' Despite the all-concealing plastic in which it was now being thoroughly wrapped, the body would be far from pleasant to handle. But after a second's reflection, he knew he should do it. The opportunity was too good to miss. Besides the payment, there was the chance to demonstrate that Peaceful Repose was a serious business, more than capable of tackling anything that Plant's could do. 'No – we'll do it,' he said. 'It'd be daft to call Plant's.'

'Maggs!' he called. 'Get the van, would you? You can drive it part of the way up here at least.' Throwing him a cheerful grin, she trotted off. Having failed her driving test for the second time only that week, she wasn't qualified to drive on the road, but Drew let her practise on the smoother sections of the field, knowing how much she enjoyed it.

The police gave their usual warnings about nobody disturbing the scene, the need for more forensic examination, and the necessity for official statements to be made by Jeffrey and the others. Drew was aware of a strange insouciance in himself and the police officers, rare where dead bodies were involved. He supposed it was partly because this particular body was so very dead, it was no longer human in any real sense. Besides, the numbness caused by the school bus crash was still very much in operation; the whole community was walking about in a state of shock from *that* catastrophe. A single mysterious old woman could hardly evoke much emotion after that. And yet, the reality appeared to be that this unknown woman was a murder victim who had been secretly buried sometime during the past year or so. Sooner or later, Drew was sure, he would be forced to care very much who and how and why and when.

Jeffrey, however, was already anxious to have his role recognised. He began to prattle nervously, as the whole group moved awkwardly down the field towards the van. 'Her flesh's all black,' he remembered. 'Like a sheep been dead in a ditch for half a year. And the bone sticking out, funny whitey-grey colour. Don't smell much, though. Not as bad as a sheep. No maggots, see. Flies can't get down that deep. Those dentures, grinning at nothing – gave me a shock, they did. All pink – not natural.'

'Okay,' Drew tried to interrupt him, 'I think we've got the picture.'

'Must've been an old lady – white hair and false

teeth.' Jeffrey cocked his head at the police, who were preparing to depart. 'Have to be a post-mortem now, eh?'

'That's right, sir,' said an officer flatly. 'And an inquest,' he added.

Drew rubbed two fingers hard across his brow, aware of a subtle pain developing. 'What a business,' he said.

'Mmm,' agreed the policeman. 'Can't recall anyone local reporting their old Mum missing – nothing nice and easy like that.' He adopted a gloomy expression. 'I hate these "identity unknown" cases. She's probably some Wino Winnie, got herself bumped off in an argument over a bottle of meths.'

Now Drew had another part of the answer to his earlier self-questioning. Just an old woman who nobody cared about. Nobody had been searching for her, worrying about her. And maybe she hadn't been murdered after all. Maybe she'd died quite naturally, out in the open last summer, and as an act of unthinking sensibility someone had buried her in the new cemetery. It had a neat touch, a nice logic which Drew found appealing, but he knew, inescapably, that it didn't ring true. *Pity*, Drew said to himself. *It's a pity she couldn't have just lain there undisturbed.* And he cast a look of such venom at Jeffrey that the gravedigger flinched in bewildered alarm.

Drew lingered after the body had been delivered to the Path Lab at the big Royal Victoria Hospital.

The Coroner's Officer, Stanley Sharples, met him in the corridor outside and clapped him on the upper arm. He looked weary and drawn.

'What's all this, then?' he said. 'Someone jumping the gun in your new cemetery?'

Drew forced an answering grin. 'Something like that,' he nodded. 'An elderly woman – the police seem to think she's probably a vagrant.'

'Funny vagrant – wearing jewellery, I hear,' Stanley demurred.

'You must have come across it before,' Drew said. 'Most people, even tramps, hang on to one special possession. It's human nature, isn't it? Even if you're living rough, hooked on drugs, as deep in the pit as you can get, you need something special to call your own. Especially women. Some lover probably gave it her fifty years ago.'

Stanley was only half-attending; Drew was irritated. Never mind that the man was in the middle of the worst disaster of his career, it was still his job to give this new case his full concentration.

'Or maybe it wasn't hers. Perhaps it's a parting gift from whoever buried her?' he went on. 'Somebody cared enough to lay her out properly, wrap her up, and bring her to my field. If they didn't care, they'd just have dumped her somewhere. Maybe they wanted her to have something nice in there with her.' Drew had seen countless instances of the modern version of grave goods; families put a bizarre assortment of objects in the coffin with their dead relatives.

'Don't get complicated about it,' the Coroner's

23

Officer begged. 'Anyway this one's going to have to wait. We haven't got time for it now. God knows, Drew, we're stretched to the limit here at the moment. I've just been talking to the mother of two boys, both killed in the back of that bus. She hasn't got any other kids. Can you imagine what that's like?' There were tears in Stanley's eyes. Drew accepted defeat.

'Okay,' he said, a heavy knot of pain and fear collecting in his chest. He didn't want to imagine what it was like to lose your family in a ghastly accident. He didn't want to listen to Stanley any more. 'Okay,' he repeated. 'I'll just wait to hear from you, then. In a week or two.'

'Don't worry son,' Stanley told him. 'We'll get around to her eventually. She isn't going to go anywhere, is she? And I can tell you already, we're not likely to find much of any use. It's going to be one that gets away – lack of sufficient evidence. Death by person or persons unknown. Usual platitudes. Even if we'd had nothing else to do, it'd come to the same thing in the end.' He eyed Drew ruminatively for a moment, remembering his past reputation. 'So – don't you go stirring things up, there's a good chap. None of your romantic amateur detecting on this one.' He smiled wanly. 'Tell you what – I'll put in a word with Fiona at the Council – make sure you get the funeral when it happens. How's that?'

'Thanks,' muttered Drew. 'But I shouldn't hold my breath – right?'

'Right,' said Stanley.

CHAPTER TWO

There was a police presence of one sort or another at the field for the next three days. Every atom of material possibly emanating from the dead woman was carefully removed from the shallow grave. 'If it hadn't been for that necklace, we might never have found her,' said Jeffrey thoughtfully. 'I was all set to give this patch a miss, as it happens. Didn't fancy being stung by the nettles.'

'What changed your mind?' Drew asked him.

Jeffrey cocked his head. 'Just one of those things,' he offered non-committally.

'And why were you out there with a metal detector in the first place?' Drew enquired belatedly. 'What's the idea?'

Jeffrey met his gaze. His strong shoulders and stalwart neck betrayed a life spent as a labourer. Drew had poached him from North Staverton Farm, despite not being able to offer steady work. So far he had dug five graves in the field and trimmed back the hedges on three sides. The railway line formed the upper boundary, with a wire fence maintained by the rail operators to augment the somewhat patchy hedge on that side. The Planning Officer had stipulated a stout boundary wall or fence, but had been persuaded that the six-foot-high hedge of mixed thorn, holly, bramble and briar was thick and prickly enough to keep intruders at bay and conceal the field's contents from over-sensitive passers-by.

At sixty-three, Jeffrey was apparently philosophical about almost everything. He lived simply, in a stone cottage with few facilities, on a quiet road half a mile out of the village. 'My granddad was a gravedigger,' he'd said, on his first encounter with Drew. 'Don't much hold with cremation myself. Burial's got to be decent, mind. Dignified.' As far as Drew could now recall, that had been sufficient reference and the post had been offered and accepted with scarcely any further discussion.

'I got thinking,' Jeffrey explained slowly. 'It's the law, you know – once a bit of ground is used as a grave, it mustn't ever be disturbed again. So it seemed to me, I should just make sure we weren't missing any treasure. Old coins and the like. See?'

Drew blinked dubiously. 'But wouldn't you find any precious objects anyway, when you were digging the graves?'

Jeffrey cast his gaze over the ten acres, and smiled wryly. 'Won't be here to see the whole field filled up,' he said. 'It's a hobby of mine, anyhow,' he added.

Drew didn't pursue it; he was just then trying to concentrate on recovering some of the momentum he felt he'd lost with the WI ladies by sending them a packet of carefully-worded leaflets.

In the following days, only moderate local interest was kindled by the finding of the body.

The weekly newspaper devoted almost all its space to stories about the dead and injured schoolchildren, but they found a few inches for the Peaceful Repose find at the bottom of an inside page. 'This has to be good for business,' Drew commented over breakfast, feeling rather gratified until Karen pointed something out that made his blood congeal.

'People'll think it's all a publicity stunt,' she said idly. 'They'll think you put that body there and then staged a dramatic discovery.'

He stared at her in horror. 'They wouldn't!' he gasped. 'That would be ridiculous.' Scanning the report, he read aloud: *Peaceful Repose Funerals opened their "environmental" cemetery three months ago, with a view to offering burials in a natural setting, with little of the ritual or trappings of modern funerals. Funerals cost approximately half the price of more traditional versions. To date, it is understood that five burials have taken place in the cemetery.* That's pretty positive don't you think? Nothing to imply devious practices.' He wiped a dramatic hand across his brow. 'You had me worried there.'

'Well, they wouldn't say it, would they?' she laughed scornfully. 'But there'll be jokes going round – you see. If nothing else, Daphne Plant'll have a go at spreading the poison.'

'Then we'll have to do all we can to identify this woman, won't we? If the police could work out how she died and where those dentures and the necklace came from, they'd stand a better chance of matching her with someone from the Missing Persons file. Though I can't think quite how–'

'Read that bit again – about who they think she

27

might be,' Karen interrupted.

Drew readily complied, pleased that his wife was taking an interest, despite her unsettling suspicions. 'Okay. Let's see – *A police spokesman revealed that the body is that of an elderly woman, approximately five feet eight inches tall, with long white hair and a complete set of false teeth. She was wearing a summer dress, and had been wrapped in a patterned cotton sheet. There are no obvious signs of violence, and a full post-mortem examination will be required before a cause of death can be established. In the light of the terrible tragedy at the weekend, this will not take place for some days. Meanwhile, the police would very much like to hear from anybody who might be able to assist in identifying the woman.*'

'In other words, they're completely stuck,' Karen summarised. 'I'm not asking for gory details, but I assume there's not much left of her face?'

'Nothing you'd want to take photos of for public consumption,' Drew agreed. 'And they're not going to go to much effort or expense to reconstruct it either. It sounds to me as if they've already decided she's just a homeless old dropout – or some mental patient let loose in the community, with no friends or family to report her missing.'

'Poor old girl,' Karen sympathised. 'Not a very dignified end – left anonymously in a field. Even a lovely field like yours,' she added hastily.

'It's not that simple, though,' Drew persisted. 'She didn't bury herself, did she? There's a mystery here, however you look at it.'

'And we all know how much Drew Slocombe

28

loves a mystery,' Karen sighed. 'Why do I get the feeling that this is only just beginning?'

'I can't imagine,' he said, widening his eyes in mock innocence. 'But I have the same feeling myself.'

Karen's answering smile was cynical. 'Oh, drat!' she sighed, as from upstairs a familiar wail announced that their small daughter was ready for her second meal of the day.

'I'll get her,' Drew offered, already halfway out of the room. 'Where's that girl?' he chirruped as he mounted the stairs. 'Where's that Stephanie Slocombe?'

It was with a familiar sense of unease that he found the image of the decomposing body from the field transposed onto that of his little girl, as she stood red-faced and wobbly, clutching the bars of her cot. It was an inevitable concomitant of his job that this happened regularly – death pushing life to the outer edges of his mind, casting its pall like a shadow. Usually he managed to push it away, or to put it to positive use, as a reminder to enjoy and celebrate each moment, but all too often he found himself acutely aware of the skull beneath the skin.

Which was, perhaps, another reason why he was going to have to find out who and why the dead woman was in his field. Until he did, he feared that she was going to haunt him.

Stanley's plea to leave well alone rang in his ears as another irritant. Drew's relationship with the police was uneasy at best, now he had set up in business on his own. When he'd left his secure job at Plant & Son Funeral Directors, rocking the boat by becoming a competitor, a lot of people had been concerned – or worse. Even if he only attracted twenty funerals a year away from his former employer, he would make quite a hole in her profits. The conventional Coroner's Officer was firmly on Daphne Plant's side, missing no opportunity to have a dig at Drew Slocombe and his Peaceful Repose Funerals. Drew's youth only made it worse: at barely thirty, he had time and energy to change hearts and minds on a substantial scale, and the reactionary funeral industry was uneasy at what the future might hold. So far, the American influence was dominant, adding a steady stream of expensive trappings to already blatantly prodigal ceremonies. Cardboard coffins and willow baskets remained the choice of a tiny minority. But everyone could sense the seesaw tipping inexorably the other way, the fickle public poised to embrace the plainer, simpler style. And everyone knew that Drew was doing his best to shift that balance.

The newspaper reported little progress the following week. Much of the relevant article merely repeated, with a few embellishments, the original facts.

Police efforts to discover the identity of the dead woman found in the new alternative burial ground at North Staverton have so far proved unsuccessful. Three Missing Persons reports have been investigated, but none of them matches the details of the dead woman. Forensic investigations indicate that she was aged between sixty-eight and seventy-five, about five feet eight inches tall, of slender build and in good health. She probably died in August or September last year. She was dressed in a knee-length cotton garment, and leather sandals. She wore a very distinctive necklace (pictured) which has been traced to Egypt, where jewellery of this sort is commonly sold in souvenir shops. It is made of bronze and is the reason why the body was found – Mr Jeffrey Chanter was using a metal detector in the field when he stumbled upon the remains. It is of no great monetary value. The police would like to hear from anyone who recognises this necklace, or who can offer any assistance in the identification of this woman.

There was a follow-up piece on the local television news that same evening, with the photograph of the necklace included.

'They've still no idea how she died then?' Karen queried.

Drew shook his head. 'Nobody's told me anything. I'm seen as a bit of an outsider now – I don't get the gossip like I used to at Plant's. They've given up digging for clues in the field, thank God. Have you seen the mess they've made?'

'Only from the window. I haven't been in the field lately. Accidentally on purpose, I suppose? The mess, I mean?'

'Probably. They do seem quite keen to get up my nose.'

Karen was knitting, a practice which Drew found amusing, and over which he teased her repeatedly. For Karen it required considerable concentration, with none of the relaxed ease he remembered from his grandmother's endless productions. 'Will she ever wear it?' he asked dubiously, every time Karen held up her effort for inspection. It was a vivid kingfisher blue and grew agonisingly slowly. 'Isn't she going to be too big for it?'

His wife pursed her lips and embarked on another row. 'You could ask Maggs to finish it for you,' he added, incautiously. 'Knitting's another of her endless talents.'

'She should get out more,' was Karen's only comment. Maggs did indeed possess innumerable skills and Drew openly marvelled at her. Eighteen years old, dark-skinned and generously proportioned, she was a person with an undeniable vocation. Officially named Marigold, she solemnly informed every new person she met that she would kill them if she ever heard herself addressed in that way. It was her firm intention to change her name by deed poll, when she could decide on a new appellation. Having somehow blundered into Plant & Son Funeral Directors for a week's work experience at the age of sixteen, she had been instantly hooked. Fascinated by the arcane details of mortuary work, deft with coffin linings, sensitive and understanding with the families, she had almost immediately announced to anyone who would listen that she was going to be an undertaker. To reinforce the point, she left school after GCSEs and begged Daphne to employ her on a permanent full-time basis – only to meet with implacable refusal. Drew had assumed that his boss was unnerved at the prospect of a young and charismatic protégée at such close quarters: a new Queen Bee, stealing her secrets and wooing her customers. Maggs had gone to another local company for six months, before Drew had made her an offer he thought she'd never accept.

'Work for me for two years, on a very small salary, and I promise to give you a quarter share in the business at the end of that time.' Maggs, typically, had demanded forty per cent. When Drew agreed, she had accepted his offer with no further hesitation.

'She must be in love with you,' said Karen sourly, nine months pregnant at the time and in no mood to tackle rivals.

'She's too ambitious to worry about love,' he said. 'This is the New Woman – haven't you noticed? They'll be ruling the world in ten years' time.'

'That body,' Maggs said to Drew the next morning, as they drove together to visit a new supplier of willow burial baskets. 'What's going to happen to her? It's a fortnight now.'

He didn't have to ask who she meant. 'Dunno,' he told her. 'I still see that long white hair last thing at night.'

'It doesn't look as if the police are making much effort,' she sniffed. 'Not when you consider it's a murder.'

'They haven't got much to go on. She might be foreign, an illegal immigrant or something. They'll never find out who she was, if that's the case.'

'She looked a bit foreign,' mused Maggs. 'I mean – the necklace and stuff.' She shuddered. 'I don't like mystery, Drew. I thought they could trace everybody these days. What about those teeth? Don't dentists put a little label on dentures?'

He laughed. 'Of course they don't. Though there might be differences between countries, I suppose. If she's a rich Arab, she'd have gone to some private bloke, probably.'

'If she's a rich Arab, her rich relations would have reported her missing.'

Drew sighed. 'There's not a lot we can do about it anyway, with so little to go on.'

'It isn't right though, is it?' she pressed on. 'They're letting the whole thing go, just because it would cost the ratepayers a few thousand to do a proper investigation. They're not doing their job.'

Drew had experience of police efforts to keep costs down. Perfunctory or non-existent post-mortems, unreliable testimonies accepted as hard fact; a quick trawl through computer records used as substitute for face-to-face inter-views. But this time, he did have a glimmering of sympathy. 'They really haven't got much to work with,' he reminded Maggs. 'And if there's no realistic chance of proving murder and finding someone to charge, you can't really blame them for admitting defeat from the start.'

'But it's all wrong,' she persisted. Drew let her have the last word. In his heart, he agreed with her, and it was pleasing to know she shared his values.

Maggs reached forward to fiddle with the temperamental tape player on the dashboard. The decision to buy a large second-hand Transit van had been fiercely argued, months ago, between him and Karen and Maggs. In the end, the cheapness and versatility had triumphed over the worry that bereaved families would find the vehicle just a step too utilitarian.

'We're going to be haunted by that body until we can lay her to rest properly,' she predicted, after a few minutes' silence.

'You're right,' Drew said gloomily.

There were, of course, more details in the police files than had been revealed to the newspapers. Prompted by Maggs, Drew made a point of calling in on Stanley Sharples a few days later, to enquire as to progress. 'Nobody claimed that body from my field, then?' he began, aiming for a brisk approach. 'How long're you going to sit on it? I assume you did eventually get around to doing a post-mortem?'

'Over a week ago, as it happens. Fitted it in at the end of Friday morning. Lucky we did – you'll have heard about the fire in the third-floor flat on Monday? We just thank the Lord there weren't any kiddies involved. We don't want any more of that for a very long time.'

'So – what did you find?' Drew had learned that with Stanley, the only way was to stick firmly to the point.

'Patience, my friend,' counselled the Officer. 'To be honest, nothing much. Cause of death is just a list of negatives. No detectable poison, no

35

broken bones, no lethal viruses. Various possible flesh wounds, all of which are most likely the consequences of natural decomposition, and nothing sinister. There's a nasty tear – a sort of gash – on her thigh, but I gather our men dropped her at one point, and the leg got damaged then. That's probably all it is. We've told Fiona she can take over at the end of the month if nothing's turned up by then. That's ten more days.' Fiona was the Recreation and Outdoor Affairs Officer for the District Council, who had somehow been landed with the task of arranging funerals for those who had nobody else to do it for them. The default choice was invariably cremation, unless there was a chance of a prosecution against anyone for causing the death, in which case a burial was deemed safer. Then, if necessary a disinterment could always be ordered, complicated and distasteful as this would be.

'It'll be a burial, won't it?' Drew said, trying not to sound impatient. 'I want to put in a formal request that she be buried in my field. It'll be cheaper, apart from anything else.'

'You'll have to speak to Fiona about that,' Stanley said, neutrally. 'We're not at that stage yet, remember. The police're getting a call a day from people whose mums've gone missing, even now. Most of them are forty-five and were last seen getting into a car with a man they've known for some time. Amazing how some folks twist plain facts to suit themselves.'

'How d'you mean?'

'It says, clear as day, in all the reports – this

woman was in her late sixties with long white hair. So these families think, okay, Mum was a bit grey around the edges, on a bad day you might think she was nearly sixty, it's worth a try.'

'They've probably had experience of police descriptions before,' said Drew dryly. 'Wouldn't you give it a shot, if you were desperate?'

Stanley shook his head. 'My mum's been dead for ten years,' he said.

Drew sighed. 'So what's your guess? Will we get an identification?'

'Very unlikely, if I'm honest with you. Not a lot to go on, you see. We think she could be foreign – not that we've any real reason for that. It seems she'd recently eaten a substantial meal – a chicken curry with plenty of rice. Good British fare. Analysis of the body tissue has thrown up one or two collapsed arteries. It's all speculation, but there's just a chance that exsanguination was the cause of death.'

'She bled to death? But there weren't any bloodstains on the clothes.'

'True. Which means we'd have to invent a whole lot of hypotheses, none of which we can prove. So we decided not to pursue it. Not worth starting hares of that sort. She was a remarkably healthy woman, you know. Excellent bones for her age. Everything as it should be from top to toe. Though her teeth must have let her down. She probably would have lived to be a hundred.'

'Unusual for a vagrant,' Drew couldn't resist remarking. When Stanley didn't rise to this, he asked, 'What about the necklace? And her clothes?'

'Clothes were interesting. No underwear – just this shapeless cotton thing. A sort of housedress, according to Helen in my office. And the patterned sheet she was wrapped in was brushed cotton, double bed size, no label or laundry mark. The shoes were made from good leather, Italian apparently. The dentures were fairly well made – they fitted her, anyway.'

'You mean she didn't pick them out of a dustbin?' Drew again couldn't hold back a hint of sarcasm. This time, Stanley reacted.

'What's your problem, Drew? *I* never said she was a vagrant, did I? I'm doing everything I can to identify her. But this isn't America. We don't keep our nameless bodies for years in the freezer on the vague offchance of finding out who they were. Not unless there's a Public Prosecutor insisting on it. Once we've checked all missing persons, and given the public as much time to respond to the appeals as seems reasonable, that's got to be it. There's no evidence of murder, apart from the obvious conclusion drawn from an unregistered burial.' The tirade looked set to continue, but Drew held up both hands in surrender.

'Okay, okay,' he begged. 'I didn't mean to criticise. I know the routine. And I'm more than happy to bury her for you. It just seems a shame–'

'Of course it's a shame,' the Coroner's Officer echoed impatiently. 'Every death is a shame. We do what we can for all of them. But this one's a non-starter, believe me. I've got an instinct for it. Dead six months or more, nobody but you showing any interest…' He spread his hands in a gesture of failure. 'Quite honestly, you'd need a miracle to get anywhere with a case like this.'

At home, life was becoming complicated by the fact that Karen was shortly to return to her teaching job after the birth of Stephanie. She had managed to string her maternity leave out longer than originally agreed, but the summer term was due to start in two days' time, and nobody was happy about it.

'I feel awful,' she moaned, when Drew got home that afternoon. 'I came over dizzy just now, when I stood up suddenly, and my back's killing me.'

'You've been carrying this great lump about, I suppose?' He indicated his ten-month-old daughter, sitting astride her mother's hip. 'No wonder your back hurts if you kink it like that.'

'Hips were designed to have children perched on them,' she told him.

'Well, in that case it's just nerves at going back to work. You look fine to me.' He treated her to a thorough appraisal, knowing how much she enjoyed his full attention. She still looked exactly like the girl he married – wide shoulders, thick hair the colour of polished oak, curves made all the more generous by maternity. But she was paler than usual, and her eyes had shadows beneath them. 'You probably ought to wean the Sprout. You've breastfed for Britain – give yourself a rest.'

Karen put her face down to the baby's, rubbing noses with her. 'Ohhh!' she moaned. 'But it's

39

only once a day, at bedtime. Please, Daddy – just a couple more months.' Together the two females looked at him, the similarity in their faces making him laugh.

'It's got nothing to do with me,' he conceded. 'I'm hopelessly outnumbered.'

'The next one'll be a boy,' Karen promised him lightly. 'Have to keep it fair.'

'No, no!' he begged. 'Give me girls, lots of girls.' He reached out and plucked Stephanie from Karen's hip, and began to dance round the room with her, singing *'Thank heaven for little girrrls...'* making the child squeal with rapture.

Karen flopped onto the sofa. 'But I do feel lousy,' she repeated, when the horseplay stopped. 'And I've got all those lesson plans to do yet. Are you sure this is a good idea?'

The agreement had been that Drew would be responsible for Stephanie's care while Karen was working. He had given himself a deadline two years' hence, by which time the burial ground would have to be attracting at least one funeral a week. Even that would leave them far from affluent. A second child, they'd agreed, would have to be deferred until then.

'We have to eat, love,' he said, suddenly serious. 'And you know what we agreed–'

'I know,' she sighed. 'I just hope you appreciate it. I just hope–' She pressed her lips together, her face tightening with emotion.

'Hey!' Drew examined her with concern. 'What's the matter, Kaz?'

She blinked several times, and rubbed a quick forefinger under her nose. 'I'm being stupid,' she

40

tried to laugh. 'It's just that sometimes I forget why we're living like this. I mean—' She flipped a hand towards the field outside '—they're all *dead* aren't they? These people you're making such a fuss about. Just lumps of rotting meat. Sometimes I wonder about how it all equates – you know? Mouldering corpses weighed against Stephanie's security and my mental health. We've both seen what it's like for women trying to work full time when they've got a young child. It's *hell*, Drew. They're whacked, trying to do it all – and then they feel guilty, resentful, all that.' She laughed again, a grating sound with no humour in it. 'Well, that's got that off my chest.'

Drew put Stephanie down on the sofa beside her mother, and knelt on the rug by Karen's feet. 'I thought you understood,' he said breathlessly, the shock of her words still choking him. 'It isn't like that – the dead can't be just tidied away and ignored. We're *all* going to be dead one day. It makes life so empty and meaningless if you don't show proper consideration for the dead.' He pressed a hand to his forehead, trying to order his thoughts. *Rotting meat,* she'd said, with unarguable accuracy. He remembered his talk with the Coroner's Officer, and the implication that even Stanley felt much the same about at least one dead person. What did it matter? That was what everyone seemed to be asking him. And when it came to trying to explain, he found the words elusive. Worse than that, he found the conviction itself was eluding him. Was he really so shallow, so capricious, that a few comments from his overwrought wife could cast doubt on his

41

whole enterprise?

'It's too late to go back on it now,' Karen said reasonably. 'I didn't mean to even suggest it. I'm just having a last-minute panic. Take no notice.' She looked down at him kindly. 'I *do* understand, really. It's only that it can seem so – *abstract* sometimes. And I'm scared it isn't going to work out. You should have had more business by now, let's face it. If only one of those schoolkids on the bus–'

'I know,' he agreed. They'd held their breath for days, in the hope that at least one family would opt for a Peaceful Repose burial for their child. In vain. Two had been cremated, two buried in the big municipal cemetery and the rest in country churchyards. Drew had done his best to conceal his disappointment.

Karen took a deep breath. 'Well, this won't get the lesson plans done. Look, Drew–' He hated it when she addressed him by name; he heard very little affection in it. 'We'll give it a term, okay? I know we agreed to longer, but I don't feel I can commit to more than that.'

He got to his feet, suddenly energetic with irritation. 'You can't do that,' he said. 'You have to give the school a term's notice. Once you go back, you'll have to stay until Christmas at least. I don't think that's such a lot to ask.'

'You think you know it all, don't you,' she snapped, echoing his tone. 'Don't forget you've got a new responsibility yourself. It won't be all smooth sailing, trying to fit Steph into your working day – even if you *don't* do any work. She'll have colds and tummy upsets, and new teeth and filthy nappies–'

'Well, it's too late to change it now,' he sum-marised, as she had done already. 'We'll just have to get on with it, won't we.'

The prickly silence that followed was becoming unbearable when Karen suddenly remembered something. 'Oh – there's a letter for you. It came second post. It looks very odd.' She picked up an envelope from the windowsill and thrust it at him. As an ice-breaker, it was only partially effective.

Drew looked at it for a moment. The address was printed on a sticky label and attached to a long brown envelope. PRIVATE AND CON-FIDENTIAL was written in capitals in the top left corner. He opened it and took out a single sheet of A4 paper.

The message was printed in crazy type in the centre of the page.

YOU ARE GOING AGAINST NATURE
CHILDREN ARE DYING
GET OUT AND STAY OUT

'Blimey!' said Drew, half joking, half horrified. 'It's an anonymous letter. Hate mail, they call it, don't they?'

'Let's see.' Karen took it from him and stared at it. '"Children are dying". That's not very nice, is it. Do they mean the children in that bus crash?'

'Presumably. Hardly my fault, though.'

'No,' she agreed faintly. 'Must be a nutter. They seem to think you're committing some crime

43

against the natural order, and this made the bus crash happen.'

'What – burying people in a field, instead of a nice consecrated churchyard?' Drew was still stunned. The phrase *hate mail* kept circling in his head: the one thing Drew couldn't bear was being hated. The idea that somebody disapproved so passionately of what he was doing came as a serious blow.

'Look, you mustn't pay it any attention,' Karen decided. 'It's not worthy of it. We'll burn it and forget all about it. I wish I hadn't given it to you now. If any more come I'll just throw them away.'

'No,' he said. 'You can't do that. I don't need protecting. It was just so – unexpected.' He forced a smile. 'We'd better not burn it, though. If they keep coming, we might have to report it.'

'To the police, you mean?'

He nodded. 'If it's a one-off, then that's the end of it. But I think it'd get to me if there were more.'

'Shit,' Karen burst out. 'This is all we need. Isn't life difficult enough without this?'

Her anger seemed at least partly directed at Drew and he chose not to react. He folded the letter and put it in a drawer of their dining table, where they kept oddments of string and useful bits and pieces. 'Let's just try to forget about it,' he said.

CHAPTER THREE

Maggs and Jeffrey often found themselves working side by side – he putting the finishing touches to his hedges, she marking out grave positions on a careful grid reference. Without formal headstones, the individual graves needed to be recorded in precise detail. 'It might not seem particularly difficult now,' Drew had said, 'but once we have fifty or a hundred people buried here, you'll see what I mean.'

'D'you reckon this'll ever work out?' Jeffrey asked, as he took a rest from his hedge-trimming.

Maggs paused in her mapping and looked at him. 'What – you mean this natural burial thing?'

He nodded. 'Out of the way spot, this. Not many people would ever dream of being buried at North Staverton.'

'That's the attraction, though,' she pointed out. 'Something out of the usual routine. They think if they can be buried here, it'll make them special. Everybody wants to be that bit different, so long as it doesn't cost too much or make them look daft.'

Jeffrey shrugged. 'So what's the story with this woman, then? The one with the necklace? Going on three weeks ago already – can't keep her in the cold store forever. Any sign of them finding who dumped her here?'

Maggs considered carefully before replying.

'Okay, this is just guessing, right? I can think of at least two explanations. First one – the woman gets herself killed, maybe by accident – some yobbos fooling about, or trying to mug her. They might not have been thinking straight, when it came to disposing of the body. Just panicked and hit on the first place that seemed quiet and un-disturbed. They might not even have known about Drew and his new cemetery. A coinci-dence.' She paused, thinking it through. 'Actually, that doesn't feel right. You saw the way she was lying. It didn't look like something done in panic. It felt more to me as if the people who buried her wanted her to have something proper. Something appropriate. This place was in the papers back last summer. They saw it and decided to put her here. It wouldn't have been difficult. Drew and Karen hadn't moved in then, and the field was open to anybody.'

Jeffrey fixed his faded blue eyes on her, unblinking. 'So – these people murdered her, and then gave her a decent burial? Bit twisted that, wouldn't 'ee say?'

Maggs wouldn't meet his gaze. 'Well – as I said, I'm only guessing. It might not have been like that at all. Maybe it *was* just a coincidence.'

He shook his head and turned back to his hedge-trimming. 'Don't believe in coincidence, me,' he muttered. 'There's more to it than we've thought on, you'll see. And it ain't no good for the business, neither. Gives a bad taste to the place.'

Maggs was scuffing the turf with her heel, trying to mark a junction on the ground to

46

coincide with the plan in her hand. 'Midway between the first beech to the west and the big hawthorn to the east,' she muttered. 'What I need is some sticks. Or big stones.' She dug her heel in deeper, attacking a tussock of coarse grass, trying to make an impression that she could find again. 'Hey! What's this?' she said, as her shoe scraped against something hard.

'Careful,' warned Jeffrey. 'Might be another body.'

'You're not joking,' she squealed, as an unmistakable bone emerged from beneath her foot. 'Look at this.'

Warily, he approached, and bent over her find. 'Too small to be human,' he said with relief. 'Been here a while, I'd say. Nothing to get excited about.'

He pulled the white shape free and held up a skull. 'Sheep,' he said. The long nose and low cranium seemed to confirm his assertion. Loose teeth rattled slightly as he shook the earth off; empty eye sockets glared blindly at him and Maggs. 'Not too common to find them in the middle of a field, though,' he said. 'Usually get dumped in a ditch. Probably brought here by a dog or a fox.'

'I don't like this,' Maggs shivered. 'What else are we going to find? I'd be scared to dig any more graves, if I were you.'

Jeffrey shrugged carelessly. 'Not going to hurt us, is it? The dead can't hurt. It might be this field was the village boneyard, years ago, where they put their dead animals. To my knowledge it's never been much good for crops. Drew's auntie let it out to grass when she could, but it always had more thistles and nettles than anything else.'

Maggs gave up her measuring and marking. 'I've had enough for today,' she decided. 'I'm not in the mood for this. That woman's going to be the first of a whole run of weird things. I can feel it.'

'Don't start all that voodoo shit,' he told her, suddenly hostile.

'What d'you mean?' She stared at him in confusion.

'Black magic and stuff. You people can't leave it alone, can you?'

Maggs was genuinely bemused. 'What people? Me and Drew?' She frowned at him. 'Can't leave what alone?'

'Don't act stupid,' he continued, looking a little uncomfortable. 'I don't know where you come from, but sooner or later, blood will work itself out.'

The penny finally dropped. 'Oh, God. You mean because I'm black? Black person – black magic? Voodoo. Jeffrey – Christ, you *know* that's crap. You should have more sense. You've seen my mum, you know how she brought me up. Isn't she the most sensible person you could ever meet?'

'Not your real mum though, is she?' he muttered.

'No,' said Maggs, on a steadying breath. 'They adopted me when I was little. It's never been a secret. I still don't understand what makes you think I'm a voodoo freak. My biological mother came from Plymouth, not Haiti.'

He nodded. 'Sorry I said anything. But it makes me sick, this stuff in the papers about satanic rituals and carryings-on. It seemed to me you were talking about that sort of rubbish.'

'All I said was it felt like the start of a run of weird things. I wasn't making some supernatural prediction. I don't know what I meant, really. I haven't seen anything in the papers about satanic rituals. Anyway, it's usually just a lot of stupid kids lighting black candles and having wanking competitions.'

Jeffrey recoiled as if she'd waved a live cobra under his nose. 'Language!' he gasped. 'Watch your mouth, Miss.'

She sneered unpleasantly at him, still smarting at his unsuspected assumptions about her, based solely on the colour of her skin. Growing up in a white family, in a small town where almost everybody was white, she had seldom been made aware of anything unusual about her appearance. Politically correct efforts to remind her of her ethnic identity had never really scratched the surface; so much else about her was remarkable that friends and teachers at school had put skin colour right at the end of the list.

'I don't think I'm the one with the dirty mouth,' she said, before turning to trot down the field to the road.

'There's a strange woman standing by the field gate,' Maggs told Drew next morning. He was in the office, playing with Stephanie at the same time as trying to do some calculations. Maggs had just arrived noisily on her bike.

49

'Probably another sightseer,' he said irritably. 'It's like Piccadilly Circus here these days. She'll want to look at the spot that's mentioned in the papers. Don't people have lives of their own any more?'

'You ought to be pleased. It's good for business. They'll remember us if one of their family dies.'

'I doubt it. They're just idle gawpers, as my mother used to say.'

'Well, this one looks as if she's here for a reason. See for yourself.' Maggs's normally good temper had yet to reassert itself after the exchange with Jeffrey the previous day. Not just that, but having too little to do, combined with some critical remarks from her mother about her weight and a spell of cold damp weather, all contributed to her gloom. Slowly, Drew got to his feet, passing Stephanie to Maggs, who took her automatically, and then gave a put-upon little frown.

'Where?' he said, going to the open door. Before she could answer, he saw for himself. And immediately he knew exactly who she was.

'Genevieve Slater,' he said, walking towards his visitor as if magnetised. 'My God.'

She had parked her car on the other side of the narrow country lane and stood next to it. They looked at each other, the eight feet of tarmac between them.

'You remember me, then?' she said. 'I thought I might have changed beyond recognition.' She turned sideways, gazing up the slope towards the unofficial grave, now reverting to its former inconspicuous state. Drew saw that she was at least seven months pregnant, and that she was

50

displaying her profile deliberately, to ensure that he didn't miss the fact.

'Of course I remember you,' he said. 'It's not so very long ago, after all.'

'Almost exactly two years. May. It seems longer.'

He remained where he was, examining her closely. She looked older than he remembered – her skin more weathered, and crinkled around the eyes. But the black hair bore no trace of grey, and was as long and thick as before. The voice was the same creamy contralto that had once appealed to him so strongly. And – as she finally crossed over and stood beside him – he noted wryly that she was still a good two inches taller than him.

She eyed the cottage with a critical pursing of her lips. 'Didn't stay long in Bradbourne, did you?' she remarked, with a tang of accusation.

'As it happens, no we didn't,' he agreed. 'But we fully intended to when–'

'Well, never mind that now. We stayed where we were in the end. Willard's contract at the university was renewed after all, and everything settled down again. Not that I should forgive you for what you did,' she added pettishly. 'In fact, I've come to call in the favour you owe me.'

'Step into the office,' he invited, suddenly aware of how they might look, standing so close together at the side of the road. 'And tell me all about it.'

The office was crowded, with Stephanie, Maggs and the newcomer. 'Would you take her for a little walk?' Drew asked Maggs, nodding at

51

his daughter. 'It's quite sunny out there now.'

His assistant frowned rebelliously and narrowed her eyes. More than once she'd reminded him that childcare was not going to be part of her job, and she had no intention of letting it become so. A glance at the obvious unborn infant newly arrived in the room carried more than a dash of disgust. Drew could hear a snide remark coming and moved to intercept it.

'Sorry,' he said firmly. 'We won't be long.'

'Don't go on account of me,' said the newcomer, summing up the situation. 'I don't want to be a nuisance.'

He looked at her as she leaned against his desk, her weight thrown back on her hands, the bulge thrusting through the gaping coat. He felt rich with it: a wealth of female power on all sides.

'I have to go,' said Maggs. 'But I don't see why Stephanie can't stay.'

Wordlessly, the woman propelled herself forward, taking a second to find her balance, and then held out her arms. Stephanie responded, twisting away from Maggs, almost leaping the gap between the two women. 'Now everybody's happy,' said Drew comfortably. 'Thanks, Maggs. I'll see you in a bit.'

He gave his visitor a chair and produced a box of toys for his daughter.

Genevieve peered through the window at the back of the office, to the burial field. 'I read about you in the local paper. You do alternative burials here, right?' she said.

'That's right.' He waited, examining in more detail her clear skin, long fingers, grey eyes, reminding himself with some embarrassment of what had passed between them two years previously, when she and her husband had wanted the same house that Drew and Karen were determined to buy, and the protracted tussle had thrown all four of them together in a disorganised jumble of conflict and bad behaviour. Through a careless piece of diary-keeping on the part of the estate agent, the two couples had met on the doorstep of the house, and the truth had quickly become clear.

Drew and Genevieve had tried to be civilised about it, but Willard and Karen had been like pit bull terriers, neither the least bit inclined to give up their prize. Their conciliatory spouses had been over-ruled. Twice they met over coffee, alone, to try to resolve the situation. And although he'd never touched her, Drew had found her to be one of the easiest people to talk to that he'd ever known. Only later did he realise quite how freely he'd talked.

It wasn't even an especially nice house, he thought now, with a rueful smile. *However did we get into such a state over it?*

But the state had persisted, made far worse by the vacillating old lady who owned the property. She liked both couples, promising each in turn that they could have it, and making the estate agent tear his hair out with frustration. The impasse dragged on until, one dramatic afternoon, Drew had decided on some concerted action. Karen wanted the house with a passion she rarely showed, so Drew took a deep breath and told the biggest lie of his life. 'My wife is in the early weeks of pregnancy,' he told the old lady. 'And I'm afraid she'll lose the baby if this stress continues. She's already had two miscarriages, you see.' The next day, the estate agent phoned to say the house was quite definitely theirs.

All might have been well, except that Genevieve heard about what he'd done, and knew he'd lied. Knew because by then she herself knew quite a lot about the Slocombes from Drew's own lips.

Now, in his office, it was like being reminded of a bad dream. Genevieve had stormed at him, making extravagant accusations, threatening to betray him to the old lady, while he struggled to stay calm, pointing out to her that his loyalties must be with his wife. 'After all,' he'd said, 'it isn't as if there's anything between you and me.'

'Isn't there?' she'd challenged him, her hair disarrayed, her chest heaving.

'Nothing,' he'd insisted, reluctantly.

She'd deflated then, wounded and humiliated. 'I thought you liked me,' she mumbled childishly.

'We wanted the same house – that's all,' he'd said perfidiously. 'I'm sorry one of us had to lose.'

'You cheated,' she'd told him. 'You don't deserve to be happy in it. But I forgive you, Drew Slocombe. You're too special to hold a grudge against.'

And Drew and Karen *had* been happy. Stephanie had somehow made his lie come true and Drew had erased the memory of his dishonesty. But Genevieve's sudden reappearance now was unsettling. Seeing her pregnant only increased his unease; it was unexpected, incongruous, and somehow inappropriate. She wasn't the right sort of woman to have a baby. He'd had the strong impression, during those previous encounters, that she was at heart very much still a baby herself.

She was playing unselfconsciously with Stephanie, blowing noisy raspberries against the child's experimental open palm, grinning widely at the chuckles this evoked. Drew tried to reconcile this picture with the worried intensity she had shown over the house purchase. Although she'd claimed that it was her husband who really wanted and needed to move, he had wondered whether that was really true. He had also wondered whether he would have behaved as he did if she'd made her appeal more personal. Would he, in the end, have fought so hard to get Karen what she wanted if he'd known for certain that Genevieve wanted it just as badly? There had been dreams in the following months where the choice had been presented and the decision far from clearcut. He found himself, in that other realm, doing almost anything that Genevieve Slater asked him to.

'So – why are you here?' he asked her abruptly. 'Not just a visit for old times' sake?'

She looked at him out of bright grey eyes and made an exaggerated grimace, wrinkling her nose and carving grooves around the edges of her lips. 'Ah,' she said. 'I suppose we'd better get to the point.' She put Stephanie down carefully, much to the child's disappointment. 'Can I sit down?'

Drew waved her to an upright chair at one end of his desk. She wore a bulky quilted coat that clearly wouldn't fasten across her bulge and long grey suede boots. She seemed to take up a great deal of the available space. He sat in his own chair, having first persuaded Stephanie to settle in her corner with a set of stacking cups to work on.

'There was a woman buried here–' Genevieve said.

Drew blinked stupidly before realising what she was talking about. 'Oh! You mean – yes, there was.'

'I think – I think she was my mother.'

A sense of doom filled Drew's whole body, heavy with the threat of trouble. He wanted very much to tell her to go away and leave him alone. But he couldn't do that to Genevieve. And besides, he was also intrigued, helplessly hooked by the promise of a story. 'You don't sound too sure,' he said weakly. He was clutching at straws; she'd actually sounded uncomfortably sure.

'Well, quite a few things fit. We haven't seen her since last summer. She had a necklace just like the one in the paper. She was seventy, nearly as tall as me, and – well, it sounds daft, but she's very much the sort of person who *would* get herself murdered.'

Drew wished he didn't have to ask such an obvious question. Such a boringly crucial question. 'I don't expect I'm going to want to hear this – but why haven't you gone to the police?' he said.

She screwed her face up again, and wriggled her shoulders inside the big coat. 'That's a bit hard to explain – though I think you of all people

56

might be able to understand. First–' She held up a hand, palm outwards, as if to slow down an oncoming rush of words and thoughts. 'First – it might not be Ma at all. If she's still alive somewhere, she's going to be furious with me for starting a police investigation. She doesn't like the police.'

'Why not?'

'Well,' Genevieve shrugged, 'she's always been a rebellious sort of person. Thinks everyone should be free to do as they like. Doesn't approve of rules and regulations.'

'She hasn't got anything to hide, has she?' He tried to sound astute, covering all angles.

'I don't know,' she admitted. 'She could have, I suppose. She tends to mix with a lot of strange people.'

'Hmmm,' Drew nodded doubtfully. 'What else? What other reasons for avoiding the police?'

She closed her eyes for a moment, and then took a deep breath. 'If it is my mother – she's called Gwen Absolon, by the way – and if she was murdered, then I think it's possible that my husband killed her.' The words came out in a low mutter, forcing Drew to strain to catch them.

He remembered Willard Slater from two years ago: tall, much older than his wife, a disconcerting mixture of absent-minded intellect and cold ambition. Drew recalled the icy look in his eyes when Willard realised he might be thwarted in his desire to obtain the Bradbourne house. No, it was not that difficult to imagine Willard killing someone.

'That's a good reason,' he agreed, the cloud of

57

foreboding coming over him again with renewed force. 'At least from your point of view, assuming you like him enough to want to protect him.'

She laughed. 'Good old Drew!' she said. 'Always straight to the point. You don't even realise how unique you are, do you?'

I could say the same of you, he thought, while prudently keeping quiet.

'It's a bit more complicated than that,' she added. 'And, believe it or not, I am trying to work out what the right thing to do would be. That's where I thought you might come in useful.'

She couldn't have known – could she? – that no other approach would work so well. 'You'll have to explain,' he said. 'At the moment it sounds as if you want to cover up a murder and pervert the course of justice.'

She shifted in the chair, leaning forward, her expression serious. 'Let's go back a bit. I assume you've been in communication with the police – after all, the body was found on your property?' Drew nodded. 'So – how interested are they? I mean, how much of a murder enquiry are they running here?'

'The timing was bad,' said Drew conscientiously. 'It came at the same time as that dreadful accident, where the schoolchildren were killed.'

'But that isn't much of an excuse, is it? Reading between the lines – or rather, seeing how much there *hasn't* been in the papers about it – I get the strong feeling that no one wants to know. They can't find any evidence, and so it's been filed away and forgotten.'

'But if you gave them some evidence – a name,

some anxieties or suspicions – they'd be very willing to open a more vigorous enquiry,' he insisted gently.

'You think so?' she said. 'That's the sort of thing I came here to find out. I knew you'd help me think it through. So – let's assume I go to them. I tell them absolutely everything I know – which isn't very much. They'll come and question Willard, and he'll laugh and tell them the idea's insane. I've been imagining things, on account of being pregnant at forty-two and being a neurotic individual at the best of times. He'll tell them my mother is a habitual traveller, off all over the world for long spells, and is fairly certain to be in Zaire or Bolivia as we speak. There's no evidence at all that she's dead, and nothing to show the body is her–'

'They could compare hair or tissue – DNA – if they had something of hers to work on. Old clothes, a hairbrush – anything, really. Presumably you could come up with something?'

'There you are, you see!' she said triumphantly. 'Why should we? We don't *want* them to identify her. We've got nothing to gain by involving them.'

'But–' Drew had a sense of being caught in a tight and insoluble maze. 'Does Willard know you think your mother is dead?'

'We haven't mentioned her for months. He's got some new research project and thinks about nothing else. He's trying to avoid real life these days. All because of this, of course.' She ducked her chin downwards, indicating the pregnant bulge. 'It horrifies him.'

'But it is his?' Drew asked boldly.

59

'Yes,' she said, with a girlish dimple. 'It's his.'

'So – let's stick with the scenario. The police turn up, ask him when he last saw his mother-in-law. What does he say?'

'I told you. He'll say, last July or thereabouts. At which time she said she'd be setting off on a new trip in a week or two.'

'Where was she living then?'

'In a basement room in a little Somerset town. I've got the address somewhere,' she said vaguely. Drew noted the imprecision with suspicion; he found it hard to believe she couldn't remember exactly *which* small town her mother had lived in. Genevieve seemed to notice his doubt, and gave a little laugh. 'She was hardly there. She moved around so much.'

'Right,' he muttered. 'This isn't getting us very far, is it?'

'Oh, it is,' she leaned forward earnestly. 'It's so wonderful just to be able to talk to someone about it. Someone I can trust.'

He had to say it. 'Genevieve – why do you think you can trust me? After what I did to you over the house? Why do you think I won't protect my own interests and go straight to the police the minute you leave here? They might come knocking on your door this very afternoon.'

She met his eyes and he recognised the power of the connection. He knew he was walking willingly into the trap she had set for him. 'Because I haven't told you enough to get you into any trouble. And – because you're you,' she said simply.

60

CHAPTER FOUR

Before Drew could sum up an adequate reaction, there was a brisk knock on the door. 'Sorry,' Drew said to Genevieve. 'I'd better see who that is.'

'No problem,' she smiled. 'I'll mind the baby for you, if you like.' She bent down to play with Stephanie as Drew opened the door. He stepped outside, closing the door behind him – suddenly the discreet undertaker.

Although not in fact wearing tweeds, the man standing on the path outside was decidedly tweedy. A scratchy-looking moustache with eyebrows to match, walking stick and gruff tones, all combined to stereotype him. 'You the funeral chap?' he demanded of Drew.

'That's me.'

'Do you do dogs?'

'Dogs! Er – well, it hadn't really occurred to me.' He pulled himself together. 'I don't see any reason why not.' His visitor cast an eye across the field; Drew supposed that this man too had read the papers, and knew what the far corner had revealed. The moustache was quivering.

'We could fence off an area for pets,' Drew said, thinking aloud. 'There might be quite a demand for it, I suppose.'

'How much?'

'Um – I'd have to think about that.'

'We'll pay two hundred and fifty for the plot and another fifty for a suitable–' The brisk tone suddenly failed, and the moustache was gripped between the man's teeth. 'You know – the–'

'We could supply a receptacle,' Drew told him. 'I think that would be an acceptable price. What sort of dog is it?'

'Labrador. Had him sixteen years. Never went anywhere without him alongside. Died in his sleep last night. Mildred's very distressed. It's been one tragedy after another this past year. She's in the car with him.' He waved an explanatory hand towards the parking area, where a large blue-grey Volvo estate sat.

Drew was slightly taken aback. 'You'd like it all done now, would you?'

'Is that a problem?'

Drew thought quickly. A labrador-sized coffin wasn't readily obtainable at such short notice. If he was to add a pets' cemetery to the services he offered, it ought to be done properly. Some human beings might take exception to sharing their last resting place with an assortment of other species – although he personally rather liked the idea. What an idiot he'd been not to think of this before! It would have made another page in the brochure he'd already produced and sent out.

Lacking a proper mortuary, he always tried to get funerals performed within three days of the death – a return to more traditional timetables which had so far appealed quite strongly to his customers. Jeffrey was on permanent standby for gravedigging. He looked the man in the eye, aware of the grief lurking just below the surface. A lot of people kept wives a much shorter time than he'd had his beloved dog...

'Tomorrow morning,' he promised. 'Will you want to be present at the interment?'

'Of course. Can we leave him here with you, then?' He stared critically at the small building behind them.

'Certainly you can,' said Drew. 'Part of this building is for the safekeeping of bodies.'

'What time tomorrow?'

'Ten-thirty? I'll need a name and address. The grave will be over there, between the two beeches–' He pointed at a corner where the field lost all sense of geometry and the hedge incorporated two sizeable beeches and a handsome oak.

The man led Drew to the car, where a shrouded figure lay stiffly along the back seat. Drew was unsure about carrying it on his own with any show of dignity. Where was Maggs when he needed her? And wasn't he leaving Genevieve alone with his baby for rather a long time? But at the back of his mind, excited calculations were going on. If people were prepared to pay two hundred and fifty quid for a dog's grave, he ought to set aside at least half an acre for them. Even one a month would make a substantial difference to his finances. Should he broach the subject of memorial plants, he wondered? Was it likely that these people would want a nice little mahonia or hellebore on the grave?

Mildred was soft and sad, peering at him hopefully from the passenger seat. 'Can you do it for us?' she asked. 'We read about you and thought this would be perfect. We haven't got much garden of our own any more, you see.'

'I'll be pleased to help,' said Drew easily. One of his resolutions from the outset had been to avoid gushing platitudes or sloppy euphemisms. Only reluctantly had he adopted *Peaceful Repose* as his trademark. He'd wanted to use something much plainer – *Natural Burials,* he'd thought – but Maggs and Karen had dissuaded him. 'You have to keep some of the reassurance,' Karen had said. 'Even ecology freaks like to think their dead person will rest peacefully.'

He hefted the rigid dog to the tiny cool room behind his office, having taken the necessary details, as Hubert and Mildred Grainger drove off forlornly without their faithful companion. This was definitely a job for Maggs, he decided. Let her phone round and find something respectable to bury a large dog in.

'Sorry to be so long,' he said, almost running through the door. 'Business, I'm afraid.'

Genevieve Slater was on the floor with Stephanie, running a toy train around the limited space between desk, filing cabinet and chairs. She looked up, her face very pink.

'That's okay,' she smiled. 'We've been getting on famously. Was it something interesting?'

Drew hesitated. 'Someone wanting me to bury their dog,' he told her, hoping she wouldn't laugh. But she allowed herself only the smallest of smiles.

Stephanie was obviously being well entertained. She crawled energetically after the train as her new friend sent it running under a chair, crowing as she went.

'Where were we?' Drew asked, knowing only too well.

'I'm not really sure,' she puffed, heaving herself awkwardly to her feet. 'I think the next move is down to you.'

He folded his arms, trying to think of something constructive to say. He also needed to physically prevent himself from offering her a hand as she got up. He would not allow himself to touch her, not even to hold her hand or support her elbow. He was afraid of the electric charge if his flesh touched hers. Trust me, I'm an undertaker, he wanted to say. Like a doctor or a ferryman – they helped you with a handclasp without a second thought. But she'd already told him she trusted him, and he wasn't sure that was a good thing. 'The next stage will be the reburial, I imagine,' he told her, striving to be businesslike.

'Not the inquest?'

'No,' he shook his head, 'it'll be another month or more before they get round to that. They won't hold up the burial for it. There isn't any need.' He slipped with relief into professional mode. 'As long as they've taken the whole range of samples, with photos and reports, they don't need the actual body any more. The verdict will probably be Unlawful Killing by Person or Persons Unknown, and the police file will remain open indefinitely – pending further evidence,' he added meaningfully.

'And will she be buried here again?'

'I hope so, yes,' he said. 'I've already suggested

it, and there isn't likely to be any objection. I'm cheaper, you see – and the Council are probably going to be paying for it.'

'There was an old tramp, I seem to remember, found dead in a ditch not far from here. What did they do then?'

'They did a post-mortem, which showed he had pneumonia and a congested heart. He died of natural causes, and Plant's did a Council funeral for him. Not quite the same thing.'

'So they don't know what my – what the woman found here – died of?'

'Apparently not,' he said carefully. 'They couldn't find anything organically wrong with her. She seemed quite robust, as far as they could tell.'

'Hmmm,' she said, with a hint of frustration. 'So all they know is how she *didn't* die. And you can't prove a negative.'

'But you *can* prove identity,' he reminded her. She didn't look enthusiastic.

They sat in silence for a few minutes, Stephanie drowsing on Drew's lap, the sun suddenly appearing through the clouds and throwing a startling brightness through the back window. The room felt uncomfortably warm and stuffy.

Genevieve put both hands on the desk and levered herself off the chair. 'I must go. I've taken up far too much of your time. You've given me plenty to think about. It was nice to see you again.'

Nice! he thought, not even bothering to stand up himself; chivalry was beyond him at that moment. Was she just going to walk away, after everything she'd told him?

'There really isn't anything I can do to help,' he said, as much to himself as to her. 'And you're wrong about one thing, you know. You have told me enough to get me into trouble.'

She frowned down at him, stately and matriarchal. 'Surely not?' she demurred. 'Put it down to the ramblings of a confused pregnant woman. Who knows – maybe that's all it is, anyway!'

He let her go without any further comment. Something told him she'd be back, and that he hadn't heard the last of Genevieve Slater and her missing mother.

The appearance of Maggs a few minutes later brought him out of his reverie. She was dishevelled and breathless, not built for running. 'I've just chased two men who were hiding in the top hedge,' she panted. 'They climbed over onto the railway line. One of them had a spade.'

Drew stared at her. 'What did they want?'

'I've no idea,' she shouted. 'How should I know? But they weren't at all pleased when I spotted them.'

'Damn it,' Drew cursed. 'This is getting ridiculous. Were they burying something too?'

'I can't be sure – I interrupted them. But my guess is they'd come to dig something up. They didn't leave anything behind, at any rate. Drew – we should tell the police.'

He wriggled his shoulders uncomfortably. 'No, no, I don't think so. It's lucky you scared them off. I shouldn't think they'll come back again. I'll get Jeffrey to do some work on that top hedge. I never imagined anybody would try to come in that way.'

Maggs snorted and slammed out of the office. Two minutes later she was back again. 'There's something in the cool room,' she said, without preamble.

'That's right.' He told her briefly about the dog people. She listened without comment, clearly wanting to move on to something else.

'What did that woman want?' she finally demanded. 'She was here for ages.'

'Confidential, I'm afraid,' he told her.

This time the slam of the door made Stephanie whimper with the shock.

Willard was home for lunch that day, but Genevieve made no effort to produce anything for him to eat. Uncomplaining, he made himself a generous Welsh rarebit, complete with dry mustard and Worcestershire sauce. Long experience deterred him from offering to make some for his wife. He carried it into the dining room and sat formally at the table to eat it.

Unusually, Genevieve followed him into the room, moving restlessly from sideboard to window, bookcase to mantelpiece, fiddling with ornaments and pausing at intervals, apparently deep in thought.

'Is something the matter?' he asked her after a few minutes, casting a swift sideways glance at her face.

'Sort of,' she admitted. 'I decided I ought to make an effort to find out where my mother is. We haven't heard from her for ages now. There should at least have been a Christmas card – she hardly ever forgets Christmas. It bothers me that she doesn't even know about this.' She gestured in the direction of her swollen belly.

Willard sighed noisily, cutting a careful corner off his toast. 'And how do you propose to locate her?' he enquired. 'You'd need to hire a private detective. The police wouldn't be interested – she's a grown woman.'

'Funny you should say that,' she murmured.

'What?'

'Look – you remember that couple – the Slocombes? The ones who beat us to that house in Bradbourne?'

His face darkened, and he fixed her with a hard stare. 'How could I forget them?'

'Well, he's in North Staverton now, running his own alternative burial ground. You must have seen the piece about a body in the local rag–'

'Get to the point, Genevieve. I want to finish a chapter this afternoon. I don't get much opportunity for a good uninterrupted session these days.'

'The point is, I think we ought to do what we can to find out whether the woman they found buried in North Staverton was my mother. No!' She put up a hand to silence his attempted response. 'Wait a minute. Just listen. He's got experience of – situations like this. We know Drew Slocombe, and he owes us a favour. He's ideally fixed to help us, and I don't think he's the type to go running to the police. In fact, I'm quite sure he's not.'

'So what have you asked him to do?' Willard

asked her wearily. 'Put his whole career in jeopardy by lying to the police for you? I can't believe you've been such a fool. There's no reason at all to think that body was your mother. She's just gone off with some new boyfriend and forgotten all about you – just like she always did.'

'That's what I told him you'd say.' She picked up a china dog, wiping dust off its head with one finger. 'This room is a disgrace. It would have been worth moving house to get rid of all this junk.'

'It's my junk,' he said. 'And I like it.'

'As you've said at least five thousand times in the past eighteen years,' she returned.

'You mentioned me then – to the Slocombe chap?'

'Oh, you were quite central to the conversation.'

'In what way?'

'I told him you were less than sympathetic to my wish to find out what's happened to my mother. That you thought I was being neurotic, and she'd turn up any day now. Which is true, isn't it?'

Willard addressed himself studiedly to his toasted cheese for two full minutes before replying. 'In that case,' he said slowly, 'I don't understand why you went to him, and I don't suppose he does, either. Doesn't it worry you that when they get to know you, just about everybody regards you as deranged?'

She flinched at the skilful thrust. 'I don't believe that Drew thinks I'm deranged,' she said softly. 'I think he understands my need to *know*.'

She lifted her head, her hands curled into fists. 'And I *do* need to know, you see,' she stated clearly. 'I very much need to know what has happened to my mother.'

Jim Kennett was an avid consumer of news items – television, radio, local and national press – absorbing the stories like a gossipy old woman and retelling them with embellishments over the bags and benches of the small old-fashioned sorting office in Cullompton. Jim had been a postman for twenty-five years, a job perfectly suited to his temperament.

The reported discovery of a dead woman in a new cemetery in a small village, a woman buried there before the first official interment, appealed to him enormously; he chuckled over it more than once. 'Jumping the gun and no mistake,' he said. 'Makes you think, though. What was in their minds – murdering her and then burying her all nice and tidy in a field that they must have known was going to be a natural burial ground?' He mused on this, while his fellow postmen ignored him. 'I mean – if you'd just killed someone, you'd bury them in a quiet place where you wouldn't expect anyone to go digging. Wouldn't you?' He looked at Pete and Fred thoughtfully, not really expecting any reply. 'So maybe they wanted someone to find her. Makes no sense.'

Pete and Fred were even more unrewarding than usual, but Jim needed to worry away at the story for a while yet. He took it home with him, and started thinking aloud over the supper table, with his wife Caroline and son Jason. 'That murder's a poser,' he began, chewing his fried liver thoughtfully. 'I was saying to Pete and Fred this morning – why bury someone in a place where you know she'll be found?'

His wife and son seldom read the papers or followed the more obscure news stories. 'What?' said Caroline.

'Two or three weeks ago – they found a body, dead six months or more, in a field which was already due to open as a natural cemetery sort of place. They still haven't identified her. It was on again last night. Asking for people who think they might have known her to come forward.'

'What's a natural cemetery?' said Jason.

'You know – where they have trees and wild flowers and bits of rock instead of proper grave-stones. It's catching on all over the place. Sounds okay to me. Time we got back to a more sensible way of doing the necessary.'

Caroline slowly raised her head from the task of removing the rind from her bacon. 'I never told you, did I?' she said. 'Last summer, when I was coming back from Taunton. I'd been to see Aunt Hilda, we'd gone shopping together, and then to a film. Uncle George had toddled off to some Masons' do – though heavens knows what they made of him. He'd already lost most of his marbles by then. Anyway I got the last train home. I saw something in a field. Looked like people burying something or someone.'

Jim laughed scornfully. 'You were dreaming,' he said. 'Besides, you can't see outside a train at night.'

72

'The carriage lights had gone out. To be honest, I thought I might have been dreaming, too. Maybe I was. It *was* a bit like a dream. Two people, and something lying on the ground. A big dark shape, it was. It could have been a person. I could see a spade, and a torch–'

'Hey! What if Mum saw them burying this woman!' cried Jason. 'She'd be famous! Where was it, Mum?'

'Somewhere between Taunton and Exeter, that's all I know. Where's this place you're talking about, Jim?'

'North Staverton,' said Jim, his hands resting immobile beside his plate. 'Right beside the railway line. Good God, woman – why didn't you say something at the time?'

She shrugged and sighed. 'I forgot about it,' she said. 'Once you get off a train, it's as if it all happened in another world. And you know how woolly-headed I am.'

'You'll have to tell the police,' said Jim, with rising excitement. 'Go and phone them now.'

She shook her head. 'I'm no good with the phone. I'll get all tongue tied. I'll pop in to-morrow and see if they're interested. But really, I haven't anything very useful to tell them, have I? They already know she was buried there. All I can do is give them a date – *if* it's the same place.'

'A date can be very important,' he told her seriously. 'Very important indeed.'

Simon Gliddon got up that morning with a sense of foreboding thick in his chest. It was the an-niversary of his wife's death. A year ago today she had been shot down, without any chance of escape, while minding her own business on an innocent holiday tour of Egypt. Simon had insisted on seeing her body when it was eventually shipped back to England. There was no other way that he could ever have believed the truth of the story he'd been told. As it was, it hadn't looked much like his wife. Her skin had darkened to the colour of antique oak; her hair had been brushed in a cloud around her head, instead of tied back in the ponytail she always wore. Only the wide plump shoulders, the stubborn jawline and the beautifully embalmed hands, wearing the wedding ring he had put on her finger, had convinced him that it really was Sarah. The image of how she had looked had remained with him constantly, only slightly dimmed after the passage of a whole year.

He had intended to go in to work as usual, hoping to drown the memories and the sudden flashes of rage in the routine tasks he would have waiting on his desk, but he decided he couldn't face it. Perhaps he owed it to his wife to remain at home, trawling through the past, wondering how he might yet ensure justice for his dead wife and punishment for those who were at fault.

The house still bore many signs of Sarah's existence. Simon had changed almost nothing – the kitchen still had mugs and ornamental plates and recipe cuttings exactly as she'd left them; the bathroom had her shampoo and body lotion on a shelf in the cabinet; the cupboard on the landing was full of her dressmaking materials. Only her clothes and shoes had disappeared, collected by her mother and disposed of in the early weeks. There was a small box of jewellery in one of the drawers, which Simon fingered from time to time, imagining the unborn daughter who had died with Sarah inheriting the objects if she had been allowed to live.

He would never marry again – of that he was certain. His father, currently on his third wife, found this inexplicable. 'She wouldn't have wanted you to be lonely, son,' he said, repeatedly. 'There's no law says you have to mourn her forever.'

Simon didn't even try to explain that he would never dare embark on marriage again. It had been too traumatic the first time for that to be within his power. He knew he could never stand there a second time mouthing those promises. He could never find the words to reveal just how gruelling his marriage to Sarah had actually been. Nobody would believe him, anyway. They'd think he was mad.

And maybe I am mad, he thought to himself. *Mad with the frustration of never being able to tell anybody how it really was. Mad with the blurring of the facts, as time goes by. Who can say, now, what was real?*

Yet suddenly, now, on this special anniversary, when he was permitted to indulge himself all day with self-tormenting memories, he remembered a man who just might understand how he felt. A man who was in a marriage that seemed, from what Simon had glimpsed of it, to be not unlike his own. He rummaged through an old address book and located the number. Perhaps the man

75

would be at home. If not, then so be it. He felt he was rolling a dice, letting fate take control.

The phone was answered on the third ring. 'Willard Slater here,' said a familiar voice.

'Simon Gliddon.'

'Hello!' Willard sounded unusually jovial. 'I was just thinking about you. Seems you've got your revenge on the old bat, then?'

'What?' Simon's mind went blank. 'Say that again.'

'The lady we all love to hate, as they used to say in the films. Come on, man, you know what I'm saying.'

'I'm sorry,' Simon spluttered, 'but I really don't know what you're talking about.'

'I understand,' Willard soothed. 'Just my little joke. So to what *do* I owe the pleasure?'

'It's the anniversary today. I wanted to talk to you.'

It was Willard's turn to splutter. 'Me? Funny sort of choice,' he said, in loud self-denigration.

'We used to talk,' Simon reminded him. 'You were always a good listener.'

'That was different. I was your tutor. And it was a long time ago. And we talked more about economics than affairs of the heart, if I remember rightly.'

'Perhaps you're right,' said Simon. And he put the phone down, limp with disappointment.

Jeffrey hadn't been very enthused by the prospect of adding a pets' cemetery to the Peaceful Repose Burial Ground. 'Have to make a fence round it,' he said gloomily. 'And keeping track of what's in there'll be no fun. All shapes and sizes. Are you going to have horses? Hamsters? It's a minefield, Mr Slocombe, I'm warning you.'

'It's too lucrative to refuse,' Drew told him. 'Look, we'll pace it out now and stick some pegs in, and you can make a start on the fence next week. Simple post and rail arrangement would probably be best.'

'Costs a fortune, that does,' said Jeffrey.

'Not if we do it ourselves. It'll keep Maggs occupied too, if she helps you. Meanwhile, we'll put the labrador here.' He pointed to a shallow hollow where the grass was tussocky and the sunlight dappled by the flickering shadows of a beech tree. 'It's a lovely spot.'

'Too good for a dog,' grumbled Jeffrey, clearly determined not to look on the bright side.

The interment next morning went well enough. Drew and Maggs lowered the plain rectangular box into the two-foot-deep grave, while Mr and Mrs Grainger sniffed wordlessly. Poignantly, they threw a doglead and well-chewed toy on top of the coffin. 'We'll never have another dog now,' Mildred said. 'We're getting too old to exercise it properly.'

Drew smiled sympathetically, though Hubert looked as if he could handle a lively dog without too much difficulty. But a dog could last fifteen years or more, and by then the man would be over eighty, he supposed. Pity to have to plan so far ahead. It was only a split second between that idea and the returning awareness that he should be doing much the same thing himself. After all, he had a family – he'd be expected to find money

77

for college fees when he was fifty, pressured to make a respectable income for at least the next twenty years, surrounded by noisy demands.

Before they left, Hubert Grainger handed over a cheque for three hundred pounds and shook Drew vigorously by the hand. 'Excellent job, excellent,' he said. 'You chose a perfect spot for the poor old boy to rest in. We read about this place in the local rag, you know. It's every bit as pleasant as we imagined it would be.' He turned and looked towards the top of the field, more or less exactly at the place where the body had been found. Drew held his breath, expecting some comment about the discovery of the dead woman, but it never came. Instead, the man went on to ask, 'All right if we come by for a visit from time to time? Just for old time's sake?'

'Of course,' Drew told him. 'That plot's yours now, to visit whenever you like.'

'D'you hear that, Mildred?' He turned to his wife, who was standing with her back to them, apparently lost in painful thoughts. 'Mr Slocombe says we can visit whenever we like.'

The woman turned slowly to face him. 'I'm not sure I'll want to do that, Hubert. It's all so sad here.'

'Buck up, old thing,' he said gently. 'It'll be all right. You see.' And he led her back to the Volvo, pausing only to nod a final thanks.

It was the first time Drew had buried an animal – although he'd once had cause to keep a dead dog in Daphne Plant's mortuary fridge – and he was astonished at how moving the experience had been. As he watched the grieving couple

78

drive away, he blinked rapidly for a few moments.

It was definitely coincidental that Drew was at the local police station to collect a burial order when the fax came through from the Cullompton Police to say there was a possible witness to the burial of the unidentified body in Slocombe's Field. 'Hey Drew – come and look at this,' invited PC Tony Stacey, who was clutching the sheet of paper. 'They're talking about you again.' He beckoned Drew to his desk and proffered the faxed message.

Witness has come forward to say she saw two people burying something shaped like a human body in the Slocombe Burial Ground at North Staverton. Mrs Caroline Kennett was on a train late at night, and saw something going on from the window. Date said to be 12th August last year. Over to you, mate. Give us a call if you'd like to interview the witness.

'Well, well. There *is* a railway line running alongside your field, isn't there?'

Drew nodded. 'But how can she have seen anything? Everything's pitch black, in the countryside, and she was on a well-lit train.'

'We can ask her to explain. Not that it helps much. Just means we have a date.'

'One that's easy to remember anyway,' said Drew casually.

'Why's that, then?'

'Glorious twelfth? Grouse shooting starts, doesn't it?'

'Not much of a shot myself,' said PC Stacey,

79

with a parody of modesty that did nothing to conceal the flash of dislike. 'Not a date that immediately thrills my heart.' He leaned forward. 'To be perfectly honest, it's the first time I've ever heard of it. Not the sort of circles I move in.'

'Well – me neither, really,' said Drew, suppressing a sigh. Yet again he'd managed to make himself look arrogant, or pretentious, by being too clever. It happened depressingly frequently and always in the company of other men. No wonder he preferred being amongst women: they never seemed threatened by displays of knowledge.

The burial order Drew had been collecting was for one Cynthia Smithers, aged seventy-two, dead of congestive heart failure without having consulted a doctor for nearly a year. Her two sons and three daughters had collectively agreed on a Peaceful Repose funeral. 'There's precious little money around, you see,' explained one of the daughters to Drew. 'And it sounds nice in your field.' Not for the first time, Drew wondered whether he'd done the right thing in keeping costs so low. For so long now funerals had made a substantial hole in almost any family's resources, and the population had seen that as no more than fitting. If you offered a cheap service, did that undervalue the person being buried? Was he making things too easy for the miserly and uncaring? The accusations had been articulated only too vividly by his former employer, Daphne Plant. *You're not doing anybody any favours, Drew. Not even yourself. If people genuinely can't afford fifteen hundred pounds or so, then there's a DSS fund to help them out. Isn't a person's life worth commemorating with some serious expenditure? All our social and personal values these days are tied up with money. By forcing them to dig into their pockets, we're saying we think death is something really important. What message are you going to be giving them? 'Just stick your old mum in this field, where she'll soon be fertilising the grass and the daisies. It'll only cost you a few hundred quid.' It'll backfire on you, Drew. Just you mark my words.*

He hadn't tried to argue with her. He saw only too clearly how it appeared to her, with her unwavering value system. Her family had been in the business for generations, fighting off threats from voracious American funeral companies, building determinedly on Plant's commitment to the local community, and its intimate knowledge of family connections. Daphne couldn't *afford* to listen to Drew. Even though funeral practices had scarcely changed in a century or more, there was no room for complacency. A natural burial ground, with its overtones of recycling and ecology, and a move away from empty ritual orchestrated by an unknown minister, just might be the future preference for a substantial proportion of the population. Drew could hardly expect his former boss to send him off with her blessing.

Cynthia Smithers' daughter quickly redeemed herself. 'Could we have one of those pretty willow baskets?' she asked. 'We'll come and decorate it ourselves, if that's all right. And we'll dress Mum up in her Sunday best.' For the next

81

day and a half, no fewer than nine members of the woman's family made free with Drew's cool room behind the office, making up for the shortage of money with an infinity of time and care and attention. Drew almost wept with relieved admiration.

'Could we put up a bird box?' asked a grandson. 'So she can be sure to have some bluetits around her? She loved bluetits, did Granny.' Drew went with him to select a suitable point on the trunk of one of the beech trees, indulging in a glowing vision of a succession of such suggestions, until the field became an overflowing paradise of colour and wildlife and individual statements of love. *Yes!* he crowed to himself. *It's really going to work.*

Cynthia's two sons dug the grave themselves, saving another eighty pounds on their bill and doing Jeffrey out of a job. They went down three and a half feet, which Drew advised was the deepest he thought sensible. After some research, he had worked out how to get the significance of this across to people, without being too graphic. 'There's virtually no oxygen deep in the ground,' he would explain, 'so the natural processes don't happen properly. And in this particular bit of ground, there's a layer of clay at about four feet, which only makes it worse. I won't go into the biochemical details, but ecologically speaking, a body is going to be a lot more useful if it's not buried too deep.' Privately, he wished they'd made it even shallower, but it was still a decided improvement on the traditional six feet.

'Er – there isn't any danger of animals – you

know–' the elder son asked uncomfortably. 'I mean – that's why burials are usually quite deep, isn't it?'

Drew smiled reassuringly. 'No need to worry about that,' he said. Bland remarks of this kind came automatically to his lips these days. He knew when to tell people what they wanted to hear. It was true, anyway, more or less. Only if the mysterious workings of the earth brought the body very much closer to the surface – and such things had been known to happen – was there any chance of a hungry badger or fox making pre-dations on the grave. Drew was keeping a close eye on his charges for this reason. Any sign of an animal digging would call for some urgent action.

The interment itself was a classic. The family – sons and daughters together – lowered their mother into the grave and covered her with flowers. She was wrapped in a sheet of pure linen, folded into the basket; her children read poems as she lay there, and shared stories about the person she had been. Weeping came and went like the scattered showers that the day had provided. Nobody mentioned God or the life to come. Drew and Maggs, standing at a distance, interested observers and nothing more, shared a moment of intense satisfaction. Afterwards, she said, 'That's what this is all about, isn't it? Give it ten years, and everybody'll be having funerals like this.'

'We wish,' he smiled. 'But yes – it said it all, when you think about it. She's a lucky lady.'

Maggs met him at the office door as he finished

with the departing family. 'The postman just gave me this,' she said. 'Second post.'

He knew instantly what it was. The same brown envelope, the same neat address label. He thought briefly about trying to conceal it from Maggs, only to conclude that there was little point. With shaking hands, he tore it open.

**YOU THINK YOU'RE SO CLEVER
IT'S THE WORK OF THE DEVIL
YOU ARE CURSED FOR WHAT YOU DO**

Maggs looked over his shoulder. 'I recognise that typeface. Comes out rather well, doesn't it?'

'What?' Drew stared at her in complete confusion. For a moment he thought she'd written the letter herself.

'It's one of the fonts on the computer. I was going through them all for our leaflets, and this was one of my favourites. Not really much use, though.' She looked at the piece of paper again. 'Hey, Drew! That's not very nice, is it?'

He laughed painfully. 'That's more or less what Karen said about the last one,' he told her. 'Typical English understatement. It's hate mail, Maggs. Very unpleasant – not the slightest bit nice.'

'But nothing to worry about,' she told him bracingly. 'Just some idiot who thinks we're the anti-Christ for giving people what they want without vicars being involved. You always get a few nutcases like that.'

'Oh? You know about this sort of thing, do you?'

She gave him a hard stare. 'Don't you start,' she warned him. 'I had all that stuff from Jeffrey.'

He was bemused. 'All what stuff?'

'He thinks that because I'm black, I practise voodoo and the black arts, or whatever they're called. Bloody fool.'

'I didn't mean that,' Drew said. 'You know I didn't.' He sighed in frustration. 'This is the second anonymous letter I've had. The first one was pretty much the same. One more and I'll have to take it to the police.'

'And what're they going to do about it?' she said sceptically. 'There's no death threat or anything. I wouldn't think they'd be very interested. And they'd gossip about it. It'd be bad for business.'

He looked at her uneasily. 'So what can we do?' he asked.

'Ignore it. Don't give them the satisfaction of being taken seriously. Don't let it spoil today, either. You've just done a really great funeral for some really nice people. Everybody's pleased with you. The sun's shining. Concentrate on the positive – it's the only way. Ignore the bad, and it'll wither away. That's what my mum always says, and it works for her.'

'Maggs, you're a marvel,' he said, automatically. It was beginning to sound like a mantra.

For the next week, Drew had no problems forgetting the hate mail; his thoughts hovered almost constantly on the image of Genevieve Slater. Was she going to contact him again? What

85

would she ask of him if she did? He had thought about her visit from every angle and never came to any other conclusion but that she had already decided the body was indeed that of her mother, and that she wanted only to confirm the fact. If this had been all, he wouldn't have minded helping her. But the body was in all probability a murder victim. It was the subject of an ongoing police enquiry, however inert that enquiry might be. Any facts uncovered about it were directly relevant to that enquiry; they should not be withheld. There was no way around that reality, as far as Drew could see.

Another scenario had occurred to him, even more uncomfortable than the first: Genevieve had fabricated the whole story about her mother as an excuse to come and see him again. He knew she liked him; there had been no mistaking the mutuality of the attraction, neither two years ago nor last week. The voice of caution repeated regularly that it would be best if he never heard from her again. He wanted it too badly. And – the biggest warning sign of all – he hadn't mentioned her visit to Karen.

He tried telling himself it was the mystery of her mother's disappearance and her husband's suspected guilt that magnetised him, but he knew he was fooling himself. However unlikely a pair they might be, the bald truth was that he found her fascinating, warm, intelligent and vulnerable. *Vulnerable?* He repeated to himself, as the word came unbidden to his mind. That, of course, was the key: Drew knew himself to be a pushover for the vulnerable. And Genevieve already knew he was capable of telling lies, big lies, when the need arose. This put him at a disadvantage. She had seen his less-than-perfect side, and this – he had to admit – made *him* vulnerable, too. Genevieve understood that it had been a bigger deal for him than it might have been for other people. Most people lied when they were buying or selling a house – it was *expected*, for heaven's sake – but Drew wasn't like that. The main thing about Drew Slocombe was his honesty.

When Genevieve did finally call, he was outside directing fence-building operations and missed it. The answerphone carried no message and dialling 1471 merely yielded the information that the caller had withheld their number. Please try again, he silently begged, somehow knowing it had been her. When the phone rang again twenty minutes later, he snatched it up.

'I thought you couldn't be far away,' her rich voice said, without preamble. 'Were you having a romantic burial under an oak tree?'

'Putting up a new fence, actually.'

'And was that sweet daughter of yours helping?'

'Luckily, no. She's having her afternoon sleep at the moment. I'm glad you called back,' he added before he could stop himself.

'Have I given you long enough to think?'

Too long, he wanted to tell her. *Anyway, what was there to think about?*

'I really don't see how you're going to avoid the notice of the police,' he began conscientiously. 'If they do release the body at the end of the month and we bury her here, they're sure to send an observer to see who turns up. It's routine in a case like this. They'd probably make sure the local papers carried the date and time for that very reason. They won't just forget the case completely, even if it seems that way.'

'I don't want you to get yourself all worked up about the police, Drew. I realise it isn't fair to you, suggesting I might know who the body is–'

'I can't see any way around it,' he admitted. 'It keeps coming back to the same thing. I know you're probably right – that they wouldn't get anywhere, even if they investigate your mother's disappearance – not unless you co-operated with them.' He spoke jerkily, the familiar cloud of mixed emotions descending yet again. 'But I can't help feeling we ought to give them a chance.'

'And I have to tell you again that Willard and I wouldn't co-operate. We haven't got anything that was hers, anyway. She didn't leave anything behind when she last stayed, and it was months ago. I'm not much of a housekeeper, but I'm sure I've vacuumed and dusted the room she used once or twice since then.'

'You underestimate Forensics,' he told her. 'If they decided to take the idea seriously, then they'd be sure to find something they could use for comparison. Don't you think it would be best if you just let them get on with it? You would at least get a proper identification – that's what you want, isn't it? And they probably wouldn't find any evidence for a murder prosecution. They haven't done so far. Why don't you compromise? I'd help you then with a clear conscience.' There was a silence at the end of the line. 'Genevieve?

Are you still there?'

'Your *conscience*,' she said, her tone icy. 'Is that all that matters to you? You think they probably wouldn't find any evidence. That's not good enough, Drew. What if they find something they're certain is a murder weapon, or blood stains on some garment of Willard's that match hers? How do I know where they'd stop?' Her voice was rising sharply, close to hysteria.

'Okay,' he said hurriedly. 'Calm down, for heaven's sake. I see your point. So – what do you want from me now?'

'Perhaps we should meet again – and I'll tell you more of the story. You could even do a bit of detective work for me – go and see if she left anything behind in that bedsit of hers, that sort of thing. I know you fancy yourself as a detective–'

'Hey!' he put in with some indignation. 'What makes you think that?'

'Come on, I read the papers. What about that business eighteen months ago – Lapsford was the name, if I remember rightly Drew Slocombe, amateur sleuth. Front page news.'

'But I wouldn't be a hero this time, would I?' he said cynically.

'Who knows?' She sounded much more cheerful, as if already sure of him. 'You might.'

He tried hard to cling to his rapidly-evaporating common sense. Instead came the faces of Stanley Sharples, shrugging off the one-too-many dead body that Drew had landed him with; of Daphne Plant, who cared little for the niceties of legal requirements if they interrupted the

89

smooth running of her business; of Karen, visibly losing faith him and his new business; of Genevieve herself, telling him in all earnestness that she really did want to do the right thing. These faces all danced and flashed in front of him, taunting him with his indecisiveness.

'I'm not making any promises,' he said feebly. 'But I suppose it wouldn't hurt to have a bit of a snoop round.'

She gave a small cheer. 'Thanks, Drew. I knew I could depend on you. Come and see me one morning next week, if you can, and I'll give you the background.'

He agreed with a sense of relief. After all, what had he committed himself to? Nothing – yet – that would give the police any grounds for serious protest. It took scarcely any effort to assure himself that going to them now would simply be a waste of their time. Let the whole peculiar story drift forward just a few more steps, before any action of that sort was required.

CHAPTER FIVE

'There's a police car pulling up outside,' Maggs observed casually, later that afternoon, a few minutes after Karen had collected Stephanie. Drew's resulting stab of guilty alarm was quickly subdued by means of a deep breath and a rapid assessment of the worst that could possibly happen. *I haven't done anything,* he reminded himself. *Yet,* he added.

He waited for the knock on the office door and opened it promptly. He knew the police officer slightly, from his time at Plant's, but had never seen the woman with him before. 'It's Graham, isn't it?' he said affably. 'What can I do for you?'

The constable was formal, but much less stiff than he might have been. 'This is Mrs Caroline Kennett,' he introduced the woman. 'She's the lady who thinks she saw something happening in your field from a train last summer.'

'Oh, yes,' said Drew, frantically trying to work out whether the visit carried any threat to his incipient arrangement with Genevieve. 'On the glorious twelfth, if I remember rightly.'

Both visitors looked at him blankly, and behind him Maggs gave a soft snort. Would he never learn? he asked himself unhappily.

'We thought it might help Mrs Kennett if she could come and see your burial ground,' the policeman continued, ushering the woman into the office. She stepped into the room nervously, as if expecting to see corpses laid out on the desk. Drew smiled at her. She looked very ordinary: anybody's mother, with neatly-cut hair and cheap-looking spectacles. The mere fact that the police had bothered to bring her was significant, he supposed. From his latest talk with Stanley, he'd assumed they'd more or less given up the whole case by this time.

'It'll look a bit different from the way it was in August,' he said. 'We've tidied it up a lot since then.'

'Well, let's give it a try,' said Graham. 'Okay?' he asked Drew.

'Help yourself.' Drew waved them towards the back door, which opened onto the field. 'You don't need me, do you?'

'Can we still see the site of the grave?' the policeman asked.

Drew pointed it out to them, the soil still disturbed; none of his official graves was yet in that section of the field, so there could be no confusion. The two set off up the path.

'What's all that about?' Maggs hissed at Drew, when she judged they were out of earshot.

'The woman thinks she witnessed people burying a body out there last August. She was in a train and saw them digging a hole, apparently.'

Maggs stuck her lips out dubiously. 'Bit of a coincidence!' she said.

'Life's full of coincidences,' he said, absently, watching the proceedings outside. 'She's nodding – look.'

'Is she? I can't see that far.'

The witness and her escort had walked up to the boundary fence, and turned to face down the slope. The woman pointed up at a tree, and then put her hand to her mouth as if thinking hard. Drew's pride in his excellent long sight was overlaid by an abiding anxiety. 'You should get glasses,' he told Maggs.

'I've got some – but I never use them,' she admitted. 'I don't often have to read faces at two hundred yards.'

'She looks fairly confident,' he said, helpfully.

'There must be loads of fields like this along the railway line,' Maggs said. 'How can she be sure it's the right one? After eight months?'

'They seem to think she's an important witness.'

'Only because she's the only one they've got. Imagine trying to use her in court! She wears glasses; train windows get steamed up; it was ages ago; and she might have been asleep and dreaming in any case. I'd love to be the prosecution cross-examining her.'

Maggs had a taste for legal thrillers, and an impressive grasp of the complexities of courtroom procedure. Drew supposed that if the case ever did get as far as a prosecution, he'd want the right person to be charged and sentenced. A reliable witness was surely something to be prized. He just wished it could all be postponed until he'd extricated himself from his uneasy connection with Genevieve Slater.

'All right?' he asked Graham when the two returned.

'It's a bit difficult,' said the woman, who

93

seemed more relaxed now. 'It was dark, you see. And I was half asleep.'

'But you thought the trees looked the same,' Graham supplied for her.

She screwed up her face. 'Well, I know there *were* some trees,' she said feebly.

'I think it's probable that you did witness the burial,' the policeman said confidently. 'And that's very helpful to us. It gives us a firm date for the killing.'

'Not necessarily the *killing*,' interposed Maggs. 'Just the disposal of the body. It might have been days later.'

'That's true,' Graham conceded, with some irritation. 'But unlikely, wouldn't you say?'

'Don't see why,' Maggs told him truculently.

Graham knew better than to argue. He guided his witness outside, turning briefly to thank Drew. 'Can't see this getting us very far,' he said quietly. 'No closer to getting an ID on the body – and we already know somebody buried her here, don't we? Still, it's as well to go through the motions. Don't want anyone accusing us of being slack.'

'I should say not,' Maggs endorsed with a serious expression. Drew inwardly prayed that Graham wouldn't realise he was being mocked. He closed the door as soon as he decently could, and gave his assistant a light cuff on the arm.

'They're not all stupid, you know,' he said.

'Oh, yes, they are,' she disagreed comfortably.

'The childcare thing isn't quite working as well as I hoped,' Drew admitted reluctantly to Karen

94

that evening; the second week of term had begun and it already felt like a month or more. 'Stephanie's very good, but when she starts walking I don't see how I'll get any work done at all.'

'But you said it would be fine. Maggs is there when you're not. And if you're both needed for a funeral, Jeffrey can stay in the office with her.'

'Maggs and Jeffrey have both made it clear they don't want to be used as unpaid childminders,' he said unhappily. 'That's the bit we didn't take into account. I suppose you can't blame them, but it never occurred to me they'd see it like that. I mean – she's so good, you can't call it work.'

'People do these days, unfortunately.' Karen sat at the kitchen table, finishing her coffee, head leaning on one hand. She looked tired and even paler than the previous week. 'It's a whole industry, looking after kids.'

'We need a granny,' he said glumly. 'Or a nice lady next door.'

'You're thirty years out of date. A *great*-granny might just have some time to spare, but the grannies are totally out of the question.'

'I know.' Drew's mother had taken a law degree in her late thirties, and was still practising in her sixties, and Karen's was running a small hotel in North Wales with her second husband. 'Maybe a grandad would be a better bet – men seem to retire more finally than women.'

'Nice idea. You just have to persuade them to leave all their friends and activities behind and move down here.'

'I'm not really complaining. We haven't had any

95

disasters yet – I was just a bit thrown by Maggs's attitude. I can't depend on her as I assumed I could.'

Karen frowned worriedly. 'We do need back-up. If you and Maggs have to go and remove a body at short notice and you can't persuade Jeffrey to take over – or he's not around – you'll be sunk. It'd be different if I worked at the Comprehensive – they've got a crèche. Primary schools aren't so enlightened.'

'They haven't got the resources,' he said pedantically. 'Look – we know people in the village. There's Jane with her twins, for instance. We could ask her if she'd mind being on standby.'

'We can't, Drew. You can't impose on people like that. They'd be sure to have something planned on the day you needed them. God – this is a nightmare.' She smacked a hand on the table in frustration, glared at him and tightened her lips. He could almost hear the suppressed accusation: *If only you had a proper job, we could afford professional childcare.*

'Hey!' he soothed quickly. 'It'll be okay. I like looking after her. She's the light of my life. If I have to, I can take her with me on a removal. It'll be another break with tradition.'

'It'll freak people out – not least the Social Services. It's probably child abuse to let them anywhere near a dead body. I'm not sure I'm too keen on the idea myself, come to that.'

'She wouldn't see anything.'

'I've got to go and do my lesson plans.' She stood up slowly, resting her weight on one hand for a moment. Drew watched her closely. 'You really don't look well,' he said. 'Pale, tired, seeing the black side of everything. What's the matter?'

She shook her head. 'On my feet most of the day – getting back into the routine. Not sleeping too well. Tired all the time. Indigestion. Nothing they invented a cure for. I'll be okay. And I miss Stephanie.' Suddenly she was crying, both hands hiding her face. She sat down again heavily. 'I wish I could just stay at home,' she wept.

'Oh, sweetheart, I'm sorry.' He put his arm round her shoulders, and ran over her list of symptoms in his head, trying not to linger on the possible diagnoses: leukaemia, Hodgkins, ME. Once a nurse, always a Jeremiah, when it came to health matters. But none of these were going to happen to his stalwart Karen. Of course they weren't.

'We'll talk about it tomorrow. Maybe you could go part-time?'

She wiped her nose fiercely, and stood up again. 'Ignore me,' she said, forcing a smile. 'Too many changes all at the same time. I'm just not as tough as I thought I was.'

'I phoned him today,' Genevieve told her husband. 'He's coming round to see me.' Willard lowered his newspaper a few inches, and threw a glance at her, sliding his eyes briefly up and down her body, as he'd done ever since they'd realised she was pregnant. She knew what he was thinking, behind those small curtained eyes: he was feeling trapped and suspicious. A child had never been part of their life plan, and her insistence on proceeding with the pregnancy had frightened and infuriated him. But his reaction had been typical: he had carried on since that first startled moment as if nothing were happening. Except that he could no longer look at her properly.

As his glance slid away, she grunted suddenly, a small '*Oof*' of discomfort. Willard's look was enough of a question.

'Just a particularly unpleasant kick from this brute.' She patted her bulge. 'Nothing that need alarm you.'

'I wasn't alarmed.' Willard was sitting at the dining table with a newspaper spread out in front of him; other papers and magazines were stacked on the floor nearby, awaiting his attention. 'You should leave the poor fellow alone,' he returned to the matter in hand. 'There's absolutely no cause for concern over your mother. Opening cans of worms – literally, I suppose, in this instance – is never a sensible idea.'

Genevieve flinched exaggeratedly at his all-too-appropriate metaphor. 'You don't care what you say to upset me, do you?' she accused.

'Not really,' he told her. 'It never makes any difference, anyway. Water off a duck's back. If it mattered what I say, things would be entirely other than they are now.'

'Your capacity for self-deception never ceases to amaze me,' she told him.

'And your lack of logic never ceases to depress me.'

'Well, at least I'm trying to do something! We can't go on indefinitely just assuming Mum's perfectly okay. I want to know, Willard. Is that too hard to understand? She might not have been the best mother in the world, but in a few weeks, I'm going to be a mother myself, and believe it or not, that does make a difference. Call me childish if you like – but the truth is, I want my own mother to be around. I need her.'

He worked his mouth as if trying to spit out this sudden dollop of sentiment, then visibly braced himself to look her full in the face. 'So – if this unidentified murder victim turns out to be your mother – and that, I suppose, can only be proven with our co-operation – you're perfectly prepared to get involved in a murder investigation, are you? With all the questions and intrusions that that involves? Possibly a trial, in the extremely unlikely event that a culprit is found. Can you cope with that, my sweet? My neurotic darling – can you actually see yourself standing up in court as a key witness for the prosecution? Can you see yourself listening to the defence call your mother a slut, a whore, a failure as a woman?'

She shrank away from him, wilting under the vitriolic blast of his contempt. 'Stop it,' she implored him. 'I'm only trying to do what's right.'

His laugh was another deluge of acid *'Right!'* he mocked. 'It takes a fully sane person to understand what's right. It's well beyond your capacity, my immature little pet, believe me. But don't let me stop you. Just you carry on in your own sweet, destructive way. Just don't expect me to be around to pick up the pieces.'

Genevieve whimpered her frustration. 'You make it all so much worse,' she whined. 'I thought I could depend on you.'

99

'I thought so too at one time,' he agreed conversationally. 'Fools, weren't we?' And he returned calmly to his perusal of the newspaper.

It was a familiar signal that he no longer wanted to talk to her, and she came very close to accepting it as her dismissal. But another nudge from the unborn child prompted her to persist.

'Willard,' she said, her tone almost normal again, 'this does involve you, you know. If my mother isn't here, then you're going to have to help with the baby. Someone's got to. Malcolm Jarvis has only agreed to come for the delivery, and to make sure everything's all right. After that, we'll be on our own.' Despite herself, her voice began to rise again, returning to the shrill tones that Willard's silence so often reduced her to.

'Millions of women face childbirth every day,' Willard told her, without a trace of sympathy. 'You should have thought of that earlier. Too late to decide you can't cope now.'

'But–' she started to say, before another kick made her pause. She continued in a voice thick with distress, 'I didn't have any choice. What else could I have done?'

Willard looked away again. 'You could have got your neuroses sorted out years ago. It's time you faced reality. You're putting two lives at risk with this nonsense.'

'If my mother was here–'

'If your mother was here, she'd tell you exactly what I've just told you. That it's time you snapped out of it. What happened is ancient history. You were twelve years old. It wasn't even *about you*. I never could see why you were so

100

screwed up over something that happened to other people.'

She leaned her head on her hands, elbows on the table, pushing her thick hair back from her face. 'It happened to *me*, Willard. Me and Brigid. Our lives fell apart and never got put back together. And now – if my mother really is dead, there's never going to be any hope of making things right.'

He stood up then, at the end of all patience. 'All right!' he thundered. 'I give up – as usual. Find your blasted mother, if that's what you want. Dead or alive, murdered or swanning around with a toyboy in the South Pacific. Just leave me out of it. I told you last year – I never want to see that bloody woman again.'

Drew got Stephanie dressed and fed and carried her round to the office. Sensing his pessimistic mood, she was unusually unco-operative, stiffening her small sturdy body when he tried to put her on the floor, clinging stubbornly to his neck. It was cold out, and the sky was a flat grey: a fit setting for Drew's gloom. The field looked bleak and unappealing. The building felt damp and draughty, all the disadvantages of an old cottage manifesting themselves at once. The office had originally been a lean-to, housing logs and tools and an ancient washtub. It had had a corrugated iron roof and whitewashed walls. Drew and Karen had replaced the roof with tiles, and erected a more solid outer wall, but it still felt insubstantial.

There hadn't been a single phonecall for two

days, apart from the one from Genevieve Slater. Maggs was going mad with boredom. The money from the labrador had already gone on fencing materials.

'I need another source of income,' Drew muttered to himself, as he tried to cajole Stephanie into taking an interest in her toys. 'Maybe I could become a childminder...'

Maggs arrived on her bike a few minutes later, and clumped noisily into the building. She wore biker's boots with enormous soles, that made Drew feel old and stuffy. 'What're we going to do today, then?' she demanded aggressively. 'The fence is finished and there's a limit to the amount of tidying up I can do.'

'We knew there'd be quiet spells,' he said. 'It was like this at Plant's sometimes. People don't die in a nice regular pattern – it goes in clusters. Any time now, we'll be doing two funerals in a day and wishing it was quiet again.'

'Dream on,' she scoffed.

Drew sighed. 'We could have a go at enlarging the car park. Widen the entrance and cut down some of the thistles and brambles. We got planning permission for twelve spaces, if I remember rightly, and at the moment you can barely get three in.'

'Twelve! Where are you going to put them?'

He shrugged. 'Eventually, all along the inside of the hedge bordering the road. It'll be tarmacked and marked out – but I haven't got the cash for it yet. Trouble is, it's a Catch 22 – nobody'll come because they can't park – and if nobody comes, we can't afford to give them a park.'

'You sound a bit down, same as me,' Maggs observed.

'Yeah, well, we might have to rethink what happens with Stephanie. It isn't going to be fair to her to have her tagging along all the time.'

'I did wonder what you thought you were doing.'

'I expected I'd be getting more business by now, and could afford to pay someone to mind her.'

'Maybe this chap'll be the one we're waiting for,' she said, nodding at the car drawing up outside the gate. As always, there was a moment of indecision as the driver wondered where he was supposed to park. Drew could see a leather coat, and the side of a man's head. He looked late middle-aged, judging by the way his head sat stiffly on his shoulders.

'Don't stare,' he told Maggs. 'Try and look busy.'

'Just don't ask me to take Stephanie outside while you talk to him,' she warned.

Drew had already guessed that the man had a newly-dead parent, or perhaps a wife, and had seen the publicity about the cemetery. He'd learned that you couldn't identify those people who'd be interested in alternative funerals just by looking at them; this man, however, seemed even less of a likely customer than Hubert Grainger had been. He was pulling off black driving gloves, and working his thin lips as if rehearsing what he was going to say, as he approached the open door of the office. 'Is this the Peaceful Repose Cemetery?' he asked. 'It's taken me bloody ages to find you.'

Drew held out a friendly hand, not so much to shake as to usher the man into the building. 'I'm sorry,' he said. 'We are a bit remote. That's part of the attraction, of course.'

'I wouldn't know about that. I don't require your services. My name's Jarvis, Dr Jarvis. I'd like to have a private talk about the body you found here last month.' His face was high-coloured, as if he'd spent the winter in sunnier climes, his hair looked incongruously dark, given his apparent age. Drew almost sighed aloud. A day or two earlier, he might have been intrigued, even excited, but the flat mood of this morning was so powerful he felt little but irritation at the loss of a potential customer and the prospect of getting involved again with the mysterious body.

Jarvis eyed Stephanie suspiciously as she sat, calmly surrounded by toys, in her usual corner. Every day Drew had added more amusements and comforts for her, until she had a play area worthy of any day nursery. 'My daughter,' he explained. 'She's no trouble.'

'Hardly the best place for her, I'd have thought,' said the man shortly. 'Don't you keep bodies here?'

'In the cool room, yes. I don't think she's at any risk from them.'

'Or they from her?' The flash of humour made some difference to Drew's assessment of his visitor. He settled the man in his best chair and then took another for himself. He did not sit behind his desk, disliking the connotations of interviews and supplication. 'Well – how can I help?' he asked.

The man chewed his lip for a moment. 'It's rather delicate,' he began. 'When I read the description of the woman you found here, and the estimated date when she must have died, I wondered whether it might be – someone I knew. I assume you're privy to more detail than was published in the newspapers, and – well – I'd like to be sure in my own mind before taking further action.'

Drew acknowledged the strong sense of *déjà vu* that had swept over him as he listened to what the man was saying: it was as if Jarvis had taken the script directly from Genevieve Slater. 'She was very difficult to identify,' he said cautiously. 'There really isn't much more to go on than clothes, dentures and the necklace. Just as the papers said.'

Jarvis became more agitated, cupping a hand tightly around his jaw as if suffering from toothache. 'Tall, elderly, slim. Wearing jewellery from Egypt – where I know she was last year – I'm *sure* it's her. She hasn't been seen since last summer by anyone in her family. I just don't understand who would have buried her here. At least – I do have a very unpleasant suspicion.' He wriggled uneasily in the chair, looking anywhere but at Drew. 'It's difficult to know how much to tell you. I realise you wouldn't want to be privy to any information that might get you into trouble.'

This is ridiculous, thought Drew. *They* must *know each other.* He raised his eyebrows encouragingly, but said nothing.

His visitor went on, 'There is one possibility the

police don't seem to have considered. If it's the woman I'm thinking of, I believe she may have committed suicide – and left instructions to be buried here, unofficially, to save all the trouble of an inquest and so on. In fact – if I can be satisfied in my own mind that it's the woman in question, I'd be happy to finance a reburial here. From a first glance it seems very pleasant.'

'Suicide?' Drew picked up the idea with considerable scepticism. 'But–'

'I know. It sounds most peculiar. That's why I'm here – I hoped you'd divulge a few more details. Set my mind at rest.'

Drew shook his head. 'I very much doubt whether I can do that,' he said. 'As I've already told you – the cause of death is uncertain.'

'But have you heard anything which would make suicide out of the question? Any further information the police haven't made public?'

Drew pressed his lips together, in an effort to control his rising temper. He was being played with – that was becoming very obvious – and he didn't like it. 'Might I ask why you've come to me?' he said coldly. 'And why you think I'd answer a question like that?'

'Because it doesn't hurt you. Because I'm desperate. Because it's the only way I can get any peace,' the man burst out. 'I know it all sounds crazy – but I'm not the only person involved. There's a family, as well.'

Drew's patience snapped. Any other day, and he might have listened with sympathy: now he'd had enough.

'If you believe you know the woman's identity,

you have a duty to go to the police,' he said firmly. 'There's nothing I can tell you. As you rightly say, by merely coming here and talking like this, you make me an accessory to the crime of obstructing a murder enquiry.' He frowned severely, and slapped one hand down on the desk for emphasis.

'But–' the man attempted '–but, just hear me out. I promise you have nothing to lose by doing that. There is absolutely no chance that I'll go to the police, and I'm trusting that you won't do so, either.'

'I absolutely can't help you,' Drew repeated. 'I don't know anything beyond what was in the papers.' He paused, remembering his conversation with Stanley. *Wasn't wearing any undies – not even knickers. Ate a substantial meal … chicken curry…* There might have been more, if he racked his brains. *What harm could it do,* he wondered, *to share these snippets with Dr Jarvis?*

As if sensing a softening, the man pressed home his point. 'If I'm right, then there's no need to take it any further. She can be laid to rest again, and nobody's going to be harmed by her remaining anonymous. Nobody but me – knowing I was more or less the one who drove her to it.'

Drew's scepticism became mixed with curiosity. *Damn it,* he thought. *Why do I always have to know the full story? It makes life so much more complicated.*

'But it wasn't you who buried her here?' he demanded. 'Because that's the way it's beginning to sound.'

107

'No, it wasn't me. Let me give you a bit more of the background. I was her GP you see, have been for thirty years or more. But I retired eighteen months ago – no, not under any kind of a cloud,' he added, noticing Drew's expression. 'I was sixty, and felt I'd done it for long enough, that's all.'

'Go on,' Drew invited him, leaning forward over the edge of the desk.

The visitor squirmed restlessly on his chair. 'I hope it'll explain why I'd much rather keep away from the police. They have an unfortunate habit of digging into the past – especially, now, where a medical practitioner is concerned. Any shadow of suspicion and they start believing they've got a serial killer on their hands. There's no character so unredeemable as an untrustworthy doctor. They'd make my life unbearable.'

'Are you sure you want to tell me this?' Drew interrupted. 'It's quite possible that I'll feel forced to pass your story directly to the Coroner.'

'I'm taking that risk.' The doctor fiddled with a button on his coat, as he spoke, but showed no sign of emotion as he told his story.

'This woman had a badly handicapped son,' he said, following the bald statement with a torrent of explanation that felt to Drew like some sort of confession. 'He had severe deformation of the spine, resulting in diminished lung capacity, chronic joint pain and susceptibility to infection. He also had poor hearing and eyesight. She wasn't the sort of woman keen to sacrifice herself to caring for him, especially when he got into his teens. But she had no choice. He was a difficult person, in many ways. Peevish, self-absorbed.

108

She never pretended to love him, and tried several times to get him into long-term residential care. Unfortunately, he wasn't quite handicapped enough to qualify under the NHS and she couldn't hope to pay for it. She had two other children, much older, and was no chicken herself. Well, in the end, she cracked. I had to choose whether to see her completely destroyed by the burden or to help her out of it. I won't go into details, but between us we brought the whole thing to a somewhat speedier conclusion than nature would have done, left to its own devices. Nathan had a chest infection, which turned to pneumonia. He was in severe distress, and was developing a new set of spinal problems as he grew to adult size. There was no quality of life for anyone concerned.'

'I'm with you so far,' said Drew, glancing at his little daughter and wondering at how things might have been in his own family circle. It didn't occur to him to doubt the man's medical credentials; as a former nurse himself, he recognised the oddly brisk detachment from a painful emotional situation. And he found himself almost as drawn into this tale as he had been into Genevieve's.

'How long ago did this happen?' Drew asked, as the man paused.

'Five or six years. I'd almost forgotten the whole thing, until early last year.'

'So what happened?'

'She came to me in great distress. Someone had accused her of killing her son, and she was frightened.'

'And what did you say?'

'I – I sent her away. I told her to stop making a fool of herself.'

'At last!' breathed Drew.

'Pardon?'

'It sounds as if you've finally got to the point. You don't really think she committed suicide, do you? The idea's completely ludicrous, given the circumstances. You're trying to get confirmation that this is your fellow conspirator and that someone murdered her, to ease your own conscience – and allay your own fears. Because if she's dead, you don't have to worry about being caught for what you did to her son.' His raised voice alarmed Stephanie, who gave an anxious bleat; Drew fell silent, wondering why he'd been so rash.

But the man seemed surprisingly unperturbed by Drew's accusations. 'You've got the wrong end of the stick, you know. I can understand your doubting my story, but you've jumped to completely the wrong conclusion.'

Drew was distracted by Stephanie, who, distressed, had crawled to him and pulled herself up to wobble unsteadily against his leg. He swung her up onto his lap. 'Sorry,' he muttered. He wasn't sure to whom he was apologising. 'You'd better tell me the rest of it.'

'They were just an ordinary family when I first knew them,' Dr Jarvis recalled, sitting back in his chair, and smiling thoughtfully at Stephanie as she played with Drew's fingers. 'Mum, Dad and two little girls. Then they fell for a third baby – quite unplanned – and it all went wrong. If ever

110

there was a good case for a termination, that was it. But she wouldn't hear of it. Anyway, there was a terrible car accident. The father was killed. Gwen was five months pregnant, and was trapped in the wreckage. When the baby was born, it was obvious he'd been damaged *in utero*. Nobody was ever really sure whether it was the psychological trauma or something more physiological that did it. She wasn't badly injured, apart from bruises and cuts–'

Drew couldn't suppress a groan. At the man's quizzical look, he explained, 'My wife was hit by a car when she was first pregnant with this one.' He nodded at Stephanie. 'We were lucky, from the sound of it.'

Jarvis shook his head. 'My patient was unlucky,' he said. 'The baby wasn't really wanted. Her husband wasn't happy about it. They were having a blazing fight in the car, just before the crash. It was a disaster waiting to happen, looking back on it. The whole family was crushed by that accident. They were like walking wounded for years afterwards. Still are, in Genevieve's case.'

Drew's heart pounded; his head hummed with the sudden surge of pressure. 'Not Genevieve Slater?' he said faintly.

'That's right,' agreed Dr Jarvis in surprise. 'Do you know her?'

CHAPTER SIX

The time had come, Drew told himself sternly, to tell Karen what had been happening. Above all, he should tell her that Genevieve Slater had turned up again. He should have done it days ago; he knew only too well why he hadn't.

Karen had been overjoyed when they'd triumphed over the Slaters and been accepted as purchasers of the Bradbourne house. 'I wonder why she chose us?' she'd mused.

'Because we're so nice,' Drew had quipped. He never told her what he'd done, never disclosed his brief intimacy with Genevieve. Karen had never even known her Christian name. He tried to, in the early days, but the moment was never quite right, and before long, it became much too late to confess. It would turn a justifiable piece of dishonesty into something much bigger, more significant, if he gave the impression that it had weighed heavy on his conscience. Much easier to try and forget the whole thing.

He had worried at first that Genevieve would find a way to tell Karen about it. But remembering how she'd forgiven him despite her anger, he had convinced himself that she would have nothing to gain by doing that. 'Well, good luck to you then,' had been her parting shot to him. 'It's been a pleasure knowing you, Drew Slocombe. Your wife's a very lucky girl.'

The shame at how tempted he'd been – the self-disgust – the horrified realisation when he awoke from dreaming about Genevieve – all came back to him now. If he mentioned her name now, linking her to the Mrs Slater from the past, wouldn't Karen know by some wifely instinct how Genevieve made him feel? Better, then, to keep her identity anonymous – at least for the time being.

Karen's good sense had helped him before, when events had threatened to overwhelm him and his inconvenient sense of justice and over-active curiosity had led him into deep waters. But she was a lot less receptive now than she would have been a year earlier. After a day in front of thirty six-year-olds, followed by collecting Stephanie and feeding her, then preparing for the coming week's schedule, she was tired and tetchy. Drew made a point of closing the office promptly at five every day and joining his wife and daughter in the cottage; Karen then frequently sent him out to the supermarket four miles away, and expected him to cook their evening meal. *How did life get to be so frantic?* he wondered.

'I had a very peculiar visitor today,' he began, when Stephanie was at last in bed and the meal over and done with. 'About that body we found.'

'Oh, yes?' Karen was slumped in an armchair with her feet up, a hand across her eyes.

'He thinks he knows who she is.'

'Why come to you about it? Hasn't he been to the police?'

'He claims to think she committed suicide

because of a threat he made to her. The police wouldn't be very sympathetic. He's a doctor, you see. He might find himself under an uncomfortably close scrutiny–'

'What was the threat?' she asked, focusing on the central point, despite her exhaustion.

'Oh – something that happened a few years ago. Euthanasia, I suppose. He says they did it together.'

'Makes sense.' She frowned, and ran her fingers through her hair; Drew observed that it could do with a wash. It looked lank and greasy. 'But why come to you? Why rock the boat when there's practically no danger of the body being identified? Sounds rather a reckless move to me.'

'Well – that's where it gets complicated,' Drew began, leaning towards her, over the arm of the chair. 'I think it could be a double bluff–'

'Oh!' Karen stiffened and put a hand to her middle.

'What's the matter?' he demanded, in alarm.

She laughed unsteadily. 'Well, if I didn't know better, I'd say I was just kicked from inside. That's exactly what it felt like.'

'Wind,' he said. 'Must be.' But in that three or four seconds, all had become clear to them both. And, suddenly, Drew lost all interest in murders and bodies and seductive older women.

The weekend came as a relief out of all proportion. Drew and Karen lay in bed until eight-thirty on Saturday morning, Stephanie dozing between them. Drew pretended to be asleep for the half hour after he woke, trying to sift through

114

the tangle of dilemmas he was faced with; he suspected Karen was doing exactly the same.

'It must have been before Christmas,' she said eventually, into the silence. 'I must be at least four months gone. God, I feel so stupid.'

'It's still not certain. You'll have to have it confirmed. Can you not buy a test?'

'If I'm four months, a test won't be reliable. The hormones all switch around at twelve or thirteen weeks. It'll have to be a scan, or a Sonicaid.' She laughed weakly. 'It certainly explains why I've been feeling so peculiar.'

It's a disaster, Drew thought despairingly; all the more despairing because he couldn't ever utter the words. These things happened to other people, didn't they? Besides, Stephanie had taken more than two years to get started – it had never occurred to him that conception could be easy. 'All that breastfeeding,' he said. 'I thought it worked as a contraceptive.'

'It does,' she said. 'Usually. I assumed that's why I hadn't started periods again. But it's not a hundred per cent. I thought – well, you know. I thought we were subfertile–'

'Yeah,' Drew sympathised ruefully. 'I thought so too.'

'I can't believe we've been so stupid! I was going to go to the clinic next week and get a diaphragm or something. I really was. I knew I shouldn't have left it this long. I can just see Dr Harrison's face – you remember he asked me what we were going to use, before Steph was a week old?'

Always quick to read cosmic meaning into

115

events, Drew had already concluded that he was being punished in some way. And it wasn't difficult to identify the misdemeanour responsible. He should never have permitted himself to feel as he did about Genevieve Slater – although how it would have been possible to feel differently, he had no idea. He should have told Karen about her recent reappearance in his life straight away. He had no idea how he was going to extricate himself from the inevitable second meeting; the involvement in her family's murky past; the acquiescence to her request that he play detective on her behalf. He was helpless flotsam, sucked in both by illicit desire and the fact of his field having been chosen as the mystery woman's burial place. He seemed to have no free will of his own in the matter.

'It might all be your imagination,' he said doggedly. 'Let's not get carried away. Anyway, wouldn't you have felt sick – gone off coffee – all that stuff that happened last time?'

'I was too busy,' she said. 'If I had felt sick, I wouldn't have had time to dwell on it. It's not like ordinary nausea – and you don't get it every time, in any case. It never even *occurred* to me.' She sighed heavily, and turned to look at him. 'Oh, Drew. How on earth are we going to manage?'

Valiantly he strove to be strong. 'It'll be fine,' he said. 'We wanted more babies, anyway. The trick is to just take it a day at a time.'

'And starve in the process,' she groaned.

They didn't return to the subject of the dead

woman in the field throughout the weekend. Stephanie was fractious and demanding; although they pretended to believe it was a new tooth coming through, both her parents knew it was a direct reaction to the tension between them. The woman who'd run their antenatal classes had made an unforgettable remark: *Babies are highly sensitive emotional barometers. When you're frazzled or worried, they'll start whinging and clinging. Once you realise that, it gets much easier to deal with.* Drew wasn't entirely convinced by the last part, as his daughter clutched his hair painfully when he tried to lie her down in her cot for the fifteenth time that evening, but he couldn't deny the truth of the basic assertion.

At the back of his mind, he could already hear Karen's voice: *I'm sorry, Drew, but you're going to have to get a proper job. One with a guaranteed income. We can't possibly manage otherwise. I can't go back to work with two babies. It'll be too complicated.*

A proper job meant abandoning Peaceful Repose, selling out to someone else. It meant going back to nursing, or starting again in something new. The idea sickened him, but it galvanised him into searching for a solution, no matter how bizarre it might be.

And the next day, it was handed to him on a plate, tied up with red ribbon and ticking like a cartoon time bomb. On Monday afternoon, three things happened within half an hour, and by the end of that time Drew's situation had been transformed.

117

Firstly, at three-fifteen, another phonecall from Genevieve came through. Drew snatched up the phone, partly in anticipation that it would be her and partly to avoid disturbing Stephanie, who was lying quietly on her side, tootling her toy train along the office skirtingboard.

'I gather Malcolm Jarvis came to see you,' she said, faintly accusing. 'And you told him you'd met me.'

'I mentioned you, yes. Was that a problem?'

'Not really. Although I don't understand what his motivation is. He hadn't seen my mother for years, as far as I know. I think he had a bit of a thing about her, when my brother was alive. She was always sort of rapacious where men were concerned. I assume he told you about my brother?'

'He did, yes. Very sad.'

'Nathan was a monster,' she said flatly. 'Self-pitying, attention-seeking. You see these angelic handicapped people on the telly, making the best of their situation, writing fantastic poetry or using computers with their toes. Well, Nathan was nothing like that. He wasn't brain-damaged – just an emotional tyrant. He never even tried to do anything for himself. Mum was his unwilling slave – he ruined her life. You could see she was over the moon when he died.'

Drew spluttered slightly at that; he was yet to hear any of his funeral customers go so far as to say such a thing. She heard him, but made no apology. 'It's true,' she insisted. 'She was like a cork out of a bottle – zipping all over the place, making up for lost time. Went overboard, of

118

course, being the selfish person she was. Never gave a thought to anybody else. I should have mentioned that Nathan wasn't altogether a cuckoo in the nest. He took after his mother in a great many ways.'

Drew cut the tirade short, feeling deeply uneasy. 'Er – where does all this leave us now? Do you still want me to help?'

'Definitely. But I know I'm asking an awful lot of you, and I'll obviously have to make it worth your while. Would two thousand pounds make a difference?'

Drew had never been offered a bribe before, but he recognised it for what it was. Conflict raged within him. For the first time he felt a real pang of fear that this whole business was going to get him into big trouble: Genevieve herself seemed to be suggesting that, with this sudden offer of money.

But two thousand pounds would oil a great many wheels. It would smooth things with Karen, and even mollify Maggs, who was beginning to cast doubts on the viability of what they were trying to do. He found himself wondering which bank account he'd put the money into, and how he'd explain it to the Inland Revenue.

'Well?' came the voice, and he realised he'd left a long silence.

'That's very generous of you.' His thought processes finally gained clarity. 'If I took a sum like that from you, I'd have to feel I was earning it. We'd do at least three funerals here for that.'

She laughed. 'Don't worry – I've got plenty for you to do. I'm going to give you a free hand to find out as much as you can about where she went after we last saw her. And if you find her alive and well – believe me, Drew, it'll be money well spent.'

His mind began to turn. *Last known address. Friends. Contacts. Interests. State of health.* He knew he was good at encouraging people to talk, that they trusted his open face and friendly manner. He could hardly wait to start. At worst, it would take his mind off other matters closer to home.

As if party to his thoughts, Genevieve spoke again. 'But are you sure you can manage it?' she said. 'What about your little girl? Could you take her with you on that sort of work?'

'Probably,' Drew was blithely reassuring. 'She's very adaptable.'

'I tell you what – leave her here with me. It'll be good practice for me, and I promise to take good care of her.'

Drew frowned momentarily, then laughed, reckless. 'Sounds great,' he said.

'Then come and see me tomorrow morning and bring the baby.'

The second event happened at four-fifteen. Stanley Sharples, Coroner's Officer, paid a visit to the Peaceful Repose Burial Ground. He walked into the middle of Drew's office without any preliminaries, and stood blocking the light from the rear window. Stanley was tall and wide, an ex-policeman with appropriately large feet and shoulders.

'This unidentified woman–' he began. 'We think she must be a vagrant, or foreign. An illegal

120

immigrant, perhaps, here without any papers. Or a refugee. We've had another look at the injury on her thigh – and gone through tests for a few of the more obscure poisons – and come to the conclusion that it's impossible to say whether or not there was deliberate injury inflicted.'

'But she didn't bury herself,' Drew interrupted, uneasily. 'You're not closing the case?' *Don't make me decide now what I ought to do. Let it hang for just a bit longer...*

'Hardly.' Stanley gave him a hostile stare. 'Haven't had the inquest yet, remember. But I doubt if we'd get any further, even if we used all the tests so far invented – and the Boss isn't inclined to take it that far. Budget won't allow it. Nobody's claimed her, so we may as well bury her and leave the file open. You never know – someone might yet come along to identify her. If they do, we've got all the samples we need for comparisons.'

'So – you're saying we can have the funeral? That we can bury her here?'

The Coroner's Officer nodded. 'So it seems. The Council are more than happy to pay your going rate – so there you have it. Funeral as soon as you like.'

Drew fought to stay nonchalant. 'Thanks,' he said. 'I assume you'll keep the necklace, dentures and clothes just in case, as well as your samples?'

'Naturally. We can match them up with anything that comes to light – but I'm not holding my breath.'

'Right,' Drew murmured. 'So it's going to be another unsolved mystery.' *Nobody can say I'm*

121

not giving him every chance, he thought, and then reproached himself for being unfair; Stanley could hardly be expected to guess that Drew had a good idea of who the body was. He foresaw a need for some intensive rationalisation in the next few days, if he was to let Genevieve have her way. Although not particularly significant in legal terms, the fact of the imminent reburial was a big psychological milestone. 'The inquest will say it's Unlawful Killing, won't it?' he said unhappily.

'Hard to see any other option,' shrugged Stanley.

'And we all assume she's some homeless vagrant, or illegal immigrant, got herself the wrong side of a drinking buddy or a gang of yobboes, who had the decency to bury her here?'

'You get a good class of yobbo round here,' Stanley joked.

'But that's the theory?'

'So it seems. As mysteries go, it's a tame one, by any standards. The only interesting part of it to my mind is that the woman didn't wear any knickers.'

Drew forced a ribald laugh, before getting back to business. 'So that's it then.'

Stanley nodded and riffled through a cardboard folder that had been under his arm since he arrived. 'You'll speak to Fiona and fix a day and time with her? I've brought you the paperwork. This has been a lucky one for you – all that free publicity.'

'Right,' said Drew again, taking the Burial Order from Stanley's outstretched hand with a mixture of relief and regret.

The third event was the arrival of Karen, forty-five minutes later than usual, to collect Stephanie; a glance at her face told Drew why she was late and what news she had for him. She was alarmingly pale, but her smile was wryly pleased. 'Due the first of September, God help us,' she said. 'At the best guess, that is. Could be at least a fortnight either way. I'm roughly twenty-two weeks, the doctor thinks. Unbelievable, isn't it? They'll do a scan next Monday, which should date it more precisely. It was highly embarrassing, let me tell you. I can't imagine how we failed to notice.'

'Never mind,' Drew consoled. 'I mean – it's wonderful news. It'll be almost like having twins.'

'Fifteen months' gap between them! Could be worse, I suppose,' she said glumly. 'Let's just hope Stephanie learns to walk before then. I said I wanted a home birth, by the way – I can't face all that hospital nonsense again.'

'Fabulous,' said Drew, pulling her to him. 'Now I'm excited.' He kissed her neck, just under the ear. 'And – I'm going to start earning a lot more money. I've got myself a new job.'

She twisted away from him, stepping back in shock. '*What?*'

'Don't panic. I'll still do this as well. But – if this works out – I might be able to do it on a regular basis. I've got a commission as a private investigator – and I've found us a childminder. Don't say I waste any time, will you?'

'*Childminder?*' She leaned down and scooped

123

Stephanie protectively into her arms. 'Who, for God's sake?'

'It's a long story,' he told her evasively. 'You'll have to speak to her yourself.' He didn't dare tell Karen she'd already met Genevieve, for fear he would blush and arouse her curiosity. 'She's pregnant herself, as it happens,' he added. 'This is only for a few days, while I try to sort out what's happened to her mother. She's paying me two thousand pounds,' he concluded triumphantly.

'Her mother?'

'Right. Her mother went missing last year.'

'Drew – is this connected with that body?'

He became instantly defensive. 'How did you work that out?'

She turned her back on him to gather up Stephanie. 'Don't tell me about it now. You'll have to give me this woman's address. You can't just dump Stephanie on her before I've even met her. When's all this going to happen?'

'I'm going to see her tomorrow. But–'

Karen sighed theatrically. 'Well, if she isn't too far away, I suppose I could manage a quick visit this evening. Come on, Steph.' She swung the baby from her hip to a tight embrace in both arms. 'Time to go home. Leave Daddy to his detective games. Say bye-bye.'

Drew didn't even try to argue, though he badly wanted to prevent the two women from meeting. 'Fine,' he said, to her departing back.

Then he softened. After all, she had more cause for anxiety than he did. He called after her. 'We'll be the envy of all our friends, with the two best babies you've ever seen.'

She didn't turn round, but he could tell she was pleased.

Behind him a voice said, '*Two* babies? Since when?' Maggs had her hands on her hips like a Jamaican grandmother. 'Nobody tells me anything,' she accused.

'We've only just found out. You're the first to know,' Drew placated her. 'Aren't you going to say congratulations?'

She frowned thoughtfully. 'I might,' she said, 'if you promise I don't have to look after either of them.'

'You're going to be too busy for that,' he promised. 'Now, listen. Tomorrow you're in charge of the office all morning. I'm taking the van, so if there's a call-out, you'll have to put them on hold until lunchtime. Shouldn't be too difficult.' One of the great improvements on his job at Plant's was the lack of urgency manifested by his clients; nobody so far had been in a rush to offload the body of their relative. Some hadn't wanted Drew to remove it at all until minutes before the burial, keeping it at home in a cool room, as had been the usual practice in earlier times. The optimum time lapse from the death to the interment was three days – long enough for families to make their preparations, and short enough for the body to be still in an acceptable condition. He made it clear on his literature that the low prices reflected a low involvement on his part. He would advise, liaise, provide the ground for the grave, but beyond that the family were welcome to do the rest for themselves, if that's how they wanted it. Additional assistance from Drew or Maggs would be charged

125

for, item by item. So far, a surprising number of families chose to go it virtually alone.

'Okay,' she shrugged, before changing the subject. 'Can I plant some flowers in the hedges?' She'd obviously decided she wasn't going to lower herself by begging him for an explanation of where he was going next day. 'Just to make it more cheerful.'

'Where will you get them from?'

She shrugged. 'Garden centre?'

Drew shook his head. 'I don't think it's as simple as that. It wouldn't be easy to get small bedding plants to survive amongst all that stuff – and we can't afford anything big. You can send out more publicity leaflets, if you like. Look through the Yellow Pages for likely places. Use your imagination. Schools, bookshops–'

'Off-licences, car salesrooms, cinemas,' she filled in for him.

'Wherever you think's appropriate. We want to get everyone talking about us. Thinking, *Hmmm – that sounds nice*. And if anyone phones with an enquiry, make it all sound blissfully straight-forward. You know all the answers to the usual questions, don't you?'

She cast her eyes up to the sky. 'Water courses no problem: no need for any special permission; hospital has to release the body to them or us; no special regulations about the coffin. How am I doing?'

'Fine. It's all yours from nine tomorrow, okay?'

'Okay. And when you get back, maybe you'll tell me where you've been.'

'Maybe,' he conceded. Then, remembering how

distracted Karen was likely to be for the fore-
seeable future, he turned back to his assistant.
'Maybe I will,' he repeated. 'I could do with some
advice.'

Karen was worse than distracted. Having abandoned her plan (much to Drew's relief) to pay
the potential childminder a visit of maternal
inspection – saying she was too exhausted – she
treated Drew to an evening of deep sighs and
half-finished sentences spiced with flashes of
irritation. Then she went to bed early, giving him
no chance to introduce the subject of the Slaters
or unidentified bodies. Preoccupied as he was
with the prospect of seeing Genevieve again, and
trusting her with his precious daughter, he felt
Karen was letting him down. She should be there
to listen to him – she was his wife, after all, and
the whole burden of Peaceful Repose rested on
his shoulders. But she seemed entirely wrapped
up in her own concerns.

And so, next morning he turned to Maggs for
the support and encouragement he was lacking.

'I think I ought to tell you what's going on,' he
said, when she arrived promptly at nine. She
watched his face intently, as she lifted off her
helmet and unwound her scarf. Her face was
purple from being whipped by the wind, and she
was breathless.

'Listen,' he said. 'You know that woman who
came a couple of weeks ago? The pregnant one?'

Maggs nodded. 'The one you knew from
before, right?'

He blinked, immediately on his guard. 'I did,

127

actually. How did you come to that conclusion?'

'The way you looked at each other. So what about her?'

'She's got an idea that the dead woman Jeffrey found was her mother. But she's not sure. She wants me to do a bit of quiet investigating, just to see if I can find out where her mother could be, before she bothers the police. She's going to pay me,' he hastened to reassure her.

'How much?'

He paused. 'Two thousand quid,' he muttered.

Maggs whistled, and stared at him even more intently. 'She's really concerned, then? I mean, there was a murder, wasn't there? It isn't just a bit of idle curiosity.' She thought for a moment. 'Drew – you're not going to get into trouble, are you? Don't you think the police would like to be kept informed?'

Drew pulled his lips back from his teeth in a parody of agonised indecision. 'Strictly speaking, I'm sure we ought to at least pass the woman's name on to them,' he admitted. 'But Genevieve promises me there'd be no way they could prove her identity the way things stand at the moment. She thinks her husband knows more than he's letting on – but she's convinced he'd lie to the police and only impede the enquiry. She needs more evidence. So – what I'm hoping is that I can find some other avenue to explore. Her work, friends – all that stuff that's got nothing to do with her family.'

'And why can't she do that for herself? If she's that worried, she ought to be the one to take the risks.'

He shook his head. 'I suppose she thinks she'd just dig a deeper hole for Willard, and that would make her situation impossible. And she strikes me as the sort of person who instinctively pays other people to do their dirty work.'

'Well, thanks for telling me,' she said briskly. 'I hope you're going to let me lend a hand? I'd make a great detective.'

'I'm sure you would,' he sighed.

Genevieve's house was in a pretty village on the edge of rising ground; Drew savoured the colourful spring gardens and aubretia-decorated walls. Nobody in North Staverton was very interested in creating a display for almost non-existent passers-by, but here things were clearly different. From the outside, the house looked modestly impressive. Semi-detached, with a curving garden path leading to a door at the side, it obviously had a good number of rooms. At the back he could see a tidy garden.

She answered the door promptly, and Stephanie crowed in apparent recognition as soon as she laid eyes on Genevieve. Drew was sure the woman's bulge had grown in the days since he'd last seen her. His insides were in a turmoil of apprehension. *Think of the money*, he told himself, but that only heightened his suspicions that he was walking into a minefield. Why in the world was she offering him such a sum? Didn't it throw all kinds of doubt on her motives? Suddenly she seemed to be going to a great deal of effort and expense to solve a dilemma she'd claimed to be rather casual about. He tried to muster his thoughts, to phrase some probing questions that would have to be answered before he committed himself to anything further. Already he was wondering if he'd been a fool to come this far.

She led him into a bright living room, the floor an expanse of polished boards, everything clean and shining. A three-seater settee and single matching chair; a television; a set of shelves containing a clock, two candlesticks, a set of china figurines and a large oriental-looking lacquered box. It was entirely different from how he'd imagined such a woman would live. She watched his reaction with a knowing smile.

'Willard insists we keep things tidy in here,' she said. 'It's the only room visitors ever get to see. We have a cleaning woman who takes complete control. I've got my own bolthole upstairs where I'm allowed to make a mess, and Willard keeps the dining room like some sort of museum, full of dreadful old stuff that was his mother's.'

'I assume you're on maternity leave?'

'I stopped about three weeks ago, at my boss's insistence. I was loafing about here, not knowing what to do with myself, flipping through Willard's piles of old newspapers, when I saw the piece about the woman in your burial ground. Good thing he *is* such a hoarder, or I'd never have known. Funny how things happen. If I'd still been working, and had had other things to occupy my time, I could probably have persuaded myself that Mum's perfectly all right – as Willard keeps insisting she is – and closed my eyes to the obvious similarities between your woman and her.'

'Where can I put Stephanie?' he asked, as the child wriggled to get out of his arms. 'Is she all right on the floor?' It was all beginning to feel so natural. Genevieve's relaxed manner, Stephanie's matching mood – why resist it? Just let her talk – there was no harm in that, after all. Act the counsellor, dig a bit deeper into the early years, when the boy Nathan was still alive. Maybe that was what she really wanted. Maybe the whole business about the dead woman would just quietly go away. Maybe elephants would learn how to play violins...

Genevieve considered the question of Stephanie's amusement for a second, looking round the room. 'There isn't much for her to play with. Did you bring anything?'

'There'll be a few bits and pieces in the van. But she gets bored with her own toys. Any old kitchen thing would do. Cardboard boxes are popular at the moment, and wooden spoons.'

'Hang on.' Genevieve disappeared through a door, returning two minutes later with an eggbox, a cereal carton, a sheet of tinfoil, a sophisticated digital weighing machine and three wooden spoons, all in a sturdy cardboard box. 'This should be fun,' she said.

'She might break the weighing machine,' he warned. 'And has the tinfoil got sharp edges?'

She crunched part of it in her hand experimentally. 'Not at all. It's too thin for that. And the weighing machine's pretty robust. She'll enjoy watching the numbers change when she presses down on it. Here, Stephanie – I'll show you.'

Drew propped his daughter in the armchair and let Genevieve present the box to her. 'The tinfoil's a good idea,' he said, conciliatory, 'so long as you don't want to use it again.'

'Plenty more where that came from,' she said. She seemed to be in efficient mode. 'Now – to business,' she announced. 'I'll make some coffee later on, but I think we should get started.'

They settled into opposite ends of the deep-cushioned sofa, Drew forced to twist awkwardly to see the woman's face. He waited for her to make an opening. It came quite quickly.

'I think you ought to have a bit of background,' she said. 'It'll explain the way things have been between me and my mother. We haven't been close – not since I was a child. I told you about my handicapped brother, Nathan.' Her face registered distaste, dislike – even disgust, as she spoke the name. But she continued calmly. 'He was born when my mother was over forty. My father died while she was still pregnant.' She looked hard at the blank television screen before continuing. 'I was twelve. We were together in a terrible car crash–'

'Yes,' Drew assured her. 'Dr Jarvis told me.'

'It goes back further than that,' she said, with a frown. 'It was all doomed from the start. Or from when she got pregnant again.' Drew inwardly shuddered; disturbed at the echo of his own life. Genevieve went on. 'She didn't want another child. She was in a foul mood for months. When he was born so damaged, she just – forgot about us. She stopped being any kind of a mother to me or my sister. We were twelve and fourteen –

132

which is a time when a girl really needs her mother. I can hardly remember a single conversation with her throughout my teenage years. It was all Nathan. He kept her up half the night, so she was always tired. When he got to five or six, he was supposed to go to a special school, but he had hysterics every time the bus stopped outside our gate, so he hardly ever went. She let him do anything he liked. But she didn't love him. He wasn't lovable.'

Drew concentrated hard. So far the story tallied with what Dr Jarvis had told him, but that hardly proved anything. He struggled to remember his supposed role: he was here to try to discover where Genevieve's mother was now, whether it was her lying in the mortuary at the Royal Victoria Hospital. It seemed reasonable to be told some of the woman's history, but it was beginning to feel as if Genevieve was unloading her personal problems onto him simply because she had finally found a listening ear. *Am I a detective or a psychiatrist?* he wondered. He also wondered how it was that none of this story had emerged when he'd known her before. Had pregnancy caused her to re-evaluate her own childhood? All he could remember her telling him then was that she had a glamorous-sounding job with the BBC. He'd listened out once or twice for her name since then – but as she worked for Radio Three, the opportunity seldom presented itself; Karen still felt young enough for Radio One to be the channel of choice, and Drew had a growing taste for Radio Four.

'I suppose if it was happening now, I'd have got

133

into drugs and ended up on the streets,' Genevieve went on, melodramatically. 'But there wasn't quite such scope then for going off the rails. Instead I immersed myself in schoolwork. My sister got herself a boyfriend when she was fifteen and more or less moved in with his family. She married him at eighteen, and I married Willard when I was twenty-three. We both – Brigid and me – had the same needs, but we found wildly different ways of fulfilling them.' She laughed, with a hard edge that made Drew wince. 'She had five children – I got my career. I've done well enough in that respect. I'm a senior producer now.'

'And then Nathan died,' Drew prompted her. 'Not so long ago.'

'It was ages ago,' she contradicted him. 'Seven or eight years, at least. He was twenty-two, and getting more impossible all the time. It was such a relief when I heard. I remember thinking that at last I'd get my mother back. But it didn't work out like that.'

Discrepancy, thought Drew with a stab of excitement – though on consideration, it didn't seem enough to mean anything. Dr Jarvis had been vague about the length of time since Nathan's death, he remembered.

'Did you hear how he died, exactly?' Drew asked carefully.

'Pneumonia or something. They always said he wouldn't live far into adulthood.'

'Did you go to his funeral?'

She stared at him, her face suddenly defensive. 'No, I didn't. I never visited him in hospital, either. I can't bear hospitals–' She tailed off, her face suddenly pale, and looked down at her bump. Her expression was very solemn – almost scared, Drew thought. 'It feels like history repeating itself,' she burst out. 'As if this is Nathan all over again. I'm almost exactly the same age she was. And don't tell me I'm crazy.'

'I wasn't going to. It's a very unnerving co-incidence.'

'Here comes the tricky bit. You probably remember my saying I thought Willard might have killed her?'

Drew nodded, not letting his face reveal how impossible it would be to forget such a detail.

'The fact is, he always had a thing going with my mother.'

'A thing?' Drew queried.

Genevieve flipped a hank of hair over her shoulder. 'He says I imagined it. Anyway, they first met when Nathan was about sixteen. My grandmother died and Willard insisted we went to that funeral – he said it was stupid to go on refusing to see each other, that it was giving me a complex. Anyway, it turned into a sort of recon-ciliation exercise – at first, anyway. I didn't have quite so many hard feelings towards my mother by then – just couldn't see that she had much of a place in my life any more. I don't see Brigid very often either.'

'Your sister,' Drew confirmed.

'That's right. She went to live in Anglesey. She's still married to Martin and they all live on a sheep farm. They haven't got any money at all.'

Drew put up a hand to stop her. 'Then surely it

would be very much in her interest to have your mother's death confirmed? Isn't there any property to inherit? Isn't Brigid going to want this business settled properly, even if you don't?'

'There isn't any property,' said Genevieve shortly. 'She gave it all away after Nathan died – not that there was very much. Caring for him had cost a fortune, with wheelchairs and all the gadgets he needed. She told everybody she was going to live as a free spirit. An out-of-date hippy. She made it work, which is the surprising part. She's got a stronger will than Brigid or me.' She fell silent, her hands twisting together in agitation.

'I'm sorry to go on about it,' Drew persisted, 'but what *was* the exact relationship between Willard and your mother?'

'I'm coming to that,' she said. 'Not that I'm going to be able to give a very coherent account. Where was I?'

'Well – money, I think. Does that connect with your decision to move house?'

'Oh, that move!' She cast her eyes to the ceiling. 'Willard was *furious* when we lost that house. He'd have killed you if he'd found out what you did.'

'You never told him?' Drew realised that he hadn't considered this aspect of his earlier encounter with the Slaters. He remembered Willard's ice cold blue eyes, the mild manner which concealed something ruthless, and felt glad the man remained ignorant of Drew's treachery.

'No, I didn't!' she said forcefully. 'I'm not that stupid!'

136

'What would he have done?'

'He'd have watched your wife for signs of pregnancy, and when there weren't any he'd have found a way to get back at you.'

'Except she did get pregnant for real three months later.'

'Willard can count,' she said flatly. 'It wouldn't have placated him. But luckily for you, things went much better for him at work than he'd expected, so we didn't need to move house after all. He thought we wouldn't be able to keep up the mortgage payments on this one, when his contract ran out. He'd been told unofficially that the university wasn't going to renew it, you see.'

'But they did?'

She nodded. 'I think they had misgivings, mind. I don't think he's very good with students, except for one or two favourites, and there don't seem to be many of them any more.'

Drew tried to turn the conversation back to something more immediately relevant. 'Your mother,' he prompted. 'You were going to tell me more about what she was up to last year.'

She didn't respond immediately; Drew felt his patience ebbing. Stephanie wouldn't be content with destroying eggboxes for much longer, and he knew they were avoiding some of the most difficult issues. 'Come on,' he urged. 'This is all very interesting, but I still don't see why you're pursuing this particular route. It's just wasting time, when in the end, if your mother *is* dead, we're going to have to square things with the law.'

Genevieve instantly adopted a hurt look, sticking out her lower lip in childish petulance.

'I'm doing this because of Willard. And because I don't think the police would be any use, anyway.'

Drew gave her a severe look. 'Those two statements are contradictory,' he pointed out. 'If they're useless, then Willard won't have anything to worry about, will he?'

'Oh, well,' she shook her head dismissively, 'you never know, do you? That's what's so difficult. I'd be so frightened–'

'Frightened?' Drew echoed. 'For Willard, you mean?' He remembered the story Dr Jarvis had told him – that he was afraid he had somehow driven Gwen to suicide because of her unassuaged guilt over what they'd done to Nathan. The doctor had disclosed a welter of background detail once it had become apparent that Drew had already met Genevieve. That, after Nathan's death, Gwen had started using her original surname of Forrester, rather than Absolon, which had been her married name. That she'd spent the years since, and all her reserves of cash, on flitting from country to country, taking up with unsuitable companions. That there had been some kind of trouble in Egypt last year, which seemed to have shaken her up. That she was very like Genevieve to look at. 'Like clones,' he'd said, with an unhappy smile. But there had been no mention of Willard Slater, no hint that he might have had reason to murder his mother-in-law.

Drew shook his head slowly. Neither account seemed credible. 'It isn't adding up,' he said.

'Then you'll just have to trust me, won't you?' she said seductively. 'I thought you'd enjoy a bit

138

of a diversion. A nice mystery to solve in your spare time.'

Drew's irritation was finely balanced with his desire to agree with her. He tried to remember everything she'd told him so far, looking for obvious evasions or inconsistencies. Perhaps everything could be explained by her being no more than a neurotic pregnant woman, over-emotional and saying whatever came into her head. It didn't work.

'This business with Willard,' he repeated. 'This "thing" you mentioned?'

'I think there was a sexual attraction between them. A few years ago, anyway, if not more recently.' She glared at him. 'Satisfied now?'

'That must have been very unpleasant for you,' he said carefully.

'Infuriating,' she agreed. 'But it explains why he turned against her last year.'

'Does it?' Drew struggled to keep up with her logic. 'So – can you honestly tell me that you think he could have killed her?'

She scowled darkly. 'Well – yes I can. Willard's a very strange man. You've seen how cold and hard he can be. And my mother could be extremely provocative.' She sighed, and looked directly at Drew, holding his gaze. 'I often think I don't know Willard at all. I look at him and he's a total stranger to me. I can't believe I've lived with him for eighteen years.'

'Hmmm,' was all Drew could manage. He thought of himself and Karen: surely they could never be strangers to each other? The idea chilled him to the bone.

'Look,' said Genevieve, more briskly, 'are you going to do it or aren't you? You sounded interested enough on the phone.'

He squared his shoulders, knowing he was already in too deep to escape unsullied, but unsure of the moment at which he'd passed the point of no return. 'I don't seem to have much choice,' he said drily.

'Of course you have,' she snapped. 'You can walk away now and forget the whole thing.'

But then he'd never see Genevieve again. 'Believe me, I'd like to,' he said. 'But the Coroner is releasing the body at the end of this week, and I've been given the contract to bury her. I'm trapped now, simply by not saying anything when I had the chance. Regardless of how I might feel about you–' he tried to ignore the lifted chin, the gratified smile at these words '–it's too late for me to speak out. What would I say? "Oh, by the way, Officer, I think you might find that this is actually a woman named Gwen Absolon. A little bird told me." Or maybe I could send them an anonymous letter giving your name: "Ask this woman why her mother hasn't been seen for nearly a year. Because she was lying in the Peaceful Repose Burial Ground." That would make them take notice, I shouldn't wonder.'

'Stop it!' she pleaded. 'Stop being so cruel. I haven't done anything to make you act like that.'

'No,' he sighed, letting his shoulders sag. 'No, I don't suppose you have. But I really wish you hadn't come to see me again, all the same.'

So he didn't have to see her reaction to that, he got up and went to Stephanie, who was toppling

140

sideways over one side of her chair, letting an arm dangle heavily: it was a habit she had, which Drew usually found enchanting. Now he pretended to be concerned that she'd land head first on the floor if he didn't straighten her. She looked up at him drunkenly, head tipped onto one shoulder, a wad of chewed eggbox in the non-dangling hand.

'What are you like?' he said to her, in a mock Devon accent. 'Crazy, you are, my girl. Sit up straight, why don't you?'

A loud sniff from Genevieve made him freeze. Jesus, she wasn't crying, was she? He forced himself not to look until he'd got Stephanie sorted out. In that half-minute, he'd hardened his heart enough for it not to matter whether she was weeping or not. It was probably all part of a deliberate plan to ensnare him, he told himself fiercely.

When he did look, she seemed very much as before – perhaps slightly pink around the nose, but nothing that couldn't safely be ignored. He decided that being businesslike was the safest option.

'Have you got the address of the last place Gwen lived?' he asked. 'That's probably the best point for me to start – though I assume you know for sure she isn't there now?'

'You assume right. She was there last summer. She gave us the address, and phoned us once or twice, apparently from there. It was a bolthole she used on and off. Just a cheap basement bedsit.'

'But–' he shook his head disbelievingly. 'Why

haven't you gone yourself to look for her? You surely must have been worrying, even before the piece in the paper, that there was something wrong?'

'We phoned the number she gave us, and a man answered. He said he thought Mum had left in July or August, without any forwarding address. I didn't see any point in going there, after that.'

Drew felt a powerful return of his earlier scepticism. Something really wasn't making sense here. But he'd had enough of Genevieve for one day; Stephanie would be wanting her lunch, and he was tiring of the effort to control all his conflicting emotions. He remembered Genevieve had had much the same effect on him, two years earlier: one minute he'd been telling a warm and sympathetic woman his life story, the next she'd seemed strange and remote. Clearly she could switch from being a perfectly capable adult to a self-obsessed bundle of neuroses and back again with no warning. He'd been mad to allow her back into his life, knowing how dangerous she could be. But there didn't seem any way out now. She wasn't going to leave him alone until he'd at least made a token effort to locate her mother.

'Just a bit more background,' he said, 'and then I'll have to be off.'

'*Background?*' she repeated. 'Haven't I given you all that?'

'I mean – apart from where she was living – what had she been doing? Who had she been seeing? What about Dr Jarvis – did she mention anything about him? I need *facts*, if I'm to be of any help.'

She sighed crossly, but her obfuscation merely piqued his curiosity. What *was* the truth of the matter? Who had Gwen Absolon been – this seventy-year-old with no strings to hold her in place? This old woman, with her complicated love life, living like a nomad? She was too intriguing a character to abandon. He deliberately brushed aside the nagging question: *What in the world am I going to tell Karen?*

CHAPTER SEVEN

Impatiently, Genevieve dumped a jumbled mass of information on Drew's bewildered ear, as he tried to keep Stephanie amused for another twenty minutes.

'Once Nathan had died, and she was finally free, she started going off round the world, doing it on the cheap, by herself. Making up for lost time – like I said. We got postcards from the wildest places. In a year or so she'd got the bright idea of taking small groups of adventurous tourists with her. None of them half as adventurous as her, of course. She did all the paperwork, visas and so on. Got them somewhere to stay and told them what to look at. They paid rather handsomely, I think. But she spent it as soon as she got it, and there were enough calamities to wipe out most of her profits.'

'Calamities?'

'People demanding their money back because they never saw a tiger, or the right sort of gazelle. Lost luggage, broken ankles. I never heard all the gory details, but she packed a fair amount onto her postcards. The worst was what happened at Giza, of course.'

'Giza?'

'You know. Where the Great Pyramid is, in Egypt. Near there, anyhow – I can never remember the name of the actual spot. There was a

144

shooting, and one of my mother's group was killed. A girl. It was about a year ago – terrorists targeting tourists to get their views aired. Very bad publicity all round and disastrous for the tourist industry, which was only just getting over the massacre at the Valley of the Kings.'

'I think I missed it,' said Drew vaguely.

'Well, it's not important. The point is, she came home rather chastened. Arrived on our doorstep one evening and was welcomed by my devoted husband. I was out at the time. She told him she felt the need of some company and when I got home she was installed in the spare room for a little holiday and he was like the proverbial dog with two tails. I freaked out, I insisted she couldn't stay for long. Then even Willard seemed to turn against her. She was only with us just over a week and I never saw her again.' Drew watched for emotion, and was rewarded by the slightest tightening of the nostrils.

'That's it?' Drew verified. 'That's all you can tell me?' *Guilt!* He told himself triumphantly. *All this is because she's consumed with guilt at throwing her own mother out. Presumably back to the grotty bedsit.* At last, something seemed to have a rational explanation.

'More or less,' she nodded. 'Hasn't she been good!' She changed the subject, clearly keen not to dwell on her actions. 'Is she always as easy as this?'

'Pretty much,' said Drew modestly, allowing himself to be diverted. 'As long as someone's around, she seems contented enough to amuse herself.'

145

'Sounds as if she'll be a doddle. I can have her any day this week, if you want to get on with it.'

'Give me that address, and I'll get started tomorrow,' he said. No, he couldn't abandon Genevieve now. Perhaps both of them were being manipulated by the ghost of Gwen Absolon. There had always seemed to be an unacknowledged but irresistible power to the fact of an unexplained death, with all the unfinished business that attached to it. Mysteries existed to be solved – like Everest; it wasn't in his nature to walk away from this one.

But he wasn't looking forward to it. He didn't anticipate success. He was going to have a great deal of explaining to do, for one thing. Karen would want to know why he was helping Genevieve – the money wouldn't be enough to convince her. And the police – God help him – would be more than a little reproachful if they ever learned the truth.

The sooner he started, then, the sooner he could claim his two thousand quid, and get back to his ordinary life. *Whatever that might mean,* he thought glumly.

Genevieve had another visitor half an hour after Drew departed. When she opened the door and realised who it was, she went instantly onto the attack. 'What the hell are you doing here again?' she demanded. 'Isn't it a bit soon for another fight?'

'I don't want to fight,' he said calmly. 'And it certainly wouldn't do you any good in your condition. I had hoped to find you in a more rational frame of mind.'

She stared at him for a moment, and then stepped back to let him in. 'Willard's not here,' she said.

'Good. We can have a nice uninterrupted chat, then.'

'I've just had that undertaker chap round,' she told him. 'He's going to do a bit of investigating. I'm paying him,' she added defiantly.

'What is there to investigate?' he asked warily.

Genevieve's face seemed to shrivel; she sat down heavily in the same corner of the sofa she'd occupied most of the morning. 'I really do have to know what's happened,' she said miserably. 'It's haunting me. I can't sleep. I claimed to think Willard had bumped Ma off – just to give Drew some reason to listen to me.'

Dr Jarvis laughed. 'I said I was convinced she'd killed herself, with the same general intention,' he admitted.

She looked at him, grey eyes filmy with self-pity. 'But why did you go to him? He must think we're in cahoots. That we've got something to hide.'

He looked at her kindly. 'I did it for you,' he murmured. 'I knew how you must be feeling.'

She sighed. 'You're retired now, you know. You don't have to keep trying to cure everybody. I'm a hopeless case, anyway. You've had nearly thirty years to sort me out, and see where it's got you.'

'I don't think doctors ever really retire,' he said. 'After all, you've asked for my services, in another context, haven't you?' He looked mean-ingfully at the pregnant bulge.

'Oh, don't!' she pleaded. 'We'll talk about that in a minute. But only if we can be sure not to start fighting again. You might as well admit you haven't a hope of winning. Willard's been on at me for months, as it is.'

He dropped his hands limply between his knees, as he sat on the edge of an armchair. 'So – is this amiable young Drew going to come up with anything? What did you find to get him started?'

'Her last known address – that seems to be where detectives usually start. And I told him the whole story of Nathan.'

'Ha!' he said. 'So did I. I hope the stories tallied.'

'I told him the truth, for what it's worth,' she said primly. 'I don't think he really understood the relevance. I'm not sure I do myself.'

'Oh, it's relevant,' Jarvis told her solemnly. 'Very relevant indeed.' He paused. 'And I hope your young friend is trustworthy, because I shared some little facts with him that could land me in a certain amount of hot water.'

'He can't go to the police now,' she said, triumphantly. 'He's left it too long. I must say, I think I was quite clever there, sucking him in so slowly. He fancies me, which helps.'

'Everybody fancies you, Genevieve,' said the doctor sadly.

They shared a long wordless moment of eye contact, with Genevieve struggling to conceal the confusion she was feeling. He knew her too well, she felt, her heart beginning to thump wildly: it was frightening, knowing that someone was so totally apprised of all one's weaknesses. It was like being in love, without any of the mutuality: it was all pain and fear and intense misery and no ecstasy. He knew the gaping holes in her character, the inconsistencies and evasions. He knew why she had to learn the truth about her mother, while being terrified of what she might discover. He knew she was utterly dependent on Willard. He knew she was virtually paralysed by her pregnancy, every trip outside the house an ordeal, every forced acceptance of what was shortly to happen to her a vicious thrust of panic. 'Stop it,' she moaned. She fell back against the cushions, and put a hand to her heart; it was thundering wildly, filling her chest with breathless terror. 'You know I can't stand it when you do that,' she complained weakly.

He smiled thinly, his eyes still on hers. 'I can't help it,' he sighed. 'You shouldn't be such a fascinating creature.' He smiled again, more warmly. 'You haven't changed a bit, you know,' he said wonderingly. 'Not since you were twelve.'

'Of course I haven't!' she spat back. 'Isn't that the problem?'

He shook his head, and stood up abruptly. 'I'll go and make us some tea,' he said. 'Or do you want something to eat? It must be lunchtime by now. I'll have a hunt in the fridge, shall I?'

'Do what you like.' She flapped a hand at him, and he disappeared into the kitchen. She stared blindly at the pile of debris left over from Stephanie's visit. She supposed she should clean it up before Drew brought his daughter back next morning – and find yet more stuff for the

149

kid to play with. It seemed like a Herculean task.

Dr Jarvis came back in under ten minutes, with a pot of tea and some sandwiches on a tray. 'Cheese, Marmite, cucumber and coleslaw,' he said. 'The bread's a bit stale, but I cut the crusts off for you.'

He put the tray down beside her, and poured two mugs of tea; Genevieve took the food and drink without comment. 'Now,' he proceeded, rubbing his hands together, 'what about you? While I'm here, would you like me to have a look? When did you last see your GP? I assume you're having visits from the midwife? Are they still happy about the home delivery?'

Genevieve turned her face away from him. 'Everything's under control,' she muttered.

'That's good to hear. You're looking well, I must say. No giddy spells? Swollen ankles? Headaches? You're damned lucky, you know, to be allowed your own way. Hospital phobia isn't generally taken seriously. But you always were a rebel.' He spoke fondly, cajolingly. 'Could I just have a glance at your record card? See if the BP's behaving itself?'

'It's upstairs,' she told him, still with her face averted. 'But I told you – everything's absolutely fine. Don't fuss.'

'It's a big event, you know,' he pursued, letting in a note of reproach. 'A lot of organising to be done. Have you got the cot and buggy and all the other stuff?' He looked curiously around the room. 'I don't see any sign of any preparations. It could all happen in another two or three weeks, you know.'

'*Two or three weeks?*' Her voice was startled; she threw him a look of pure horror. 'What makes you say *that?*'

'Experience, my dear,' he smiled. 'Something an old-fashioned family doctor can still lay some claim to. You've never been able to establish an exact date, and since you refused to go for a scan, it can only be guesswork. From the look of you, I'd say the head's already well down in the pelvis. Now I don't want to say anything to alarm you – just reassure me that you've been seeing the GP or midwife regularly, and that you've at least got the basic essentials standing by.'

'Yes, yes,' she said firmly. 'Everything's under control. I told you. But ... you will come as well, won't you? I can't do it without you.'

'I'd be privileged to attend, so long as your own GP has no objection,' he assured her. 'You'll have to introduce me as a friend of the family. He'd be within his rights to feel intimidated by having a retired doctor breathing down his neck.'

'No problem,' she smiled bitterly.

His sandwiches finished, he got up to go. 'It'll be all right,' he said vaguely. 'We'll find out what happened to Gwen, one way or another. Don't forget – that body might yet turn out not to be her at all.'

'A wild goose chase, you mean?' she said gloomily. 'No – I'm sure it's her. The Egyptian thing, the age and height. But why do they say she had white hair? Mum's hair was dark grey.'

The doctor shrugged. 'I've heard of it happening – the acids in the soil leach out the pigment, and leave it white. Or maybe she dyed it.'

'Why would she dye it white? It would make her look so old. I sometimes think that's another reason why she steered clear of me and Brigid – she wanted to pretend she was fifty, and having daughters less than ten years younger than that would rather give the game away.'

'We'll probably never know now,' he said dismissively. 'Bye, then, Gen. I'll see you soon. Look after yourself, won't you.' And he leaned over her for a paternal kiss on the cheek. The tickle of his moustache sent shivers through her. *Just like a real father*, she thought to herself, wriggling in her chair.

Stephanie was to spend the next day with Genevieve – Drew had been careful not to disclose the 'Slater' – after he had stoutly endorsed her suitability for the task. 'She'll be fine,' he insisted. 'Genevieve was bored, sitting about all day doing nothing much. She'll be happy to have somebody to play with. She said it would be good practice!'

'Can she do nappies? And mouth-to-mouth resuscitation?' Karen demanded.

'*Anybody* can do nappies,' said Drew impatiently, trying to ignore the other part of the question.

'I suppose it'll be okay,' said Karen grudgingly. 'I just feel irresponsible, letting Steph go to somebody I've never met.'

'Stephanie can look after herself,' he said.

'Don't be stupid,' she snapped. 'She's ten months old.'

'Joke,' he defended lamely. He tried to make

152

amends. 'I won't leave her there all day – not at first, anyway.'

'We should have asked for references,' gloomed Karen, as a final word. She was going to break the news of her pregnancy to the Head of the school that morning, with the warning that this time she was unlikely to be coming back, and she was not looking forward to his reaction. 'But then, we're desperate, aren't we?'

Maggs's attention to publicity for Peaceful Repose Funerals included trying to get Drew more bookings as a speaker. Not only did some groups pay well for the talk, it was a key way of generating more business. She was also planning to have a think about other services they might offer. 'Flowers, for example,' Drew had suggested. 'Could we have a garden area with dahlias and sunflowers that could be cut and sold for funeral tributes? That'd provide some colour, too.'

'Could do,' shrugged Maggs.

'And the pets' area. We've got to publicise that. Draft an ad for the paper, and I'll look at it this afternoon. I should be back about three. I'll phone in every couple of hours, to see if there's been any news. Pity we can't afford a mobile, but there it is.'

'Can't afford anything, mate.' For a girl of eighteen, Maggs had a remarkable grasp of financial matters. 'The Smithers haven't paid up yet.'

'Pity. That'd keep us going for a bit. It's so galling,' he burst out. 'There's Daphne Plant swimming in money. Makes four hundred pounds' clear profit on every funeral. And we're counting every penny.'

'Give us time,' she said. 'You've gotta have faith.'

'Maggs, you're a marvel,' he said, for the thousandth time. 'Now I'm off. See you.'

His first visit was to Gwen Absolon's basement bedsit. 'I don't expect you'll find anything,' Genevieve had warned him. 'All her stuff will most likely have been chucked in the dump by now.'

He found the house quite easily, in a small side street in Shepton Mallet. The basement rooms had their own entrance down a flight of steps. A very large woman who appeared to be in her early sixties answered his knock; her girth filled the doorframe so he could see almost nothing of the passage behind her. 'Oh, hello,' he said. 'I'm looking for a Mrs Absolon. This was the last address we had for her. She was here until July or August last year, I think.' He raised his eyebrows and waited, knowing his boyish looks almost invariably charmed women of this sort of age. But they didn't seem to be having much effect on this one.

'Never heard of her,' said the woman. She wore an iron-grey two-piece outfit, her hair a similar shade: she put Drew in mind of a battleship. Something about the jut of her breast, the solid stance as well as the colour tones.

'Could I ask how long you've been here?' He treated her to his most charming smile.

She pushed out her lips in an unselfconscious

154

pout of deliberation. 'Almost four years,' she said grudgingly, going on to reveal further details almost in spite of herself. Drew thought he recognised the signs of loneliness. 'Heard about it in the corner shop,' the woman confided, 'and snapped it up. Suits me very nicely, too.'

'And you don't know anything about the person who was here last summer?'

'I know quite a lot about her, as it happens. If we're talking about the same woman. And one thing I know is that her name was not Gwen Absolon.'

'Forrester!' Drew remembered. 'She sometimes called herself Forrester.'

'Well, that's different,' said the woman comfortably. 'Wendy – Gwendoline – Forrester occupied the room behind mine – at the back. Not there very much though. And what business might it be of yours?' There was little of challenge or suspicion in her voice: she seemed in no hurry to move, either to admit or exclude him.

'Gwendoline!' Drew murmured. 'I'm sure it's the same person. But I don't know anyone who calls her Wendy.'

'Oh, that's just me. I'm funny about the name Gwen, that's all. Long story. And my question still stands,' she added, fixing him with small sharp eyes. He began to wonder whether she was somehow well ahead of him in the direction their exchange was taking. He wished he'd taken the time to prepare a convincing cover story. As it was, he'd got no further than a faint hope that he'd find some of Gwen's possessions left behind. He struggled to be inventive.

'You see, I'm her only living relative. She's my aunt, and we haven't heard from her for a long time. She sent us this address, but nothing since then. My wife insisted I come in person, to try and find out what's going on. We didn't have a phone number or anything.'

The woman made herself even bigger, puffing out like a toad. 'Left it long enough, haven't you,' she accused, with implacably folded arms. 'The room's been relet long since. There's a Mr Lawson in there now. He works nights, so we can't disturb him.'

'Can I just ask – did my aunt leave suddenly?'

She considered for a full minute. 'Well, as it happens, she did disappear rather abruptly. I assumed she'd gone away on one of her trips, but then the landlady came to me in September, asking if I knew why no rent had been paid for the back room. We went in together, and found it left quite neat and tidy, but with quite a lot of things still there – as if she'd intended to come back. Now don't you go thinking we've helped ourselves,' she continued, pointing a stubby finger at Drew's chest. 'It's all in a cupboard out in the back passage. We were going to keep it for a full year before taking it to a charity shop.'

'I wonder if I could have a look at it?' he said.

Again the extended finger. 'Can you prove you're a relative?' she demanded.

'Not really. My name's different from hers. I could describe her – that would prove I knew her. I wouldn't want to take the things away – just have a quick look through them, in case there's a clue as to where she is now.'

The huge woman eyed him closely. 'Couldn't you just show me?' he cajoled.

She melted without warning, shuffling backwards to allow him ingress. 'Come on, then,' she said. 'I don't see any harm in it. Everyone's so suspicious these days, expecting the worst. If you turn out to be a burglar or a conman, the laugh'll be on me, won't it.'

'I'm harmless, I promise,' he laughed. 'My name's Peter Stafford. My grandmother was Gwen Absolon's sister.'

'Great-nephew, then,' she remarked, giving him no time to regret the dishonesty he had just perpetrated. 'I wouldn't know any of my great-nephews from Father Christmas.'

'How did *you* come to be living here?' he asked, before he could stop himself. Her change of manner was seductive, a surprise that only fuelled his curiosity. 'If it isn't a rude question, I mean – how did you come to be looking for something like this?'

'No harm in asking,' she replied calmly. 'It's a sorry tale of bad planning, in essence, combined with bad luck. What happened to me could have happened to anybody. My husband and I bought a large house with a huge mortgage, at the wrong moment. With hindsight it's obvious we were too old to take on such a loan. He fell ill – the value of the property plummeted. We had to sell at a massive loss, abandoning life insurance in the process. When he died, I found I'd got virtually nothing. If I'm careful, and don't live too long, the residue will see me through here. It's surprisingly comfortable, actually. Very liberating, in a strange way. Do you know what keeps me going?'

Drew shook his head, guessing she'd say something banal like television or stamp collecting.

'The Internet,' came her astonishing reply. 'I bought myself a computer, and made sure I rented a place with its own phone – and now I'm in touch with the whole world. You interrupted me, as it happened, just as I was talking to a man in Zimbabwe.'

'But isn't it very expensive?' Drew wondered. 'Being on the phone all day long?'

She smiled, her broad face oddly impish. 'It pays for itself,' she said. 'I've always been a quick learner, and now I can create websites better than a lot of people. Never judge by appearances,' she added tartly, noticing Drew's expression. 'The Internet is the great leveller, in case you didn't know.'

'But it doesn't earn enough to get you out of this—'

'Hovel?' she supplied. 'No I'm not stupid enough to think it's going to last. I've a nice little niche at the moment, but people are quickly realising they don't need someone like me. It gets easier all the time, and they can do it for themselves. But we're digressing. The cupboard's there – look. It isn't locked. I think I'm going to leave you to it.'

'I really appreciate your help,' said Drew. 'And it's been very nice to meet you. I didn't catch your name, Mrs–?'

'Henrietta Fielding. Good luck finding your aunt. Personally, I think she's probably dead.' Before Drew could react to that, she had gone into her room, through a door halfway down the passage, and closed it firmly behind her. Why did she say that? he thought.

In the cupboard were three Sainsbury's carrier bags, two pairs of shoes and a small pile of loose books. One bag contained clothes, neatly folded and rammed down hard; another held papers, mostly letters, but also including brochures for Nile cruises and a reporter's notebook. The third was heavier and more angular, the sharp corners of the contents threatening to break through the plastic. Emptying it carefully in the shadowy passage, Drew found a framed photograph; an alarm clock; a prickly tropical seashell; two pebbles; a bag of small stones with runic symbols engraved on them; a carved wooden box containing a few pieces of cheap jewellery; a sterile medical pack containing syringes, needles, dressings and swabs; and an impressive Swiss army knife. It took him a few moments of inexplicable joy before he understood that the act of unpacking the bag was powerfully reminiscent of opening his Christmas stocking as a child. Every item seemed to glow with a kind of magic. The runestones carried an atavistic thrill; the pebbles might have come from the most sacred spot on earth. The photograph was of a teenage boy, head flopped oddly to one side and a hostile look in his eyes, despite the half-smile on his lips. The unfortunate Nathan, Drew presumed.

Amongst the papers were letters from the Inland Revenue, an old passport, confirming her identity as Gwendoline Absolon, and two folded newspaper cuttings. Both described a shooting a short distance from the Great Pyramid in Giza on 12th April the previous year. A young married woman had been killed. Her name was Sarah Gliddon and she had been pregnant. She was twenty-seven, and had been the youngest member of a tour party led by an independent British guide specialising in such tours. The party in question had spent two weeks visiting the oases of Egypt, and were on the last day before flying home. The shooting had been the work of a single terrorist: suicidally foolish, given the presence of a dozen or more armed tourist police. The gunman had been killed before he could do any further damage. Mrs Gliddon had been the only casualty. The Egyptian Government claimed it as a vindication of their policy of high security, even though desperately regretting the death of the young woman; they pointed out that on the same day a tourist had fallen off a Nile cruiser and drowned, and another had suffered a fatal dose of sunstroke in Luxor. Drew snorted at this strange logic, while sympathising with the authorities plagued by such determined acts of destruction.

There were two hand-written letters, which Drew unfolded and read, as he sat back on his heels in the gloomy corridor. The first was from a man called Trevor.

Luxor, 18 July

Adorable Gwen,
When are you coming to see me? I'm missing you terribly. In fact, I'm planning to come to the UK in a couple of weeks' time, so I hope I'll see you. Will you

be off on one of your jaunts, I wonder? I'll turn up at your address, anyway, and hope for the best.

Remember you read my runes last time you were here? I think you put the Evil Eye on me, telling me there'd be health problems and setbacks of all kinds. I blame you entirely for what's been happening here. You're a witch – you know that.

Did that bloke get off your back? Just say the word and I'll settle his hash for you. Nobody would ever connect him with me, would they?

I'm writing this on the deck of Sammy's felucca – remember those long evenings we spent up here? I'm in a sentimental mood. Ignore me. I don't know what I'm saying. There's nobody here to talk to tonight.

I will come and find you, lovely Gwen. Don't go away.

Trevor

If it hadn't been for the postmark, smudgily showing the date as less than a year previously, Drew would have assumed this was a letter from Gwen's distant past. Knowing the recipient to be seventy, he read it carefully again; with a glance over his shoulder, he slid it into his pocket. It didn't take a detective of unusual powers to work out that here was another possible candidate for involvement in the woman's death. A recent lover had to be included in the equation. And who was the mysterious 'bloke'?

The second letter was still in its envelope, bearing a second-class stamp, but the postmark was illegible. Inside, however, was a crisply lucid communication, dated early January of the previous year.

161

Dear Mrs Absolon

Further to our discussion last month, I would like, please, to take up your offer of a place on your next trip to Egypt. I trust that it will include at least two oases, as well as a chance to explore the Great Pyramid and other sites near Cairo. I am glad you agree with me that this arrangement has the virtue of satisfying both our needs. I look forward to receiving confirmation of dates in the near future. You can reply to the above address without any anxiety.

Yours truly

Sarah Gliddon (Mrs)

The return address was in Salisbury.

Drew held the sheet of paper in his hand for some moments. This was from the girl who'd died in the terrorist attack. Her stilted use of English, the strange references to 'satisfying both our needs' and 'without anxiety', made him wonder if there was a hidden subtext. He tucked it into his pocket with the first one.

He felt he was getting to know Gwen Absolon, little by little. He wished he could have met her; she sounded quite something. The bag of runestones intrigued him, and he fingered them curiously. 'Telling the runes' could, of course, have been a cynical little party trick, designed to break the ice in her tour groups, or to give herself an aura of mystery. The reference to them in the letter from Trevor did at least tell him that she used them, and usually carried them with her when she travelled.

162

He flipped quickly through the reporter's notebook from the second bag, noticing that it was half full of jottings; lists, mostly, with a few addresses and odd lines of description. One page contained a list of six names – amongst which was that of Sarah Gliddon – headed by the dates 31 March to 13 April. Beside Sarah Gliddon's name, the word *Free* had been inserted, in brackets.

The absence of money, passport, birth certificate, pension book, hairbrush, suggested she had at least taken a handbag with her when she left the bedsit. Although the other residents might have helped themselves to cash, they would hardly have bothered with worthless personal items. Squatting back on his heels, the lino dusty beneath him, Drew slowly fingered the items again. If they were indeed the entire sum of the worldly goods of Gwen Absolon, he supposed he should view them as pathetic. She was little more than a vagrant, lugging a battered assortment of basic articles from place to place, going virtually unmissed for months after her last disappearance. But 'pathetic' was not the word which came to mind. Rather he felt an admiration not much short of awe for someone who travelled so lightly through life.

He was getting a sense of a woman who knew where her priorities lay. A person with clear values and total self-sufficiency, and a minimalism that liberated her to an extent that most people could barely dream of. She didn't need a kitchen full of gadgets, or even a family; she was content with a series of intimate encounters which passed easily when the passion evaporated. Drew suspected that this Trevor had been importunate, a nuisance who didn't know when to let go – though perhaps the fact that Gwen had kept his letter refuted this idea. Such affection as Trevor professed must have at least given her a pang of warm feeling. Had he turned up, as promised, and found her indifference so wounding that he killed her? If so, how would he, presumably a stranger to the area, have found Drew's burial ground?

As he pondered, Henrietta Fielding poked her head out of her room. 'Still there?' she said. 'Found anything?'

'Nothing to say where she might have gone,' he admitted. 'Just a collection of odds and ends, really.'

'Can I make you a coffee? I've got some free time now. Sorry if I was abrupt before.'

He got up, wincing as he straightened stiff knees. 'Thanks very much,' he beamed at her. 'I could do with one.'

The bedsit was larger than he'd expected, with a high ceiling and generous light. A stainless steel sink and new-looking cooker occupied one corner; Henrietta's computer hummed in the diagonally opposite corner, on a big oak table, with a scanner and printer ranged alongside it, together with a stack of floppy disks and CDs. The bed was narrow. Drew had a vision of Henrietta's large body overflowing its sides.

She moved economically, barely lifting her feet off the floor. *She must weigh over twenty stone*, thought Drew. He wondered what it was like,

164

carrying such weight around all the time, never escaping it, getting stuck in narrow theatre seats, glared at on trains, giggled at in the street. Her arms were huge, her neck invisible. Her heart must be quite an impressive engine, he mused, to keep such a monumental body functioning, day in, day out.

'You said you thought she must be – dead,' he said, trying to sound wary and nervous: normal people could often barely utter the word, and Drew was doing his best to come over as a normal person.

'Well, it stands to reason,' she said calmly. 'Women of her age don't go missing the way she did. They don't run away from husbands or have bizarre midlife crises.'

'She didn't act like an old woman, though.'

'But, she must have been over sixty, although she was very well preserved. Straight back, lovely head of hair. She didn't leave any pills or potions anywhere, so I assume she was in perfect health. It's funny, isn't it – trying to guess at people's lives? Especially when there's so little to go on.'

'I hardly remember what she looked like,' Drew ventured. 'She hadn't gone white, then?'

Henrietta Fielding shook her head, her own pate only lightly sprinkled with silvery strands. 'Not white,' she demurred. 'A lovely strong iron-grey. Long and thick. I admit I envied her that hair.'

Drew pulled a wry face. 'I do remember she always had it long, but apart from that, I can't really say–'

The woman made no attempt to finish his

sentence for him, but watched him with an intelligent curiosity. Drew had an uncomfortable feeling that she was reading his thoughts, summing him up. He struggled to keep the conversation going. 'I know she travelled a lot.'

'Indeed she did,' came the ready response. 'She was away for a month or so last winter and she told me she'd been overseas for much of the previous year. I saw her off on her spring trip, as it happens. She seems to have travelled very light. Didn't bring much back with her, either.'

'So – you saw her last during the summer? Would you be able to put a date on the last time you actually did see her?'

'Oh, my word. That's a tall order. I'd have to think about that one.' She put a hand over her mouth, and stared hard at a point on one wall for some moments. 'I have no recollection of any particular encounter,' she said at last. 'Wendy just wasn't there one day. I'm only guessing, but it must have been late July – the schools had just broken up. You might have noticed there's a big comprehensive just over the road.' Drew shook his head. 'Well, there is, and they're very noisy at break times. I think I do remember saying something to Wendy about the blessed peace of school holidays.' Her face brightened. 'And I asked her if she had any more travel plans in the offing. She said there was nothing definite, but she certainly wasn't intending to spend the winter in England. Oh – I remember. I went away myself for a long weekend – early in August. Wendy wasn't here when I came back.'

'Do you remember the dates?'

'Hmmm. Let's see. I went to stay with my old schoolchum Grace. It was her birthday – the 9th – while I was there. Something like the 7th to the 10th I would imagine?'

Drew frowned. 'It all sounds very worrying,' he said, trying to assume the role of long-lost nephew. 'Don't you think so?'

'I did worry a little, I must admit,' she said. 'I even toyed with the idea of reporting her missing to the police. But you know how it is. People come and go. If you live in a place like this, you expect a degree of transience. And Wendy travelled so light, and seemed to have so few ties, I persuaded myself that she'd gone off on a whim.'

'How long did she actually rent the room?'

'Oh, years,' came the surprising reply. 'She arrived a few months after I did.'

Drew tried to think. 'You said you thought she was probably dead,' he reminded her.

'Yes. When she hadn't been back for her bags by November or December, it seemed likely that she'd been in an accident, or taken ill. Or something like that,' she ended, with an atypical imprecision that jarred on Drew's ear.

He eyed her sternly. 'In that case, you certainly ought to have reported it to the police. What if she's been lying in a hospital all these months, and nobody knows who she is? She could have had a stroke, or lost her memory. And if she is – well – dead, there must be an unidentified body somewhere.' He pulled himself up short, sensing thin ice.

Henrietta Fielding's eyes twinkled incongruously. 'It never occurred to me that I might be the person responsible for her,' she said calmly. 'I took it for granted that she had other friends and relatives who would alert the authorities if they were concerned.'

'But they obviously didn't,' Drew responded. 'Otherwise you'd have had the police here, examining her things.'

'Whereas all I've got is you,' she smiled.

Drew felt he'd reached an impasse. He'd let his persona slip, losing sight of his role as worried relative. He sipped his drink, playing for time, and hoping Mrs Fielding hadn't noticed his lapse. The coffee was good, and the biscuits accompanying it were far from Sainsbury's cheapest. Henrietta might be in reduced circumstances, but she wasn't living like a poor person. She drank her own coffee without speaking, apparently quite content to let the silence continue.

'Well, thank you very much,' Drew said at last. He could think of nothing more to ask her, apart from a blurted 'Did you murder her? Had she upset you in some way?' – thoughts he clearly couldn't voice. The full extent of the indecipherable background facts depressed him. 'You've been very helpful.'

'I don't think you'll find her,' she said gently. 'It's been too long, and evidently she's left too few clues. I hope you weren't due for a big inheritance from her?'

Drew forced a laugh. 'Oh, no – I don't think so. At least I can tell my wife I tried. I'll just pop everything back in the cupboard.'

'Don't be silly. Take it. It's of no use to anybody

else, and if she does turn up, we'll tell her Peter Stafford took it all. She'll know where to find you, won't she?'

Drew gulped and nodded. 'She ought to,' he croaked.

CHAPTER EIGHT

In the office, Maggs had run out of work by eleven o'clock. Although dry outside, it was overcast and uninviting – and besides, she had been instructed to stay close to the phone. She tried positive thinking – visualising a succession of customers, visiting and phoning, with at least three new funerals booked and agreed by the time Drew came back. There could be no argument about the satisfaction level of the families involved in those few burials they had conducted so far – so why hadn't they passed on word to all their friends and relations? Though, she admitted to herself, even if they had, it would be unlikely that further deaths would yet have taken place in their immediate circle.

Doodling idly, she let her thoughts turn to Drew and Karen's new baby. It worried her, the way they hadn't bothered to make proper provision for Stephanie – the best outcome now would be if Karen gave up work altogether and stayed at home to look after her own children. If Drew had more time to himself to get on with doing his job properly, there was every chance that Peaceful Repose would take off in a big way. Maggs could think of a dozen sidelines they could offer, if only they could get themselves better organised. Eventually, they should aim to build a chapel of some sort, so people could have a proper ceremony – not necessarily religious – in comfort. As it was, they had the option of using the village church only three hundred yards away – but that didn't suit the majority of their strictly secular customers. They wanted a place to gather, out of the rain, with somewhere to plug in a tape or CD player. Despite the clear proscription of any such building in the field, according to the planning permission, Maggs had every confidence that there would be some way around that in the future. *Petty bureaucracy,* she decided, dismissively.

At half past eleven, she had a visitor. The sound of a car engine alerted her and she reached the window in time to see a woman getting out of a minicab. The cab didn't drive away; apparently she had asked the driver to wait for her. Maggs met her at the office door. 'Hello again,' she said.

Caroline Kennett looked very uncomfortable; she glanced up the sloping field towards the infamous grave. 'Oh – er – hello,' she faltered. 'I hope you don't mind–'

Maggs was wary. 'Didn't bring the policeman with you this time then?' she challenged.

'No – he said he wouldn't be needing me any more. I didn't turn out to be very useful, I'm afraid. He seemed to want me to be so *certain* – and I just kept getting less and less sure. I came back to see if I could remember anything on my own. Do you mind if I just have a little walk around?'

Maggs considered this with deep suspicion. The story of the buried woman was still very unclear to her, and this visit from the only witness seemed distinctly significant. Why couldn't she leave it alone, especially as she'd been given the brush-off by the police?

'All right then,' she nodded. 'Can't see any harm in it.'

She went back into the office, taking care to keep watch on the woman through the back window. This time Mrs Kennett went directly to the grave, much more confident than she had been when in the company of the policeman. The minicab waited patiently; Maggs wondered how much it had cost to come here again. Unless Mrs Kennett had an extremely dull life, it seemed quite a bit of trouble to go to in the circum-stances.

Had she perhaps invented the story of being a mere witness to the burial? And now, was she having one final check to make sure there were no incriminating details to be found? Perhaps on her previous visit she'd noticed something that could give her away. Maggs's imagination began to run riot, as it often did, as she continued to watch the woman, wishing she had her glasses with her. When Caroline bent down, reaching her hand to the grass at her feet, Maggs had no idea what she was doing.

'Damn it!' she muttered to herself. She was tempted to run up for a closer look, but it would be too late; whatever the woman was doing, she'd have finished by the time Maggs got there. She was already leaving the site of the grave and walking slowly up to the fence by the railway, as she had before. Crossly Maggs withdrew her scrutiny and tried to get back to her work. She was writing busily when the woman tapped on the office door.

'See what you wanted?' Maggs enquired.

'Oh, I don't know,' said the woman worriedly. 'It's all so difficult. But those trees–' she pointed at the tall oaks on the roadside '–they do look very much how I remember.'

Maggs shrugged. 'Difficult,' she agreed.

'Well, I must get on,' Mrs Kennett said fussily. 'I'm supposed to be visiting my Aunt Hilda, but when I got to the station, I decided to come here again. The minicab's costing a fortune, but I wanted to put my mind at rest. By the way–' she added, 'there's a very nasty smell up there. I think there's a dead animal or something. Near the railway line. It's quite strong.'

'I'll go and look,' Maggs promised. 'Thanks for telling me.'

She waited for the woman to leave, then went to investigate. It was true – there was inescapably the whiff of putrefaction. She followed it determinedly, finally discovering the source.

'Yuk!' she gasped, holding a hand over her nose. 'Wait till Drew hears about this!'

On his way back from Henrietta Fielding's, Drew remembered his promise to Maggs and called her from a phonebox. She took some time to answer; when she did, she was breathless. 'Too busy to answer the phone?' he demanded.

'You could say that,' she puffed. 'It was as quiet as the you-know-what until an hour ago, and then things started to happen. The police are here now – somebody's made a complaint about us. Some nutcase, accusing us of paganism and witchcraft. Your friend PC Graham Sleeman came with some other bloke. They're not bothered – it isn't against the law, anyway, to be a pagan. But I had to show them round. Oh – and that Kennett woman came back again. I don't know what she wanted, but she said there was a smell, and I found a stinking dead cat wrapped up in a sheet, by the railway line. Remember those two men with the spade that I chased away a couple of weeks ago? It must have been them that left it there.'

'What have you done with it?'

'Nothing. I thought Jeffrey could deal with it, next time he's here. The stink's awful. Very bad for business.' She went back to her earlier topic. 'Why do you think she'd come back again? It seems a bit fishy to me—'

'Can't you do it?' Drew interrupted her, evidently still focused on the dead cat. 'It won't need much digging.'

'I might,' she said unhelpfully. 'I'll see how I feel. Oh, and that Jarvis chap phoned. Wouldn't tell me anything. Patronising git.'

'Sounds like a busy morning,' Drew said brightly, hoping to divert her. 'But nobody wanting a funeral?'

'Not a soul,' she told him dolefully. 'When will you be back?'

'Mid-afternoon, I should think. I'm going to collect Stephanie and report on my progress to Genevieve. I've got some more questions for her.'

'Enjoy yourself,' Maggs said with a burst of irritation, and slammed the phone down noisily.

Drew sat in the van with a large jotter pad on his lap; he had bought it specially at a nearby stationer's. He was working on a flowchart, starting at the top with Gwen Absolon alias Wendy Forrester, and following threads downwards, via Genevieve, Willard, Dr Jarvis, the Egypt shooting, Sarah Gliddon, Trevor, Henrietta Fielding and Brigid. He knew he was merely feeding in every name he'd come across so far, with little or no resulting enlightenment. He wrote: *Jealousy/suicide/blackmail* alongside the listed names, and then added *Runestones?* next to Trevor. Consulting Gwen's notebook, he added the names from the list that he guessed was the tour group she'd taken to Egypt. Stephen and Felicity Fletcher, Maggie Dobson, Janet Harrison, Karl Habergas. He supposed he should try to trace them all, ask them when they last saw Gwen, discover whether they could throw any light on where she might be now. He was confident that he hadn't left anything out, but he was no further forward.

The pressure of the imminent burial – or reburial – of what he now firmly believed was Gwen Absolon's body made Drew's head hurt. In his mind, it was a deadline (a word he'd learned not to use in the funeral business), and he badly wanted to solve the mystery before the burial took place. He couldn't waste time sitting in the van trying to think. He'd already spent half an hour staring at the jotter, struggling to build a picture of the dead woman from the conflicting comments he'd heard. *Hair colour?* he had

175

written, underlined twice. Henrietta Fielding had said it was dark grey, yet the woman in the grave had white hair. Of course, it might have lost pigment while in the ground. He'd heard stories of dark-haired people turning ginger after they'd been buried for a few months – but understandably, there was little hard evidence. And the white had been so white – he'd seen it for himself, and it had been mentioned prominently in the newspapers. It was definitely something he would have to pursue.

Although not as final as a cremation, the bureaucratic hassle of disinterring a body for further forensic examination was enough to make it a highly unusual occurrence. Drew didn't think he could face the idea of that – more police presence in his burial ground, more suspicion and bad publicity. If there was to be any increased police interest, following new facts or leads, then it was in his own best interest to produce it within the next few days.

Remembering the newspaper articles about the shooting in Egypt, Drew wondered whether there was any sense in trying to locate Gliddon, husband of the dead Sarah. He should probably visit the widowed man and ask if he'd ever met Gwen – and whether he knew why *Free* had been written alongside his wife's name in Gwen's list. He assumed Gwen would have visited him to offer her condolences after Sarah had been killed, or at least attended the funeral of her slaughtered charge. He needed to know whether she had seemed depressed or unstable – whether anything might support Dr Jarvis's suggestion of suicide. Given Genevieve's volatile nature, and the past tragedies that the whole family shared, he found it entirely credible that Gwen too had been given to mood swings. Had she perhaps talked about anyone threatening her, or causing her concern? The long list of questions was wearying: he put the jotter down on the long seat beside him and turned the key in the ignition.

Throughout the day he had repeatedly felt an impulse to return to Genevieve's house. He told himself he wanted to be sure she was taking proper care of Stephanie – but just as much he wanted to lay eyes on her again. There was a quiet thrill at the prospect. Even better, his researches of the morning had produced some genuine progress, and he now had more than enough to talk to her about. Whether she had ever heard of Trevor, in particular. And had Gwen actually spoken to her about the Egypt tragedy? Had Willard acted especially oddly last summer? Questions galore – but much more important than that, he wanted to look into those grey eyes again.

By two o'clock, he was driving into her village's main street. He promised himself he would work that evening – telephone the Gliddon man, re-read all the papers he'd taken from the bedsit. He wanted Genevieve to get value for money. And if he stayed at her house long enough, he might witness the return of the elusive Willard, and perhaps assess for himself whether the man could be a murderer.

In fact, neither Genevieve nor Stephanie seemed

177

particularly pleased to see him. They were in the back garden, despite the cool weather, cuddled together on a rug with a book. Drew spotted them as he went to the side door, and savoured the tableau. His sturdy little daughter was cradled in the pregnant woman's arm, as Genevieve reclined gracefully against a contraption apparently designed specifically to prop you up as you read a book in the garden. The intimacy was not merely physical: both heads bent over the book in rapt attention. Genevieve's long raven hair was loose, and hung in wavy hanks over her shoulders. Trevor's letter, and the word *witch*, flashed into his mind.

'Hello!' he said heartily. 'You two seem to be getting on very well.'

Both faces turned towards him, oddly alike in expression. Neither smiled; both pairs of eyes seemed preoccupied. 'You're early,' said Genevieve. 'Case solved already?'

'Far from it, I'm afraid. But I haven't come back empty-handed. I need to ask you a few questions before I can go any further.'

She made no move to get up. Unprompted, Drew felt a wave of longing rush through him, a huge desire to kneel down beside her and hold her in his arms. Gritting his teeth, he held his ground, eight or ten yards away, and focused on murder; dead bodies; unofficial graves. To break the uncomfortable silence he told the story of the cat.

'Just after you came to the burial ground, Maggs saw two men running away. They were carrying spades. Well, now she's found a dead cat in the hedge, where they were hiding. I guess that's one little mystery solved.'

'Oh?'

'Well – I assume they wanted to bury it some-where. Maybe they live in a flat or something. Like the man and his wife with the labrador – they said they hadn't got anywhere to put it. Cheeky of the cat people, though. I could have charged them for the service.'

'Doesn't a dead cat make you think of anything a bit more sinister?' she asked him, her head on one side. He met the beautiful eyes full on. A harmless pleasure, surely...

'Um – no, I don't think so. What did you have in mind?'

'It doesn't matter. It's my fevered imagination. We've been reading this – look.' She held up the book, and Drew recognised *Where the Wild Things Are* from his own childhood. 'It's going down very well. I think we've been through it six times so far. I know it off by heart.'

With a sense of capitulation, he walked forward and sat down on the rug, two or three feet away from Genevieve. 'Now, can I ask my questions?' he pleaded.

'Go on then,' she invited him. 'Though I ought to get you some coffee or something first.'

He waved that aside, and launched into an account of his morning's discoveries, such as they were. He omitted the runestones, but tried to include everything else. 'So – have you ever heard of Trevor?' he finished.

She shook her head. 'Definitely not. Sounds like some passing ship in the night who didn't know when to keep going: my ma collected lots of those.'

'That's what I thought,' Drew nodded. 'But it's possible he did come over to see her, and she angered him enough to provoke him to murder her. God knows how we'd begin to trace him now, though.'

'We wouldn't,' she said flatly. 'If that's what happened, then he's going to get clean away with it.'

'The other thing is this shooting in Egypt. I think I ought to try and speak to someone who was in the tour party. I've got what looks like a list of names – although no addresses.'

'I think Willard knows who they are,' she said vaguely. 'He helped her to write to them all, when she came back here after it happened. He persuaded her it would be diplomatic. He's quite keen on Egypt, as it happens – it was one of the things they talked about a lot. He worries about the country's economy when something like that shooting happens.'

Drew blinked; it was hard to envisage someone worrying about Egypt's economy in the face of so much else to get upset about. Genevieve noticed his bemusement.

'It's not as weird as you think. His subject is economics. Egypt's a stabilising influence in the Middle East, and when things start to slide for them, the whole area's at risk. Or so he says. I can't say I take much interest.'

'What is his job, exactly? You never did tell me.' Drew asked, as casually as he could manage.

'He's a senior lecturer in economics at the

University of North-East Devon,' she replied readily, almost as if waiting for the question. 'It used to be a technical college – quite honestly, it's rather a joke to call it a university. But don't tell him I said so. He fits in a bit of history or sociology as well if anyone's missing. Jack of all trades, is Willard. He's cruising towards retirement now, cutting down on his hours. Mind you, he's more enthusiastic than ever when it comes to acquiring knowledge. He's taken to the Internet in a big way.'

The image of Willard produced by Genevieve was fragmented and contradictory, not much helped by Drew's recollection of him two years earlier. The man was a real enigma.

'Are you planning to go back to Radio Three after the baby's born?' he asked.

'Absolutely,' she said with force. 'I'd go mad, stuck here on my own all day.'

'That's a shame,' said Drew, without thinking. 'Because it looks as if all your maternal instincts are in the right place.' He nodded at Stephanie, still roughly turning the pages of her book and jabbing at the monsters with an excited forefinger. 'I'll be expecting her to start saying *let the wild rumpus start* in the middle of the night, now.'

Genevieve laughed sceptically. 'This is easy. I'm happy to devote a few hours to a nice little person like Stephanie. Besides, at the end of the day, she goes home. A helpless puking baby is going to be quite a different prospect.' Again he glimpsed the flash of fear he'd seen before, a spasm that pulled her face into a blank mask of paralysis.

'Do you think you could ask your husband for those names?' Drew forced himself back to the business in hand. 'It would be very helpful.'

She looked doubtful. 'I suppose I could. He never throws anything away. But aren't you clutching at straws? It must have been months after the Egypt thing that she died. I think you'd do better to concentrate on where she was and what she was doing in August.'

'You're probably right,' he sighed. 'But at the moment, Egypt seems to be cropping up so often that I don't feel I can just ignore it.'

She screwed her mouth sideways in an exaggeration of uncertainty. 'I'll have to think of a reason for asking him,' she said. 'Or he might get suspicious.'

Drew shied away from any further examination of Willard's role in the business: his brief, as he understood it, was to try to find some alternative perpetrator. He kept his thoughts firmly focused on the morning's finds. 'If he and Gwen wrote to all the people,' he said slowly, 'would they have done it on the computer?'

'Of course! Willard does everything on the computer. How clever of you! We can go and find the addresses now, without ever having to ask him!'

'Won't he know?'

'Not a chance. I've learned how to cover my tracks. Come on.'

Following slowly up the stairs, carrying Stephanie and trying not to move too closely to Genevieve, Drew recalled every single fairytale in which boys are lured into danger by beautiful women. Hansel into the gingerbread house; Kay and the Snow Queen; the Prince and the Little Mermaid. He thought of every story he'd been told about lovers being caught by outraged husbands and savagely punished. Going upstairs with Genevieve felt like the first step on a very rocky road.

In Willard's study the computer had to be switched on, the password given. 'How do you know his password?' he asked in a whisper.

'Easy. We used to have a Persian cat called Beulah, the love of his life. It's the first thing he'd think of. But he doesn't know that I know.' She giggled girlishly, tapped keys and clicked the mouse, humming cheerily to herself, until they were scrolling through numerous files with Egypt in their title, dating back to the February of the previous year. It took four or five minutes to find what they wanted. They'd tried *Egypttours* and *Egyplett* with no success, but *Egypadds* yielded a complete list of names and addresses, including that of a Simon Gliddon, with *Sarah* in brackets after it.

'I'll print it for you,' Genevieve said, and proceeded to do so.

Drew took the opportunity to inspect the room. It was a typical academic's study: books lined one whole wall, and stacks of papers sat on the desk in the middle of the room. A large abstract oil painting dominated the wall opposite the window. Drew suspected it was worth about as much as a large and powerful car. Along the floor, filling the whole length of the wall containing the window, were stacks of newspapers and magazines. Drew counted seventeen piles.

Stephanie rocked restlessly in his arms, anxious to get down and explore. 'No,' he told her. 'Keep still a minute.'

The printer was whirring into life, and a sheet of paper was disgorged. Genevieve laughed as she brought up the three or four document files that she'd already noted were the last visited. 'Just in case he checks back,' she said. 'The dates'll be wrong, of course, but I doubt he'll look closely enough to notice the details.'

Drew watched idly at first, but was suddenly galvanised by the name of one of the files. *HenriettaF.* Sensing his sudden tension, Stephanie began to whimper, and then squeal – mercifully, as Drew quickly realised; he didn't want Genevieve to notice the change in his manner. 'Hey!' he soothed his daughter. 'Not long now, poppet.'

Genevieve handed him the printed list of names and addresses. He folded the sheet of paper, and slid it into his pocket. 'Thanks,' he said. 'Now we'll be going. Can I leave Stephanie again tomorrow?'

Genevieve spread her hands welcomingly. 'Any time,' she grinned. 'We're best mates already.' She came up close to him – much too close – and kissed the child on the cheek. 'Bye, baby. Thanks for the company.'

Stephanie continued to grizzle. 'She's tired, I expect,' he apologised. 'We'd better be off.'

'Thanks for what you've done today,' she said graciously. Then she chuckled. 'Mum would have loved all this, you know. Causing so much

184

mystery and confusion. She loved to be the centre of attention!'

Drew jiggled his daughter, and managed to hush her enough to venture one last question. Each time he met Genevieve, he became aware of all the things she hadn't told him, all the things he couldn't begin to understand. 'It might help me to get one thing clear,' he began, 'if you could give me some idea of how you actually felt about your mother. I mean, in the last few years. Since Nathan died.'

Genevieve sighed dramatically. 'Heaven protect us from New Men, and their *feelings*,' she said. 'There was a time when such questions would have been considered irrelevant at best, and embarrassing at worst. Now *feelings* are regarded as a vital element in everything that happens.'

Drew frowned his disagreement. 'When we're talking about murder, surely you can't ignore emotion. You've told me a story that involves jealousy, guilt, regret – and then you make jokes about the person at the centre of it.'

She frowned, and he realised she was close to tears. As if to confirm his perception, she gave a noisy sniff. 'I know,' she laughed shakily. 'I'm all over the place. I thought we'd already established that.'

'So – what's the answer?'

'To what?' She ran a hand through her hair. 'Sorry – what did you ask me?'

'How you really felt about your mother.'

'Ah, yes. I thought we'd covered that as well. How would you feel if your mother had given every atom of her attention to your younger

185

brother, and then took herself off on an orgy of self-indulgence when he was out of her way? I don't think there are words for it, really. You'll have to use your imagination.'

'Resentment? Loneliness? Longing?' he hazarded, before becoming aware that he was pushing too hard. And what was the point? If Genevieve had killed her mother, she wouldn't have hired Drew to investigate her death.

She seemed to have regained her composure. 'I'll give you an example. When I got my job at the BBC, selected out of two hundred applicants, she didn't react at all. Never said a word when I phoned to tell her. She wasn't remotely interested. If I *had* loved her as a child, all that sort of thing was killed later. I didn't hate her, just left her out of my calculations – as she did me. So, when she came back, wanting to be friends again, sucking up to my husband, I wasn't inclined to meet her even halfway. I was hurt and angry. I didn't think I needed her any more. I wanted her to go away again and leave me alone–'

'You wanted her dead,' said Drew quietly.

She stopped, shaking her head. 'That never occurred to me,' she said. 'It truly didn't. The miserable truth is that I wanted, even then, for us to get back to being a normal mother and daughter. But I knew it was hopeless. Absolutely hopeless. When she came here last year she was just looking for somewhere to crash out for a bit. Where she'd be looked after and have someone to talk to. And I couldn't bear having her here. She never asked me anything about work, or my interests. And I didn't trust her an inch with Willard. It was gruesome.'

'So – you feel guilty now, and that's why you want everything sorted out? If your mother's still alive, you want her support, and if she's dead, you want – well, what *do* you want?'

'You're more or less right,' she smiled weakly. 'Guilt, curiosity – Christ, Drew, why do you keep asking me to give reasons? Wouldn't you want to know whether your mother was alive or dead, and if dead, then how and when and by whom? Isn't it all perfectly understandable?'

He watched her for a moment. This was a repeat of the day before: when he tried to push her for something concrete, she turned into an emotional mess and made him feel unacceptably aggressive. And maybe she *was* being perfectly straight with him. In any case, he could hardly claim he was being used when she was paying him so handsomely.

'Thanks for that,' he said wearily. 'Now, I'm really going. Madam's got a wet bottom.'

'Oh – change her here. That bag of nappies is in the bathroom.'

'I'd better be quick, then. She's going to fall asleep any minute. Which way is it?'

She showed him along the landing, past two closed doors, to the generously-sized bathroom at the end. He found the nappies and knelt on the floor, lying Stephanie on a tufted bathmat. Deftly he effected the change, and bundled her back into her clothes. She watched his face throughout, in the way she had, as if awarding him marks for efficiency.

CHAPTER NINE

'I buried the cat,' said Maggs, as soon as he walked into the office, having delivered Stephanie to Karen. 'It looked as if it'd been strangled with wire or something. It's throat was a horrible mess. The police didn't even seem to notice.'

'Nasty,' said Drew automatically.

'Drew – something's going on. That complaint – well, people are stupid, I know – but would they have made something like that up? And after you got those letters – well, I wondered if there was a connection. It's all beginning to feel a bit scary, don't you think? What if people come round at night and interfere with the graves?'

'Nothing goes on at night,' Drew told her with robust confidence. 'Nobody can get in.'

'They can. Easily. The top hedge is full of gaps. And it wouldn't be difficult to climb over the gate. What if there are Satanists who come here and do horrible things? That would explain the letters – if somebody's heard something or seen something, and thinks it's you at the centre of it.' She laughed fleetingly. 'Listen to me! Only a little while ago I was telling Jeffrey he was mad to think the same sort of thing.'

'What about this conversation with Jeffrey? You've mentioned it twice now. Sounds as if he got under your skin.'

'Well, yeah – he did a bit,' she admitted. 'We found a sheep's skull, and I said something perfectly innocent and he started raving on about voodoo. You know what,' she said, on a sudden thought, 'I bet he's been mouthing off in the pub, and someone's picked it up and got everything totally out of proportion. And somewhere along the line, one of them's gone and called the police.'

'And that was *before* you found the cat?'

'That's right.' They looked at each other. 'So – that means that somebody *wanted* the police to start snooping about. To find the cat and decide there was something to the story they'd been fed.'

'Steady on!' Drew protested. 'That would be seriously malicious.'

'Like the hate mail,' she reminded him.

Drew refused to be shaken; he waved a dismissive hand at the idea that he was under any real threat. 'It must be just kids messing about,' he insisted. 'Who's going to take all that trouble just to – well, to do what? And it didn't work, anyway, from what you say – the police didn't take any notice of the cat.'

'Well, that was mainly thanks to me,' she claimed, with a show of false modesty. 'I pretended to think it must have been hit by a train, and they seemed to go along with that.'

Drew sat down at the desk and tried to change the subject. 'Things are complicated enough without this,' he decided. 'I'm not even going to think about it at the moment. How did you get on with the leaflets?'

'Never mind the leaflets,' she said, suddenly

189

intense. 'I told you that Caroline Kennett came back again this morning, didn't I? She wanted to try and settle in her mind whether it really was our field she saw from the train.'

Drew sighed. 'And did she?' he asked.

Maggs spread her hands non-committally. 'She thinks the trees look the same,' she said. 'I'd say it had to be our body she saw. Bit of a co-incidence otherwise.'

But Caroline Kennett didn't seem to matter much more than dead cats to Drew; his head was full of Genevieve, and what she wanted him to do.

'Listen, Maggs,' he said with some force, 'I need someone to help me untangle this body business. Last time, Karen–' He stopped. Last time, Karen had driven around with him, stood beside him when he confronted suspects, offered invaluable insights into what must have happened. This time, Karen was distant and distracted, hardly knew what Drew was doing, and cared even less.

'Come on, then,' Maggs encouraged. 'It's about time you remembered who your partner is around here.'

'But first you've got to promise you won't say anything to the police. Not until I say you can, anyway. I know it's risky. I could probably lose my livelihood, and worse, if it gets out that we've been withholding information relevant to a violent death. Even though I gather from Stanley they're not actively pursuing a murder investigation, that's not going to count for much.'

'You could go to prison,' she said, with an un-nerving relish.

Drew laughed weakly. 'I doubt if it would come to that. So far, I'm not actually withholding any real evidence. At least–' he frowned, wondering whether the suspicions he had and the material he'd found in the basement cupboard constituted real evidence. 'At least, it's all supposition at the moment,' he asserted firmly. 'Anyway, she hasn't even been buried yet.'

'Not long now, though. Is the burial your cut-off point? Get it all sorted out by Friday?'

He huffed a cynical laugh. 'I wish,' he said dourly.

'So tell me what you found out today,' she invited.

He went to fetch his jotter pad from the van. Putting it in front of her, he tried to explain who everybody was, and how he thought they might fit into the picture. 'She was a bit of an outsider,' he concluded. 'She doesn't seem to have been really close to anyone.'

'But – poor woman!' Maggs burst out. 'Having that awful son to look after, and being abandoned by her whole family. It reminds me of my mother – forced into caring, whether she wanted to or not.'

'What do you mean? Your mother isn't forced to care for anyone.'

'Not now she isn't. But when they adopted me, they were looking after their son. He was hooked on heroin from the age of sixteen, and he died when he was twenty-five. They kept him at home. Otherwise he'd have been living rough on the streets.'

Drew stared at her. 'How did they manage

191

that?' he demanded. 'Most addicts leave home and never go back. And how could they adopt a baby in those circumstances?'

'I wasn't a baby. I was four, and it wasn't easy. None of it. The *point*, Drew, is that I know what it's like. And my sympathy's all with this dead woman.'

'Which explains why you won't help me with Stephanie,' he realised.

Maggs scowled at the floor, and then nodded. 'Sort of,' she agreed. 'I'm never going to fall into that trap. I've got better things to do with my life than minding someone's kid – even my own. So I'm never going to have any.'

'Good for you,' he said sourly. 'Meanwhile, I think you're wrong about Gwen Absolon. She was a lousy mother to the girls, just when they most needed her. Whatever the handicapped son was like, she's got no excuse for abandoning them the way she did.'

Maggs checked herself, clamping down on the arguments he could see forming in her head. 'So – what exactly does this Genevieve want you to do next?' she demanded.

Drew approached this question with cautious eagerness; he wanted to hear how his answer sounded, whether it carried any credibility. 'Well,' he began, 'she isn't primarily interested in bringing a killer to book. She just wants to be sure it wasn't Willard who did it. I think she genuinely does believe it could have been him.'

'But that's the *impossible* part – don't you see?' Maggs glared at him. 'You can't prove a negative, not properly. The only way you can be certain it wasn't Willard is if you find the real killer. Otherwise, you've failed.'

'No.' Drew shook his head. 'If that was true, there'd never be any case for the defence. Don't try bringing logic into the law – there's probably any number of ways Willard could prove his innocence. And obviously, Genevieve doesn't want him to know she suspects him. It might be a peculiar marriage, but it seems to be fairly stable. If he thinks that she thinks he's capable of murder, I imagine it could rock the boat something chronic.'

'If you ask me,' Maggs asserted recklessly, 'Willard, Genevieve and Dr Jarvis are all in it together. Trying to muddy the waters. It's usually the family in this sort of case, you know.'

'Is it really?' he said with mock seriousness. He reminded himself how young she was, how little she knew of the realities of life. Disappointed, he began to think she was going to be much less help than Karen would have been.

'No. Drew – honestly. They sound a strange bunch to me,' Maggs insisted.

'You saw Genevieve. Did you think she seemed strange?'

Maggs cocked her head to one side, considering it. 'Well, she was all over you,' she offered. 'Fluttering her eyelashes. And too sloppy over Stephanie. As if she was busting a gut to make you like her.'

Drew winced: you didn't talk about 'busting a gut' in reference to a heavily pregnant woman. And he didn't like the acuity of the girl's observations. 'Well, I thought she was just being pleasant,' he argued.

'So you think her story makes sense, do you? What about the doctor chap? Does Genevieve think he could have driven the woman to suicide?'

'I didn't ask her,' he said irritably. 'We hardly mentioned Dr Jarvis.'

'The suicide idea's crap, anyway. Even if someone promised her to do the midnight burial while she was still alive, they'd never carry it through. Not when it came to the point. Can you imagine it? So the doctor's telling you porkies for some reason.'

Drew nodded impatiently. 'But if he'd killed her, why would he come here afterwards and introduce himself? He'd stay well away, keep his head down.'

She mused on this, and then said, 'He was probably scared that we knew more than the papers were saying. That they'd identified the dentures or something. So he worked out that the safest thing would be to pop in here and do a bit of digging.'

'That's Jeffrey's job,' Drew quipped. 'Anyway, that doesn't fit with the way he came across. He definitely didn't know Genevieve had already been here – he was genuinely shocked by that.'

'So? That doesn't mean anything.'

'That's enough.' Drew abruptly stood up. 'We're not getting anywhere just talking about it. We need more information. I'm going to contact Simon Gliddon – the husband of the girl who was shot in Egypt. If ever there was anyone with a legitimate grudge, it's him.'

'What? Now?'

'It's worth a try.'

'Before you do, there's a few more things that happened while you were out. Then I'm going home – okay?'

She filled him in on two phonecalls and a summary of some of the ideas she'd had for increasing their income. 'We ought to build a chapel,' she mentioned casually.

Drew snorted. 'Okay, I'll bear it in mind,' he told her. 'For when we're all millionaires.'

'I had another thought,' she ploughed on, undaunted.

'Oh, yes?'

'You could hire yourself out as a sort of non-religious minister. What's the word they use? Officiator, or something.'

'Officiant, d'you mean? Taking funerals? Doesn't that mean I'd have to be in two places at once?'

'Not really. The family usually supply bearers – and really there's no need for a conductor. If they wanted one, it could be me. But it would make everything even more – you know – cosy. I think it'd be great. And you could charge them the same as ministers get.'

He thought about it for a moment. 'Well, yes,' he murmured, 'I could probably do that. I've seen other people make a mess of it enough times to know how *not* to do it, at least. Thanks, Maggs. That one *is* worth thinking about.'

'You see – the only way you're ever going to make ends meet is to offer a whole lot of different services,' she pursued eagerly. 'If we made willow baskets here too, and grew plants and baby trees in a greenhouse, we'd be able to keep almost everything they paid us. We could charge seven or eight hundred pounds, flat rate, and do quite nicely on two or three funerals a week.'

'Not with Karen not working,' he reminded her. 'On top of her salary, it would have been enough. As it is, we're going to need a bit more than that. But you're heading in the right direction,' he added encouragingly.

'Thanks, boss,' she grinned. 'See you tomorrow.'

'See you,' he responded cheerily.

He fished Willard's list of names and addresses out of his pocket, and dialled 192. Directory Enquiries found him the number he wanted with ease, and he went straight on to key it in. The phone was answered on the third ring. A youngish, male voice said, 'Gliddon.'

'Forgive the intrusion, Mr Gliddon, but I wonder if I could speak to you about your wife?' Drew found himself stammering, once again unprepared for the reality of the conversation.

'My wife's dead,' the voice barked impatiently.

'Yes, I know. In tragic circumstances. The thing is – I've been asked to make a few investigations–'

'Are you the police?'

'No, no. Nothing like that,' Drew said hastily.

'In that case we have nothing to say to each other. I'd appreciate it if you didn't invade my privacy again.' And the phone was dropped, noisily and unambiguously. Drew was left staring disbelievingly into the receiver.

196

I should have invented a better cover story, he realised, and pulled his jotter towards him, to try out a few ideas. But he'd blown his only chance with Simon Gliddon.

It was only a minute or two before he'd decided that the basic gist of what he'd told Henrietta Fielding wasn't too bad. It seemed sensible to present himself as a relative looking for Gwen Absolon. No, he corrected. *Somebody with something for her. The offer of a job, or the possibility of some money due to her.* There was no need even to hint at the idea that she might be dead. He wondered whether Gliddon would have been any more forthcoming if he'd opened by mentioning Gwen. Somehow, he didn't think so.

He ran his finger down the sheet of names and addresses, pausing at the least common surname: *Karl Habergas* with an address in a place called Hemlington. Drew located a map and eventually found it, barely twenty miles away.

'I'm going this evening,' he decided. 'No time to lose.'

He definitely felt better for having told Maggs the whole story. He was encouraged and touched by her positive attitude and enthusiasm; it made a big difference having a partner, he concluded. The only snag was going to be preventing Maggs from detecting the real depth of his feelings towards Genevieve. Because if Maggs could work it out, then Karen was bound to be at least one step ahead of her.

Karen was decidedly dubious when Drew told her he was driving forty miles, there and back, to visit a man about Gwen Absolon that evening. 'Are you sure he'll be in?' she asked.

'No, but I don't want to phone first. I don't want to give him the chance to turn me away. If I just arrive on the doorstep, he's far more likely to speak to me.'

'Haven't we been here before?' she sighed.

'You're going to have to get used to it,' he warned her. 'I'm just not capable of letting these things slide by.'

'Maybe you ought to join the police force. I don't suppose you're too old. And think of the pension!'

He shook his head. 'I like to specialise.'

'You're just a child, Drew Slocombe. You want the icing but not the cake. I ought to stop you going off to see this man. For all you know, he's the one who murdered the woman.'

Drew paused. 'That never occurred to me,' he said with a laugh. 'You should get together with Maggs. She invents implausible scenarios every two minutes.'

'Oh, she knows all about this, does she? Is that wise? At this rate you'll both be in trouble with the police.'

'She sulked until I told her. So far we haven't done anything illegal, anyway.'

'Oh no. Just withheld important information concerning a murder enquiry, in full knowledge of what you're doing.'

'If I can just get a handle on what happened to the woman in our field, I'll go straight to the police,' he promised, wondering as he did so whether he could honour such a commitment. 'I

198

really feel I'm getting somewhere now. The burial isn't till Friday – I'm giving myself until then to see if I can work out what's happened to her. The thing is, we're still not really sure it's who we think it is.'

'Sounds fairly definite to me,' judged Karen, surprising Drew as she so often did. 'From what you've said, which admittedly isn't much, it's all too neat to be anybody else.'

'Well, if it is, and if she was murdered, then the police are going to be very glad of some definite leads, aren't they?' he said firmly.

Karen turned away. 'I think you're crazy,' she said. 'Just playing silly games.'

Karl Habergas answered his door five seconds after Drew rang the bell. Drew realised he'd been expecting a big blond Nordic type, with sturdy legs and clear blue eyes. Instead, he found himself looking down on a small man in his fifties, almost bald and wearing heavy-framed spectacles. He looked unnervingly intelligent.

Drew had worked intensively on his cover story during the drive to Hemlington. 'Good evening, sir,' he began politely. 'I'm really sorry to trouble you, but I'm looking for a lady by the name of Gwen Absolon, and I understand that you went on one of the tours she organised last year.'

'She certainly isn't here,' said the little man shirtily. 'And it's a long time since that trip. What do you want her for, anyway?'

'Well,' Drew tried to appear confident, 'I work for one of the larger tour companies, and Mrs Absolon has been highly recommended, as a leader of groups of older folk. We're in very urgent need of a substitute guide, starting this weekend, and her name came to mind. The trouble is, we don't seem to be able to find her.'

'How did you find *me?*' Habergas demanded.

Drew improvised. 'A Mrs Fletcher gave us your address. I understand she was in the same group as you? She and her husband have just booked a tour with us, for July this year, and she overheard our dilemma when she was in the office this morning. She said Mrs Absolon was an expert guide. She also said that if anyone in the group would have kept in touch with her, you'd be the one.'

The man seemed to assimilate this with no sign of suspicion as to its veracity, and Drew trembled inwardly at the smoothness with which the lies tripped off his tongue. Drew, the straight guy, who valued his own integrity above all else, turned out to be as good a liar as they come. *But I'm not harming anyone by it,* he told himself. *It's a necessary means to an end.*

'I didn't keep in touch with her,' Habergas said, rather sadly. 'Although I liked her. Very much. Didn't the Fletcher woman tell you what happened to our group?'

'She said there'd been a terrorist attack which had tragic consequences, and that the tour leader behaved with absolute efficiency. She couldn't speak highly enough of her.'

'Did she give you the details?' Habergas asked, with an odd eagerness. 'Because if not, I'd be more than happy to fill you in. It's true that Gwen coped admirably. But, to be honest, the

Fletchers didn't really witness much of what happened. Perhaps they weren't so affected–' He tailed off, staring down his quiet street as if gazing over the sand dunes of Egypt.

'If you'd like to tell me, I'd be more than happy to listen,' Drew offered gently, marvelling at how simple his task was turning out to be. The man was clearly still traumatised by what had happened, and evidently had nobody he could confide in. 'Often it's a lot easier to tell a stranger about something like that,' he ventured.

'Come in, then,' Habergas invited, as if he'd waited for this moment a long, long time.

He led the way into a stuffy back room, filled with a large table and several chairs. Two cats occupied the chairs closest to a grimy Rayburn. There was a strange mix of smells: fried onions, damp washing, and something medicinal: the sweetish, repulsive odour that Drew associated with chemotherapy patients, from the time he spent working as a nurse.

'I'll just go and tell Mother we've got a visitor,' the man said. 'Won't be two ticks.'

'Mother?' echoed Drew.

'She's upstairs. I'm looking after her. They weren't feeding her properly in hospital and nobody ever told her what was going on. She's a lot happier here.'

Drew smiled weakly, shades of *Psycho* hovering at the back of his mind. Karen's comment was also impossible to forget. *Perhaps he's the one who murdered her...*

'Oh, it's all right,' the man assured him. 'She's not going to die.'

201

We're all going to die, Drew wanted to tell him. And if Mother was having chemotherapy and had been allowed home, and must be at least in her mid-seventies, then her chances of surviving longer than a few months must be minimal.

It took Mr Habergas a few minutes to settle into the story. 'I'm not sure how it's going to help you,' he said. 'I have absolutely no idea where Gwen is now.'

'I expect we'll soon find her,' said Drew easily. 'I don't suppose she's gone into hiding.'

'No,' said his host thoughtfully. 'No, I don't suppose she's done that.'

Clearly Mr Habergas had harboured an affection for the woman, and Drew found himself feeling sorry for the little man, with his dying mother and his post-traumatic stress. He hoped the forthcoming debriefing would be therapeutic – and that he wasn't being too irresponsible in inviting a reliving of the story and then leaving Habergas to deal with whatever stirred-up emotions were thereby invoked. *I can always come and see him again,* he promised himself guiltily.

The man cleared his throat, and leaned forward in his chair. 'I'll tell you all I remember,' he said. 'I warn you, it could take some time. I hope it'll show you what I mean about Gwen, at any rate.'

Karl Habergas was an excellent storyteller. It took him more than half an hour to describe for Drew everything that had happened that morning in Egypt, and when he'd finished, Drew almost felt he'd been there himself At first he'd chafed at the wealth of detail, the seeming irrelevancies, but the force of the story quickly gripped him, and he lost all sense of time. He was no longer an acute investigator searching for clues: he was simply a listener, letting the tale unfurl as it would.

'We were actually at North Saqqara, not Giza, as some of the papers reported. It's all part of the same general area, and we never bothered afterwards to correct the mistake. Gwen had arranged for us to have a minibus and a guide, and spend the whole day touring the pyramids. It's a set itinerary, which was very tame after the adventures we'd had in the oases, where tourists hardly ever venture. The guide was on autopilot, diving into tombs and mastabas more or less at random and telling us a whole lot of garbage. We all knew more than he did, I think. Sarah had studied Egyptology, and knew the place inside out. But it was the last day, and none of us was in the mood to argue.

'After a bit, the guide gave up, and went back to his vehicle, leaving us to explore on our own. I wanted to see Mereruka's mastaba again – I remembered it from the first time I ever went to Egypt, as a new graduate. The carvings are wonderfully lively and irreverent. I've always been attracted to the man. After all those vainglorious Pharaohs, he comes as a refreshing relief. I went there with Gwen – she likes the hunting scenes. We were mostly in different rooms, but bumped into each other now and then. The Fletchers were doing rubbings in King Teti's tomb. That's a nice little pyramid, by the way. Anyhow, the thing is, you do have to spend quite a time in these places to do them justice. We had all day, and were determined to make the most of it. It was high noon, or just after, and hot. But we were all quite seasoned by then and not at all bothered by the climate. We also had the place more or less to ourselves – the tour parties are all rounded up at seven am, poor wretches, so they can be scooted out again before the sun gets up steam.

'Maggie and Janet were off somewhere with Sarah. There's such a lot to see – mastabas galore. Sarah liked Ti, for some reason. We didn't worry about them. Gwen was a perfectly competent guide – she knew when to let people do their own thing, and when they needed help. She knew the importance of free time. And she insisted, over and over, that Egypt was as safe as anywhere, once you understood the basic rules.

'Maggie and Janet are a couple. They've lived together for twenty-five years, and are great value. Very funny, scholarly, self-deprecating. I'd never spent time with lesbians before, and they were a real eye-opener. They could read each other's minds. They took to Sarah, and she was grateful for their company. In some of the remoter spots, a woman alone is likely to be regarded with disapproval, so she usually teamed up with them, and they went to several places as a threesome.

'Gwen and I didn't even hear the gunshots when they came. Neither did the Fletchers. Stephen and Felicity – rather a depressing couple, to be honest. Always hinting at disappointment and criticism. She got tummy trouble at the Farafra Oasis and was rather limp after that. I must admit, it surprises me a little that she speaks so highly of Gwen now. I suppose she's had time to reconsider.'

'That must be it,' agreed Drew hastily, inwardly wincing at his near-mistake.

'Anyway, the first we knew, our guide came running in shouting "Madam! Madam! Come quickly. There is bad trouble."

'We came out into the sunshine, having no idea what to expect. There were about ten tourist policemen clustered round, guns bristling, some of them kneeling on the ground. You could smell cordite or whatever it is, and there was an awful silence. Everything seemed very small and far away. We ran up the sandy path to where we could see Maggie and Janet, arms round each other.

'When we got there, with the guide, one or two of the policemen turned their guns on us, their faces terribly tense and pale. Vehicles were rushing towards us – all sorts of officials coming out of the woodwork. I didn't know where to look, and still had no idea what had happened. Finally, I saw the two bodies, first one then the other, about fifteen feet apart. Sarah was in a sort of heap, her bottom in the air. I recognised her shorts first. Her head was pressed into the sand, sideways – just a mass of blood and hair. They said afterwards that three bullets had hit her in rapid succession. One in the top of her head, one in the neck and one somewhere lower down. He must have been swinging his gun as he fired. The other body was a man, still holding a heavy-looking gun. He was not quite dead – his chest was heaving, and one hand was opening and shutting. I think he died as I watched him – the breathing slowed and then stopped.

'Nobody said anything. It was all over in seconds, the story spoke for itself, and everyone was just so frightened and shocked, they couldn't find words. Gwen went very shaky for a minute or two, and held onto me for support. The Fletchers were still down in Teti's tomb, and a handful of other tourists were beginning to assemble a little way away, shepherded by some of the police. I don't think any of us imagined there'd be any more shooting, although the police were obviously extremely sensitive to any sudden movement. They'd failed, you see. They were there, at all the big sites, to prevent precisely this from happening. But you can't prevent terrorism. The man probably had the gun in an innocent-looking bag. He would have looked the same as a tour guide, or a souvenir-seller. They're supposed to check everybody on the site, but after months or years when nothing happens, they inevitably get slack. But they were onto him very quickly. He only fired those three bullets, straight at Sarah. They claimed afterwards that he singled her out deliberately, though we'll never have any real idea why.

'Gwen was desperately upset by what had happened. She must have felt it would do enormous harm to her reputation. One of the first things she said was, "Well, that's the end of my career as a tour guide." We kept assuring her that there was nothing she could have done, but we couldn't convince her. I suspect she also felt rather guilty.

She hadn't liked Sarah, you see.'

'Oh?' Drew interrupted for the first time. This was clearly important.

'Just one of those things between women, I suppose. Sarah did nothing to make herself likeable, I must say. She was rather stolid, unsmiling and intense. Rather demanding, too – always making sure Gwen knew exactly what she expected from the trip. Gwen seemed to resent her at times.' He shrugged, as if animosity between women were just another of life's many mysteries.

'Anyway, although it was in all the British newspapers, they didn't make anything like as much of it as they did the Hatshepsut shooting two or three years ago. It was all a bit "Ho-hum, here we go again," especially as only one person died. The gunman was the usual fundamentalist nutcase, apparently. We thought he may have objected to Sarah's shorts. She was a bit overweight, and – well – you could see rather a lot of flesh. Her top was tight-fitting, too. But that's so ironic, because she actually had a lot of time for Islam. She loved the muezzin calls and the commitment to regular prayer.

'The aftermath wasn't as ghastly as it could have been – mainly thanks to Gwen. She shielded us from any more unpleasantness with great skill. We were due to fly home the next morning anyway, and after we'd all given statements to the police that evening, we were free to go as planned. Gwen stayed behind to be with poor Sarah and to meet her husband when he flew out. I think he had her flown home eventually for cremation. I'd rather expected to be informed of when it was, so I could send flowers, but there was no contact.

'I haven't seen any of the group since we arrived back in the UK on the thirteenth of April last year. I sent Gwen a Christmas card, but heard nothing from her. I'm rather sorry about that. She and I got along very well. In fact–' he smiled shyly, and dropped his eyes to the table '– I did hope, just for a day or two, that we might – well, keep in touch afterwards. And maybe something a little bit more. If it hadn't been for that Trevor chap–' He shook his head angrily. 'But you don't want to hear about that. It's got nothing to do with her performance as a guide.'

Drew tried desperately to find a pretext for encouraging this intriguing diversion. All he could manage was 'So – who was Trevor?'

'Well,' Habergas hesitated. 'He had been with us at Giza earlier that day, but then he went off alone. He wasn't with the group, but he'd known Gwen from a previous trip – he lived in Luxor, I think – and seemed to be following her about. I heard him arguing with Sarah, too. Something about Moslem women being oppressed. Sarah was very tactless, you see – she'd go up to women in the street and ask them questions. Of course, hardly any of them understood her. Only some of the very young ones had any English.'

'Silly girl,' said Drew with due pomposity. 'I'm surprised Mrs Absolon didn't warn her not to behave so recklessly.'

'Perhaps she did,' Habergas offered loyally. 'But Sarah wasn't a person to heed advice, I'm afraid.'

'And this Trevor person also tried, from what you say?'

'Not exactly. He just told her she was an ignorant little fool who had no idea what she was talking about.' Habergas clearly recalled this moment with some relish. 'He was an odd chap – a loner, I suppose. But Gwen liked him. After he showed up, she hardly noticed me,' he admitted sadly. 'Even when I gave her the necklace.'

Drew held his breath, but said nothing; a flicker of an eyebrow was all he permitted himself.

'It wasn't anything much. Just a thank-you present. I gave it to her the day before the shooting. I didn't want to make a public display of it, so I just gave it to her in Cairo, when no one was looking. It was nice – nothing too elaborate or expensive. I think she liked it.' The wistfulness was hard to bear.

'Well, that's more or less it,' Habergas summarised. 'It was undeniably traumatic and it coloured the whole holiday retrospectively. I'd saved for years to do the trip, and I enjoyed it enormously until the last day. I haven't been abroad very much, which is why Gwen's laid-back style suited me so well. I went on a Nile cruise in my twenties, and saw all the temples and tombs and so forth, and have been a keen amateur student of Egyptology ever since. But I was attracted by the modern Egypt, too – the oases in particular. We had freedom combined with security, whilst getting well off the usual tourist trail. Another terrible irony is that we'd only visited a popular tourist site on that very last day. We were desperately unlucky to be at that place at that particular moment.'

He stopped speaking, perhaps reliving the emotions of that momentous day in the heat and sand.

'I appreciate your hearing me out. You didn't have to.'

'I was glad to have the background,' Drew said heartily. 'It confirms our decision to offer Mrs Absolon some work, when we find her. She sounds absolutely what we're looking for.'

'It would be nice to see her again,' said Habergas. 'You know how easily people drift apart. I spoke to Janet on the telephone some-time last summer, when we floated the idea of a little reunion, but concluded that it wouldn't be very much fun, under the circumstances. Since then, I've just drifted back into my old life. As one does. And now, perhaps–'

Drew took the signal to leave. He had Trevor, necklace, Sarah Gliddon and all to ponder over – more than enough to justify the forty-mile round trip. Effusively, he thanked the man again, and wished him well, silently congratulating himself on the success of his cover story and the sincerity of his good wishes.

But Habergas had one last surprise in store for him. 'You're not really looking for her to give her a job, are you?' he said, as Drew stepped out of the house. 'Nobody would employ a woman over seventy these days.'

Drew had no choice. 'Oh, yes,' he said earnestly. 'I assure you we make no discrimin-ations based on age.'

210

The man looked him steadily in the eye. 'I think you're a detective,' he said. 'I think you're hoping to blame Gwen for Sarah's death – just like her husband did.' Before Drew could summon up any further bluster, Habergas continued. 'But I've told you the absolute truth, whoever you are. How you use it is up to you.'

CHAPTER TEN

Maggs didn't go directly home after leaving the office. Instead she headed for the village of Fenniton, and rode her motorbike straight past the Slaters' house. She'd looked them up in the phonebook – there was only one *W Slater*. She slowed for a quick look, but not enough to attract attention to herself. Somebody was in – the light was on in the front room, but the curtains were not yet closed, and a figure was moving about inside.

She rode round the next corner and dismounted. The bike was quickly secured to a lamppost and she walked back the way she'd come. It was getting rapidly darker and she assessed the chance of anyone seeing her as minimal; cars passed sporadically, but beyond that there was no sign of life. Everybody was indoors: eating, watching television, getting their kids to bed.

As she approached the house, she saw Genevieve Slater close the curtains of the lighted room. Her arms were stretched upwards, displaying the curve of her pregnancy in all its enormity.

Maggs slid through the front gate and up to the window near the fence dividing the house from next door. Anybody walking past might well see her – but thankfully there were no pedestrians in sight. Pressing her ear to the lower section of window, she listened intently. Nothing. Not a word. Either they weren't speaking in the room, or the glass was too thick. It was a few minutes before she realised– *Double glazing!* Designed to keep sound at bay.

Muttering crossly to herself, she stood upright and tried to find a chink in the curtains to peer through. Finally, at one edge, she found a space big enough to make a spyhole. Unfortunately, a small holly bush grew directly below it, making access highly uncomfortable but she persevered – after all, she was a detective now – and was rewarded by a scene of apparent domestic harmony.

Genevieve was on the sofa, legs propped on a pouffe in front of her. A man sat in the single armchair holding up a newspaper, so Maggs could only see the top half of his head. He was tall, with a big head, to judge by the length of his legs and the width of his brow.

As she crouched against the prickly bush, Maggs heard the engine of a motorbike. She thought for one heart-stopping moment that someone had stolen hers. Standing up, she peered into the street and saw a youth of about her age draw to a halt outside the house and lean his bike carefully against the kerb. He took off his helmet, and walked through the front gate. Maggs hurriedly crouched low again, praying he hadn't seen her: explaining what she was up to would be a real challenge. An inspiration came to her, and she quickly unbuttoned her trousers. If she was caught, she would pretend to be having

213

an emergency pee in the bushes.

But it seemed she would not be required to explain herself. The young man walked purposefully up the path to the door at the side of the house. When the doorbell rang, Maggs observed the reaction inside the room. The man looked round the edge of his paper but retained his grip on his reading matter; he obviously had no intention of going to the door. He said something to Genevieve, who likewise made no move to get up. Maggs watched the silent scene in suspense. 'Hurry up, one of you! Go and answer the door!' she muttered.

Eventually, in an obvious huff, the man set his paper down carefully and got to his feet. He disappeared out of the room, and Maggs heard the key being turned in the door around the side of the house. She crept out of the holly bush and moved towards the corner.

'Yes?' came Willard's voice, full of suspicion.

'You don't remember me, do you?' came a light voice with a lilting Welsh accent.

'No, I bloody don't. Who the hell *are* you?'

'Now, don't be like that, Uncle Willard. I've come all the way from Anglesey.'

'Good Christ! It's Stuart, isn't it? I haven't seen you since that horrific Christmas when your whole family descended on us. You must have been about twelve.'

'That's right,' said the visitor cheerfully. 'Can I come in? I'm on an errand from my Mum, mainly. I'm having a year out, see, catching up with some of my relations. Thought it might be fun to drop in on you, specially as Mum wants to know if you've heard anything from Granny. She's getting really worried. Talking about calling the police if she doesn't turn up soon.'

'Oh, bloody hell. You'd better come in.' The door slammed and Maggs heard no more. She returned to the window and waited in vain for the two men to reappear. Instead, Genevieve got up and went slowly out of the room – presumably in answer to a summons from the hall or kitchen. Maggs sighed, and started to leave. At least she'd learned something, she consoled herself.

Next morning, Drew heard Maggs arrive before he'd finished his breakfast. 'What's she doing here so early?' he asked Stephanie, Karen having already left for work. His daughter fluttered her eyelashes knowingly, but offered no explanation.

When his assistant knocked on the front door, instead of letting herself into the office, he knew something must have happened. She burst into the hallway as soon as he let her in and stood there looking tragic.

'Auntie Sharon's got stomach cancer!' she announced dramatically. 'They say she's only got a few weeks to live. She told my mum last night.'

Drew stood his ground, aware that if he so much as raised a hand, she could well throw herself at him and start weeping on his chest. That wouldn't be a problem for him, but he wasn't sure how she'd feel about it afterwards. 'Poor lady,' he said.

'She's only thirty-nine!' Maggs protested. 'And there's nothing they can do for her. She must have had it for months – she's been feeling poorly and drinking gallons of indigestion stuff.'

'They wouldn't have been able to cure it,' Drew said gently. 'Treatment might have added a few months to her life, but it wouldn't have been at all pleasant. They remove your stomach and you have to live on gunk that's specially prepared. It really isn't any fun.'

'Anyway – I'm going to go and see her now,' Maggs told him firmly. 'She's always been my favourite Auntie – I used to stay with her in the summer holidays. She's great.'

'Where does she live?'

'The other side of Bradbourne. Not far. I'll be back by lunchtime.'

'Isn't she in hospital?'

'No – she discharged herself. She doesn't believe in hospitals.'

'But–' Drew tried to remember his plans for the day. 'I really need you to mind the office.' With anybody else, he supposed he might be accused of insensitivity; with Maggs, he could say what he liked.

'Sorry,' she shook her head. 'I wouldn't be any use to you, the state I'm in. Let me just go and make sure she knows – oh!' A flurry of tears drowned what she'd meant to say. Drew abandoned his efforts not to be too kind, and patted her on the shoulder.

'Go on, then,' he said. 'It's obviously come as a big shock.'

'Thanks,' she sniffed. 'I'll be all right later on.' She wiped her nose on the back of her hand, and gave herself a shake. 'Actually, I've got things to tell you,' she remembered. 'I went to Fenniton last night and had a bit of a snoop at your lady-friend's house. They had a visitor. A boy called Stuart, who calls the man Uncle Willard. Looking for Granny, he said, Interesting, eh? I think I've earned a morning off, helping your investigation in my free time. I promise I'll be back by one. You do understand, don't you?'

'Course I do,' Drew said. 'You've got to go.'

'You can phone Genevieve and tell her she doesn't have to mind Stephanie this morning.' Maggs seemed reluctant to leave, loitering in the doorway, evidently torn between her allegiances to work and family.

'Yes, I'll do that,' he agreed. 'Go on.'

She grimaced. 'It's all right when they're actually dead, isn't it?' she said thoughtfully. 'It's the dying that's a bummer.'

And at last she was heading down the path, pulling on her crash helmet as she went.

Drew gathered Stephanie's things and carried her round to the office. He was aware of a definite feeling of relief at not seeing Genevieve again so soon, mixed with frustration: time was going by, and he ought to find something constructive to do with his morning.

He set Stephanie down in her usual corner, and arranged a selection of toys within her reach. As he tried to order his thoughts, he found that something was niggling him: some crooked piece of logic to do with Genevieve's mother. Genevieve couldn't pursue her own investigations into Gwen's death because she might attract police attention... But why should this be a worry? Why should Genevieve asking questions about Gwen

217

Absolon – her own mother – be any more suspicious than Drew Slocombe doing so?

It could only be the case that someone else, somewhere, already had reason to think the Slaters were involved in Gwen's disappearance. If someone had heard Willard shouting at her, or see him in a compromising situation with her – that person might well come to damaging conclusions if questions came to be asked. If it was true that Willard had killed Gwen, and then vowed to Genevieve that he hadn't, she might be reluctant actually to confront anyone who could provide proof that he was guilty. If the painful truth had to come out, it would be better coming at one remove from somebody sympathetic, like Drew.

The only witness to anything that Drew was aware of was the Kennett woman on the train, and she had claimed only to see two people digging a grave in the late evening of 12 August. Drew realised he could at least check whether Willard had an alibi for that date. He could ask Genevieve if she could remember where her husband was that night although, seeing that it was now nearly eight months ago, the chances were very doubtful.

It was past the time when he should have arrived at Genevieve's house with Stephanie, and he still hadn't phoned her. He assumed her veto on phonecalls had now been lifted and he rang the number that she'd given him.

There was no reply. He let it ring for ninety seconds, giving her time to get out of the bath, in from the garden, down from a loft ladder. He visualised her at the bottom of the stairs in a terrible broken heap. He imagined her labour had started and she was having strong contractions in rapid succession. He considered shutting the office and rushing to her side. Or calling an ambulance. It never crossed his mind that she might have gone out deliberately, abandoning her promise to look after Stephanie.

Stephanie had strewn cotton reels, crayons, small plastic bottles and painted wooden bricks in a careless semicircle around her. She was now crawling resolutely across the room to the filing cabinet. Drew was aware that she could hurt herself if she tried to pull herself up by the drawer handles and they came flying open – so he was meticulous about keeping the cabinet locked at all times. He therefore paid little attention when she began to do exactly as he'd expected. Grasping the handle of the second drawer up, she pulled hard. At first it held, and she began to take her weight on her feet, though with a decided wobble. The handle was just too high for her to get a useful purchase, but she persisted. The next Drew knew, there was a sound of metal sliding on metal, a startled cry from the child, and then a loud knock. The drawer had acted just as Drew had imagined it would, hitting Stephanie hard with its sharp lower edge. It caught her just above the eyes. By the time he'd rushed over and picked her up, she had a bleeding gash at least three inches long.

It was her first real accident, and Drew's heart stopped at the sight of his bloodstained baby. She stared at him in shocked amazement, before closing her eyes and going limp in his hands. 'Oh, God!' he cried. 'Wake up, Steph! Hey!' It was long seconds before his nurse training took effect and he thought to check the pulse in her neck, and listen to her breathing. Both seemed reasonably normal. He was lifting the telephone receiver to call an ambulance when she began to scream. Her hands fluttered in front of her face, touching her head tentatively at first, and then pressing both temples. The screaming increased, pain and panic combined. Blood flowed down her face, and Drew eventually realised it was in her eyes, gumming them up, blinding her. That must be the main cause of her panic. 'Hey, hey!' he soothed. 'Hush, Steph. Daddy's here.' His words were lost in the noise his daughter was making.

'Good God, what's happened?' came a man's loud voice in the doorway. 'Here – let me see.'

Drew clutched Stephanie defensively to his chest before recognising Dr Jarvis. The 'Doctor' part filtered through his frenzy, and brought a flash of relief. He relaxed his grip slightly.

'She hit her head,' he said, superfluously.

'It always looks worse than it is,' said the doctor calmly. 'She's more frightened than damaged, I'd say.'

'She was unconscious at first,' said Drew urgently.

'For how long?'

'Oh – well, a few seconds, I suppose. I was phoning–' He looked at the receiver in his hand, unable to remember how far he'd got in dialling 999. There was silence at the other end, so he assumed he'd left the task unfinished. 'Only a few seconds,' he repeated.

'Probably just a faint, then. Now, little lady, let's wipe this mess away, shall we?' He looked at Drew enquiringly. 'First aid kit?' he suggested.

Drew shook his head, cursing his oversight. 'I'll run and get some stuff from the house,' he offered, handing the child to the doctor. 'I'll be very quick.'

Stephanie's screams had subsided into whimpers; Dr Jarvis pulled her hands away from her face and rocked her soothingly. 'Poor little girl,' he said. 'Poor old head.' He brushed wisps of hair away, where they risked getting stuck in the coagulating blood. Drew left him, the beginnings of disabling relief threatening to paralyse his legs if he didn't hurry.

He found lint, antiseptic, a soft towel and a bowl for warm water in barely a minute. Running back to the office, he prayed there'd be no need for stitches; a scar would inevitably result, and the idea appalled him. In the tiny lavatory and washroom alongside the cool room that served as a mortuary, behind the office, he ran the hot tap until the water came through warm. Together the two men wiped away the blood and made every effort to mollify the injured child. Dr Jarvis, like many retired doctors, still carried some medical supplies in his car, including butterfly sutures. 'Always come in useful,' he remarked. 'These ought to be more than enough – and they shouldn't leave a scar.'

Drew's gratitude knew no bounds. In no time the wound was cleaned and dressed, the swelling minimal. 'Pity it wasn't a bit higher up,' said the doctor. 'It might have been just a bump, then. How did it happen, anyway?'

Drew indicated the filing cabinet to the doctor's bewilderment. 'The drawer came open,' he explained. 'She was pulling herself up by the handle.' Only then did he notice that the cabinet's key was protruding from its lock, on the top left-hand corner, above the first drawer. Neither he nor Maggs ever left it there; they were scrupulous about taking it out and putting it away.

Somebody had opened the cabinet and left it unlocked. Not Maggs – she'd left the office before him the previous evening and hadn't come in here that morning. And not Drew – he was certain of that. And not Karen, surely? She took no interest in the paperwork of Peaceful Repose.

Somebody had been in his office since five o'clock the previous afternoon and gone through his records.

For the rest of the day, puzzles swirled round Drew's head, clamouring for solutions. The afternoon had been spent rocking Stephanie, singing to her, telling her stories, letting her regain her confidence, while trying to keep her awake, as Dr Jarvis had advised. Maggs had returned at one, as promised, and expressed genuine concern at Stephanie's accident. When he described how valiant Dr Jarvis had been, she posed the question Drew had completely forgotten to ask in the midst of the panic over Stephanie. 'What did he come for?'

He shook his head in self-reproach. 'He never got round to saying. I took Steph back into the house as soon as he'd patched her up, then I heard his car driving away. I wonder what he wanted.'

He told Maggs the cause of Stephanie's accident; she confirmed Drew's assumption that she hadn't touched the filing cabinet for at least the past two days.

'How's Auntie Sharon?' he asked warily.

'Angry,' she said. 'With herself for taking so long to accept she was really ill, and with the doctors for being so certain it'll kill her. And with God, too. Oh – and she wants one of our graves,' she added as an afterthought.

For a while they each attended to routine office affairs. There had been a larger than usual delivery of mail, which Drew left Maggs to process and respond to as appropriate. He went back to the filing cabinet, trying to ascertain whether anything was missing.

The plan of the burial plots was the most vital document, and that seemed to have been untouched. Copies of correspondence; ideas for publicity; newspaper cuttings; a list of all the doctors in a wide surrounding area; catalogues from suppliers – everything in its place, neatly labelled and apparently undisturbed. Only the top drawer of the three actually contained anything; the middle one, which had injured Stephanie, was equipped with hanging files, but every one was as yet unfilled. In the bottom drawer they kept teabags, sugar and biscuits. Nothing in the way of paperwork.

'Whoever left it open must have found the key,' he muttered. 'Not that it would be difficult.' He kept the key in the little unlockable wall cupboard above the filing cabinet.

'What?' Maggs asked, from the desk. 'Did you say something?'

'There must have been an intruder here last night, and yet there's no sign of any disturbance. The door hasn't been forced. Karen didn't say she heard anything.'

'It must have been Jeffrey,' she said. 'He knows where you keep the key. He'd have been looking for something.'

Drew was only half convinced. 'But he shouldn't come round here at night. Why would he do that?'

'Search me,' she shrugged.

'I'll speak to him about it.' After all, it was his fault Stephanie hurt herself. He shouldn't go into the filing cabinet for anything. *Why would he?* he repeated to himself.

Maggs put down her pen, and sighed. 'Maybe he wanted to check the positions of the plots. Maybe one of his cronies showed an interest in having a grave here, and asked for a particular spot. He could have been in to see if it was clear.'

'He knows what's clear. He doesn't need to look it up on the plan.'

'Well, ask him,' she said impatiently. 'Your trouble is, you do everything by guesswork, when you could save loads of time by just *asking*.'

'Do I?' He was startled. 'Is that what I do?'

'Sometimes,' she said. 'It's a man thing. They don't like to admit they don't know everything.'

'Not me,' he said uncertainly. 'I learned a lot from a man last night. He told me the whole story of that shooting in Egypt.'

'What – the girl in Gwen Whatnot's tour party?'

'That's the one.' He gave a smug smile. 'I went to visit Karl Habergas, and he described the whole thing to me. He's a funny chap – lives with his old mother.'

'Bloody hell! Not another carer?'

'I'm afraid so. Sounds as if she's terminal.'

'Like Auntie Sharon,' Maggs remembered, her mouth drooping solemnly.

'I suppose so. By the way – who's going to be doing the caring for your auntie, if she can't stand hospitals?'

She narrowed her eyes at him defensively. 'We're all going to muck in,' she said curtly. 'I'll be there at the weekends, mainly. It's different with her, though. I like Auntie Sharon. She's not going to be bad-tempered and whingeing and demanding things all the time.'

A new silence ensued, but they both knew more talk was imminent. Drew spoke first. 'There was no reply from Genevieve when I tried her this morning,' he said. 'Maybe I ought to have another go? She was meant to be minding Stephanie for me again.'

'Irresponsible cow,' remarked Maggs. 'You can't trust her an inch – I told you.'

'She might have gone into labour – or be ill.'

'She looked fine last night. Probably taken that boy out, to show him around. He had a very strong accent. Welsh, I think. Sort of sing-song.'

'If he's her sister's boy, he's from Anglesey.

225

That's an island off the coast of North Wales,' he added; Maggs's ignorance of geography was an ongoing theme between them.

They were interrupted by the phone. Fiona, the Council Officer responsible for funerals, wanted to confirm the date for the burial of the nameless woman. 'It's a bit sooner than I expected,' she admitted. 'I'd have thought they'd want to keep her a few more weeks – but there've been twenty post-mortems this month already, and the fridges are overflowing. Everyone's trying to go on holiday now spring's here, and quite honestly, the sooner we bury her the better. They've taken all the samples they can think of, or so Stanley says. What can you offer me, Drew? Your first Council burial, eh?'

Drew forced a laugh. 'We thought Friday,' he said. 'Stanley told me already that you wanted it done soon. We more or less decided then that Friday would be best.'

'That's okay. It makes no difference to me. I usually try and turn up – but I don't feel very involved with this one. No family or anything.'

'No identity,' Drew reminded her, feeling he had to say it, in spite of the sharp stab of guilt it gave him. 'Sounds as if the police've been too busy to worry about her much.'

'You can say that again,' Fiona agreed emphatically.

'That's how it goes sometimes,' Drew continued. 'Twenty post-mortems is a lot. You'd think at least one of them would fancy a nice natural burial, wouldn't you?'

'It'll catch on,' she assured him. 'People take

time to change, that's all. It's a lovely idea. I'm tempted myself, if I'm honest.' Fiona was thirty-seven. Drew inwardly sighed.

'Ten-thirty okay?' he asked.

'Perfect. Can you quote me a price, so I can get things sorted out this end?'

'Will there be a minister?'

'I think so, yes. Got to keep up appearances. The police want it put in the paper – I'll get it in for Thursday. Unless you want to do that for me?'

'I will if you like. All part of the service. What do you want it to say? It'll look funny under *Deaths*, with no name.'

'Maybe I'd better do it. Try to make a news story out of it. A follow-up to the stuff they did when you found the body.'

'With the minister, and cardboard coffin, all services, purchase of plot – four hundred and fifty,' Drew said, answering her earlier question having totted it up in his head.

'Is that all? Look, Drew – unless a person has specified cremation, I think we might be able to give you all the Council funerals from now on. I'd have to get it confirmed from higher up – but I don't think there'll be a problem. That's if you'd like them? And if you can keep it at this sort of price. The main cemetery costs nearly twice that, with Plant's doing it – even for the Council.'

'Well – thanks very much,' he said slowly, hardly believing his luck. 'Though Daphne's not going to like it, is she?'

'That's business,' Fiona laughed. 'She'll survive. She's tough as old boots.'

Maggs waited a moment after Drew had hung

up, before remarking, 'Funeral definitely on Friday, then?'

'That's right. And she says we can probably have all the Council burials from here on.'

'Hey! That's fantastic! And Daphne's going to be upset, right?'

'Right. I just hope I don't bump into her for a while – she'll scratch my eyes out. Anyway, what were we talking about, before Fiona phoned?'

'Genevieve Slater, of course. What else do you talk about? And I was just wondering whether you've told Karen all about this.'

Drew eyed her furtively, saying nothing. Maggs elaborated. 'I mean, she ought to know you're taking a bit of a risk, getting involved. If you're arrested in the middle of the night, for playing games with the police, she isn't going to like it.'

'She knows the basics. But she's got other things to think about at the moment. It isn't a problem for her. She trusts me.'

'Does she? I'm not sure I would.'

'Okay,' he held up his hands in surrender. 'It's just – I can't let it drop now. I don't like loose ends. I don't like injustice.'

'You don't like anybody to think you're less than perfect, either,' she said. 'That's not meant nastily. But you always have to follow a thing through, don't you? Like setting this place up. Most people would just dream about it, but never actually do it.'

'That's nothing to do with perfection,' he said uncomfortably. 'That's just one-track-minded-ness.'

'Well – that's part of it. Whatever you call it –

you're doing it again now, aren't you? Most people would back off. Just let the woman get on with it herself, sort out her own life. But you won't do that, will you?'

'I can't,' he said. 'You know I can't. What about the money, for one thing? It would be the worst possible thing to do – to give up now. Where does that leave us with the police?'

'It's okay,' she smiled. 'I'm on your side. You're a lot like me,' she said, with an affectionate tap on his shoulder. 'I couldn't let it go now, either. Must be why we make such a good team. Your charm and my common sense; your sense of justice and my ambition – we're going to be un-beatable.'

'I'm sure you're right,' he said. 'All we need now is to earn some money and save my children from starvation.'

'What about all these Council funerals we're going to get? Things are looking up, Drew. I knew they would. All you have to do now is figure out who killed Gwen Thingummybob, preferably before Friday, and we'll be laughing.'

'Ha, ha,' he said.

Karen was far more angry than Drew had expected when she got home and found her daughter had been damaged. He followed her into the house, trying to convey the truth of what had happened, only to be faced with a cold anger that ranged far and wide in its accusations. She stared grimly at her daughter's injured face. 'I thought I could trust you,' she said. 'I thought she'd be safe with you.'

Drew felt a matching coldness. 'I'm not some hired childminder,' he said quietly. 'She's my daughter as well. I care about her every bit as much as you do. I'm as careful as anybody could be to make sure she doesn't get hurt. I locked that drawer last time I used the cabinet – I knew she'd climb up it sooner or later. I made sure it wouldn't tip over on top of her, and I *always* locked the drawers. I don't know why I'm even bothering to defend myself. It's as much of a disaster for me as it is for you. You're only getting worked up because you feel guilty for not being there for her. It won't leave a scar. She's got no lasting ill-effects. Little kids bump their heads all the time.'

'Guilty!' Karen screeched, and opened her mouth for a renewed onslaught.

'Stop it!' Drew ordered her. 'Calm down. I can see it's been a shock, and I'm sorry. But you're not helping, going on like this. Get a grip, okay?'

He told himself he was speaking so coolly because Stephanie was on his knee, and would be upset if he shouted. Because Karen was pregnant, and shouldn't get herself over-excited. But he knew it was something much less compassionate than that. For the first time, he found himself disliking his wife. Disliking her predictable female hysterics, her rush to attack and blame him, her involuntary recoil from Stephanie because she was damaged. He was disappointed in her, if he was honest with himself.

'As I said, she isn't permanently injured,' he said with finality. 'She's been seen by a doctor. These things happen. We'll have to get used to it.'

Karen said nothing more, but left the room quickly. Drew was sure she was crying, but he made no attempt to follow her.

After Stephanie was finally in bed, and Karen was busy with lesson plans in the dining room, Drew tried to assess his day. The morning seemed a long time ago; the previous evening a forgotten era. Hadn't he been on the verge of grasping something about Genevieve and Willard and the dead woman, something important, when Stephanie's accident had happened? He couldn't remember what it had been, and soon gave up trying. Tomorrow was Wednesday. Only two more days to the funeral for the unidentified, murdered woman who'd been found in his field. He sighed with resignation. What did it matter? he said to himself. If nobody else cared about her, why on earth should he?

The same old answer bounced back. He cared because it was unthinkable not to. Because if you didn't care, you didn't deserve to live. If you didn't make some sort of effort, Fate would drop a great hand out of the sky and pluck your child away from you. You had to do what you could to keep things straight. If Genevieve Slater had dubious reasons for wanting her mother's death explained, then so be it. It was the explanation that counted. He didn't need to follow the logic, or approve the motives. He didn't even need to obey the letter of the law. All he had to do was follow his own instincts, keep an ear out for the voice of his conscience, and let the rest take care of itself.

And just now, his conscience was murmuring *Karen* in his ear. He had been cold and distant with his wife, when all the time he knew how hurt and frightened she was. And tired, and guilty. She was going through a low time, and a large part of the responsibility for that lay with him. He urged himself to stand up and go to her. To tell her he understood, assure her it would be all right. But his legs wouldn't obey. Dimly, he was aware that there was something stronger at work within him than his conscience, and he was alarmed by it. Something irresistible was in control of his actions. The image of Genevieve Slater's grey eyes and wild black hair, her ivory skin and ready laugh, was superimposed on that of his suffering wife.

There were two obvious courses of action open to him. He could phone Genevieve and tell her he wanted no more to do with her. He would bury her mother on Friday and leave it at that. No more investigating. But he'd already let Maggs convince him that this wasn't in his nature – that it wasn't a serious option for him. So that left the second choice: he could knuckle down to completing his enquiries as fast as possible. Square things with the police and make the whole business official. No secrets. Uneasily, he ratified his decision. Tomorrow he would devote the entire day to visits, phonecalls, questions and serious detective work.

CHAPTER ELEVEN

Karen still wasn't very communicative the next morning, but she raised no objection when Drew told her he was leaving Stephanie all day with Genevieve again, provided – he qualified silently – he could get hold of her first to make sure she was at home. He hadn't mentioned the previous day's lapse to Karen; any hint that Genevieve might be unreliable would send her into a spin. As it was, Karen merely shrugged impatiently when he tried to apprise her of his intentions. 'Fine, fine,' she said inattentively, rummaging in her school bag. 'I know I had that list some-where...'

Drew didn't try to help. Karen's job involved more papers, leaflets, instructions, than he could begin to comprehend. She lost something vital most mornings.

Eventually she'd gone, and Drew set about the routine of clearing up the breakfast debris and preparing Stephanie for her day.

Jeffrey arrived at nine, with a view to establishing the exact position of the grave for the new burial. 'Do Council funerals have a special area?' he asked doubtfully.

Drew tutted reproachfully. 'Of course they don't. Remember what we agreed – unless people specifically ask for a particular spot, we follow in rotation. The new one can go next to

Mrs Smithers. It makes it much easier for the paperwork, apart from anything else. By the way, Jeff-' he tried to sound casual, friendly – 'have you been into my filing cabinet? I found it unlocked yesterday, and I couldn't think who else it might have been.'

The gravedigger's lean face darkened. 'I have not,' he said hotly. 'What would I want with a filing cabinet?'

Drew shook his head slowly. 'I thought it was unlikely. But nobody else knows where we keep the key. Although I suppose it's not that hard to find. And how would anybody get into the office? That's kept locked at night, too.'

'That lock-' The man scoffed. 'Not worth tuppence. Anybody could get through that.' It was true that Drew's security arrangements were rudimentary: there was a Yale lock on the office door that didn't always clip properly when the door was pulled shut. Drew had been cavalier about it until now. 'Who'd want to break into an undertaker's?' he'd laughed. 'There's nothing here to steal.' Now he felt less sure.

'Well, there isn't anything missing, so not to worry,' he said, with a brief frown. Of course he should worry, he told himself; the office was in the same building as his home, where his wife and daughter slept. Intruders could be violent. It was irresponsible to say the least not to take the matter seriously. 'Right,' he continued, referring Jeffrey back to the matter in hand. 'You can mark the new grave out today, but don't start digging until tomorrow afternoon. If it rains, we'll have a horrible mess.'

Sullenly, Jeffrey nodded. 'I know what I'm doing,' he muttered. 'I'm going to leave two foot clear from the lid to ground level. Is that all right with you?'

'Should be fine,' Drew said. 'I doubt if there'll be anybody here. You and Maggs and me can lower it. She'll be in a cardboard coffin.'

'Is she here?'

Drew shook his head. 'Not yet. I'm taking the coffin to the hospital this afternoon, and bringing her back in it. She'll have to be well wrapped up.'

'Plastic sheeting?' Jeffrey widened his eyes in mock surprise.

'Certainly not. I've got a length of hessian standing by. And the coffin's packed with newspapers. She won't start leaking in that short time.'

'The worms can finish what they started, then,' said Jeffrey with a twisted smile.

'Dust to dust,' said Drew lightly. 'There's no escape.'

Jeffrey shrugged and turned to go.

Drew made a mental note to be back from Genevieve's by three-thirty in order to catch the mortuary before it closed at four. The coffin was waiting in the cool room, already prepared by Maggs the previous afternoon. One of her tasks for today was to pack in the newspapers and cut a generous length of hessian. She'd also promised to collect some foliage to put on top of the coffin. 'I'll cut some greenery from our garden,' she told him. 'That'll look nice.'

Both she and Drew had been surprised at the simplicity of arranging funerals in the new way, having worked in traditional undertakers' premises. 'You realise how much time is spent just faffing about,' she remarked, after they'd completed their first burial in mid-January. 'I suppose they have to look as if there's a lot to do, to justify the expense.'

'You're absolutely right,' said Drew. 'I would say we've done barely an hour's work each, plus Jeffrey's gravedigging, and it's all been perfectly dignified. Better than a cremation, by a long way.'

'No comparison,' Maggs had confirmed.

'And thank God we don't have to worry about those bloody cremation papers,' he added, for good measure.

'A right old rip-off.' They'd sighed in complacent agreement, envisaging a steady stream of natural green burials, with themselves as pioneers.

It was still going to happen, he insisted to himself now. It was just taking a little longer than they'd hoped.

He didn't, in the end, try to phone Genevieve. The prospect of her once more failing to respond was so disagreeable that he found he couldn't face it. It was more than likely that she could ignore a ringing telephone, for no better reason than she didn't feel like answering it. Or she was apprehensive as to who might want to speak to her. So he resolved to drive to Fenniton anyway. It would give him time to think. And, as he turned the corner into the main street of the pretty little village, he remembered what it was he urgently needed to ask her.

Leaving Stephanie in the van, he went to knock on the door, craning his neck first to scan the back garden for any sign of Genevieve. Everything seemed quiet and still. He wondered how much useful investigating he could accomplish with his daughter coming along for the ride. He wondered, indeed, what he ought to do next if he couldn't see Genevieve first. He could try and trace the Fletchers from the Egypt tour, and the lesbian couple. He wanted to locate Trevor-from-Luxor, too, but hadn't the slightest idea how to go about it. And he supposed he should try and speak to Dr Jarvis again before the day was out, to establish a reason for the previous day's unexpected visit.

Just as he was thinking he might try the back door, he heard steps inside. A key was turned, and a bleary young face appeared. 'Yeah?' came a husky voice. 'Who is it?' There was a Welsh lilt to the accent and Drew quickly made the appropriate connection.

'Is Mrs Slater in?' he asked.

The youth regarded him warily. 'Who're you?'

'My name's Drew. She looks after my little girl sometimes. I was hoping–'

'Hi, Drew!' came Genevieve's musical voice. 'You're bright and early!'

It was nine forty-five. He wondered if Willard was upstairs somewhere, too, still in his pyjamas. 'Sorry,' he said. 'After yesterday, I thought I should try and spend the whole day–'

She interrupted him quickly. 'Ah, yes. No problem. Bring her in, and I'll run and get dressed. This is Stuart, by the way. My sister's

237

son. He's staying here for a day or two.'

'Pleased to meet you,' Drew threw over his shoulder, as he went back to the van for his daughter. Her welcoming grin was a treat to see. Her damaged head was discoloured from the bruising, but the wound was already knitting together, a thin line of scab giving her a piratical scowl.

Quelling a renewed burst of anxiety at the appearance of a scruffy and possibly untrustworthy teenager in the house where he proposed to leave his child, Drew waited for Genevieve to reappear. When she did, he told her he had one or two questions for her. Stuart obligingly slouched out of the room, leaving them alone; Drew waited for her to ask what had happened to Stephanie's head, but she gave no sign of noticing anything was amiss. His unease increased. How was it possible to overlook something so glaringly alarming as a baby's gashed forehead? He remembered her failure to answer the phone the day before, her even worse failure to refer to it now. Wouldn't a normal person be apologetic, remorseful? Wasn't it a fairly major bit of letdownhood? He almost decided he wouldn't leave his baby with her, ever again. He almost decided he was never going to come back, never again going to give in to the undiminished delight of being with her.

But first, he had to ask his question. 'August the twelfth last year,' he began quickly. 'Is there any chance you can remember where you and your husband were on that date?'

'Glorious twelfth, eh?' she smiled disarmingly.

238

'Well, we certainly weren't shooting grouse. I really haven't any idea. Neither of us keeps a proper diary. We write engagements and appointments on a calendar, but it will have been thrown away long since. I might come up with something, if I think hard enough. I couldn't guarantee I'd be right. Why do you ask?'

Drew hesitated; he had a strong feeling that he should hold his few cards close to his chest from here on. Even though he was officially working for Genevieve, her own dubious role in the story made things a lot more complicated. On the other hand, his reason for naming a particular date in August must be fairly obvious, in which case prevarication would only look silly.

'Somebody's turned up who thinks she saw a body being buried in my field on that evening,' he said. 'If you could prove for certain that Willard was somewhere else on that date, he's much more likely to be in the clear.'

'Okay,' she said slowly. 'That gives me an incentive, doesn't it. What day of the week was it?'

'Saturday.'

'It would be,' she laughed. 'And August, too! All the usual routines fall apart in August. I wish I could say we were in the Bahamas, or on a cruise of the Seychelles, but sadly I can't. But don't despair. I might come up with something, given time. I guess we can assume one thing, at least.' She flushed like a young girl, and glanced at her abdomen. 'It must have been sometime in August when this thing got started.'

Drew, his mind tuned to gestation periods, did his own rapid calculation. 'When did you say it

239

was due?' he asked.

'Nobody seems to know exactly,' she giggled. 'I don't suppose it'll be much longer. The doctor says the head's well down.' Drew observed something furtive in her manner as she said this, her eyes sliding away from his. But he could think of no possible reason for her manner. *Unless,* he thought wildly, *the whole pregnancy is a hoax, and she's got a pillow strapped round her middle.* For a moment, the idea seemed almost feasible: there was a definite suggestion of a little girl playing houses about Genevieve. *Probably why Stephanie liked her so much,* he thought.

'We haven't got very much time,' he reminded her. 'The burial's on Friday, and I would really like to have something definite by then.'

'Why?' she said, with disarming simplicity. 'Why does that matter?'

Drew frowned. 'It matters mainly for my own peace of mind. The police will change down a gear after the burial – though I must say they seem to be about as low-geared as you can get already. Even so, I have to protect my own interests. Once that body is buried in my field I'm going to feel even more responsible.'

'You mean, you're coming over all guilty about not telling the police everything you know?'

'Something like that,' he agreed.

'Well, I'm quite happy to have a deadline,' she said breezily. 'If you think you can find out the truth in two days, I'd be the last person to try and stop you. But what happens if you don't make it?'

'I don't know.' *But I do know that it might not be what you want to hear.*

240

'But—' she began, scratching her lower lip with a long forefinger, 'from the point of view of the police, the burial doesn't matter too much – am I right? They've kept all the evidence they need – photos and samples and stuff. Haven't they?'

He nodded. *Photos, weights, measurements, observations, hair samples, scrapings from under fingernails.* The list was a long one – so many fluids and specimens could be removed from a single body, however decomposed. It was true that they were unlikely to want to inspect the original again.

'So the deadline isn't really Friday, is it?' she persisted. 'In *my* mind, it's the birth of this little monster.' She tapped her bulge.

'Which makes things a bit tricky,' Drew remarked. 'It sounds a bit unpredictable as an end date. What happens if I haven't found anything by then?'

'Then forget it,' she said lightly. 'I'll be able to say I tried.' A bump from outside the door distracted her. 'That must be Stuart,' she said. 'Apparently Brigid's worried about our mother and asked him to find out if I knew where she is.'

'He seems a rather unlikely spy,' Drew said.

'Oh no,' she disagreed. 'He's a *perfect* spy. I bet you he's listening behind that door this very minute.'

'If so, he'll be able to tell your sister that a dead woman, who is very likely to be her mother, is being buried on Friday, with no identification and some distinctly worrying evasiveness where the police are concerned.'

'Hey!' she protested. 'Why so sharp, all of a

241

sudden? I thought you understood.'

He looked her full in the face, the creamy neck bare where she hadn't fastened the top button of her shirt, the lips pushed out in a slight pout. She was glorious, he admitted to himself. And terribly dangerous.

'I don't know that I do understand,' he said carefully. 'I have a feeling I'm being used. Two weeks ago, everything was desperately urgent. Now you don't seem to care what happens either way. Did something change?' Still in his arms, Stephanie was getting bored, wriggling to get down. 'Can I let her go?' he asked. Genevieve shrugged, so he set the child on the floor and sat on the sofa beside her.

Genevieve remained where she was, standing beside the window. She sighed and appeared to droop like an unwatered plant. 'I'm sorry, Drew,' she said. 'I've treated you very badly, I know. It's just that – it's quite difficult to concentrate wholly on my mother when I'm about to go into labour at the age of forty-two. It's scary.' Her eyes bulged, and a hand fluttered against her chest. 'Plus,' she continued. 'I have sort of changed my mind about Willard. He's been–'

Drew was about to caution her, on the assumption that the nephew might well be listening at the door, when the youth himself made a sudden appearance. 'Sorry to interrupt,' he said, with a disarming grin, 'but I wanted to ask you something, Auntie Gen.'

Genevieve eyed him distractedly. 'What?' she said.

'Am I allowed to use Uncle Willard's computer?

242

He's left it on. I haven't played any of my games for three days now, and I've got withdrawal symptoms. I promise not to be on it for too long – but as you've got a visitor–' He held up a CD with a rueful grin. 'I brought a few with me, just in case.'

'Oh,' she flapped a dismissive hand. 'I suppose so. Will it work, though?'

He nodded quickly. 'Oh, yes. He's got more than enough RAM on that Pentium II of his. I won't disturb anything. I'll make sure it's as I find it when I finish.'

'Go on, then,' she said.

'Bit cheeky,' Drew commented when the boy had gone. 'Aren't people's computers like their cars – not for any old Tom, Dick or Harry to use when they like?'

'I expect Willard told him he could use it,' she said vaguely. 'He probably left it on for him.'

'I suppose I'll have to get Stephanie set up with her own website in another year or two,' he mused, stroking the little girl's cheek. 'I feel I've got left behind somewhere. I'm the only person I know without an e-mail address.'

'I don't think you're missing much.'

The conversation was going nowhere; Drew came to an abrupt decision. 'Look,' he said, lifting Stephanie onto his lap, 'it's obvious you've got things on your mind. I won't leave Stephanie with you today. The main thing is that date – August the twelfth. I haven't really got any more leads or ideas that I need bother you with now. I've got a lot of detail on what happened in Egypt, when that girl was shot – I've got a full list

243

of people I want to talk to. Maybe I should just get on with it. Meanwhile, I think you should tell that boy that he's right to be concerned about his granny.' His unspoken disapproval was strong enough to penetrate her distraction; she sighed again, but more in exasperation than shame or concern.

'I'll tell Stuart that we think his gran's dead, okay? But I'm not going to say anything about the body, or your burial ground.'

Drew shook his head in disbelief. 'That's ridiculous,' he said flatly. 'You make death sound such a casual thing. You can't just tell a kid, *We think your gran died last year sometime. But we're not sure.* Death doesn't lend itself to equivocation. If someone's dead, you're supposed to inform the authorities. Get a death certificate. Close bank accounts.' His voice was getting loud and Stephanie was staring frowningly up at his face.

'Sorry, baby,' he said to her. 'I didn't mean to alarm you.' He picked her up and pulled her gently to him. 'We're going home now.'

'Drew,' Genevieve said his name slowly, cajolingly, 'don't be cross. I'm not feeling too good today. I had a bad night. I must have sounded terribly callous just then. It's only that I've accepted my mother's dead and will never see this baby. I've done my grieving about that–'

'It's all right,' he interrupted her. 'You've already explained. I just think you could give your sister the chance to get *her* grieving done, as well.'

She raised her eyebrows, and blinked deliberately. 'Brigid grieving?' she echoed, with an expression very close to a sneer. 'She wouldn't know the meaning of the word.'

'But she's worried enough to send Stuart down here.'

Genevieve sneered again. 'He was coming anyway. He's spending a year bumming around, and this is as good a place to freeload as any.'

Drew could see she was strained; even speaking seemed to be an effort. Much of the gloss of his early encounters with her had rubbed off by now, and he thought he was seeing something more like the real person. Without the ready grin, the warm eye contact, she ought to have come across as much less attractive. Unfortunately, this was not the case. She seemed vulnerable and frightened: a cornered animal, angry with her persecutors. If anything, Drew was now even more determined to understand her – and why she had approached him in the first place. A reversal had taken place in the last few moments. He had been annoyed at her coolness; wounded at her failure to notice Stephanie's poorly head, on the verge of walking off and leaving her to her own family chaos. But he couldn't do it.

He sighed, and shifted Stephanie to a more comfortable seat in the crook of his arm. She was getting too heavy to be lugged around, he noted, and remembered at the same instant that she would soon be ousted from such cosy physical intimacies by a new sibling in any case. It seemed impossible – against nature. *This* was his baby. He didn't want another one.

'Okay,' he said. He looked at Genevieve. 'You're calling the shots – you're paying me, after all. Tell me what you want me to do.'

She swept a hand lightly across her brow, as if to organise her thoughts. '*That* hasn't changed,' she said. 'Find out what's happened to my mother. Full stop. If that body is her, then what happened to her? I wish you wouldn't keep *asking* me this. I don't know why you can't just get it into your head that the assignment is really very simple.'

'If it was that simple, you'd save yourself some money and go to the police,' he said coldly.

'And the police would do bugger all,' she snapped back.

'They'd give you a definite identity, at least.'

'Right. And then, as I've said time and time again, they'd crawl all over our lives. And yours, now you've got so involved. You said it yourself on Monday – there's no going back now.'

He could hear fear spicing her voice, a tremor that seemed to have something to do with her physical condition. She put both hands across her bulge in a gesture that seemed more for her own protection than the baby's. Drew was puzzled. There was something about the baby that he hadn't grasped. Something central to the way Genevieve was behaving and thinking...

'Well, we've got a couple more days,' he said reassuringly.

'So – are you leaving Stephanie here or not?' she asked, showing clearly that she understood his caution. 'I am usually quite reliable in that respect, you know,' she added.

There was still one piece of unfinished business. 'Where were you yesterday then?' Drew demanded. 'I rang and rang and you never answered the phone.'

She blinked. 'I thought you'd just changed your mind without telling me,' she said. 'I never heard the phone.'

Slowly she went out into the hall and picked up the telephone. 'There's no dialling tone,' she said, holding it out to him triumphantly. 'It must be out of order.'

'Have you had any calls in the last couple of days?'

She shook her head. 'Not one – but then we don't get that many anyway.'

It was never easy to relinquish a sense of grievance, however misplaced it might be. Drew found himself having to do some rapid backtracking. 'I'm sorry,' he said softly. 'And yes, if it's all right with you, I'll leave Stephanie for a few hours.'

'That's what I hoped you'd say,' she smiled, holding out her arms for the child.

In the van outside, Drew paused for a moment's consideration. He had a trail to follow – broken and faint as it might be – and some glimmering hints at the edge of his mind as to what could have happened to Gwen Absolon. Perhaps it was the out-of-order telephone that had done it – but for whatever reason, his mood was optimistic for the first time in days. He went over what he knew, using his jotter pad as an aid.

Shooting in Egypt, 12 April. Five surviving group members. Trevor. Sarah's husband.

Returns to England a few days later, to basement bedsit. Stays a few days with G & W Fenniton.

247

Ructions with Willard. Something missing here?!
Henrietta Fielding.
  Probably unhappy or guilty about the shooting. Dr
Jarvis. Nathan? Memories stirred up. What happens
next? Another job? Money worries? Dates?

With some excitement, he began to feel his thoughts coalesce. He remembered the file title on Willard's computer – *HenriettaF* – and shivered at the implications of the connection. Conspiracies and collusions should be assumed, if there had indeed been a deliberate murder. After all, Caroline Kennett did say she'd seen two people digging in the field. Unfortunately, he had to delete Henrietta from that particular role: if she'd been seen by Caroline, her hugeness would surely have been a major element of the story.

He tapped his pen against his teeth. One name jumped out at him: *Dr Jarvis.* The man had called to see him, and been diverted from his purpose. He'd wedged a printed card on top of Drew's front gate before getting into his car. Drew had retrieved it later, when Stephanie had been settled after her accident.

The card stated: *Malcolm Jarvis MD. Fir Trees, Grange Lane, Woodleigh.* The phone number began with a code that predated the 01 that all numbers now started with. That made it at least five years old, and Drew suspected it had been printed rather longer ago than that; the corners were fraying, as if it had been in a pocket for a considerable time.

Woodleigh wasn't far away. Drew had no hesitation in pointing his van in that direction.

CHAPTER TWELVE

The house was set back from the road, with a garden full of spring flowers and shrubs just coming into leaf. There were mullioned windows, and a front porch with a mature wisteria draping heavily over it. It fitted the man perfectly, to Drew's mind.

He rang an old-fashioned bell by means of a leather thong attached to the clapper, wondering whether it would be loud enough to rouse a sleeping doctor to a midnight crisis. Apparently it was. The door was opened quickly, and the retired doctor greeted him with a welcoming smile.

'How's the invalid?' he asked, looking over Drew's shoulder as if expecting to see Stephanie following him.

'Fine, thanks to you,' said Drew.

'With her mum today?'

'No,' said Drew hesitantly. 'Genevieve's got her.'

'Has she?' was all Jarvis said to that.

Drew chose to ignore the implied doubt as to the wisdom of using Genevieve as a childminder. 'You never told me why you came to see me yesterday,' he prompted. 'I'm having a bit of a go at clearing up the mystery of what's happened to Genevieve's mother. On behalf of Genevieve. I assumed you had something more you could tell me.'

'Come in,' Jarvis invited. 'It isn't much, but it

might fill in one or two gaps for you.'

They went into a large, light living room with a richly coloured Chinese carpet on the floor. Drew had an impression of shades of blue throughout – curtains, cushions, carpet, paintwork. It was cool and pleasing. There was no evidence of a female presence in the house. No cooking smells or cardigans on the backs of chairs. No sentimental knick-knacks or hand-stitched rugs. Drew's assumption that he was dealing with a lifelong bachelor had so far taken no knocks.

Drew appreciated that he needed to tread a careful path between taking the man into his confidence – on the grounds that his initial approach ensured his innocence – and making a naïve disclosure of everything he had gleamed so far. Drew had been accused of naïveté more than once in his life, and it was a failing he strove to amend. The exact role of Dr Jarvis in the fate of Gwen Absolon was very far from clear – he might yet prove to be instrumental in whatever had befallen her.

He waited, quelling the temptation to embark on a string of probing questions. The ball was very much in Jarvis's court; sooner or later he would surely lob it back.

'Let's see now,' mused the older man, legs crossed comfortably as he reclined in a Parker Knoll armchair, 'I think I filled you in quite comprehensively as far as Gwen's background was concerned. It might not prove to be directly relevant, of course, but at least it gives you more of a picture.'

Drew found himself wondering just how closely Jarvis had been monitoring his progress. Did Genevieve give him a daily update? He contented himself with a nod of agreement.

'I probably ought to have elaborated a little on the subject of Willard.'

The transparency took Drew aback. Obviously the doctor had spoken to Genevieve and she had revealed her worries – genuine or not – that Willard had been involved in Gwen's disappearance. So now, rather than stick to his threadbare story about suicide, he wanted to endorse Genevieve's line, in the hope that Drew would find it doubly credible as a result. He almost laughed. Was the man really so stupid? Did he think Drew was stupid? Either way, the net result was to cast even deeper doubt on the Willard story.

'Go on,' he invited, keeping his face bland.

'Willard was very fond of Gwen. Although they didn't meet very often, they found they had a lot in common. Interests and so forth. They eventually developed a very close relationship.'

'Genevieve has already told me this,' Drew pointed out.

'Has she?' Jarvis paused. 'Well, now you've had it confirmed.'

'How would you say it helps my investigation?'

'Well – there's a very real possibility that Willard carries some – perhaps all – of the responsibility for Gwen's disappearance,' Jarvis said carefully.

Drew lost patience. 'Yes, yes, I *know* all this,' he rapped out. 'It's Genevieve's whole reason for not wanting to go to the police. It's the thing she keeps coming back to. Except–' He remembered her starting to say something about changing her mind about Willard, and he'd cut her off.

'Yes?'

'Nothing.' Drew clamped his lips together. 'Would you tell me exactly when you last saw Gwen?' he asked after a moment.

'It must have been sometime in July, I think, a few weeks after all that hysteria over Nathan's death. I just happened to see her in the street in Bradbourne. We'd parted on a rather awkward note, but she was pleased enough to see me – or so I thought. We went for a cup of tea.'

'And how was she?'

'Tired. Rather low in spirits. But I managed to cheer her up. I could always do that. We talked about trivialities – nothing that might push us back into the earlier disagreements about Nathan. She seemed reluctant to talk about any of that, anyway.'

'What colour was her hair?' Drew asked suddenly.

'Same colour it always was.'

'Which was?'

'A sort of dark grey. The colour of–' he cast his eyes around the room, landing on a pewter jug sitting on the mantelpiece '–that jug, more or less. I know why you ask. The dead woman's hair is white, if the newspaper account is to be believed. It happens, you know.' His show of professional expertise left Drew unmoved. His efforts at supporting Genevieve were endearing in a way; Drew had little doubt that he was trying

252

to protect her. There was no way that anything the man said could be taken at face value. *He probably made a very good doctor,* Drew thought ruefully. Telling people what they wanted to hear, colluding with spouses to conceal harsh truths – and always taking the easy way out of a sticky corner. Yet, paradoxically, he found that he *did* believe the story about Nathan and his untimely end. It had the ring of truth, and nothing Genevieve had told him contradicted it. Besides, he had the feeling that the man could be highly susceptible to the entreaties of a clever woman.

'Have you ever been married?' he asked, suddenly. The question hung for a moment, while Jarvis examined it.

'Once,' he admitted. 'About a hundred years ago. She left me. I still have some of her shoes under the bed.' He tried to smile deprecatingly at this eccentricity, but it was swamped by a wave of self-pity. 'I don't seem to be very good with women,' he added sadly.

Nor men, Drew thought unkindly. 'But you got along well with the Absolon women – Gwen and her daughters? The family doctor they all loved and trusted for years?'

'Oh, yes. They knew they could trust me. I always did what they expected of me. I still do,' he concluded.

'It sounds like a very – *intimate* – relationship.'

'You could say that, I suppose.' The doctor met Drew's eyes with his own watery gaze. 'Yes, I loved them. They were everything to me – Gwen especially. That's why you've got to find out what happened to her.'

It felt like a dismissal, but Drew held his ground. 'So why leave it so long? Why not start searching for her six, nine months ago? Where did you think she was all winter?'

'I tried to find her,' Jarvis defended himself. 'I kept asking Genevieve where she was.'

'And what did she tell you?'

'She said she didn't think Gwen was feeling very well-disposed towards any of us any more, and she'd probably gone to some remote foreign country to forget all about us.'

'And you believed her?'

'Why wouldn't I? Especially as she'd been so upset by the Egypt business. I could see she might want to spend a few months on a beach in the South Pacific, just to get over it.'

'But now you don't think that's where she was?'

'Not now you've found the body,' the doctor said. 'Of course not.'

'So you're convinced it's Gwen,' Drew said.

'I am, yes.'

'Why?'

'Because of something Stanley Sharples mentioned to me a few days after the body was found.'

Drew's surprise was only momentary: of course a doctor, even a retired one, would be acquainted with the Coroner's Officer. Stanley had been in his job for ten years or more.

'What was that?' he prompted.

'The woman wasn't wearing any underclothes. No bra or pants – nothing. That's my Gwen. She was well known for it, among her closer friends. And it's something her doctor would be likely to discover at some point. If we'd been talking about a young girl, it might not be of much importance, but Gwen was seventy. How many women of her age do you think go round with no knickers?'

Touché thought Drew, happily.

In the van, he ran over the encounter again. *Forget suicide* he thought. He didn't believe Gwen had ever been afraid of repercussions over her son's death, or soon got over any such nervousness.

'There's a message for you,' said Maggs, as soon as he got back to the office, having collected Stephanie from Genevieve's house, where he had permitted himself to stay for only ten minutes. 'You're to ring a woman called Marjorie Hankey as soon as possible. Her husband died, but she doesn't want him buried here.'

'What?' Drew was distracted, trying to put Stephanie down, but she was sleepy and clinging. 'Oh – I'd better phone her.'

'Tell me about your morning first,' she demanded. 'Any further developments in our murder investigation?'

Drew shook his head impatiently. 'Maggs – you can see I'm struggling here. At least straighten the cushions for me. Come on, Steph – let go. Just have a little nap, okay?' It occurred to him that she was probably thirsty, and there was no doubt that she wanted a new nappy. There was always something, just when he wanted to sit down and assemble his thoughts into some sort of order.

Sullenly, Maggs arranged a bed of cushions in

the corner, but made no further move to help. 'It's more like a dog's bed than a child's,' she muttered.

He pulled his daughter away from his chest and deposited her in the cushions. It was suddenly wonderful to have the use of both hands again, despite the grizzling protest from Stephanie.

Five minutes later, he was calling the mysterious Mrs Hankey. She answered on the first ring. 'Hello?' she said, in a strong voice.

'This is Drew Slocombe from Peaceful Repose Funerals. I understand you wanted to speak to me?'

'Yes I do.' The briskness was unusual in a new widow; he wondered whether Maggs had got the story wrong. But no. 'My husband died last night. He's at the Royal Victoria Hospital. I remembered your talk, a few weeks ago, and I must admit you impressed me. Although not perhaps in the way you might have expected.'

Drew made a self-deprecating murmur, still waiting to know what she required of him.

'I've got a funeral director from Garnstone to arrange a cremation. Unfortunately, Harold had a horror of burial, otherwise I might have been tempted to use your cemetery. The thing is, I very much liked the way you addressed us last month, and I want somebody genuine like you to take the service. Well, *service* might be the wrong word. We're not religious, you see. Hymns would be grotesque. There's no reason to drag God into it at all. But I did wonder whether you'd be interested in, well – orchestrating things? Is that something you'd be able to do?'

'Very much so,' said Drew, trying not to sound too excited. 'When is the funeral to be?'

'Well, if it's all right with you, we've booked it for Tuesday afternoon next week. Two-thirty. Are you free then?'

'I'm sure I can be.' The problem of Stephanie jabbed at him: wild thoughts of leaving her with Desmond in the Crematorium office flew round his head. But this was an opportunity not to be missed. It felt like a gift from a guardian angel. Despite Stephanie's all-consuming needs, this was definitely turning out to be a good day. 'I'm rather tied up tomorrow and the next day – would it be all right to come and see you over the weekend, to discuss what you'd like me to do?'

'Of course. Saturday morning would be the most convenient for me. Let me give you my address.' As soon as she mentioned East Caddling, he remembered her: the critical woman in the Women's Institute audience. The one who had seemed so outraged by his ideas. It just went to show – you never knew the effect you were having on people, he thought smugly. 'Would you give the funeral director my details, or shall I do it?' he asked. 'They'll want to know who's officiating.'

'I already said I'd approach you,' she told him. 'I'll let them know you've agreed.'

He made the appointment for Saturday, and put the phone down. 'I don't believe it,' he said to Maggs, who'd been listening in from the cool room next door. 'She wants me to officiate at a cremation. Looks like your idea was spot-on.'

'How much is she paying?'

'I've no idea. Ministers charge about seventy quid, so I'd better go for that. The undertakers are sure to tell her what the usual rate is. Humanists are more expensive, though. They reckon they give a more personal service, and spend more time with the family.'

'Make it a hundred,' she advised. 'That'll cover the travelling. It's not Plant's, is it?'

'No – somebody from Garnstone. The Co-op, I expect. American-owned. I should get a letter from them to confirm the day and time. They're not going to know what to make of it.' He laughed at the image of the confused professionals. 'But what if I make a mess of it?' He stared at her in sudden panic. 'I don't have any idea what to do. I'll get the timing all wrong. I'll press the button for the curtains before we've finished. Oh, God, what have I done?'

'Pull yourself together,' she said unfeelingly. 'You've seen it done enough times. You can't possibly be worse than some of those vicars, just reading a few lines from a book.'

'The idea is to be better,' he reminded her. '*Genuine* was the word she used. How can I be genuine when I've never met the man?'

'You'll be okay,' she said kindly. 'People like you, Drew.'

'That's all right then,' he groaned.

Karen was late collecting Stephanie, and Drew's more positive frame of mind was beginning to degenerate as his daughter whined and clung to him. She had just dropped into a light doze when Karen arrived. 'I can smell that body,' Karen said, as she came into the office. 'Haven't you got it sealed up?'

'Two thick layers of hessian, the coffin packed with newspapers and the top tapped on,' he said. 'But sealed – no, not really. You know the routine. We believe in biodegradability here. No plastic, no zinc linings or inch-thick solid oak. I can't smell anything.'

Karen's upper lip twitched and her nostrils flared. 'Well, I can,' she repeated. 'And it's revolting.'

'It'll be gone soon,' he told her. 'And about time too. I think that woman's been a jinx on me, ever since we found her.'

Karen tried to scoop up her daughter without waking her, but Stephanie's head flopped back with a jerk. Focusing on her mother as she woke up, she scowled and began to whimper. 'Come on, you pest,' Karen said grumpily.

Drew wanted to tell her about the officiating job, and his progress with the detective work, as well as asking her what sort of day she'd had, but Stephanie's wails prevented any of that. He hadn't liked hearing his daughter called a pest, either: even as a joke, it jarred on him. 'She's not a pest,' he protested mildly. 'She's been as good as gold all day, until we got back here. Especially considering her head probably still hurts.'

Karen glanced swiftly at him, not letting her eyes meet his. 'I wanted a cup of tea, and a rest,' she said. 'Now I'll have to entertain her, as well as trying to do lesson plans, and phoning the parents of one of the kids at school who wrote *Fuck Off* all over his reading book. He's only six – I suppose I

259

should applaud his spelling skills. I don't need it, in any case. I don't need any of this.'

'Leave her here, then,' said Drew sharply. 'I'm not going anywhere.'

'And let her breathe in the gases from a dead body? It's probably poisoned her already. It's really making *me* feel sick.'

He gave a scornful laugh. 'That's what they used to think in the Middle Ages. You know perfectly well you can't catch anything from a body – unless it's got anthrax or one or two other rare things. You're just being hysterical.'

Without another word, she leaned Stephanie against her shoulder and marched out.

Drew clenched his fists and screwed his face up as if expecting some great blow to fall. The dislocation of his mood of self-satisfaction was exasperating. He and Karen had been cross with each other before, had disagreed and sulked – but this was different. She didn't look like the same woman. And he didn't feel like her husband. Restlessly he went to the small window at the back of the room and looked out over the burial field. Maggs was there with a spade in her hand, pushing back encroaching grass from the path they'd made from the car park to the first graves. This had been a topic of much discussion, as had most elements of the new business. Drew had wanted to leave natural grass to provide pathways. Maggs and Karen had both demurred, reminding him how wet grass could be, and slippery. They had persuaded him to lay a triple row of bricks in a curving diagonal from one corner to its opposite, with a few side branches off it. Generously, he admitted he'd been wrong: not only did the path make walking easier, but it helped immensely in the necessarily precise recording of where each grave was. The effect was unobtrusive, but even after only a few weeks of spring growth, the path was threatening to disappear entirely.

He went out to talk to her. 'Jeffrey ought to be doing that,' he said.

She shrugged. 'He's gone. I suppose he thinks marking the position of a grave is enough for one day. I enjoy doing it, anyway. If people can't see the paths, they'll trample any-old-where and churn up the ground.'

'Good thinking,' he nodded.

'What's going on?' she burst out suddenly. 'Are we just going to bury that woman and forget about her? Have you been to see the daughter again today?'

'I'm still supposed to be investigating it,' he said, uncomfortably. 'But I don't think she cares very much. Her baby's due in a few weeks, and she's a bit distracted by that.'

'Is that boy still there? The nephew?'

Drew nodded. 'Bit scruffy. But quite friendly, I suppose. It might be nice for Genevieve to have him around.'

'What – as an unpaid nanny, d'you mean?' Maggs was confrontational, and Drew hesitated before answering.

'I didn't mean that. And I really should be trying to think it all through again. I wish I could just dump it all on the police, to be honest. Especially now I've got to do this officiating. If

261

that works out, I can stop being a private detective.'

'Before you even start,' she said, with a thread of contempt he couldn't ignore.

'Hey! That's not fair! I think I've done pretty well for an amateur.'

'So who killed her?' demanded Maggs with her youthful directness.

'Right. Let's see now.' He met her challenging gaze with a little smile. Somehow talking to Maggs, with her gusts of unpredictable emotion and bold lack of deference, was always refreshing. 'First choice still has to be Willard even though Genevieve seems to have changed her mind on that. She's worried about the police thinking it was him, though.'

'What if she's protecting someone else – a lover, maybe – and pretending it's Willard because she wouldn't mind getting shot of him. Willard didn't look much like a murderer to me, when I saw him through their front window.'

Drew laughed. 'You know what a murderer looks like then, do you? Besides, if she'd really wanted to set Willard up as a suspect, wouldn't informing the police anonymously have been a better option?'

Maggs scowled. 'Suppose so. But Willard just looked too ordinary.'

'Just bear in mind that practically anybody can commit murder,' he said. 'Ask any prison officer. They usually say the murderers are the most ordinary, the most pleasant, of all their charges.'

'I know,' she said. 'So what other suspects are there?'

Drew looked around his field, savouring the serenity. 'I'm not going to get into that now,' he decided. 'But it seems to be coming a bit more clear. I feel as if I'm getting closer to the truth.'

Maggs clearly felt she was being shut out. 'Good for you,' she muttered.

Twenty minutes later, she came bouncing into the office, her mood restored. 'Tell you what,' she said brightly, 'I'll go and see the nephew at the weekend, if he's still there. I'll hang about round the corner and try and get a chance to talk to him. He's a biker too, so that'll give me an excuse. Get some background stuff on the family. And I think you should give it a rest. If you think about something else, all sorts of new ideas pop into your head when you're least expecting them.'

'You're a wise woman, Maggs,' he said. 'But I can't ease up now. I know exactly what I've got to do next. And try and keep out of Genevieve's sight. She'll recognise you, and I doubt if she'd approve of me confiding in you. If you do go, don't go falling for that boy's big brown eyes.'

'As if I would,' she said innocently.

Karen wasn't happy about Drew going to see Marjorie Hankey on Saturday morning. She sulkily crashed her way through some tidying up in the main bedroom after he'd told her that evening, then ran the vacuum cleaner around the room like a weapon while he was trying to undress Stephanie for bed. The child lay on the duvet, sucking her thumb and looking uneasily from one parent to the other.

'I'll do the garden in the afternoon,' he promised brightly. 'Or anything else you want me to. And we've got all day Sunday free. We could have a trip out – you'd like that.'

Hearing himself, he winced; platitudes were the fallback position when feelings were taboo. He knew only too well what Karen wanted from him, but his arms refused to obey her silent plea for a hug. Karen's need for warmth and consolation was like a wind in the room – a grasping sort of wind, tugging at him insistently, like Stephanie sucking on her thumb. But the thumb put up no resistance, unlike Drew. The more needy Karen became, the less capable was he of responding. He reproached himself fiercely, but it did no good. Silently popping shut the fastenings on Stephanie's sleepsuit, he gave up the attempt. *Can't be the perfect husband all the time,* he thought defensively. Besides, everything would work out in the end. It always did.

But he could not deny the quivering fear in the pit of his stomach. Karen and he had always been more than just 'husband and wife'. They were – or had been – something much more powerful than that. Her happiness had been his, her choices and judgements always the best for him too. It had all been so natural, so effortless – until now. Except the move to Bradbourne, when he had gone out on a limb. Risked a secret lie to get Karen what she wanted. Risked a fate-tempting dishonesty that made him shiver to recall it. Any other falsehood might have been buried long before in the general impedimenta of daily life. But that one had been special. He had evoked a child where none yet was, after almost two years of trying to conceive. How had he dared, he wondered now? No wonder he was being forced to pay for it.

The expected punishment would obviously have been perpetual childlessness. Instead, he was to have two babies, when all he wanted was one. A much more cunning, and potentially lethal, revenge. And there was absolutely nobody to blame but himself.

'No point in arguing about it,' he said lamely, when the vacuum cleaner eventually fell silent.

'Who's arguing?' said Karen frostily. 'You'll do what you want to – as always. You never take any notice of what I say.'

He recognised how far from grace they had fallen then. When words like *always* and *never*, spoken with anger and resentment were conscripted into the conversation, stereotypes began to take over. They would soon cease to be Drew and Karen, friends and lovers, become instead a pair of faceless puppets going through the motions of a marriage, where nothing was real. Until they could no longer keep the façade intact. *I won't let that happen*, he promised himself. *As soon as I find out what happened to Gwen Absolon, I'll make things right with Karen.*

Thursday was less like spring than summer. May was with them and the world was green and golden. Drew woke with his thoughts like crystal droplets, his worries firmly locked away. Today he was going to get to the bottom of the mystery of Gwen Absolon.

He had already asked Directory Enquiries for the telephone number of the lesbian couple from the Egyptian tour, and the first thing he did after opening the office was to dial it. From what Habergas had told him, the women were both over sixty and unlikely to be out at work. And, indeed, a friendly voice answered on the fifth ring. 'Janet Harrison,' it said.

'Oh, hello,' Drew said, equally friendly. 'I'm very sorry to disturb you, but I wondered if you could help me. You don't know me – my name is David Spencer, and I work for one of the main overland travel companies. I understand you were on a trip with a Mrs Gwen Absolon last year?'

'How did you get my name?' she asked, immediately on her guard.

'From a Mr Karl Habergas. He was on the same trip. You probably remember him.' A nasty moment, Drew realised. What if she went on to ask where he'd got *his* name from?

'So what do you want?'

'Well–' he laughed as naturally as he could. 'It's just that we can't seem to locate Mrs Absolon. We'd hoped to persuade her to fill in for us on one of our upcoming tours. It's designed for older people, and she seems to have all the right skills for the job. You don't happen to know where we might find her, do you?'

'I last saw Gwen in Egypt, last April,' said the woman crisply. 'Since then I have spoken to her once on the telephone, and that's all. I have absolutely no idea where she might be now.'

'Do you have an address for her? Even an old one?'

'I'm sure it would be of no help to you now. She used a box number in London for bookings and so forth. I'm sure you'll have something much more up to date than that. Frankly, whoever you are, this all sounds slightly iffy to me.'

Drew laughed again, with even less conviction this time. 'I expect it does,' he said. 'I knew it was going to be a long shot – but we've been badly let down, you see, and it's a case of panic stations this end–'

'You'll never find her,' the woman said, unexpectedly. 'She'll be long gone by now.'

'Gone?' echoed Drew.

'Out of the country. When that shooting happened, she said, there and then, that she would be giving up the job. It sounded as if she meant it. She and that boyfriend of hers – Trevor something – are probably backpacking in Thailand as we speak.'

Drew managed one final laugh. 'Lucky lady,' he said.

'Whether she is or not, I think you'd better give it up. You'll never find her,' Janet Harrison reiterated.

He rang off thoughtfully. The woman's efforts to throw him off the track had been just that bit too earnest. Gwen, he concluded, had asked Maggie and Janet – and perhaps Habergas and the Fletchers too – to divert anybody who might come looking for her. 'I'll be uncontactable,' she would have said. 'I never stay in one place for long.' And because of the bond of the catastrophe that had struck in Egypt, because they had no reason not to help Gwen, they would have agreed.

But why mention Trevor? Why drag his name into the conversation? Was it because they mistrusted him somehow, and wanted to make this clear? Was it just extra padding on a flimsy story? Or was it some kind of test, or password? If the questioner reacted with recognition to the name, further information would be disclosed.

Drew hummed with energy. Whether or not he could wrap it all up before tomorrow's burial no longer seemed to matter so much. He was like a bloodhound with the scent clear before him; like a crossword addict with enough clues filled in to feel he'd broken the back of the puzzle. He just needed to be patient for a little while longer. But – he had to admit – there was at least one whole blank corner yet to be completed. For that he needed another word with Stanley Sharples, Coroner's Officer.

Stanley was only accessible in the mornings. After that, he took himself off on mysterious errands, visiting relatives of the deceased, chasing up laboratories, beyond the reach of the telephone, ignoring all suggestions that he carry a mobile with him. Stanley was a law unto himself, and as long as he satisfied his job description, nobody much complained.

Drew phoned and caught Stanley in the mortuary of the Royal Victoria as he witnessed yet another post-mortem. Being the only person with blood-free hands, he picked up the receiver. 'Sharples,' he said.

'Drew Slocombe here. Just a quick question – something that's niggled at me about this body we're burying tomorrow?'

'Fire away,' Stanley invited, his attention more than half on the catastrophically damaged liver being extracted from the corpse on the table.

'Well – you're sure there's no chemicals, no poison, in her system, aren't you? I mean – seeing as how we bury them so shallow, without anything to stop leaching – it's as well to be sure.'

'We didn't find anything.'

'You analysed her hair?'

'We did, son.' Drew held his breath; it was touch and go. 'She'd bleached it white, you know. Funny thing – but then, that's women for you. The roots hadn't grown back, so it must have been quite recent.'

'Really? How odd,' Drew said. 'Well, bleach isn't going to cause too much of a problem. Thanks, Stanley. That's all I wanted to know.'

She was frightened, Drew told himself, with a certainty he could hardly account for. Hiding away in that bedsit, scarcely speaking to anyone. Encouraging people to think she was going off to the other side of the world. Dyeing her hair white, not long before her death, when she'd always wanted people to think she was ten or twenty years younger than her actual age.

Now all we need to know is who she was afraid of, Drew concluded complacently. And he could think of only three possible answers to that.

269

CHAPTER THIRTEEN

The remainder of Thursday passed in comparative inactivity. Since Drew had reached the conclusion that he could weather the burial the following day in spite of not having concluded his investigations, his new-found confidence seemed to get stronger as the day wore on. He dated it from the moment when he realised that Genevieve had been at home, with a dead phone line, all along when he'd tried to call her. A silly, irrelevant detail, perhaps; but it had strengthened something in him. Restored a faith that had been sliding away. There was more about Genevieve that he didn't yet understand – but he hoped he would before long. She was hiding something, something deeper than guilt over her mother's death: it could be guilt over the years of estrangement, and it might well be part of the original impulse to try to find the truth about her mother – but he sensed it was somehow peripheral to the assignment she'd given Drew. That, he felt sure now, was an obligation Genevieve had chosen to delegate simply because she had other, more pressing, things to think about.

The burial began to look more like a catalyst and less like a deadline. Letting it go ahead without getting distracted by thoughts of missed chances and burned bridges might well be the best line to take. As Genevieve had rightly reminded him, and Stanley had only that day confirmed, all the evidence was safely stored away in vials and on slides, waiting for the key that would unlock its secrets. Nothing would change that. Better to take a little more time and be sure of coming to the right conclusion, than to simply abandon the investigation, or risk getting it wrong.

He could have gone to see Marjorie Hankey today after all, except that Stephanie might have been a nuisance. Besides, he'd earned a quiet day in the office, he told himself. And Stephanie had earned some quality time with him, too. Leaving Maggs to answer the phone, he took his daughter for a walk in the sunshine around the field, pointing out the primroses in the banks, the blossom on the hawthorn.

In one of the lower corners, where the hedge ran alongside the road into the village, his foot caught a piece of brown sacking, half-hidden under a low-growing bramble. At first he ignored it, intent on watching an early butterfly with Stephanie. Then something snagged his memory, and with a flicker of apprehension, he bent awkwardly and pulled at it with his free hand.

It came easily, falling open as he tipped it up. Something feathery rolled halfway out; as he lifted the sack, a cock pheasant fell onto the ground. Drew sighed with premature relief. Somebody must have been poaching, and had thrown his kill over the hedge in panic when in fear of detection. Or they'd left it here deliberately, meaning to come back later. The bird hadn't been dead for long, as far as he could tell, although there was a faintly unpleasant smell. Harmless country behaviour – Drew didn't grudge one of the locals a bit of free meat. But there was something else still in the sack. With Stephanie's eyes following every move, he upended it again.

A head fell out, landing on the stump of the neck. It was a fox, the ears half-pricked, the lips drawn back in an ugly snarl. The eyes were open, though horribly glazed. Here was the source of the smell. In the open air, the stink was much worse; Drew recoiled, clutching Stephanie close. He kicked glancingly at the head, knocking it sideways, and started back towards the office at a trot. How could he have let his child see such a thing?

'What's the matter?' Maggs demanded, as he strode into the office and set Stephanie down in her corner.

'More dead animals,' he said shortly. 'I'll have to go and bury them. They stink.'

'Wait a minute,' she ordered, frowning, 'what sort of animals? Is this another of those – things? Like the letters and the cat?'

He hesitated. 'I hadn't thought of that,' he said. 'I thought it must be poachers.'

'But what is it?'

'A cock pheasant and a fox's head,' he told her. 'In a sack, under some brambles. Hardly conspicuous. I assumed someone had just chucked them over the hedge.'

'They wouldn't be under brambles in that case, would they?' she said reasonably.

He shook his head. 'Christ knows,' he said. 'But

I can't just leave them. Especially not that head. It's grotesque.'

'Just when I thought all that stuff had stopped,' Maggs sighed.

Drew looked at her. 'You're a bit worried by it, aren't you?' he realised.

'Well, you must admit it isn't very nice,' she said.

'It's not worth even thinking about,' he told her reassuringly. 'Honestly, Maggs – I don't want you to get in a state over it. It's stupid and ignorant, but it's not hurting us, is it?'

'Not yet, no,' she said. 'But it might be the start of something really horrible. When are you going to do something about it?'

'Like what? The police have already been here over that black magic nonsense. They're not going to be very keen on coming again, are they?'

'They might be if you showed them those letters.'

'I can't do that. I threw them away,' he said. 'I decided they didn't deserve any more of our attention.'

Maggs slumped back in the chair in exasperation.

'And I'm going to bury those things out there, too. We can't let this nonsense get to us,' he repeated.

The funeral on Friday of the officially unidentified body lasted barely five minutes. The weather had changed completely; it was damp and drizzly, and the grave looked alarmingly shallow, even to Drew. Police Constable Graham Sleeman

273

turned up, as did Fiona from the Council. The retired vicar from Bradbourne, who conducted all the cheap and brief funerals, had been asked to officiate. 'We should have a minister,' Fiona had said, when discussing the arrangements with Drew. 'What if this woman was a devout Christian?'

Drew couldn't tell her that he was almost certain she wasn't. 'A minister's no problem,' he had reassured her. 'We're not consecrated, but we're more than happy to have the usual prayers and so forth.' He hoped Gwen wouldn't mind.

Drew and Maggs stood, hands folded, having assisted Jeffrey and Constable Graham Sleeman in lowering the flimsy coffin into the grave. Graham had been called into service with little notice. 'What would you have done if I hadn't been here?' he demanded. 'You'd never have managed with only three of you.'

'We would,' Drew contradicted him. 'It just would have been less dignified. It's one of the things we're trying to change – all that stupid ritual about getting the box into the hole without huffing and puffing. You'll notice we haven't got plastic grass, either.'

The earth from the grave was piled up two feet away, leaving space for people to stand at the edge of the hole. Because of the rain, Jeffrey had thrown a groundsheet over it, where normally he simply left it uncovered. So far, all but one of the families had elected to fill the grave in themselves afterwards, tramping it down as they went, seeing the whole process through to its natural conclusion.

Drew felt a pang of guilt as the vicar stumbled over the point where he should say the dead person's name. *Gwen Absolon,* he said silently, hoping it counted just as well as if he said it aloud. He tried to imagine the woman as she must have been in life, but the blurred and blackened flesh that was her present reality was too vivid in his mind. The stink had hit him that morning when he went into his cool room, and the bottom of the coffin had been unpleasantly damp when he'd taken his corner to carry it out to the grave. She was a leaking putrefying mess of matter now, and it was hard to inject any sense of significance or awe into the disposal of her remains. Genevieve had been right not to come. What they were doing here wasn't important; they were merely allocating the dead body of this woman her little bit of space on the earth until the decaying process was complete and she melted into the soil. *I'll plant a little tree on the grave,* he thought. There was a natural burial ground in Carlisle which put a tree on every grave, so that the one-time field would eventually be a dense woodland, sprouting out of a hundred human bodies. Drew had suggested it to all his customers, but few so far had embraced the idea.

As the final words were uttered, and Maggs shivered in the cold drizzle, Drew cast his eye around the field, surveying his domain from the railway at the top, to the road at the bottom, trying to visualise it full of graves, a permanent memorial to himself as well as to the occupants of the ground. He was in the vanguard, a pioneer of a new way of dealing with death. In spite of worries about Karen, perplexities over Gene-vieve, the knowledge of pain and trouble ahead, there was always a stab of self-satisfaction at what he'd done in initiating this field. His zeal was undiminished, regardless of the financial con-straints and the practical problems.

An estate car came slowly along the road, head-ing towards the centre of the village. It slowed as it reached his house, and almost stopped. The hedge was high enough to obscure most of the vehicle; all he could see was a grey roof. Then it crept level with the entrance to the burial ground and he could see it properly. There were two people in it, their faces turned towards him. It was too distant to recognise them, even with his long sight, especially through the rain-spattered windows, but the car seemed familiar. He supposed it was locals, curious about the little funeral going on so quietly and simply. Of one thing he was sure – it hadn't been Genevieve. He knew that from the thump of disappointment that took place inside him.

He had half-expected somebody from the press to turn up, despite a small piece on page three of the previous day's newspaper, giving the brief facts that the body remained unidentified and would be buried in North Staverton, where it had first been found. *Woman killed and buried, found, examined, and reburied, identity unknown.* It wasn't much from which to make headline news, he admitted. A sad little mystery – that was all.

But that was wrong. Genevieve wasn't a sad little person by any means, and he didn't think her mother had been either. It all came back to

Genevieve. Every time he woke up in the night, or lifted his attention from work, the image of Genevieve Slater came before his eyes, luminously attractive, magnetically compelling. He could no more abandon the prospect of seeing her again than he could abandon Stephanie, his adored little girl. And the sudden awareness of this shocking truth almost brought him to his knees with guilt and fear.

The grey car moved away. Returning his attention to the final moments of the burial, he forgot all about it. The vicar had closed his prayerbook, and his head was bowed as he led the tiny gathering in a moment of silence. Drew heard Fiona sigh, and wondered what she was thinking. He knew her as an unusually caring person, often letting herself become emotional over the solitary deaths in sordid bedsits for which she took responsibility. She did her best to ascertain religious denominations, family history, and any friends there might be. While relatives often behaved with grim callousness, apparently afraid of being made liable for hefty funeral costs, friends would remain diffidently absent for fear of being seen as pushy. 'I'm only a friend,' they'd say, even when Fiona discovered they'd faithfully watched over and supported the deceased for twenty or thirty years. 'If there's one thing I've learned,' she told Drew some time ago, 'it's that blood ties are very over-rated. We pay lip service to family connections, but do bugger all about them. Give me a devoted friend any day.'

How was she feeling, then, about a body with no name? A person she couldn't begin to get to know? She was clearly uneasy about this un- orthodox and unceremonious funeral: the absence of a chapel, the sheer anonymity of the whole exercise, must be difficult for her – although many of her funerals had graveside services. When only two or three mourners attended, a full service in a chapel could be embarrassing, even grotesque. Even so, he supposed she would have liked the option.

It was over. Jeffrey was already shovelling the earth onto the coffin lid, and Drew hoped it would withstand the weight at least until nobody was watching. It was habit, he supposed, that still made him flinch from certain unsavoury realities of the business. Made him continue to want to protect families from having to witness what was really going on. Most wooden coffin lids caved in within a few weeks of the burial, which was a curious fact, given the lengths some families went to, ordering solid oak and pretty linings. *Please don't let us have to dig her up again,* Drew silently prayed, as he turned to walk back to the office, alongside Graham.

'That the end of it, then?' Drew ventured.

'Can't see it going anywhere now,' the police- man replied. 'Nothing much to go on. There's usually one or two likely ones on the Missing Persons file – but not this time. Not a soul seems to have missed her. Sign of the times, I suppose. Asylum-seeker, maybe. Gang of louts going too far and panicking. Or a foul-mouthed old loony, chucked out of a psychiatric ward and onto the streets. Plenty of likely scenarios.'

'Maybe,' said Drew, biting his lip. He hadn't

known how much he cared about Gwen Absolon, until he'd heard how she was regarded by the rest of the world. He didn't want to let her lie there, forever labelled as a 'foul-mouthed old loony', or a lost and rootless foreigner.

'Pity your man ever discovered her, really,' mused Graham. 'Just a lot of wasted time and money to put her back where you found her.'

'Whoever did it must have had a conscience,' Drew said, unable to stop talking about it.

'How do you work that out?'

'They could just have dumped her in a ditch, or the river. But they gave her a nice tidy burial instead. Makes you think.' He stopped himself before he betrayed any more of his feelings.

Graham was inattentive. He turned to look back at the field. 'What's that new area for – over there?'

'That's our new pets' cemetery,' said Drew. 'By special request.'

'And good luck to you,' grinned his friend. 'I have to admit you deserve it.'

On his way to see Marjorie Hankey that Saturday, Drew played a Paul Robeson tape on the temperamental machine in the van. The deep male voice provided a welcome antidote to the embarrassment of females in his life. The songs might be sentimental, but at least they referred to nothing more complicated than manual labour, simple aspects of existence. Women's motives and emotional games were getting much too confusing for him. Once he had relished the warm fertility, the absence of competition, consequent on living and working with females. Now he was starting to find it cloying, confining. He tried to imagine Graham or one of the men from Plant's getting embroiled as he had done. They wouldn't have stuck with it for a minute, letting Maggs and Genevieve, Karen and Stephanie, ensnare him with their conflicting needs and opinions. And now here he was, on his way to see yet another woman, with emotion seeping out of her, no doubt, and a bagful of irrational demands.

He should have had more faith, especially after the phone conversation on Wednesday. Mrs Hankey was as brisk as ever, although he did notice momentary lapses of attention, a film across her eyes as if the truth were lurking at her shoulder, threatening to pounce if she relaxed her vigilance for a moment. Each time it happened, she clenched her fists tightly – an act that looked painful, given her swollen, arthritic finger joints.

They sat side by side on a high-backed settee and Drew took notes. 'I don't want a lot of trivia,' she told him. 'I see your job as steering us down the narrow line between cold anonymity and slushy sentiment. I liked the things you said about death in your speech the other week. There's something refreshingly robust in your attitude – your *manner*.'

He made an anxious face. 'I hope I can get it right for you,' he said.

'You can't be any worse than one of those crematorium ministers,' she assured him. 'I've been at funerals where they've obviously been thinking about something completely different.

280

And I can't abide those singsong voices they put on. Just speak naturally and keep it simple. My son said he'd stand up and give a little eulogy, too. And we'll play a bit of music.'

Thank goodness for that, thought Drew; the prospect of having to fill a full twenty minutes had been one cause of his original panic. 'Was his death expected?' he asked. This had always been one of Daphne Plant's favourite questions to people coming to arrange a funeral. Drew had assumed it guided her in how much sympathy to manifest, though it had niggled him the first few times he heard her use it. Now, God help him, he was doing the same thing.

Mrs Hankey eyed him narrowly. 'I'm hoping for better than that of you,' she said tartly. 'My husband was seventy-nine and suffered from the normal aches and pains you associate with a man of that age. We expected that he would die one day, but hadn't quite bargained on it happening this week. Death is all the more extraordinary, don't you think, for being both utterly pre-dictable in a general way, and frighteningly unforeseen in specific cases. Harold was very ill for a week beforehand, and we had the sense to talk briefly about the possibility that he would die. On his last day, I could tell that he felt something had changed. A kind of *shift,* if that makes any sense. But we needn't dwell on that. I don't want you to go into that sort of detail. Just see us through the ritual aspect of it. He'd probably have wanted something even plainer – no real ceremony at all – but I want to do this for myself. I can't just let him go without marking the moment in some way.'

Drew knew what she was talking about now, knew he could give her what she wanted. It was just a matter of being in the right frame of mind, and avoiding the usual clichés and euphemisms.

'Yes,' he agreed, 'I understand.' He was in no way surprised when he looked into her face and saw tears like splashes on the powdered cheeks. Violent little tears, which had shaken loose without her consent. Drew took a risk. 'Don't try to deny the sadness,' he advised. 'There's no shame in being sad.'

She managed a little laugh of self-reproach. 'It's this damned stiff upper lip,' she said. 'I can't help regarding tears as weak. Now listen – I don't want you to make me cry at the funeral. If you could manage to be genuine without getting too close to the bone, I'd be grateful.'

The phrase lingered in his mind, as he invited her to feed him a few salient facts and they planned the sequence of events on Tuesday afternoon. *Genuine, without getting too close to the bone*. It made him think of Genevieve and the strange, contradictory service she was asking of him. She was saying much the same thing. *Find out the truth, but don't get in too deep – don't get me into trouble, or rock my family's boat*. It made a bit more sense now, after this encounter with Marjorie Hankey. Hadn't someone once said that human beings could only bear so much truth?

Aware of Karen's displeasure at this whole weekend exercise, he did his best to keep the meeting brief and, after forty minutes or so, tried to bring things to a conclusion. 'You haven't taken many notes,' Mrs Hankey observed. 'Are you sure you'll remember everything?'

'I think so,' he assured her. 'It's quite simple, after all. We start with my introduction, then the first piece of music. Then Colin does his piece about his dad. Me again, followed by music and the committal. I'll jot a few thoughts down when I get home, but I don't think I'm likely to forget anything.'

'I was impressed that you did your talk to the Women's Institute without any notes,' she said. 'That suggests confidence – and a degree of sincerity. People find that very appealing.'

He gave a little shrug. 'I'd be worried about losing notes,' he smiled. 'I prefer to rely on my head. I'm glad you approve.'

'I should think a lot of women approve of you, Drew Slocombe,' she told him. 'You're a most personable young man.'

Receiving such a compliment was a lot more difficult than being honest about death, he discovered. The accident of boyish good looks combined with a genuine liking for women was probably all that accounted for his appeal; he could take credit for neither of them. A quiet 'Thank you' was his only response.

They parted company without ceremony. Marjorie Hankey stood at her door, dispassionately watching Drew climb into his van. If she was surprised or disconcerted by its age and lack of gravitas, she betrayed nothing of this on her face. Still warm from her approbation, he drove directly home, trying to compose Tuesday's funeral address in his head.

He heard Stephanie crying upstairs before he reached the front door. It was an angry grizzling and sounded as if it had been going on for some time: a tired, frustrated sound, designed to get on any adult's nerves. The kind of crying that Stephanie almost never went in for. He hurried into the house, following the sound, impatient to assuage or console. He saw Karen standing oddly in the kitchen doorway with the phone to her ear, her face white and strained.

'I keep telling you, it's nothing to *do* with me,' she was saying. 'My husband's here now – you can speak to him.'

She met his eye, and he read anger, fear and a terrible mistrust. Before he could move, she'd thrust the phone into his hand. It could only be Genevieve. Genevieve, who'd called with un-guessable betrayals intended to sour things between him and Karen. Stephanie's wails filled the house like broken glass, jabbing at him, making him desperate to go to her. He held the phone at arm's length and pointed up the stairs with the other hand.

'I'll go to her,' Karen said tightly.

Tentatively, Drew finally addressed the phone. 'Hello?' he said. 'Drew here.'

The intonation at the other end was faintly familiar. 'I seem to have upset your wife,' came a rich female voice.

'Who is that?' Drew demanded, beyond his usual politeness by this time. Stephanie was quieter now, but Karen's hostile face still hovered before his mind's eye.

'Henrietta Fielding. You remember – you told me you were Wendy Forrester's nephew, or some such nonsense. It's taken me all this time to find out who you really are. And before you ask, I'll explain how in a minute.'

But why is Karen so upset? Drew wondered, even as a wave of guilt swept through him. *She doesn't even know who this woman is.*

Being caught out in a lie rendered him speechless. 'Er–' he tried.

'I understand she's been buried in your field – again.' She chuckled, a warm sound. 'It would seem that the body you found – the one in all the papers – was our Wendy. Funny how the whole picture falls so neatly into place when you've got all the pieces.'

All the pieces? Drew made an effort. 'Are you asking me or telling me?' he managed.

'Just making sure you know that I know. Look – I was hoping not to get involved in this. The problem – or maybe it's the solution – is, there's a man called Trevor just turned up, saying he has to see Wendy. He's coming back again tomorrow. Quite honestly, I don't think he's a very nice character.'

He knew better than to believe her. 'So this is just a friendly warning? What did you say to my wife?'

'Well, she kept asking me what my connection with you was – she seems to be a bit on the possessive side, poor darling. I judged that it might be unwise to share the whole story with her, so I prevaricated. Asked her to give you a message. She seemed reluctant to do that.'

'We have an office telephone line,' he said briefly. 'My wife has her own concerns, without being expected to handle messages for me.'

'But what are you going to do about this Trevor character?' she reminded him.

'Nothing, I don't expect,' said Drew. 'Unless you've given him my name and address, he's surely never going to connect me with his friend. And since he's presumably left it nearly a year before looking for her, I don't get much sense of urgency about his enquiries. I should also point out that the body buried here has not been formally identified. Its identity can only be based on pure supposition.'

Belatedly, he remembered the computer file: HenriettaF. *Willard*. That must be her source of information.

'You're taking a very big risk, you know,' she murmured. 'You should never have become involved. And you should put some hard work into learning how to lie effectively. I knew I'd seen your face before. Did you know your local paper has put all its back issues onto a website – pictures and all? I found you in one from last October, when you got permission for your burial ground. Took me a little while, I admit, but I had plenty of time. So now I know all about you, Drew Slocombe.'

So what good would effective lying have been? Drew asked himself, strengthened by the knowledge of her secret link with Willard.

'So you've given Trevor my address,' he continued. 'Otherwise, I can't see the point of your call.'

286

'He seemed so upset, poor fellow. Terribly worried about his elderly girlfriend – especially when I told him she hasn't been seen since last summer. It would have been cruel to send him away with nothing.'

Drew's laugh was bitter. 'Thanks very much,' he said, and put the phone down.

Upstairs everything had at last gone quiet, and he took a few steps towards the staircase. Before he reached the first step, the phone rang again.

It was Henrietta. 'Look–' she began, 'I think you should come and see me. Tomorrow, if you can. I can't say that I'm on your side, exactly, but you seem a nice enough young man, and I'd hate you to end up with a criminal record, just for helping out a soft-headed thing like Genevieve Slater.'

'You know Genevieve?' Drew was surprised at the admission.

'I know *of* her,' said the woman.

What was there to lose? Quickly, Drew agreed, before remembering his earlier promise to Karen. 'No,' he amended hastily, 'not tomorrow. I can probably manage Monday, quite early. I'll have to bring my little girl.'

'I'll see you on Monday then.'

'What did she say that made you so cross?' Drew asked Karen, who was sitting on the bed with Stephanie, playing with a jigsaw.

'It wasn't so much what she *said*,' Karen told him tightly, 'it was the *fact* of her. You seem to spend most of your time in intimate conversation with strange women, and it's getting up my nose. When they start phoning here, when I'm in the middle of doing ten things at once, my temper just won't stand it. I never said I'd be your secretary, and I'm bloody well not going to.'

The Slocombe family did not go out at the weekend. It was wet and windy, and besides, they couldn't agree on anywhere to go. Karen embarked on a major appraisal of baby clothes and equipment, making a list of new requirements; Drew was shaken at the lack of enthusiasm the process elicited. When Stephanie was on the way, euphoria had been a perpetual condition for both of them. He trembled for his second child, aware that Karen evidently had as little anticipatory pleasure in the idea of it as he had.

He tried to address the issue when he took her a mug of tea halfway through the afternoon. 'Do you think we've used up all our love on Stephanie?' he ventured. 'Does that happen?'

She sat back on her heels, several piles of tiny garments spread out on the floor in front of her. 'I hope not,' she sighed. 'But I knew a girl at school where the parents seemed to have no love for her at all. It was so awful. Her older sister had big birthday parties and lovely new clothes, and poor Anne was like a neglected orphan. One birthday, she invited me and some others to a party – when we got to the house, there was nothing happening. Her parents were furious with her. It was terrible.'

'We'd never be like that. We'd have the NSPCC after us. Anyway, there must have been more to it. Maybe she was the result of an affair, or something.'

Karen shrugged, and then burst out, 'It's just – there isn't enough *time!* I feel as if I'm trying to run up an escalator that's going down very fast. And I feel so tired and useless. Look how long it's taking me to do this simple job. I'm not doing my schoolwork properly, either. The class is behind in number work, and I can't get myself to do anything about it. I just lose my temper with them. It's an absolute nightmare.' She looked up at him, resentment clear on her face. 'And then you go charging off after some idiotic murder that nobody else is interested in. Taking Stephanie into God knows what danger. Okay, so you're getting paid for it, but you should be earning that money doing what you set out to do. I don't like getting calls from strange women at weekends, unless they want you to do a funeral for them. I know it sounds like whining, but I really believe you're not taking me into consideration at all these days. I feel as if I'm carrying this whole thing all by myself.'

A lesser woman would have burst into tears at this point; Karen was dry-eyed and despairing. Drew couldn't move for the pounding of his heart. He'd gone badly wrong somewhere, and he couldn't help suspecting it was when he allowed himself to start this new baby. That had been careless at best; culpably selfish at worst.

'I'm sorry,' he mumbled feebly.

She looked at him hopelessly. 'Sorry? But you're not going to do anything about it, are you? Before you know it, the funeral business will have withered away and you'll be a full-time private detective. That isn't what I want, Drew. Let me make that very clear. It's dangerous and it's silly. And I can't let you take Stephanie around with you when you're doing it.'

'I've no intention–' he began.

She shook her head impatiently. 'It's money at the root of all this. If that woman had never offered you two thousand pounds to find her mother, you'd have had the sense to stay out of it. Wouldn't you?' She hooked a finger round the bridge of her nose, and rubbed it fiercely. 'Maybe you wouldn't,' she decided. 'But now she's paying you, you're under some sort of obligation. It's all a ghastly mess, and I want you to get yourself out of it as quick as you can.'

'Then help me,' he challenged her; a remnant of spirit asserting itself at last. 'Like you did last time. I'd never have got to the bottom of that one without you.'

'I seem to remember ending up in hospital, and you practically losing your job. As a precedent, I don't think that has much to recommend it.'

'Even so, it was nice to have you on the same side,' he said, sadly.

'I haven't got time. I told you. All I'm asking is that you do what you have to do to earn the money she's offering, and then get right out of it. She's poison – I can feel it.'

He didn't dare argue. He didn't dare say: *Some poisons are too attractive to resist.* But he resolved to do as she asked. If he could find the strength.

CHAPTER FOURTEEN

He accomplished his appointment with Henrietta Fielding with Stephanie sitting in her buggy,
watching the huge woman with silent and
fascinated interest. After ten minutes, however,
he began to suspect that there was very little to
be gleaned, in addition to what she'd told him on
the phone. She sat, monumental, in a wide armchair, and played verbal games with him, like a
monstrous cat toying with a mouse.

'Not a squeak out of Trevor since I spoke to
you,' she began. 'Nothing further to report at all,
in fact.'

'Could you give me a description of him?'

'Middle-aged hippy. Thin, unkempt. Unreliable. A drifter.'

'But determined enough to come in search of
Gwen after a year or more. Important enough for
you to contact me about him.'

'I wanted to get him off my back. To pass the
buck, if you like.'

'You did that when you gave him my name and
address. Why did you need to speak to me again?'

Her eyes twinkled, as she glanced from Drew to
his daughter and back again. 'I'm sure I told you
– I'm a keen observer. I wanted to see how you'd
react, where you'd go from here. I don't get out
much, and the computer gets wearisome after a
while. Perhaps I like a bit of excitement.'

Drew had not forgotten the computer. 'You're in touch with Willard Slater, aren't you? That's how you know about Gwen being Genevieve's mother, and about me being asked to find her.'

'It isn't *quite* that simple,' she said. 'But it's near enough. I know that Genevieve contacted you because she can't abide not knowing what happened to her mother. Reasonable enough. But Willard and I don't waste much time discussing his wife. It's Egypt that interests us. Modern Egypt, that is. You know, it's most regrettable, the way some countries are perceived as having only a past, with nothing of significance happening in the present. Like Greece and Italy. My husband and I made several trips to Egypt together – we spent our honeymoon there. Willard has a fine mind, you know. I enjoy our exchanges enormously.'

Drew smiled at the picture that came into his mind: Willard and Henrietta shoulder to shoulder, discussing the minutiae of Egyptian economic policy. Except they didn't do it shoulder-to-shoulder; they did it keyboard-to-keyboard. 'Have you ever actually met him?' he asked curiously.

She shook her head. 'Actually, no. We found each other through a current affairs newsgroup. Even though we're only twelve or fifteen miles apart, there seems no point in getting together. It isn't that kind of relationship.'

'Or Genevieve?'

She shook her head. 'Never,' she said flatly. Drew was unsure whether he could believe her.

'So – it was a complete coincidence when

Genevieve's mother came to live in the same building as you?'

'Gwen had told Genevieve she was looking for a bedsit, somewhere quiet. Willard sent e-mails out to several of us – it must have been a couple of Christmases ago – asking if we knew of any cheap places. And I responded. Simple, really.'

'So you have quite a lot of contact with Willard?'

Henrietta frowned slightly. 'Not really, no. No more than anyone else in the newsgroup. We were in touch quite frequently after Wendy got back from Egypt. She seemed a bit down, and I wondered why. Willard told me all about her involvement in the shooting – obviously it was relevant to our joint interest, as well. You know, it wasn't a normal terrorist attack – if it makes sense to call such a thing "normal". The gunman wasn't with an organisation.'

'Oh?' Drew's interest blossomed. 'What do you think that means?'

'Well, from what we can gleam – and Willard does know people out there, that stupid girl had been going round talking to the local women, encouraging them to fight for their rights. One of them was a young student of English – she understood more than the others. She went home all fired up, and her father saw red. He happened to be one of the most reactionary chaps around. It sent shockwaves through Cairo – they like to think of themselves as pretty progressive compared to places like Algeria and Saudi.'

The account she'd given was more or less consistent with that of Karl Habergas.

Stephanie began to bang her heels on the lower struts of her buggy, a sure sign of restlessness. 'I'll have to go,' Drew decided. 'If that's all you wanted to tell me?'

'Expect a visit from Trevor,' she said. 'He might be just the person you need to complete your investigation.'

He swallowed the *How?* and *Why?* questions. He thought he understood this woman better now. A lively mind trapped in an almost immobile body, with little to do all day but weave links between unlikely people. She must have thought she'd gone to heaven when Drew called on her looking for Gwen Absolon. Yet he strongly suspected that she knew nothing about what had in fact befallen Gwen once she left her bedsitter for the last time. She was getting there as slowly, perhaps, as Drew was himself. His competitive streak quivered at the idea of a race to the finishing post.

'Well, it's been very interesting,' he said neutrally, getting up to go. The prospect of a rival excited him, as he was sure it excited her.

Maggs was obviously annoyed when he arrived in the office. 'You're never here,' she complained. 'This is getting ridiculous. The phone's been red-hot all morning, and I don't know what I'm supposed to be doing.'

Drew took a deep breath. 'Okay, I'm here now. I'll try not to go out again today. Who phoned?'

'Who do you think?' she muttered, flicking a hand at the notepad on the desk. A neat list had been made on it. *1. Mrs Slater. 2. Mrs Hankey. 3.*

Daphne Plant. 4. Mrs Slater. 5. Fiona.

'Daphne Plant?' he queried in surprise. 'What did she want?'

'She didn't say exactly. My guess is she's heard you're officiating at the funeral tomorrow and she wants to know what's going on.'

'The Garnstone undertaker must have told her. You can't keep anything secret in this business. Still – maybe that's good. It might lead to more work.'

Maggs gave an explosively mocking laugh. 'You're joking!' she said. 'Daphne's not going to recommend *you*, is she?'

'I don't see why not. It's no skin off her nose. It's not the same thing as doing burials, taking business away from her. Officiating's something different altogether.'

'She doesn't like you, Drew,' Maggs told him grimly. 'Hasn't that got through to you yet? You've rocked her boat too many times. Before you came along, her life was a lot easier.'

'She was spoilt,' he said obstinately. 'I'm not doing her any harm. If she's giving people what they want, she'll get plenty of business, whatever I might do.'

'And Mrs Slater phoned,' she reminded him. 'Twice.'

'So I see,' he said, hoping he sounded casual. 'She didn't leave any message?'

'Just that she'd like you to call her. Mrs Hankey the same. Fiona wants the account for the burial asap. I told her we'd post it today.'

'You can do that. We told her four fifty, didn't we?'

'Does that include a tree? She said she thought a tree would be nice.'

'Did she?' Drew was pleased. 'We could do something for another twenty. That's still a lot less than she'd have had to pay for a cremation.'

'And you wonder why Daphne's miffed with you! You know she makes at least a hundred quid profit, even on the contract funerals.'

Drew gave her a sceptical look. 'Where d'you get that from?'

'Work it out yourself. Seeing that there's at least – what? – eight or nine a year, you'd be doing her out of something like a thousand a year. That's not far off the total phone bill, just to give a for instance.'

'Maggs, you're a marvel,' Drew said. 'A brain like a computer.'

'It's not difficult,' she said impatiently. 'Other people just don't make the effort.'

'Before I forget – did you see young Stuart over the weekend?'

She frowned and shook her head. 'No, I didn't. I was with Auntie Sharon.'

'Both days?'

She nodded, and put up a hand to forestall further questions.

'Phone the Slater woman, will you?' she said. 'The sooner she's out of our hair, the sooner everyone'll be happy.'

Except me, thought Drew guiltily.

When he returned her call, Genevieve enquired briefly as to how the burial had gone. Drew gave an equally brief reply.

'Can you come over?' she asked next.

'What, now?'

'That would be nice.'

'Sorry,' he said, painfully. 'I can't. Maggs needs me here for the rest of the day. And tomorrow I'm officiating at a cremation. It'll have to be Wednesday. Can you tell me why you want to see me?'

'Nothing special,' she said, in a purring tone. 'It's just nice to talk to you. And perhaps we should assess where we've got to in investigating what happened to Mum. I hate to say it, but I'm not sure you've earned your pay up to now – have you?'

'I haven't stopped working on it,' he assured her. 'In fact, I think it might all be coming together at last. There've been one or two new developments.'

'That sounds intriguing. Stuart's still here, by the way. He's being very sweet. But he's decided to look for a job, so he's going to be out most of the time, once he finds something.'

'So he's going to be a permanent fixture, is he?' It occurred to Drew that he might usefully have a word with Stuart. Another angle on the family background wouldn't be a bad thing.

'Well, for a few months, anyway. He's got a place at Newcastle University in the autumn. This is one of those year-out arrangements, where you just footle around wasting everybody's time.'

For the first time, Genevieve sounded her age. Drew wished he could tease her about it, but he was too acutely aware of being ten years her junior. *Like Habergas and Gwen*, he thought suddenly. He contented himself with a short laugh, before confirming their appointment. 'I'll be there at four on Wednesday – after Karen's collected Stephanie. Okay?'

'It'll have to be, I suppose.' He could hear the suppressed reproach, the not-quite-gracious acceptance of the delay. *What does she do all day?* he wondered. Maybe digging into her mother's fate was really little more than time-killing while she waited for her baby to be born.

As Monday wore on, Drew began to feel increasingly nervous about the next day's funeral. In his head, he could give the perfect eulogy, neither too sentimental nor too brusque, personal but also general. True without being platitudinous. 'Death comes to us all,' he rehearsed aloud. 'But the death of our own loved one always feels like a unique event. For that family, that particular circle, it is of course unique. And nothing afterwards is ever the same again. The pattern has to be redrawn, the loss accommodated...' So far, so good, he assured himself. Even if he just paraphrased the usual Funeral Service words, it would sound fresher and more plausible than the normal hackneyed routine.

Something about the need for a ritual to mark the changed circumstances. The respect due to the dead person; the long life now finished; the inescapable ruthlessness of death ... no, that was a bit too strong. It probably wasn't a good idea to remind everyone quite so explicitly that their turn was sure to come. He walked up and down the office, practising, repeating a good phrase, hoping it would stick in his memory. It was okay, he assured himself. It was going to work. He planned to charge ninety-five pounds for his services, and he reckoned Mrs Hankey was getting pretty good value for money.

Stephanie was quiet all day, eating her lunch without fuss, and taking a long nap afterwards. She slept deeply, lying on her back, arms flung out, a solid little body. Absorbed in his rehearsal, Drew paused now and then to look down at her on her cushions. She provided a perfect antidote to thoughts of mortality and loss. Stephanie was his link to the future now. She would remember him when he was dead; she might even take over the business, expanding, transforming, innovating. There was land in abundance all around them, scope for all kinds of enhancement. Growing up here, in the beauty and peace of the village, she would be more than happy to put down roots.

Crossly, he shook himself. It wasn't fair to map out her future like this. She might want to live in New York or Japan, to become a dentist or a stockbroker. Anything, he reminded himself, was possible. And – damn it – what about the new baby? It might be a son, intent on taking over the business from Drew, ambitious, avaricious, single-minded. Drew was deeply alarmed to discover how stubbornly unenthusiastic he felt at the prospect of a boy child.

Karen fetched Stephanie ten minutes later than usual. She looked pale and seemed to move

299

stiffly. 'Are you all right?' Drew asked her.

'I twisted my back at lunchtime,' she admitted. 'I was doing playground duty, and stretched to catch a ball someone threw at me. It just caught me a bit awkwardly. It's nothing. My balance is a bit off these days. It'll be better tomorrow.'

'If it isn't, you're to take the day off. In fact, perhaps you should phone now. Give them a chance to get a supply teacher organised.'

'I can't, Drew,' she said. 'The kids are behind as it is. Supply teachers are really bad news these days – I'd have to work three times as hard when I went back again.'

'You can only do so much. These targets and stuff are impossible, anyway – you're mad to drive yourself into the ground over them.' He was beginning to raise his voice in admonition, as seemed to happen every time he tried to talk to Karen these days. She turned her back on him, bending down to gather Stephanie into her arms.

'Aargh,' she groaned, and slowly straightened up again. 'Can you lift her? It doesn't want to bend.' She pressed a hand to her lower back. 'This is ridiculous. I don't know what's the matter with me.'

Drew looked into her face, which was even paler than before. 'Come on,' he said, more gently. 'You're going to lie down. And you are definitely not going to school tomorrow. Have a lazy morning, at least.' He attempted a disarming grin. 'And then, in the afternoon, you can mind Her Ladyship while I officiate at a funeral. See? It's all worked out fine.' The state Karen was in, he felt confident that she'd go along with the

300

idea. Despite her irritation at his going out on Saturday, she liked the prospect of his becoming a regular alternative officiant, and Drew knew it.

'Worked out fine for you maybe,' was all she said, before allowing herself to be ushered into the house and onto the settee. Drew made her a mug of tea and a honey sandwich, earning himself a warmer smile than he'd had for many a week.

Drew hadn't been prepared for the smirks and snide comments in the office at the crematorium, when he arrived fifteen minutes ahead of the scheduled time for the Hankey funeral.

'Is this going to be a regular thing – or did you know the bloke?' Desmond asked him.

'I didn't know him. It's all part of my new venture, in a way.' He was fiddling with a stack of slim service books, which the crem provided; they contained a number of variations on the basic Funeral Service, along with a selection of the most popular hymns. He realised they'd been removed from the chapel when it became clear that this was to be a non-religious funeral – he didn't know whether to be gratified or unnerved.

'I thought you only did burials,' Desmond pursued. Another realisation hit Drew: the manager of the crematorium was unlikely to be favourably disposed towards someone actively working to diminish the proportion of cremations.

'That's right,' he agreed. 'But this is something extra. Non-religious officiant. It came out of the blue, to be honest, but if this one goes well, I might try and do some more. You could help spread the word for me.'

Desmond pursed his lips. 'We'll see about that,' he said, sceptically.

The chapel was fuller than Drew had expected. Five rows were filled completely, on both sides of the aisle, and a scattering of mourners occupied some seats nearer the back. A huge clock hung on the rear wall, over the door, so there could be no excuse for over-running. Drew had already ascertained that there was another funeral following directly after this one. He breathed deeply, and tried to remember everything he'd learned from his time working at Plant's.

The funeral conductor and bearers were all strangers to him. He'd exchanged a brief word with the conductor, agreeing that the mourners should be seated before the coffin was carried in, and that Drew would take all responsibility for playing the music at the selected intervals. Two switches were discreetly hidden under the lectern – one to operate the sound system, one to close the curtains around the catafalque. Normally, the minister only used the latter – an organist was usually in charge of the music. But Marjorie Hankey had dispensed with organ music. 'Harold hated it,' she said.

The ceremony passed in a whirl for Drew. After his brief introduction and the opening burst of taped music, the son spoke haltingly of his father, with two or three small family anecdotes, and a nicely-worded acknowledgement of how hard it was to sustain a successful father-son relation-ship. Everyone looked moved.

Drew then embarked on his eulogy. Without notes, he looked from face to face, gesturing now and then at the coffin, making no attempt to avoid the reality of why they were there. The widow kept her eyes on his face, serious but tearless. Other people were nodding, a few frowning, but he thought he could sense a growing relaxation, a gathered feeling as if they trusted him. A glance up at the clock told him he had spoken for six minutes, which was more than enough. He finished, with the words, 'We will say goodbye to Harold now, each in our own way, as we listen to a piece of his best-loved music. At the end of the music, the curtains will close, and we will take our leave.'

He let them sit for just over a minute after the curtains had done their jerkily automated turn. The symbolism was unavoidable, especially after Drew's closing words, and the people in the chapel all seemed to exhale at once. That was that, then. They'd done their best to mark the moment and follow the dead man's wishes – now they could get on with the rest of their lives. Drew began to walk towards the side door, where the conductor was standing, ready to throw it open. Between them, they escorted everyone outside – an awkward part of the proceedings in most cremations. Everyone waited to see if there was a strict sequence – whether close family should line up to shake hands with the rest – what they were supposed to do once outside.

Flowers were laid out in alcoves, with the names of the day's dead on little labels. It was the one and only chance the family had to inspect them; knowing how much money could be spent on a simple tribute, it was incumbent upon them to at least go through the motions. Drew stood self-effacingly beside the conductor. He was slightly surprised when the man palmed a small brown envelope into his hand, with a tight smile and nod. It dawned on him that this was his fee. At Plant's, the ministers had all been sent a cheque for their services at the end of each month. Cash in hand seemed oddly quaint and patronising.

Marjorie Hankey was surrounded by friends, most of them of a similar age to herself, and the great majority female. Drew hadn't thought to ask whether she'd like him to announce that there would be refreshments served somewhere afterwards – on the whole he believed it was bad taste to make any such reference. Was it per-missible to slip away now? he wondered. He couldn't think of any reason why he might still be needed – but neither did he want to look im-patient to be off.

As he dithered, the widow broke out of the enclosing group and came up to him. 'You did that marvellously,' she said. 'I don't know how I'll ever thank you. It was exactly what Harold would have wanted – I could feel his approval. Nobody could ask for anything better.'

Drew blinked. 'I'm glad you're – satisfied,' he began.

She leaned towards him, and lowered her voice. 'You're going to be in great demand, you know. You have a rare talent for capturing the right tone. Don't let anything spoil it, will you?'

He smiled. 'I'll do my best,' he said.

'I mean it,' she said, louder, her natural asperity winning through. 'At your age, you've got everything still ahead of you. You could really make something out of this work you're doing. All it needs is for the word to spread, and for a few people to take the plunge, and you'll be setting the tone for all funerals in a few years. Most of us hate what the American undertakers are doing, but not many have the courage to do anything about it. I can't tell you what a difference you've made to me. When Harold was ill, I found myself dreading the funeral, with all the insulting platitudes and dreadful insincerity. I bless the day I found you, Drew Slocombe. If you ever want a testimonial from a satisfied customer, you know where to come.'

Drew could do little more than shake her hand and depart. The sense of fulfilment was like being coated in warm honey; he wanted to go away and savour it. And Marjorie's words had excited him; if she was right, and his idea did take root in the general community, he might well find his life taking a dramatic turn for the better.

It was close to four o'clock when he got home. Calling in at the office first, he found Maggs with a shorter list of phonecalls than on the previous day, but a look of agitation on her face.

'There's a man here,' she hissed. 'Look!' She pointed out of the small back window, overlooking the field. Drew could see a figure in a long brown coat, standing beside the new grave. The head was bowed, the hands clasped; as he watched, the man clumsily knelt down on the grass near the head of the grave.

'I think I know who that is,' Drew said. 'If I'm right, then we've got quite a bit to talk about. I'll give him a few minutes and then stroll out for a chat.'

'He's been here nearly half an hour already. He walked up and down the field a bit, to start with, and then seemed to decide it was the new grave he wanted. I've been keeping out of the way – I don't want to put my foot in it by telling him anything he's not supposed to know.' She looked at him searchingly. 'You haven't been keeping me very well informed on all this, you know,' she reproached. 'I thought we were supposed to be working on it together?'

Drew sighed. 'There hasn't been much time. Anyway – you haven't asked me how the funeral went.'

'I can see it was okay. You're practically glow-ing.'

'It was *fantastic!*' he told her, with exultation. 'You should have heard what Mrs Hankey said. She was as pleased as anyone could possibly be. And they paid me – look.' He dug out the brown envelope and opened it. Five twenty-pound notes were neatly folded inside. 'Look, she's even given me more than I asked. We'll be rich, Maggs, if this catches on. Your faith will be rewarded.'

'I never doubted it,' she said casually. 'But maybe there's just a few hurdles to jump before we're earning a thousand quid a week.'

'Each!' he said, wildly.

'*Obviously* each.' She folded her arms majestic-

306

ally. 'Meanwhile, you'd better go and interview your witness, or whatever he is. He looks as if he might be leaving.'

The man outside had got to his feet, and was rubbing his hands slowly together. Drew made for the door. 'Hello!' he called, hoping he sounded more friendly than challenging. The man was still fifty yards away, and although he looked right at Drew, he made no sign that he'd heard him speak.

The long brown coat turned out to be made of leather, very creased and stained, but nonetheless genuine. It confirmed Drew's conjecture that this was Trevor. Trevor who lived in Luxor, who had known Gwen Absolon and written to her about runes and plans and past romance. He was bearded, thin, hollow-cheeked. He walked carefully down the slope towards the road, glancing briefly from Drew's face to the ground.

When the distance between them was four or five feet, the man stopped. 'You the owner of this place?' he asked. Before Drew could answer, he added, 'You'll have to shout. I'm very deaf.'

Drew nodded wordlessly, wondering how to convey all the things he wanted to ask. 'Come into the office,' he invited loudly, with an exaggerated sweep of his arm towards the building. 'We could have some tea.'

The man cocked his head on one side consideringly. 'Why?' he said.

At least it looks as if he heard me, Drew thought. 'Why not?' he said.

The visitor smiled at that, and ducked his head in a jerk of acceptance. Drew led the way. He

307

fished teabags out of the filing cabinet, and reached milk down from a shelf. The cool room had a tap, and he quickly went to fill the kettle, which also lived on the shelf, well out of Stephanie's reach.

He clattered with mugs for a few moments while the man sat on one of the chairs, leaning an elbow on the desk. Drew remembered how agitated Daphne Plant would become if a customer strayed into the office – where they might read letters to ministers, or funeral accounts. *No such paranoia here,* he thought smugly.

'You know whose grave that is?' Drew said, looking out of the window at the spot where the man had knelt.

'I hope it's my friend Gwen's,' he replied. 'Otherwise I've just said goodbye to the wrong person. Not that it would matter much,' he added.

'You didn't come to the burial. I assume you read about it in the paper?'

'What? Oh – the burial. No.' He looked at the floor until Drew produced a mug of tea which he took in both hands. 'Did anybody?'

Drew shook his head. 'Not really,' he said.

'She died last year – is that right? I did see the papers. Mrs Fielding showed them all to me, on her computer. Damn clever, that – pictures and everything. Even showed her necklace – the one poor old Habergas bought her. I felt a bit bad about him – seeing he was so keen on the old girl. I buggered off to Tangiers, anyway, after that business at Saqqara. Should have left him with a clear field from the start. She'd probably have done all right with him.'

So: another piece of confirmation that the body had indeed been that of Gwen Absolon. But then, he'd stopped doubting it a long time ago.

There was something strangely anachronistic about his visitor. The coat; the old Etonian accent; even the mention of Tangiers: all seemed redolent of the thirties. And yet he was probably only just over fifty at most. Drew sipped his own tea and tried to move things along a bit.

'I think I found a letter of yours,' he said, trying to speak clearly. 'Amongst her things.'

'You know who I am, then?'

'I think so. But I could be wrong.'

'My name's Trevor Goldsworthy. And yes, I wrote to Gwen. She was a good friend.'

'Your letter didn't mention Saqqara,' Drew observed.

'No. I didn't want to upset her.'

Drew reminded himself that this could very easily be Gwen's killer. He also remembered Maggs's caution about revealing the identity of the body in the grave. Reasons for suspecting Trevor's motives were legion, and yet Drew found himself compelled to trust him. Impatiently, he tried to resist. The man could be a spy, or a drug dealer, for heaven's sake! That was certainly what he most resembled.

'I last saw her in Saqqara, though,' Trevor continued obligingly. 'The day of that shooting. She was in an awful state, of course, and turned to me for comfort. I like to think I rose to the occasion, in my own small way. So much work involved when something like that happens.' He grimaced expressively. 'Not that she seems to have had much feeling for the girl,' he added.

'Oh?'

'Well, she couldn't conceal a certain grim sort of satisfaction. *At least it wasn't any of the others,* she said. *Maybe there's something in religion after all. Allah seems to have got it right for once.* Afterwards, she decided to take a break from the tours. Said she'd see if she could straighten things out with her daughters, once and for all.'

'How long had you known her?' Drew asked loudly. It seemed the question got across loud and clear.

'Ages,' Trevor said. 'On and off, mind you. We'd meet up in North Africa, Cyprus, Turkey – that sort of area. My old stamping grounds.'

Drew adopted an encouraging, interested expression, hoping for more detail. He was only partially gratified. 'I really wanted to see her again,' Trevor groaned, with a glance out of the window. 'I never thought she'd go and die on me.' For the first time, he showed signs of grief. 'I can't believe I won't see her again,' he said, wonderingly. His eyes filled with tears.

Drew waited for the little storm to pass. It wasn't long in doing so. 'You've got it nice here,' the man continued. 'Gwen's lucky.' Then he remembered. 'They put her here before, didn't they? The bastards who killed her. Jumped the gun and buried her before the place was even open. And now you've put her back again.' He shook his head painfully, and rubbed a hand down one side of his neck, under the ear. 'Ouch,' he groaned. 'Must've slept awkwardly last night. Damned sore.'

'Do you know Genevieve?' Drew asked suddenly, having been careful not to deny or confirm the man's analysis of Gwen's fate. Trevor looked at him, frowning. 'Genevieve Slater,' Drew repeated more loudly.

'You mean the bitch daughter? Never met the bloody cow, and hope I never do.' He fixed his eyes on Drew's, his look hard and bitter. 'She broke Gwen's heart.'

Drew couldn't bring himself to pursue this line of enquiry. 'Your letter,' he said hastily. 'The one in Gwen's things.' Trevor watched his face intently, in the effort to catch his meaning. 'You said a man had been bothering her. You said you'd "settle his hash", if I remember right.'

Trevor sucked his upper lip, thinking hard. 'That's *right*,' he said slowly. 'The Gliddon chap – Sarah's husband. Some nonsense about suing her for dereliction of duty. He started on about it even before the body was back in the UK. Bereavement takes some people like that, of course.'

Drew raised his eyebrows. 'You know,' Trevor said. 'Anger – it's a natural response to pain or grief. Quite irrational, of course. Nobody could blame Gwen for what happened to Sarah.'

CHAPTER FIFTEEN

Karen's mood seemed to alternate between anger and a flat depression that Drew had never seen before. On the whole, he preferred her angry. 'You've been back for over an hour, and never even bothered to pop in to see how I was,' she accused, the moment he stepped through the door. 'I saw the van, and assumed you'd come here first, before the office. Stephanie's been grizzling for most of the afternoon, and my back's worse, if anything. Thanks for asking.'

She was lying stretched out on the sofa, with Stephanie in the crook of her arm, fast asleep. The sense of being doused in cold water combined with the increasingly familiar blanket of guilt, paralysed him in the doorway. He couldn't deny the truth – he had forgotten all about her. The relief of an afternoon without his daughter, not to mention the dazzling success he'd made at the funeral, had outweighed any worries he'd had over Karen's strained back.

'It didn't occur to me,' he told her truthfully. 'When I got into the office there was a man visiting the new grave. I could hardly risk missing the chance to talk to him.'

'The new grave?' In spite of herself, she showed interest. 'It wasn't the murderer, was it? Revisiting the scene of the crime?'

'Who knows?' Drew knew better than to rush

things. 'He certainly seems to have known her pretty well. Knows the daughter, too – or knows *of* her, at least.' He was treading carefully, now.

Karen leaned her head back. 'You know, this business isn't going to do us any good publicity-wise, in the long run. People are going to associate the field with something unsavoury, if they remember the story at all.'

'Believe me, I wish it hadn't happened as much as you do. I'm going to give it another week or so, follow up one or two ideas, and if they don't lead anywhere, I'll tell Genevieve I can't do what she wants. I don't think she'll be very surprised.'

'She won't ask for her money back, will she?'

'Not if I can convince her I've done everything possible. When her baby arrives, she'll most likely be too busy to worry about it any more. At least she's got a grave to visit that is virtually certain to contain her missing mother. And if she does decide to talk to the police, she can probably establish her mother's identity from the samples they've taken. She only needs to provide a hair, or bits of old skin on clothing, or bedding.'

Karen wrinkled her nose. 'And wouldn't that land you in real trouble with the police?'

He put up both hands, palms outwards. 'Let's hope not,' he said. 'Now – let's change the subject. Ask me about the funeral this afternoon.'

She was contrite then, her own forgetfulness as culpable as his had been. And although his excitement and self-satisfaction had mostly evaporated, he gave her a full account of his first outing as an officiant, including the approving words from Marjorie Hankey.

Drew expected Wednesday morning to drag, but the reality turned out very differently. Karen insisted she was well enough for work, and drove off determinedly, leaving Drew and Stephanie frowning at each other in the kitchen over a stack of unwashed dishes and toast crusts.

Before he could even open the dishwasher, Maggs let herself in through the back door, eyes wide with excitement.

'Have you seen what's happened?' she demanded.

Drew stared stupidly at her. 'What are you talking about? And didn't we agree you wouldn't use this door? Karen wants the office and house kept separate—'

Maggs shook her head impatiently, and then pointed out of the still-open back door. 'Look!' she ordered.

A crude wooden cross was visible, halfway up the field, decorated outlandishly with a variety of apparently slaughtered animals. It stood perhaps five feet high, rammed into the ground where the grass had been left uncut, some distance from any graves. As if magnetised, Drew went outside for a closer inspection.

A dead hare hung from one arm of the crosspiece; a crow from the other. The top of the vertical was crowned by a roughly-woven wreath, and below it dangled a badly damaged rabbit, tied to the stake with a tight cord. All the bodies seemed to be seriously mangled and at least one was unpleasantly smelly.

Maggs followed close behind. 'Yuk!' she said.

'It's much worse when you get near it. Do you think it's that black magic stuff? Didn't you hear anything?'

He shook his head, trying to remain rational. 'Not very clever magic,' he said critically. 'I thought they usually put their crosses upside down.'

Maggs tutted. 'It's *serious*, Drew. What if somebody sees it from the road? We'll never live it down. How could they do it, with you just there in the house?'

'We sleep at the front,' he said. 'And it wouldn't necessarily make any noise, just pushing a stake into the ground.'

'They must have come in a car,' she pointed out. 'Unless it's the neighbours.' The neighbours were a very ordinary family, twenty-five yards away. Beyond them, the village centre started, comprising four dwellings, a church and a straggling farm. Drew shook his head.

'Not the neighbours,' he said with certainty.

'What're you going to do?' she asked.

For reply, he gripped the lower part of the offending object and yanked it upwards. It came out of the ground easily, and he found himself holding it upright as if in some bizarre religious procession. He threw it hastily to the ground, and left it there. 'I've got to get back to Stephanie,' he said. 'Let me think about this. There has to be some reason behind it. Some kind of message.'

'Will you tell the police?' He was already striding back to the house, and she was trotting to keep up with him. He gave no answer to that question for some minutes.

'If I report it, it'll get into the papers,' he said finally. 'And the police can get themselves in a bit of a twist about this sort of thing. They link it up with all kinds of nonsense, and the whole thing can get blown out of proportion. And they've already had that report of trouble here. At worst, it's someone who thinks there's some special significance to a burial ground which makes it a good place for their highly unpleasant practices. But I don't think it's that. I think it's a sort of protest, from some religious nutter. It's probably the same people who left that sack under the brambles, and sent those letters. They were probably going to hang up the pheasant and the fox's head, as well as all this lot.'

Maggs was not mollified. 'Horrible,' she shuddered.

'They haven't disturbed any graves or done any damage,' he pointed out. 'It could have been a lot worse.'

'And it might be yet, if you don't stop them,' she warned.

'They'll stop,' he said with confidence, 'if we don't give them any sort of satisfaction. Ignoring it is by far the best strategy.'

'Well, I think it's scary. Where did they get those poor animals from?'

'Roadkill, I expect,' he said, thinking about the flattened crow and the mangled rabbit. 'Though I admit it's unusual to see a hare killed by a car.'

'I saw one last week,' she remembered. 'The day of the burial. It looked as if it'd just been hit. It might even be the same one. It was on the

316

dual-carriageway, a mile this side of town.'

'They must have picked it up that same day – otherwise magpies and things would have cleaned it up in a few hours.'

'They must be mad,' she said. 'Aren't you scared?'

'Not a bit,' he said bravely. 'But I'll tell you what – we can fix up some security lights, and fit a lock on the gate. We should have done that before anyway.' Busy with Stephanie and all her equipment, he sent Maggs ahead to open up the office. At least they'd have something to do that morning – phoning for prices and options on security systems.

But the prospect was a depressing one. He had wanted his cemetery to be open, available to visitors at any time, a place of peace and sanctuary. Intrusion and desecration hadn't entered his head as a potential hazard. Security lights would pollute the natural peace of the field, masking the night sky and implying a defensiveness he did not want to feel.

Puzzlement over the source of the sinister crucifix, combined with gloom over the compromises he was being forced to make, made for a restless morning. The only relief came from an intriguing piece of news gleaned from another phone call from Fiona at the Borough Council Offices. She called to say she had confirmed her decision to refer all the Council funerals to him, apart from those which specifically requested cremation. This was a coup for Peaceful Repose, and would seriously upset Daphne Plant. 'At least it was never really a formal contract with

Plant's,' Fiona told him. 'Just custom – or habit. We never made any real commitment to use them.' Drew knew already that it was deemed advisable to use an undertaker based outside the town where most of the deaths took place. A 'contract' funeral was done cheaply, at unpopular times of day, and the complex sensitivities of the business meant that local undertakers preferred not to be seen performing them too close to their own sphere of operation. Hence Plant's, from Bradbourne, five miles outside the city where Fiona worked, had been ideal. Drew was acceptable for similar reasons. 'As long as you're sure it won't reflect badly on your own business?' Fiona added.

He paused for a moment. He would be burying homeless addicts, tramps, solitary hermits with no locatable families. Bodies found under hedges, dead of exposure and neglect. The detritus of society, unclaimed and unfunded when it came to the disposal of their mortal remains. 'No, I'm not worried about that,' he told her. 'It'll be a privilege.'

'I'm going to enjoy working with you, Drew,' she told him. She laughed, as if she'd just thought of a good joke. 'Incidentally – there's another reason I phoned you – you know that woman you buried for us last Friday? Well, someone's sent us five hundred pounds to pay for the funeral. Anonymously. A wad of twenty-pound notes in a plain brown envelope, delivered by hand. It says *For funeral costs re: unidentified body at Peaceful Repose Cemetery.* Plain enough.'

'But that's–'

'More than your account comes to. I know. Embarrassing, isn't it? But you'll have to take it. Get a few trees or something with the change.'

'Have you told the police?'

'No – that never occurred to me.' He could hear her tapping a pencil against the desk. 'I suppose I ought to, now you mention it. She *was* murdered, after all. Or so we're assuming.'

'She didn't bury herself, as Maggs keeps reminding me. A crime was committed – we can't get away from it. Who on earth would send a large sum of money like that?' He wasn't asking Fiona, but himself. And only one answer came back.

Genevieve Slater. The bitch daughter with a guilty conscience and some crazy mixed-up ideas about making amends. Surely, it had to be Genevieve. Trevor Goldsworthy looked as if he couldn't spare one twenty-pound note, let alone twenty-five, and he couldn't see any reason for Dr Malcolm Jarvis to start throwing money about.

Stephanie spent most of the day in her usual corner of the office. The moment Karen came to collect her, Drew was pulling on his coat, and unhooking his keys to the van from their place by the door.

There was no sign of anyone else in the house apart from Genevieve. This time she let Drew in before he could ring the doorbell. He'd forgotten how tall she was, how straight-backed and regal. She smiled widely, meeting his eyes in a long gaze, but he was not so carried away that he

319

missed the lines of strain around her mouth.

'Are you all right?' he asked.

'Oh, yes. As well as can be expected. I've got the bugger of a backache, that's all. Had it all day, and can't get comfortable. You'll have to take my mind off it.'

She led him into the living room, and eased herself down into a corner of the sofa. The bulge of her pregnancy seemed like a separate entity, perversely clinging to her, spoiling her shape. She let her legs flop open, ungainly and untidy, so the unborn child appeared to sink into the space between.

'Did you want a cup of tea?' she asked with a little frown.

He could see that she had no intention of getting up again. 'I'll go and make some for both of us,' he said. 'I'm sure I'll be able to find every-thing.'

'Give me a shout if you can't,' she told him, her words broken off by a little moan. 'Christ, this is getting beyond a joke. I won't sleep a wink tonight if it doesn't ease up.'

Drew hovered in front of her, trying to remember what he and Karen had done to alleviate late-pregnancy aches and pains. All that occurred to him was that she'd slept on a bizarre arrangement of pillows, which allowed her to lie face down, as she preferred. He couldn't recall any backache.

'When exactly are you due?' he asked.

She shook her head irritably. 'I don't know. We keep changing our minds about precise dates. This month sometime, I think.'

'What did the scan say?'

'I never had a scan.'

Drew wasn't surprised. 'Well – the midwife usually has a pretty good idea, from the way the uterus grows. I never quite mastered all the details, but I seem to remember a whole lot of dating tricks.'

She looked at him in bewilderment. 'Are you telling me you were a *midwife?* I thought you were a nurse?'

He laughed. 'That's right – only a nurse. But we all had to do a few weeks in Maternity. I've forgotten most of it now. When Stephanie was born, it all went out of my head. Seeing my own baby born wasn't anything like the textbooks, or any of the deliveries I'd watched.'

'Oh, well,' she tried to smile, 'never mind all that now. Make some tea and we'll get down to business.'

In the kitchen, Drew wrestled with something odd in her manner. Was it normal for a woman within days of delivery to dismiss all discussion of the subject? Although understandably nervous, especially if this was her first child, it struck him as peculiar that she should be so evasive. Maybe she just didn't think it was relevant to the business between them. And she was probably right about that.

She took the mug of tea from him with a trembling hand. He sat at the other end of the sofa, twisting to face her. 'So – how do I earn all this money you're giving me?' he said. It crossed his mind to ask her directly about the five hundred pounds handed in to the Council offices, but it seemed somehow rude. Insensitive – like asking how much a present had cost. She probably hadn't expected Fiona to mention it.

She forced a smile at his question. 'I'm sure you've done your best,' she said. 'I didn't give you very much to go on, did I?'

Drew remembered Trevor's words. *The bitch daughter.* From Gwen's point of view, translated through Trevor's friendship and grief, this might be evidence of selfishness or worse on Genevieve's part. But, of course, that didn't mean she'd murdered her mother. If she had, it would be sheer insanity to pay someone to investigate the death.

And where was Willard?

'I've seen Trevor Goldsworthy,' he told her, in some trepidation. 'He came to visit the grave yesterday.'

Genevieve frowned. 'Who?'

'He knew your mother in Egypt – and other places, apparently. Sounds as if they were quite close.'

She screwed up her face in a disarming attempt to recollect. 'I don't think I ever knew him. She had loads of peculiar people in her life. She met them on her travels. Most of them sounded like losers. How did he know where to find her grave?'

Drew hesitated. There was no good reason for withholding information from Genevieve, especially as he was ultimately answerable to her, but something warned him it might be a mistake to mention Henrietta. He chose compromise. 'The place where your mother used to live – it seems Trevor called in there and they directed him to me.' The over-simplification jabbed at his conscience, but Genevieve seemed satisfied. At least, she didn't query his explanation. Instead she put a hand to the small of her back and groaned. Then she seemed to hold her breath, leaning forward and staring at the sofa cushion between her legs. 'Oh God!' she grunted. 'I think I've wet myself. This is very embarrassing.'

Drew recognised the sweet-sour smell that rose from the fabric. For a moment he was transported to the delivery room where Stephanie had been born, the sharp scary moment when the midwife had taken a long plastic instrument to Karen and ruptured the membranes. He stared at Genevieve. 'Your waters have broken,' he said. 'You're in labour, aren't you?'

She stared back at him. 'Am I?' she said, looking scared. 'Your guess is as good as mine.'

'Come on,' he said. 'Remember the antenatal classes. Let's keep calm. Where's the phone number for the hospital? Is your case packed? I guess we should call an ambulance. That backache – it looks as if it might have been the first stage of labour. It happens like that sometimes. When did it start?'

'Ages ago. This morning. It just got worse and worse.' She put both hands across the bulge of her belly, fingers outstretched, and shook her head, as if in denial. Her eyes gleamed with anger, and anguish.

'Don't worry,' Drew soothed her. 'This is going to be a nice quick delivery, I bet you. No time for any drugs or unnecessary interference. Just show me where you've put everything, and I'll see you get to the Maternity department. I don't think we should waste any more time, though.' As he spoke, he watched her hold her breath again, as if seized by some inescapable outside force, and tuck her chin down on her chest. She was pushing, in the classic posture drummed into women at antenatal classes. 'Very good!' he said, automatically. 'But if we don't bustle, the baby's going to be born on the sofa.'

She looked up at him, breathing fast, her eyes losing focus. 'What?' she said. 'What's happening? Everything's horribly wet.'

'Take your trousers off,' he said. 'I'll go and find you something else to wear.'

He ran upstairs, locating the main bedroom without difficulty, and casting a hurried look around it. The bed was unmade, a jumble of duvet and newspapers and a rather grey-looking T-shirt. The dressing gown on the back of the door was far too flimsy to be of use. Flinging open the wardrobe door, he spotted some sort of knitted coat, long and voluminous. He grabbed it, and ran back to Genevieve with it. He found her pushing again, having made no effort to undress as he'd instructed.

Taking a deep breath, he knelt in front of her. 'Let me,' he said, and started to pull the baggy maternity trousers down. She had to lift her bottom to help him; for a moment, he thought she wasn't going to co-operate. Then she heaved herself up, and the garment came away. The smell of amniotic fluid grew stronger, the strangeness of it sharpening his wits, forcing him to face what was happening. 'Lie down,' he told her. 'I'd better try and see what's going on.'

'I'm not having it now, am I?' she said stupidly. 'I thought it was supposed to hurt.'

'It is,' he said. 'But some people get lucky. You look to me to be in the second stage, already. You've had at least three pushing contractions. The hospital's more than twenty minutes from here – the ambulance could take that long again to reach us. Sorry, but I think we're going to have to cope on our own. Where's your husband? I ought to phone him. And I'll have to call the hospital. It's illegal to deliver a baby without medical assistance – unless you've absolutely no choice, that is.'

Something he'd said seemed to get through to her, and she looked at him with wide-open eyes. 'Call Dr Jarvis,' she said. 'I want Dr Jarvis.' And she recited a phone number. Drew went out to the phone in the hall, stretching the cord and propping the lounge door open, so he could watch Genevieve at the same time. He asked her to repeat the number, as he pushed the buttons.

There was no reply after ten rings. 'I don't think he's there,' he told her, just as she began another unmistakable push. She'd swivelled round on the sofa, and was now almost horizontal. He wondered if he'd done the right thing, telling her to lie down; she looked a lot less comfortable that before. Dropping the phone, he went back to her, picking up the knitted coat and wondering how he'd ever get her into it.

'Where's your husband?' he asked again.

She shook her head, and grimaced to indicate

ignorance. 'No idea,' she managed eventually. 'This is amazing,' she added. 'It hardly hurts at all. And I was so terrified.'

A suspicion began to dawn in Drew's mind. 'You have booked in at the hospital, haven't you?' he demanded.

A look of childish cunning crossed her face, followed by a parody of regret. 'I'm afraid I haven't,' she admitted. 'I did try to. I actually phoned them once, to ask what I ought to do. But I never got through to anybody who could speak any sense.'

'But Doctor Jarvis would have done it for you. Has he been doing the antenatal checks?'

'Not really. I told him my GP was handling everything, but that I'd like him to be with me, as a friend. The truth is, I haven't got a GP. There was never any need. I've never been ill.'

'But your husband? Didn't he insist?'

'I told him the same story. I said I'd arranged for a home birth, with midwives and everything. He washed his hands of it all. He knows he'd never get me inside a hospital.' She gasped, and held her breath for another dramatic push. Drew watched the changing shape of her belly as the baby prepared to make its entrance. Genevieve continued breathlessly, as if it were as important to expel the confession as to give birth to her baby. 'I can't go near hospitals, you see,' she panted. 'I'm phobic. Always have been. It's like trying to make myself step into a furnace.'

Before another contraction could cut off any more revelations, Drew forced himself to look at her vulva. There was a segment of dark hair

326

clearly visible, even between pushes. Another five minutes or less, and there'd be a third person in the room with them. He experienced a crystal-clear moment of decision. Either he could panic – rush round trying to gather up towels, scissors, hot water, dial 999, tell her to stop pushing. Or he could stay calm, give her the comfort and support she needed, catch the baby as it arrived and use whatever came to hand for the after-math. His training counted for nothing in that moment. Something much deeper took hold of him, some visceral confidence that babies get born regardless of circumstances. And it was exciting, in many different ways.

'It's nearly here,' he told her. 'We'd better just let nature take her course.'

But Genevieve had opted for a belated hysterical panic. 'Help me!' she cried. 'I'll die, I know I will. And the baby's going to be deformed. I've known all along. It isn't right. It's a monster. I don't want to see it, Drew. Take it away, will you, as soon as it's out. Please!' She gripped his hand, digging her nails into his flesh.

'Come on,' he adjured her. 'Don't be silly.' He stroked the hair from her brow, looking into her eyes. As if a button had somewhere been pressed, his own body began to take an active part in the proceedings. He was hot, flushed with the drama, and physically responding. He almost laughed out loud when he realised. Childbirth was famously non-sexual, a universal turn-off to husbands and partners. Some men, by all accounts, couldn't face sex with the woman again for months, after witnessing the gross ravages to the genital region wrought by the birth process. Drew had felt no such excitement with Karen during her labour. He wondered what Genevieve would make of it, if she knew, and resolved firmly that she was never going to find out.

She pushed again, and the sliver of head became much larger. 'Fantastic!' he encouraged her. 'It's almost here.'

On the next contraction, she cried out, a sound full of despair and terror, and flung her head from side to side. Almost no progress was made. 'You have to help,' Drew told her. 'This is the crowning. It needs your co-operation.'

'I can't,' she whimpered. 'I'm too frightened.'

'You must,' he said sternly. 'There's no going back now.'

Afterwards, she told him that there was nothing he could have said more guaranteed to convince her than that. Closing her eyes, gritting her teeth, with tears sliding down her cheeks, she screamed her way through the great final push. The baby surged into the world, twisting and turning to free its own shoulders, and landing glistening on the unprotected sofa cushions with a brief splutter.

As Drew grasped it, with the intention of placing it in Genevieve's hands, the front door slammed. As he looked up, he met the eyes of a tall, gaunt, elderly man in the doorway.

'Willard!' gasped Genevieve.

CHAPTER SIXTEEN

Genevieve's husband was much less substantial than Drew remembered him. In two years he seemed to have aged considerably. It took him a long, long moment to grasp what was happening. The baby coughed, and squeaked; the room was flooded with the smell of blood and fluid and sweat. Drew grabbed the forgotten coat and tried to drape it over Genevieve. His over-riding emotion was one of guilt. Kneeling on the floor, bending over another man's wife in an attitude of acute intimacy, he felt he'd been caught in a flagrant act of adultery.

Willard took two steps towards the sofa, his face a ghastly grey-white, and then crumpled, in unreal slow-motion. 'That's bloody typical,' Genevieve squawked.

Drew felt a rising hysteria. He'd walked into a madhouse, occupied by people who made insanely light of death and birth equally. All it needed now was the nephew, Stuart, to stroll in wearing full biker's regalia.

The baby, almost forgotten, lay quietly on Genevieve's bare belly, its arms spread out, pressing into the warm skin. 'You've got a daughter,' Drew observed, almost casually. 'She looks perfect to me.' Examining the infant's face, he saw the lips flush red, and then the whole body change from lifeless pewter to a rosy pink.

'I'll have to find something to wrap her in,' he said. 'It isn't very warm in here.'

Genevieve ducked her head awkwardly, the flesh under her chin pleating as she tried to see the baby. 'Help me sit up,' she demanded. 'I can't see her properly.'

Drew put a hand under her arm and hauled her into a better position. Her T-shirt had ridden up until he could see the bra underneath. 'You should put her to the breast,' he said. 'It helps expel the placenta. I'm going to have to cut the cord in a minute, too.' He looked around distractedly, wondering where he might find a suitably sterile knife.

Genevieve looked from the baby to Drew and then to Willard, who was evidently regaining consciousness. 'Blistering festering hell,' he muttered. 'Shit-scattered sodding cunt.'

Genevieve looked back at Drew, her face a caricature of disbelief. There was a moment's silence, and then she burst out in a shriek of laughter, making the baby flinch with alarm. 'Did he say what I think he said?' she spluttered. 'He must have gone mad. Willard *never* swears.'

Drew's head was whirling. Somebody certainly seemed to have gone mad, and he was beginning to wonder whether it might be him. But once a nurse, always a calm influence in a crisis. 'People often curse when they come round from a faint,' he said. 'It's as if their inner censor has been disabled.'

'Inner censor!' Genevieve echoed, still giggling. 'Oh!' she added abruptly. 'Something's happening.'

The muscles of her now flaccid belly had visibly contracted, and she involuntarily held her breath. 'Oooh,' she sighed. 'The sofa's never going to be the same again, is it?' The placenta, huge and purple, glistened between her legs. A substantial amount of watery blood came with it.

'I'll have to clean the baby up – and get her something to wear. You ought really to go up to bed.'

'I will in a minute,' she said. 'Put that coat thing over us for now. You'd better see to Willard. Sorry, Drew,' she added. 'This must be a hell of a lot more than you bargained for.'

Forcing himself to be methodical, Drew quickly established a degree of order. The baby was obviously in good condition, opening her eyes and staring with interest at Genevieve's face. Willard stared at the baby with a similar fixed attention. He was now sitting up on the floor, long thin legs sticking out in front of him, his face an entertaining mixture of a score of emotions. Suddenly he said, 'She's got my ears. Look!'

Drew collected bowls, buckets, water and a knife from the kitchen. Then he ran upstairs and found a warming cupboard well stocked with towels and blankets. He told Genevieve he was going to dial 999, so she could be taken to hospital for a proper examination.

'No!' she said loudly. 'Absolutely not. Try Dr Jarvis again, if you like – but I'm not going to hospital.'

'She's phobic,' said Willard conversationally. 'Hasn't been near a hospital since she was twelve.'

'So I gather,' said Drew, too busy to consider the full import of this information, but he hesitated, the phone in his hand. Then he pressed the Redial button, hoping Dr Jarvis would answer this time. As he did so, he glanced at his watch. It took several seconds for the hands and numbers to make sense. 'Half past *seven?*' he said stupidly, listening to the ringing tone in his ear. 'It can't be.'

'It is,' Willard confirmed. 'It's nearly dark outside.'

Dr Jarvis answered the phone just as Drew was about to put it down. He promised to be there in fifteen minutes. Drew then phoned Karen, who was almost hysterical with worry.

Genevieve embarked on a struggle to attach her daughter to a nipple, and, when it finally worked, shed tears of belated emotion. She rummaged clumsily in the pocket of the coat for a hanky, and brought out a handful of objects. A crumpled tissue, a tampon and two ticket stubs were scattered on the floor beside her. 'Oh, look,' she said to Willard, 'these are our tickets for *West Side Story*. Remember we went up to London to see it and stayed the night in the Regent Palace Hotel? I can't have worn this thing since then.' She squinted at one of the scraps of card. 'Twelfth of August,' she read. 'Why does that date ring a bell?'

'Glorious twelfth,' said Willard inanely.

Drew closed his eyes for a moment. 'I think you've just given your husband a cast-iron alibi for the murder of your mother,' he said. After what he'd just been through, he no longer cared about betraying any secrets.

Dr Jarvis arrived as promised, and Drew handed over to him with minimal ceremony. They'd broken practically every rule in the medical handbook anyway – let the doctor, retired or not, sort it out. There was obviously no cause for medical concern, apart from Willard, who continued to look very grey and shaky. Mercifully, he'd been so preoccupied by events in his living room that he hadn't even looked at Drew long enough to recognise him as the rival housebuyer encountered on the Bradbourne doorstep.

Drew himself was shaking as he drove home in the van. His sexual stirrings at the climax of the birth continued to cause him severe pangs of guilt and self-disgust. Although his lust had physically abated, he still felt hot all over at the memory of Genevieve half-naked in front of him. He reran the whole experience, savouring the various thrills and shocks, finding moments to chuckle over, alongside the feeling that he'd disgraced himself. He hoped he'd be able to convey to Karen just how hilarious the returning husband had been. That, he decided, was going to be the most prudent angle on which to focus. She'd understand why he'd forgotten to phone her, how he'd managed to lose three hours in the whirl of activity. She'd laugh when he described Willard's faint and his creative curses when he was coming round. She'd be moved by the easy birth, in the face of Genevieve's terror of the medical aspects of becoming a mother. Wouldn't she?

Genevieve's hospital phobia was something Drew still hadn't fully taken on board, and he gave it some belated consideration. He was appalled that she had never intended to present herself to the Maternity department when the time came; it was one thing for a terrified teenager to deny her pregnancy to herself and the world, but for an educated woman in her forties to behave in such a way seemed incredible. Presumably she had lied to everyone concerned, going through the motions, listening to instructions, while all along planning to sit tight and let things happen, to go it more or less alone. Was such a thing possible in the present day? An elderly primagravida such as she was would never have been allowed to arrange a home birth. And if she had been strong – or stupid – enough to simply let it all go over her head, what did that imply about other areas of her life?

What, above all, did it imply about the things she had told Drew concerning her mother?

He tried to put himself in Genevieve's place, assessing what her priorities must have been. Her evasions and sly looks, the childishness and the petulance – they could all be attributed to the pregnancy. Strange behaviour on Willard's part was hardly surprising, when on the verge of retirement, he'd been landed with a first baby whose mother was prepared to risk the lives of both herself and her child.

The wretched woman must have been tormented by conflicting needs – to discover the truth about Gwen, to keep her marriage intact, and to get through the ordeal of childbirth, which was very likely to result in her being taken to hospital, however horrifying that prospect might be. Drew shivered with compassion. No wonder Genevieve had seemed half crazy at times.

He remembered the couple as they had seemed two years earlier. Willard so ruthless and determined to get his way, Genevieve placatory, maintaining a veneer of good behaviour, befriending Drew as her softer strategy for getting the house. It hadn't worked, because he'd put Karen's wishes above Genevieve's – but she'd got to know him in the process. She must have felt a sudden surge of hope when she realised that he had a connection with the disappearance of her mother. It must have felt like a gift from heaven.

She hadn't been trying to seduce him, or destroy Willard, or obscure a murky, undiscovered truth. She hadn't been in cahoots with Dr Jarvis. Genevieve, lost, lonely, and more than a little unbalanced, had simply offered him payment for services rendered. Seeing her and Willard together in that living room, their new baby throwing their pretence of normal married life into turmoil, had convinced Drew of that. Having him investigate the circumstances surrounding Gwen's death had been a way of convincing herself that she really cared – and a way of giving her life purpose as she waited in limbo for the birth of her child.

'She's mad,' said Karen emphatically, later that night, having heard the story. 'There's no other explanation.' She was in bed, and Drew was about to join her; but her manner was so un-inviting, he hesitated, wandering barefoot around the bedroom, tidying clothes and putting socks in the dirty washing basket.

He resisted the urge to defend Genevieve.

But he thought again of the teenage girls who somehow hoped that if they didn't say anything their pregnancy would just go away. That the whole thing must be some ghastly delusion, because the reality would be too much to deal with. He wondered, belatedly, whether there was any baby equipment in the Slaters' house. Surely Willard would have had the sense to see that at least some basics were standing by? Otherwise, it would involve poor old Dr Jarvis in some hasty summoning of district nurses and social workers to provide the necessities. And wouldn't that be appallingly humiliating for two professional people more than old enough to cope with parenthood?

'We all have moments of madness,' he said. 'I don't suppose she can help it.'

'All I can say is – trust you to get involved,' Karen grumbled. 'Mind you, if you hadn't been there, what would have happened?'

'It would have been pretty much the same. It was the easiest delivery you can imagine. She never even realised she was in labour. Proves a point – they say labour hurts more because women expect it to. If she'd known what was going on, she'd probably have rolled around in agony all day. And yet she said she was totally terrified of the whole thing.'

Karen pulled a face; envy, disapproval and

grudging admiration all evident. 'You can't help worrying about the baby, can you?' she said, in a more mellow tone.

'She's a nice little thing,' Drew said, a trifle wistfully.

'Oh, you!' Karen burst out. 'You're too good to be true, aren't you? Birth, death they all come so easily to you. All in a day's work. You're sickening sometimes.'

'But–' he began, with no idea at all how to react to her sudden attack, 'I don't–'

A noise outside interrupted him: an outburst of high-pitched screeching that set his nerves on edge. It seemed to be coming from the field at the back of the house. 'Good God! What's that?' he said.

'Sounded like animals,' she said, clutching the duvet to her chest. 'You'd better go and see.' The noise came again, as harsh and jangling as before.

'Are they fighting or what? I've never heard anything like it.'

'We haven't lived through a mating season in the country before,' she said, more calmly. 'That's probably all it is. Just so long as the foxes aren't digging up your bodies. That *would* be embarrassing.'

'I'll have a look,' he said. 'Maybe I can see something from the spare room.'

It was a moonlit night, and dark shapes were visible in the field. The scattering of trees threw shadows across the grass, and the new fence around the pets' cemetery made a neat pattern of light and shade. Movement caught his eye as he tried to find the source of the noise. He was right

337

– it *was* animals. Slowly he made sense of the scene. A rounded creature, silvery in the moonlight, was engaged in a tug of war with something slighter and more agile. They were at the place where he had flung down the grim crucifix that he and Maggs had found. *Fighting over the body of the hare,* he realised. Again the shrill screech emerged from one of the combatants. As they shifted and struggled, he could see they were a badger and a fox, each determined to seize the carcase. If he hadn't known otherwise, he might have thought it was the hapless object of the battle that was screaming.

Before he could decide what to do, the badger suddenly broke loose, the prey in its mouth, and began scuttling towards the railway line at the top of the field. The fox pursued, in aggressive bounds, but it was clearly defeated. No further sounds emerged, and Drew tiptoed back to bed.

'Nothing to worry about,' he whispered. 'Just nature, red in tooth and claw.'

Karen had snuggled down under the duvet, with her back to Drew's side of the bed. She was no longer interested. 'Should be just up your street, then,' she muttered, without turning over.

Drew decided he should update Maggs after the events of the previous day. He told her about the ticket stubs in the coat pocket. 'If the Kennett woman was right about the date when she saw the body being buried, from the train – then it wasn't Willard,' he concluded.

'You mean it wasn't him who *buried* her,' she said pedantically. 'He might still have killed her.'

'In that case, there'd be at least three people involved in her murder. Possible, but somehow it doesn't seem very likely. And where would he have kept the body?'

Maggs pouted. 'Are you sure that a theatre ticket is proper evidence? They could have bought tickets but never gone to the show.'

'That's true,' Drew admitted. 'But we can check with the hotel. She told me its name. A famous one. Um–'

'Hilton? Savoy? Waldorf?'

Drew shook his head. 'No – not so expensive. Two words. It'll come in a minute.'

Maggs waited impatiently for thirty seconds, and then said, 'Never mind. Assuming they are off the hook, where does that leave us?'

'Good question. It might mean that Genevieve won't want me to investigate any further, if she's convinced herself that Willard had nothing to do with it. She's got her baby now – that was a kind of deadline all along.'

Maggs watched him closely. 'You don't want to stop, though. Do you? Too many loose ends. You don't want to leave that grave without a name. It'll niggle you for years. People will remember the mystery. It's a hobby with some nerdy blokes – great unsolved murders. You'll get visits from people who think it just *might* be their long lost cousin.'

Drew ignored this typical Maggsian flight of fancy. 'Besides, we owe it to Gwen Absolon,' he said. He gave a deep sigh, and looked thoughtfully out of the window. Suddenly it came to him. 'Regent Palace!' he said brightly. 'Regent Palace

339

Hotel. That was where they stayed.'

'Congratulations. That should be easy to check. Now – that horrible cross. It seems we didn't pull it down quickly enough. There was a chap at the gate just now, when I arrived. Said he'd seen it. Said he'd told the blokes in the pub about it last night, and they all decided they weren't happy for "that sort of thing to be going on round here".' She mimicked the West Country accent. '"'Tis master queer, that 'tis. There's been no such business as 'e, till that Slocombe turns up."' Reverting to her normal speech, she added. 'It could lead to real trouble, if anything like that happens again.'

'Trouble?' Drew echoed, trying to pay attention. He'd been obsessively reliving the events of the day before, remembering Genevieve naked and vulnerable, scarcely listening to what Maggs was saying.

'If people think we've got weird goings-on like that, they'll think twice before burying their relations here,' she spelt out. 'Won't they? It'll be bad for business. We've got to do something about it.' She spoke slightly louder and more slowly than necessary.

'Okay,' he nodded irritably, 'I get the drift. I just don't see what we *can* do.'

Before she could offer him any suggestions, there was a small crash and a wail from Stephanie's corner. The child had crawled over to a metal wastepaper bin and tried to use it to pull herself up. It had toppled over and sent her tumbling onto the floor.

'She's going to start walking soon,' Maggs

observed coolly. 'She won't stay in that corner, then.'

'She doesn't stay in it now,' he remarked.

'No,' said Maggs, putting a wealth of meaning into the single word.

Drew sighed. 'All right. I know what you think about having her in here. It won't be for much longer. Karen will have her when term finishes.'

'Which is the end of July. More than two months away. Look – I think you should find a minder. An au pair, or something. You're not giving the business enough attention, Drew. You know you're not.'

As always, he felt an uneasy mixture of adult affront and boyish humiliation when told off by someone so much younger. Her words were so obviously concerned, so deeply sincere, that the affront quickly evaporated. They were partners, after all. And in recent weeks, she had demonstrated all the good sense and commitment he could have asked for.

The phone took things off in yet another direction. It was Olga, the office assistant at Plant & Sons Funeral Directors. Drew listened to her with a sense of being saved.

'Daphne asked me to ring you,' Olga began. 'We've got a family here who'd like an alternative officiant. The deceased is a woman of fifty-four. Breast cancer, I think. They want cremation, but nothing religious. Somebody's mentioned your name to them. They're wondering about an ashes plot in your field.'

'Great!' he said, hardly able to credit what he was hearing. 'When?'

'They'd like to meet you first. Can I send them round when they leave here? They're in a bit of a rush.'

'Absolutely. Can you give them directions?'

'Daphne can. Thanks, Drew. I was just checking that you'll be there, really. Looks as if things are taking off for you, doesn't it?'

'Maybe they are,' he agreed, not sure he believed it himself. 'Let's hope they like me!'

Olga murmured something he didn't catch, and he wondered what she thought of his new role as officiant. At least this wasn't threatening any competition for Plant's, unlike his burials. The persistent preference for cremations amongst the population was a cause for regret, but this latest development promised to do a lot to reduce the frustration. 'Thanks, anyway,' he said. 'I'd better do a bit of tidying up before they get here!'

She laughed politely and rang off. Drew looked round the office, at the dozing Stephanie in her cluttered play corner, at the suspicious lack of papers on the desk, and wondered what the approaching people would make of it. *They'll just have to take us as they find us,* he decided

Maggs was surprisingly worried by the impression they were going to make. 'Steph's sure to wake up and want a drink or something,' she warned him. 'And she'll fill her nappy, or throw a wobbly. It'll look so unprofessional.'

'We've done it before,' he reminded her. 'She usually rises to the occasion very well.'

Maggs ran a hand through her dense hair, and scowled at Drew. 'But – has it occurred to you

342

that she might have put people off? That she's the reason we haven't had more business?'

He stiffened defensively. 'Not really,' he told her. 'I think people like it. It shows we're human. I'm trying to take the fear and distance out of death and funerals. You know that – I shouldn't have to keep saying it. What's your problem with it?'

She wriggled her shoulders. 'Oh, I don't know. I think it's this business in the field. And Karen's more depressed every day. Isn't that enough to be going on with?'

'Karen depressed?' he repeated, wonderingly. 'Is she?'

'Of course she is. Who wouldn't be? Every time she tries to imagine this time next year, she must want to jump under the next train that goes past.'

He sat down at his desk, and stared unseeingly out of the window. He'd known, of course, but the knowledge had been kept hidden, while he distracted himself with other matters. With Genevieve Slater. 'What am I supposed to do?' he muttered.

Before a reply could emerge, his eye was caught by a car coming through the gate. Two people occupied the front seats, and he watched them slowly get out, casting curious glances around the field.

One was a woman, and she went to open one of the rear doors of the car. The other was a man, and he began to walk towards Drew's office. 'I'd better go and meet them,' he said, heaving himself out of the chair.

By the time he was out of the door, the woman

343

was holding a small child over her shoulder and the man had almost reached the office, so that he and Drew were only two feet apart. 'Come in,' Drew invited. 'I assume you've come about the cremation that Plant's are arranging?'

'Right. Vicky and Nigel Gardner. It's Vicky's mother who died.'

Drew experienced the familiar warm tingle of satisfaction that came with every new funeral. It was the feeling of *rightness*, of being invited to do what he'd been born to do, of being able to help another family through this great crisis in their lives.

'And you'd like me to officiate – to conduct the actual ceremony for you?' he supplied smoothly.

'We'd like to discuss it with you, yes,' said the woman. She was narrow-shouldered and fair, her eyes filmed from excessive weeping. Drew recognised the look: even with make-up to hide the ravages beneath her eyes, the lids were un-mistakably pink and the whites veined with red threads. Drew couldn't avoid making a mental comparison with Genevieve, also coming to talk about a lost mother, weeping, admittedly, but very far from ravaged by it.

'Come into the office,' Drew ordered, holding open the door for them. 'Excuse my daughter – I look after her while my wife is at work.'

Maggs was standing in Stephanie's corner, looking down at the child. For a moment Drew saw a confused glance pass between the visiting couple; initially they assumed he meant the dark-skinned teenager was his daughter. Then Stephanie stirred and began a soft babbling and

344

they noticed her on the cushions.

The woman made an inarticulate sound of pleasure, and gently pulled her own child away from her shoulder. 'Look, Billy – there's someone for you to play with,' she chirped. 'Can I put him down beside her? They might keep each other amused. How old is your little girl?'

'Nearly eleven months,' he said. 'She's not walking yet.'

'Billy's nine months. He's getting to be quite a lump.' She deposited her small son with some relief next to Stephanie and for a few minutes the four adults observed the comical wariness of the infants as they took full cognizance of each other.

'This is nice,' said the woman eventually. 'Not like you'd expect an undertaker's to be.'

'Actually–' the husband began, before checking himself and casting a questioning glance at his wife. Since she offered no interruption, he continued. 'Actually, we had thought of asking you to do the whole funeral. But – well – we heard some story about peculiar goings-on here, and it made us a bit nervous. I probably shouldn't be telling you – it makes us seem a bit gullible, I suppose, but we couldn't feel entirely comfortable after what we'd heard.'

Maggs pushed forward. 'What have you heard, exactly?' she demanded. 'I bet you it isn't true.'

Vicky Gardner replied. 'We wouldn't normally listen to gossip. But two different people have mentioned it to us. Ever since that body was discovered here, and the papers made such a thing of it, they say you've been – having unwanted attentions. From Satanists, and witchcraft, and stuff like that.' Hurriedly she forestalled Maggs's outraged intake of breath. 'I'm sure it's all been highly exaggerated,' she said. 'But look at it from our point of view. We just couldn't live with the worry that the grave might be desecrated. I mean – we think this is a lovely idea, and we're very keen to bury Mum's ashes here. It's just – well, you must see…'

She tailed off, and Drew put a restraining hand on Maggs's arm. 'Yes, I see,' he said gently. 'And it's up to us to find ways of setting people's minds at rest. It was courageous of you to explain it to us. We had no idea there was such widespread gossip going on. Inevitable with a new venture like this, I suppose. Now, perhaps we should talk about how you want the cremation to be conducted.'

When they'd gone, with the date and format of the funeral all arranged, after a swift confirmatory phonecall to Plant's, Drew heaved a sigh of relief. He'd agreed a package with them, whereby he would conduct the funeral, collect the ashes afterwards and inter them in a special plot in the field, all for a hundred and twenty pounds. 'That's less than you'd pay a Church of England minister for the same services,' he told them, and they seemed more than happy.

Maggs was still disgruntled. 'We've got to sort out this gossip about Satanic rituals,' she told him firmly. 'Make a hundred per cent sure it doesn't happen again. I know we're sorting out security lights, but what about getting a dog which could live outside at night?'

'Tricky,' he demurred. 'There are so many places people could get in, if they were really determined. A hedge isn't the same as a high wall, or barbed wire. And Karen doesn't like dogs. But you're right – we must do something. I'll ask Jeffrey if he's got any ideas. Where is he? I haven't seen him all week.'

'There hasn't been anything for him to do,' she reminded him. 'He's been ditching for the farm. I wondered when you'd notice he was missing.'

Drew shook his head impatiently. 'Don't get at me, Maggs. I've got enough to worry about as it is.'

'*Sorry,*' she snarled. 'I thought those people would have put you in a better mood.'

'Me!' He stared at her. '*Me* in a bad mood? I thought it was *you.*'

The negative atmosphere – or perhaps just plain hunger – set Stephanie off, and she started a whining complaint. 'Lunchtime,' Drew announced, glad of the diversion. 'And after that we'll talk about security for the field.'

But things didn't go according to plan; another phonecall interrupted the feeding of Stephanie. Maggs answered it, and passed it quickly to Drew without explanation. It was Dr Jarvis.

'Genevieve asked me to phone you,' he began. 'She wants to thank you for everything you did yesterday. It was a miracle you were here. She'd led me to believe she'd got full medical back-up for the birth, as you probably realised. I've only just found out that she hasn't even got a GP. She hadn't seen anybody at all, apart from me. It makes me tremble to think of it now. It really is

347

miraculous that you were here,' he repeated. 'Your medical training saved the day.'

'I don't think it did,' Drew disagreed. 'It was the easiest labour imaginable. I had no more idea than she did that anything serious was happening, until the waters broke. How are they?'

'Fine. Unbelievably. It's all quite bizarre. There's no equipment – the baby sleeps on Genevieve's chest most of the time. She's got it wrapped in an old cashmere shawl that was Gwen's, apparently. It's feeding magnificently, and seems to find the whole business quite acceptable. It happens like this sometimes – the baby takes control, and everything falls into place. Makes you want to burn every book that's ever been written on the subject.'

'What about Willard?'

'He's hiding in his study. It's all too much for him – not surprisingly. I think he can be relied on for some basic shopping and that's about it. The nephew's still around, too, which is a big help. He seems very sensible.'

'Where was he yesterday? There was no sign of him while I was there.'

'He's got himself a job at a local cinema. Works afternoons and evenings. Seems all set to stay until he starts his degree course, if they'll have him.'

Drew tried to think. 'Dr Jarvis – what about Gwen? What am I supposed to do now? Have you spoken to Genevieve about it?'

'Not since the baby arrived, no.'

'You know, of course, she was worried that Willard might have killed her mother,' Drew ventured. 'At least, that's what she told me. But now it looks as if he's got an alibi.'

He changed the subject swiftly. 'Has she chosen a name for the baby?' he enquired.

'Not as far as I know,' the doctor said stiffly. 'When I saw her she was considering Apricot – but I think I talked her out of that.'

Drew laughed. 'Well, thanks for phoning,' he said easily. Give her my best wishes when you see her.'

'You don't understand,' the doctor said. 'She wants you to go and see her – today. As soon as you can. That's what she wanted me to tell you.'

'Let me go instead,' Maggs suggested. 'I'll say you can't get away, and I'd love to see the baby.' She grimaced at the blatant untruth. 'I'll tell her she can give me a message for you if she likes.'

'She won't like it,' Drew warned her. 'And she'd be furious if she knew I'd told you everything.'

'Well, I'll be better than nothing. And I might pick up some clues that you've missed. I might get a chance to chat with the nephew after all.'

'I doubt he'll be there. He works at a cinema, apparently – probably won't be home till eleven or so. You can't stay that long.'

'No,' she agreed regretfully.

'I'm really not sure about you going at all,' he persisted. 'Genevieve isn't likely to want to talk to you. She hardly knows you.'

'Can't I just ask her if she wants you to continue with your detective work? I can easily say you're tied up here, running the business, but you thought it would be rude if nobody showed up.'

Drew was handicapped by his conscience. The birth had changed things substantially, and the aftermath with Karen last night had fixed his resolution not to see Genevieve again. 'Oh, all right then,' he said snappily. 'You can go after we close this evening – if you don't mind doing it in your own time.'

CHAPTER SEVENTEEN

The rest of the afternoon was unusually full of activity. An enterprising travelling salesman for a coffin manufacturer found his way to Peaceful Repose Funerals, and did his utmost to persuade Drew that he had a need for a stock of oak veneer coffins with satin linings. Drew pointed out the lack of storage space; the ideology of his business, which favoured less substantial containers for the deceased; the unrealistic prices he'd be expected to pay. The man had an answer to everything, but he eventually left unsatisfied.

Maggs drafted more advertisements for the pets' cemetery, to be inserted in the county magazine and a local newsletter. 'We ought to fence off another corner for ashes plots,' she suggested. 'And do some special ads for them, as well.' Drew agreed, bolstered by the prospect of yet another untapped source of income.

As if to confirm the feeling of progress being made, someone then phoned with an enquiry about natural burials; his old mother was fading slowly away in a nursing home. Drew assured the caller that they could provide a full service at low cost, and that he could be contacted at any time.

'I'm going to have to get a mobile phone,' he concluded afterwards. 'Otherwise I can't guarantee to be there to answer people's queries. Nursing homes won't even wait till morning, usually. And it would be nice to think I could go out in the evening sometimes.'

When Karen collected Stephanie, Drew made a special effort to greet her with a smile. 'How was your day?' he asked, grasping her by the shoulders, and kissing her. 'It's good to see you,' he added.

She looked at him suspiciously. 'Why? Has she been playing up?'

'Not at all. She's been fine. She even had a little friend to play with this morning. And I'm officiating at another cremation next week. Nice people.' He stopped himself, having resolved to keep the focus of the conversation on Karen, rather than his own concerns. 'How was school?'

She shrugged. 'Heavy going,' she admitted.

'We'll have to do something about that,' he assured her. 'You'll get ill at this rate.' Remembering Maggs's comment about depression, he wondered whether he was already too late to make a difference.

Karen shrugged again. 'Not much we can do about it, is there,' she said gloomily, confirming Drew's fears. 'Come on, then, nuisance. Let's get your tea.' She lifted Stephanie slowly, wincing as she did so, and left the office.

The customary sense of freedom hit Drew as soon as she was out of sight. With Stephanie gone, it was as if a great ball and chain had been disconnected from his leg. He wanted to run outside alone or go for a long drive in the van, just because he could. Yet he knew he ought to use this free time to work at being an undertaker. He eyed the telephone blankly, wondering who he might call to further his own prospects. With a recurring sense of self-disgust, he could think of nothing and nobody but Genevieve Slater.

He tried again to concentrate on other things. Restless, and angry with himself, he got up abruptly. Outside, in the last few hours of daylight, spring was growing more rampant by the day. There was blossom on the hawthorn and primroses along the edges of the field. Birds were inexhaustibly working at parenthood. Drew decided to go for a circuit of his domain.

From the office, he turned to his left, walking alongside his western boundary until reaching the fence around the pets' area. The grave of the labrador was still very visible, a solitary hummock amongst the thickening grass. Drew tried to calculate how many similar graves he might fit into the space, and how they ought to be arranged. Even a dog or cat needed to be recorded properly; he would have to devise a grid reference system, similar to the one for the rest of the field. Knowing the British passion for pets, families would visit the grave of an animal at least as often as that of a deceased relative.

The fence came to an end at the top of the field, where the railway ran along the far side of the hedge. As Drew reached it, a train passed by; he stood watching it, feeling the age-old excitement that everyone experiences at the sight of passengers hurtling along to an unknown destination. The glamour of travel, of movement at speed, never faded. The woman who had witnessed what had almost certainly been the unauthorised burial of Gwen Absolon must have done so at this very spot. The hedge had grown appreciably since then – there were few sections of it now where anyone inside the train could see into the field, unless they stood up. Last August, he had only just made his intentions public, in his campaign to win planning permission and community approval for the new cemetery. The people who buried Gwen had quickly seized their opportunity.

The original resting place, where Jeffrey had made his discovery five weeks earlier, was now no more than a patch of earth; the grass was beginning to grow over it once more. The woman had been reburied lower down the field, further to the east. Drew stood beside the first grave, and tried to imagine the sequence of events. What a struggle it would have been to carry the dead woman from the road; how nerve-racking, trying to dig quickly in case a car, or a train, passed by. Why, he wondered, hadn't they waited until later? Until the last train had gone? Did they have to be somewhere else, to achieve an alibi, or to avoid being missed?

He recalled again the snug way the body had been lying, the cloth wrapped tidily around it, the ground tamped firmly down. Perhaps he was being fanciful, but it seemed to him that there had been something almost compassionate in the way it had been done. They had taken care not to allow any soil on her face – something that Drew himself had always found very distressing. Even when burying the labrador, he had made sure it was well wrapped up first.

The presence of the Egyptian necklace had to

be significant. It would have been so much more sensible to remove it, if the identity of the body was to remain undiscovered. He ran once more through all the clues and connections, searching for the one that would give him the key. For some nudge he could give the mechanism that would bring everything clicking into place.

'Are you all right?' Karen's voice penetrated his musings: an unwelcome interruption. She was standing at their back door, a hundred yards or so distant. He frowned, trying to hold onto his thoughts, and raised a hand to wave assurance to his wife that all was well. Something prevented him from calling back. You didn't shout in a cemetery – you didn't disturb the ghosts lying all around you. He remembered reading in a book of folklore that a buried corpse was likely to walk again, if given enough provocation. Some were so persistent in their refusal to lie down that their exasperated survivors dug them up again and burnt them. This, Drew suspected, was one strong but unacknowledged motive behind the wholesale swing towards cremation. It left the living free and clear to get on with their lives.

He slowly wandered back to the office, where Maggs was about to leave. 'It's five o'clock,' she told him. 'Are we locking up now?'

The odd look she gave him chimed with Karen's call from the kitchen to check on his wellbeing. He was evidently behaving strangely in some way, but there didn't seem to be much he could do about it. He nodded agreement, before locking the front door, and exiting through the back with Maggs.

'Try and keep an eye out for any more goings-on in the field,' she lectured him. 'Listen out for cars late at night – there can't be much traffic through here after dark. I think you should make the gate harder to open. Put a chain round it, with a padlock. We need to do something ourselves until the security lights and locks are fitted.'

Drew pulled a reluctant face. 'What if we need to get out quickly? Things like that always make me nervous – as if we're barricading ourselves in, rather than keeping intruders out. We'd be sure to lose the key in an emergency.'

Maggs tutted impatiently. 'Well, it's silly to leave it all so vulnerable to outsiders, after what's gone on. And if something else does happen, the locals are going to be onto it right away. They're building it up into some kind of village scandal as it is. We really don't need that, you know.'

'I know,' he said submissively. 'And I will do something – I promise. After we've had supper, I'll tie the gate up, and make sure there are no obvious breaches in our so-called security. Okay?'

'It'll have to be, I suppose,' she accepted ungraciously. 'Now, I'm going home for my tea, and then I'll scoot over to the Slaters' house. And you ought to phone the Regent Palace Hotel – see if they really were there when they said.'

'I was going to,' he said with dignity. 'Don't stay long, will you? People with new babies don't like visitors getting in the way.'

'She *asked* you to visit, remember? Things can't be in too much of a state if she was prepared to see you.'

Give her my love, he wanted to say. *Tell her I miss her.*

At the Slaters' house, Maggs caused a subdued disturbance. Willard had let her in, the puzzled frown on his face provoked by her attempt at explaining who she was. He led her into the lounge where Genevieve sat in an armchair, the baby lying along her thighs wrapped in something that looked like an old cardigan. There was a strong, unpleasant smell in the room, which Maggs quickly located as coming from the sofa. It was generously stained and looked wet. 'Somebody to see you,' Willard mumbled to his wife. 'Must be some sort of health visitor.'

Genevieve glanced at her with no sign of recognition. 'I'm not doing anything wrong, as far as I can see,' she said defensively. 'She's still alive, anyway.'

'No, I'm not a health visitor,' Maggs said, stifling a giggle. 'I probably know as little about babies as you do. Don't you remember me? I'm Drew Slocombe's partner. Business partner, I mean. He couldn't come, so he sent me instead.'

'Cheeky little bastard,' Genevieve said carelessly. Maggs did giggle at that, despite the shock she felt at hearing the majestic Genevieve stoop to such language. Genevieve gave her a closer look. 'Yes, I remember you now. The girl who didn't want to play nursemaid. I'm beginning to understand how you feel.'

Maggs chose to ignore this. 'He's told me all about your mother,' she said briskly. 'We work closely together, you see – he couldn't really keep it secret. I'm interested, anyway.' She realised she was trying to convince Genevieve of her detective credentials. It didn't seem to be working very well.

'I'm not,' said the woman wearily. 'Not any more. You'll have to put the whole thing down to pre-baby panic. I was completely terrified, you know. It must have sent me a bit loopy. I wish now I'd left it alone. Let the dead bury the dead – isn't that what they say? If my mother's off my back, who am I to complain? She'd never have been any use to me anyway, not after all this time.'

Maggs thought of her own mother and felt a flash of sadness at how wickedly some people could waste their most precious relationships. 'But Drew's in too deep to stop now,' she persisted. 'He wants to follow it all through to the end – so he can get things straight with the police if need be.'

'I'm not stopping him,' Genevieve said. 'He knows that. It's just that I don't really care very much any more. I admit I got myself in a bit of a state about it, but I'm all right now. So – what do you think of her?'

Maggs gave the baby a brief glance. 'Looks fine to me,' she said quickly. 'I'm not really into babies.'

'They're nothing like as complicated as people tell you. She seems to know what to do without much input from me. Stuart does the mucky bit, bless him. Not that there's been much of that yet. He tells me it all starts tomorrow, with oceans of ghastly yellow stuff. Willard's pretending nothing's happened – stays out as much as he can, and then sits in front of the computer when he's here. I don't know when he last had anything to eat. Stuart does a bit of cooking, luckily, or we'd probably starve.' Genevieve shifted uncomfortably. 'I don't seem to have worked out how to put this little thing down.' She closed her eyes and leaned carefully back in the chair. Maggs hovered, having found nowhere to sit: the smell from the sofa was still causing her to take shallow, disgusted breaths. 'So,' she said firmly, 'Drew's going to carry on with his investigation. He doesn't really feel he's earned the money you gave him yet.'

'He saved me a fortune yesterday,' Genevieve said. 'I thought I was going to have to summon a private midwife – but he did it all instead.'

'If you had someone booked, you'll probably have to pay her anyway,' Maggs told her.

Genevieve shook her head. 'I didn't. I hadn't even got as far as that.'

'You must be mad,' said Maggs with feeling. The older woman looked at the girl with eyes full of a sudden naked pain. 'You could say that, I suppose,' she whispered, 'if a bone-deep phobia can be called madness. There is no way I could ever step inside a hospital. They'd have to give me a general anaesthetic first, and keep me under the whole time. I couldn't even go for an abortion. So I didn't have any choice. I've never had my own doctor, in case he ever insisted I go to hospital for something. So being pregnant had to be a completely non-medical event for me. I'm sure I've broken any number of laws in the process.'

Maggs tilted her head sideways, considering the dilemma. Clear-sighted as always, she made an obvious connection. 'It's like your mother's death,' she said. 'All handled unofficially – outside the law. I shouldn't wonder if you buried her in that field.' She looked at the baby again. 'Birth and death – you're equally careless about both. You think you can do everything in your own sweet way.'

Genevieve gave a throaty laugh, humourless and harsh. 'I didn't bury my mother in your field. If I had, why on earth would I have then asked Drew to investigate it?'

'Conscience? Double bluff?' Maggs suggested. 'Keeping your husband from guessing what you'd done? Loads of reasons.'

'I didn't, though. I absolutely swear to you.'

Maggs could think of nothing more to say. The brief certainty that she'd resolved the whole matter quickly evaporated. Apart from the sincerity of Genevieve's denial, there appeared to be a more than adequate alibi, if Drew got confirmation from the Regent Palace Hotel. But she couldn't help feeling disappointed that she couldn't prove Genevieve guilty immediately.

The smell and the frustration were both urging her to make an early departure. 'I'll go now,' she said. 'Is there anything else you want me to tell Drew?'

'Tell him he doesn't owe me anything. Tell him I'm sorry to have lured him into my madhouse.'

The stirring of the baby, and Genevieve's instant tense reaction, drove Maggs quickly out of the room. 'I'll let myself out,' she muttered, to the

360

oblivious woman. But as she reached the front door, she heard a key turning in the lock from outside, and it opened towards her.

She recognised the nephew, Stuart, with some gratification. 'I thought you were going to be out till late,' she said, with a familiarity which seemed to take him aback.

'What?' he said, staring at her. 'Who might you be, then?'

'It's a long story,' she said. 'I hear you're holding everything together here. Quite a hero, from the sound of it.'

He closed the door behind him, and stood close to Maggs in the small hallway. 'Are you one of the neighbours?' he asked.

'No – and I'm not a health visitor either,' she grinned. 'I'm from Peaceful Repose Funerals, if that means anything to you.' She watched his startled reaction closely, not knowing how much of the story he'd been told. She decided to venture further. 'Where your grandmother's buried?'

Her gratification intensified, as he gripped her arm, and brought his face within an inch of hers. 'What do you know about my grandmother?' he hissed, glancing up the stairs and towards the lounge door, as if afraid of being overheard. 'Look – we can't talk here. Give me a minute and I'll take you for a drink.'

'Okay,' she said nonchalantly, wondering if he could see the way her heart was thumping. 'I'll wait outside for you, shall I?'

They walked to a nearby pub, which turned out to be so upmarket that anyone wanting nothing more than a beer was regarded as peculiar. There was nowhere to sit, other than nasty little tables arranged much too close together. Maggs eyed it with distaste. 'Call this a pub!' she grumbled.

He grinned at her. 'It's terrible, isn't it? But I can't go far – Genevieve's going to need me in a bit.'

'How come you're so good with babies?' she asked, as they stood together at the bar.

'Eldest of five,' he shrugged. 'It just seems to come natural to me.' Carrying both glasses, he led the way to the remotest table he could find, and arranged himself and Maggs so they both had their back to the rest of the customers. 'Now,' said Stuart firmly, 'tell me what you know about my gran.'

Maggs was tempted to plunge in with the whole story as far as she knew it, only omitting the somewhat far-fetched idea she'd harboured that Genevieve and Willard had killed Gwen between them. But she wasn't at all sure how Drew would react if she did that. Stuart might be on Drew's list of suspects, and it would be naïve to say too much at this stage.

Instead, she said carefully, 'Your aunt approached my boss, wanting him to help her find out what became of your gran. It looks very likely that an unidentified body that was buried in our field is actually her.'

She watched him closely for a reaction. 'Your *field?*' he repeated, apparently bewildered.

She explained briefly about Peaceful Repose.

'And has your boss come up with anything?' the boy asked. 'What about the police?'

Good question, thought Maggs. 'They decided not to go to the police until there's something more definite to tell them,' she said. 'At the moment, it's all guesswork and supposition.'

Stuart blew out his cheeks, and shook his head wonderingly. 'Wait till my mum hears all this!' he said. 'She thinks Gran's still overseas somewhere – mind you, she was beginning to get worried. That's one reason she wanted me to come here. To see if Genevieve knew where she was. She'd asked Genevieve on the phone, but she'd always got fobbed off.'

'And what did Genevieve say when you asked her?'

'She said she didn't think there was any cause to worry, and why didn't I stay with them a bit. Give myself a change of scene. It's a strange sort of set-up they've got here. Willard not here most of the time, and I'm beginning to think my aunt's not right in the head. She never bought a thing for that baby, you know. I had to go and get nappies, and some woman from the clinic brought a bag of clothes this morning. And do you know what she wants to call it?'

Maggs shrugged.

'*Apricot!*' he burst out with profound scorn. 'What kind of a name is that for a baby?'

'Could be worse,' said Maggs feelingly. 'So – what about your gran? Can you think of anyone who might have killed her and buried her in our field? Last summer, it was. There's a witness who says it was on the twelfth of August. Your aunt and uncle say they were in London that night, at a play and then a hotel. We can find out whether that's true, of course.'

Stuart widened his eyes. 'You're not suggesting Aunt Gen did it, are you?'

Damn! thought Maggs. *I was going to keep quiet about that part.*

'Well, we had to keep an open mind,' she said quickly. 'Anyway, when did you last see your gran?'

'I last saw my gran six years ago, when I was thirteen,' he said. 'She wasn't one for family visits. According to my mum, she was never really right after my uncle Nathan died. I expect you know all about that.'

'Not right – in what way?' she enquired.

'It must have been the grief, I suppose. She just went crazy, rushing off to foreign countries, never telling anybody where she was. She sent post-cards now and then, but never told us where we could find her.'

'I see.' Maggs tried to sound encouraging, but her companion had just caught sight of the clock above the bar. 'Did you ever meet Nathan?'

'Oh, yes!' he said readily. 'He was in a thing called PHAB – Physically Handicapped and Able-Bodied. We had a junior group at our school and there was a sort of exchange once – like with French schools. I wasn't really involved – I'm needed on the farm too much in the summer – but I did go out once or twice with them. Nathan had a girlfriend who'd come along too.'

'Was she handicapped as well?'

'Sarah? No, no, not at all. She was very healthy. Pushed his wheelchair for him. Funny couple, but she obviously really loved him. Must have been devastated when he died. Though I never heard anything about her again.'

Sarah... mused Maggs. *Now where did a Sarah fit in?* 'So – what was Nathan like?'

He thought for a moment. 'He never took much notice of me. I thought he was a bit self-obsessed to be honest. But he must have been different with Sarah. She was mad about him – at least that's how it looked to me at the time. He was quite good-looking, in a way,' he offered. 'Big grey eyes with long lashes.'

'How old would he have been then?'

'He was twenty, and she was more or less the same. They were in the senior section. She's probably married with kids by now. Forgotten all about him.'

'Probably,' Maggs agreed carelessly. 'Do you want another drink?'

'No thanks – I can't stay any longer,' he said. 'I told Aunt Gen I'd only be half an hour. I'll see you again, maybe?'

'Maybe,' she shrugged, delightedly aware that he was reluctant to tear himself away. 'Give you a break from babycare!'

'Yeah,' he grinned. 'I'm no saint, you know. Caring's all very well for a while, but I've got my own life to live.'

Maggs sighed with relief. 'You don't know how glad I am to hear that,' she told him.

'I'll be going, then,' he said again. 'You've told me quite a story.' He scratched his head dis-tractedly. 'I need to have a proper think about it all. If someone has murdered my gran, then we'll want to see justice done. It's no good Genevieve thinking we can just carry on without telling anyone. She's not the only person in this family.'

Next morning, Maggs was early at the office, eager to bring Drew up to date on her encounter with Stuart. But Drew was there even more punctually, with other matters on his mind.

He and Jeffrey were standing awkwardly beside the desk when Maggs walked in. The atmosphere was full of tension; both men wore solemn expressions. 'What's happened?' she demanded. 'And where's Stephanie?'

Drew looked at her without speaking; she could see he was wondering how much to tell her.

'You may as well give it to her,' Jeffrey mumbled. 'Don't hold back on my account.'

'I caught Jeffrey putting up another of those – things,' Drew said. 'Only this time it had a bat and two rabbits attached to it. Stephanie's gone to Sally Harris's this morning, by the way – the woman in the village with the twins.'

Maggs blinked. 'Bats are protected,' she said foolishly. 'You're not allowed to kill them.'

'Bugger that,' snarled the gravedigger. 'I find bats in my roof, I'm goin' to kill 'em, protected or otherwise.'

'But *why*?' Drew pleaded, clearly not for the first time. 'You're not some sort of Satanist, are you?'

Maggs guffawed at that. 'Course he isn't,' she said scornfully. 'I bet you someone put him up to it. He'd never come up with that on his own.'

Drew frowned. 'I suppose only an insider

would know the best times to do it – and the places you can get in without coming through the gate. I chained it shut, like we said,' he told her.

'Why do you always feel guilty when something bad happens?' Maggs asked impatiently. 'Come to that,' she added, as a thought struck her, 'it was probably me that gave him the idea. Remember I told you we'd been talking about voodoo, weeks ago now?'

Drew shrugged his shoulders helplessly, and she turned to Jeffrey. 'How much did they pay you to mess things up for us with this rubbish?' she demanded.

The man stared at her stonily and said nothing.

'We thought you were part of the team,' said Drew reproachfully.

Maggs chewed her lip. 'I know who it must have been,' she announced. 'There's only one person who'd want to put us out of business before we get too popular.'

Drew seemed to come to life. He might be a bit feeble at times, Maggs thought, but he was never stupid. 'You mean Daphne Plant, don't you?' he said quietly. Keeping his eyes on the gravedigger, he repeated, 'Daphne Plant. That's right, isn't it, Jeffrey?'

'Might be,' the man mumbled. 'You'll never prove it, though.'

Maggs felt a surge of rage. 'Oh, yes, we will!' she said. 'We'll give the whole story to the papers. It'll be a challenge to Daphne to sue us for libel. And she won't dare do that, because the story'll be true.' She laughed shrilly. 'How about it, Drew? Isn't that what we should do?'

'It's an idea,' he agreed, slowly. 'But the papers would never co-operate. They'd want evidence first. And we couldn't give them that until we'd been to the police and made a complaint. Better just to go to Daphne direct, I should think.'

'And the letters!' Maggs remembered. 'Who sent those letters?'

Jeffrey looked genuinely confused. 'Don't know about no letters,' he asserted.

'Daphne herself must have done it,' Drew concluded. 'She surely wouldn't have involved anyone else – and I don't think Jeffrey even knows how to turn a computer on.'

'The devious cow,' stormed Maggs. 'And everyone thinking she's so respectable! Pillar of the community.'

'She must have seen us as a real threat,' Drew muttered. 'I never thought she'd take me so seriously.'

'But ye can't go to the police, can 'ee?' Jeffrey burst out. 'On account of that murdered woman out there, and you knowing more than you've let on. If the police get wind of what's been going on, it's trouble for you, Drew Slocombe.'

Drew crumbled, in the face of this sudden attack. 'I don't know what you're talking about,' he stammered.

'Oh, yes, you do. People coming to weep over the grave, cars coming past and stopping when they think nobody's looking. That grave's had more visitors in the past week than all the rest put together. For somebody with no name, that's a bit strange, to my mind. And if I were to go and tell the police about it, they'd have some nasty

368

questions for 'ee. Wouldn't like that, I dare say?'

Drew took a deep breath. 'When have you seen these people?' he asked. 'I only know of one man, who came a few days ago.'

Maggs backed him up. 'Yeah – I've only seen one man, too. And he was from the Council – wasn't he, Drew? Came to check everything had been done properly.'

'Bollocks!' said Jeffrey nastily. 'Don't you try your lies on me, girl. Council workers don't kneel in the grass blubbing over an unknown corpse. I saw 'un, when I passed by.'

'All right, that's enough,' said Drew, regaining control. 'We'll leave it for now. Just tell me, Jeffrey – do you still want to work for me here?'

'Work?' the man laughed derisively. 'Call that work? Buggerin' about with willow baskets and reading stupid poems over dead dogs?'

'I take it that's a no,' Drew returned, with dignity. 'In that case, I'd prefer not to see you around here again. Think yourself lucky we're letting you off so lightly. Maggs, we have things to do. We've wasted too much time already.'

'Right,' she said.

Drew and Maggs spent much of the morning debating her encounters of the previous evening. Drew was openly dismissive of her theory that Genevieve could have been responsible for her mother's death. 'Of course it wasn't Genevieve,' he insisted. 'It did cross my mind, but it makes no sense to think it might have been.'

'It starts to make a lot of sense,' Maggs countered. 'She hasn't told you a single word of truth from start to finish. Did you phone that hotel?'

'I think she's told me the truth as she sees it,' he disagreed quietly. 'And no – I got sidetracked by this business with Jeffrey. I'll do it in a minute.'

'They won't tell you anything unless you pretend you're the police. And I bet you daren't do that.'

'Watch me,' he said crossly, and grabbed the phone. Sparing no expense, he tapped in 192 for Directory Enquiries, and quickly got the number for the Regent Palace Hotel in London West One.

Refusing to meet Maggs's satirical eye, he plunged in when a voice announced that he was speaking to the hotel in question. 'Oh, hello. This is the West Somerset police here – I need confirmation of a booking you had last August. A Mr and Mrs Slater are claiming that they stayed the night of the twelfth with you. Would you check it for me, please?'

'Just hold the line,' came the unsuspecting voice. After a pause, in which he could hear a computer keyboard being tapped, he was told, 'Yes, I can confirm that. A double room, for a Mr and Mrs W Slater on the twelfth of August last year. Is that all you need?'

'Have you any way of knowing whether they did actually take up the booking? I mean – they didn't just reserve it and then not show up?'

'Definitely not. We have details of their payment, meals taken, room service – they were definitely here on that date. Though I can't say exactly what time they arrived.'

'That's very helpful. I'm much obliged to you.'

He put the phone down, just before Maggs let out a shriek of admiring laughter.

'I'm much obliged to you,' she mimicked. 'You sounded like somebody's butler.'

'They told me, though,' he smirked. 'They were definitely there that night.'

She squinted at him sceptically. 'All you know, Mr Clever Detective, is that two people calling themselves Slater stayed there. Oldest trick in the book – using someone else's name.'

Drew paused, and then shook his head. 'If they did, then that means there were at least four people in the conspiracy to kill Gwen – and I don't believe that.'

'Why not? Doctor Jarvis, Trevor and the Slaters – it would all fit quite nicely, if they were in it together, as a team.'

'You might as well throw in Henrietta Fielding and Karl Habergas while you're at it. You've got a full half-dozen then. And we wouldn't have a hope in hell of ever discovering what happened, because they'd all be lying their heads off. But I don't think it's anything as complicated as that.'

'Maybe Dr Jarvis was right all along – she committed suicide, and they all agreed to bury her, according to some sort of last request.'

'No.' Drew shook his head. 'There's some connection between all these different strands. If we put together every single thing we know about Gwen Absolon, we might work out what it is. But just now, what I should really be doing is driving over to Plant's and confronting Daphne with this story of Jeffrey's. The trouble is, I'd much rather face a suspected murderer with a wild set of accusations than do that.'

'You have to be subtle,' Maggs advised him. 'Let her think you're scared of tackling her – and then drop it on her when she's least expecting it. Preferably in front of a whole crowd of influential people, like doctors and nursing home matrons.'

Drew chuckled. 'If only,' he said, feeling more cheerful.

Maggs nodded towards the window. 'Looks as if we've got visitors. They look familiar.'

'It's the labrador people – the Graingers,' Drew said. 'How sweet. They've come to see the grave.'

'It's a wonder they haven't brought a bunch of flowers,' said Maggs sourly. 'Some people don't have anything better to do than dwell on the past. Imagine getting that morbid over an animal!'

'Don't be so heartless. Just for that, you can take them up the field. Do a bit of work for a change.'

Any chance of a sharp riposte was interrupted by the knock on the office door. Sticking her tongue out at Drew, Maggs pulled open the door, and adopted a saccharine smile. 'Good morning,' she said. 'Mr and Mrs Grainger, isn't it?'

'That's right,' Hubert Grainger confirmed, his voice gruffly surprised at being so swiftly identified. 'We were wondering if it was convenient to visit Seti's grave?'

'Our dog,' came the milder voice of his wife, as Maggs blinked at the odd name.

'Yes, of course,' gushed Maggs. 'Just follow me round this path, and I'll take you up there. You might not remember exactly where it is, otherwise.'

'Oh, I think we will,' said Hubert. 'But you're welcome to escort us.'

'*What* did you say your dog's name was?' Maggs asked curiously, as she strode ahead of them along the diagonal path towards the pets' area.

'Seti,' supplied Mildred.

'Ah,' Maggs murmured. 'Nice.'

'You seen to have had some new burials since we were last here,' the woman continued, pausing to cast a comprehensive glance across the field.

'Only two, I think,' Maggs replied. 'It's been a bit quiet for weeks now.'

'Really? Why's that, then?'

'It just happens like that. People seem to die in waves. It was the same when Drew worked at Plant's – you know, the undertaker in Bradbourne? But now we're starting to pick up a lot more business. Soon we'll be rushed off our feet. Of course, it's going to take time for people to make the change to our sort of service. Death rituals are very entrenched, and people are incredibly conservative – we knew that when we started. We think it'll turn round, though.'

'I'm sure you're right, dear. And meanwhile, you can do a nice sideline in pets, perhaps?'

'Well,' Maggs laughed, 'so far, you're our only customer. Here we are, look.' She stopped at the modest mound that was their dog's grave. Grass was beginning to grow over it; the absence of a marker made it difficult to identify.

'Hubert – we must put something here to show where he is,' the woman said. 'We can do that, can't we?' she turned to Maggs.

'Within reason. We prefer something wooden, or a living plant. Drew did say initially that he wouldn't allow stone memorials, but now he's decided a piece of natural rock would be acceptable.'

'That sounds nice – doesn't it, Hubert?' Mildred looked up at her husband, her expression a mixture of beseeching and a sudden acute grief. Maggs was bewildered.

'There, there, old girl,' he soothed. 'Keep a grip.'

Mildred Grainger sniffed and then squeezed her nose tightly between her thumb and forefinger. Maggs began to withdraw, wondering how anybody could be so attached to a dog. As if reading her mind, Mildred spoke to her.

'It's not just Seti, you see,' she apologised. 'We had another loss last year, and now anything to do with graves or dying can start me off.'

'Mildred!' her husband remonstrated. 'The young lady doesn't want to hear about our problems.'

'That's okay,' Maggs assured him. 'People often like to talk when they come here. It's understandable.'

'No, no – Hubert's right,' Mildred insisted. 'We should keep our grief to ourselves. I'm all right now.'

'I'll leave you, then,' said Maggs and strode away before they could embarrass themselves further.

In the office, she and Drew watched the couple potter around the graves. 'They had another loss last year, she said,' Maggs told him, 'and this is bringing it all back.'

'They said something about that when they first came here,' Drew remembered. 'Something about it being one tragedy after another. Sometimes trouble does come in spades.'

Maggs tried to busy herself with some paperwork. Drew continued to gaze out of the window. 'They're a long time up there,' he remarked, fifteen minutes after the Graingers had been left alone at the graveside. 'What on earth can they be doing?'

Maggs glanced in their direction. 'At least they're not kneeling in the wet grass,' she said. 'They must have some sense.'

Drew sighed heavily.

'What's the matter?' she asked.

'Need you ask? Jeffrey. Daphne. Karen. Genevieve—'

'They're going,' she interrupted. Together they watched the elderly couple make their way slowly down the field. Drew went to the back door of the office, and stood conspicuously, in case the Graingers wanted to speak to him.

'All right?' he asked politely, as they reached him.

'Yes, yes – thank you,' Hubert Grainger responded. 'We've put our minds at rest.' He looked back over his shoulder, oddly, not at the dog's grave, but further to the east.

'Good,' said Drew, a little mystified. 'That's good. Any time you want to come, feel free.' They disappeared around the side path, and he heard car doors slam a few moments later.

'What did he mean?' wondered Maggs. 'Putting

their minds at rest?'

'Probably heard rumours of witchcraft, like everybody else,' said Drew. 'Came to make sure the dog hadn't been dug up.'

'Funny name it's got,' she said. 'Setty. What sort of a name is that?'

'Oh, for God's sake!' Drew protested. 'We've got better things to do than worry about a labrador's name. I've got this cremation next week, where doubtless Desmond's going to make more snide remarks. And what the hell am I going to do about Daphne? How *could* she be so underhand? Bribing Jeffrey! It wasn't fair to him, apart from anything else. She must have known it could lose him his job.'

Maggs huffed a sarcastic breath. 'Don't get your knickers in a twist over Jeffrey,' she admonished. 'He knew what he was doing. If it'd been up to me, I'd have wiped the floor with him. He *betrayed* you. He's not worth bothering about.'

'And then there's Karen. I should spend lots of time with her this weekend. If you're right about her being depressed, she's going to need plenty of TLC.'

'I'll be doing a bit of that myself. I said I'd spend all day Sunday with Auntie Sharon. You wouldn't believe the stuff they've sent home with her! Her bedroom's like something out of *ER*.'

'Sounds grim,' he sympathised. 'Are you sure you can face it?'

'I'm going to have to. Though I'd rather deal with a dead body any day.' She heard herself and gave a horrified laugh. 'Listen to me! I really do love Auntie Sharon, you know. She's always good to talk to – I just have to try and forget she's ill. Don't you think?'

'Sounds the right sort of attitude to me. Nobody wants to be labelled as a cancer patient. It makes people forget who they really are.'

One of their companionable silences ensued, though neither of them now made even a pretence of being busy. Drew flipped through a trade magazine, reading with detachment an article on the escalating takeovers of British undertakers by the American-owned SCI. He found himself taking a degree of satisfaction in the inexorable march of sanitised, synthetic, over-priced funerals. Sooner or later, the population would rise up in protest, and that could only be to his direct benefit.

Maggs didn't appear to be doing anything at all. She sat in the wooden chair near the window, humming tunelessly to herself, apparently lost in thought. Suddenly, she stiffened. 'Sarah!' she said. 'Does that name mean anything to you?'

'Hmmm?' he mumbled. 'What d'you say?'

'Sarah. Somebody connected with Gwen Oojamaflip was called Sarah.'

'That's right. Sarah Gliddon. The girl who was killed in Egypt.'

'How old was she?'

Drew sighed, and accorded her his full attention. 'Twenty-seven, I think. I tried to speak to her husband, remember? He slammed the phone down on me.'

'Well, Gwen's handicapped son – Nathan – had a girlfriend called Sarah. She'd be that sort of age now. Stuart told me a bit about her. Said she was terribly fond of Nathan. She must have been devastated when he died.'

'It's a very common name. So what?'

'Well – how about this? What if it was the same girl? She kept in touch with Gwen, and decided to go on one of her trips. When she was killed, Genevieve somehow figured out who she was, and was so furious and jealous about her Ma still hanging on to memories of Nathan, she flipped and did her in. Makes sense, doesn't it? She's crazy enough for that, isn't she?'

'Absolutely not,' Drew disagreed vehemently. 'You've got to stop thinking it was Genevieve. You're getting obsessive about it. Unless you can stay open to the whole range of possibilities, you're just wasting time.'

She looked downcast. 'Maybe I was getting carried away. Right – you're right. It was a daft idea.'

'Well then,' he said, more calmly, 'let's stick to facts, eh?'

'Yes, boss,' she said meekly. 'But I bet you there is a connection somewhere. You said you were looking for connections.'

'That's true. Now who can I ask about women called Sarah, I wonder?'

They both knew there was only one possible person.

CHAPTER EIGHTEEN

The weekend started reasonably well. Karen was noticeably more cheerful, and Stephanie marked her eleven-month birthday by standing unsupported for several seconds, crowing triumphantly. 'She'll be walking before she's a year,' said Drew excitedly.

'I was two days under ten months,' said Karen. 'But I didn't talk until I was one and a half. They thought I was mentally defective.'

'I've no idea how old I was,' he sighed. 'I don't expect I was much of a prodigy.'

'You were thirteen months walking, and at fifteen months you knew a hundred words,' she said with authority. 'I asked your mother.'

'Amazing,' he laughed. 'First, that she can remember, and second that I was so articulate.'

'It's good that Steph won't be an only child,' Karen ventured, alerting Drew to the fact that she was in the mood to talk. 'I was always wishing I had brothers and sisters.'

'I wasn't,' Drew said, with feeling. 'Never much good at sharing, me. And I didn't see how my Mum would ever cope if she had more kids. She seemed impossibly busy, just with me.'

'Did you have an imaginary friend? Or kids to play with next door?'

'Nope. I had a cousin Nanette, who cried if I so much as touched her, and wore clothes she couldn't bear to get dirty. She was horrible – like a doll. She came with her mother sometimes, and I was supposed to play with her. I had no idea what I was meant to do.'

'You've turned out quite well, then, considering,' she said with a grin.

'It wasn't so bad. Later on, I felt quite grown up, coming home on my own to an empty house and getting the supper started. It was nice having all that space.'

'A child of your time,' she remarked. 'Latchkey kid.'

'Doesn't happen now. They go to after-school clubs, or someone's paid to meet them from school. Never get a minute to themselves, as far as I can see.'

'Yes,' she mumbled, clearly following another train of thought. 'Drew–'

'What?'

'I've told the Head I'm definitely not going back after this baby. I'm going to stay at home, whatever happens. That's all right, isn't it?'

He felt cold; a stiff breeze of responsibility chilled him to the bone. He turned his head away from his wife and daughter, struggling to give an acceptable reply. 'It – well – it changes things,' he said. 'It puts more pressure on the business. We'll have to do some sums, to see whether it'll work.'

'We won't need to buy much,' she persisted. 'We can get by without new clothes, and I can grow veg in the garden. I'll get Maternity Benefit for a bit. And maybe by the winter, you'll be bringing in a lot more money.'

'I haven't had that two thousand quid yet,' he

380

admitted. 'I'm not sure she'll ever actually give it to me. I'm not sure I can rely on her promises.' The reference to Genevieve was rash, it brought a renewed flood of physical reaction that took his breath away. He was full of a terrible ache, guilt and sadness finding expression in his bloodstream and nervous system.

'You'll get it,' said Karen fiercely, 'if I have to go and demand it myself. She's caused enough trouble, without withholding payment from you. You've earned that money – every penny of it.'

He laughed weakly. 'Perhaps you're right,' he said. 'And when we get it, we'll buy a lot of sensible things, and save the rest for the electricity bill.'

At weekends, the office phone was redirected to the house, so that Peaceful Repose calls and personal ones all rang through on the instrument in the Slocombes' kitchen. When Drew answered it at twelve forty-five on Saturday, just as Karen was ladling out thick tomato soup into bowls for them both, he had no way of knowing just how important a call it would turn out to be.

'Is that Peaceful Repose Funerals?' came a female voice. On Drew's confirmation, it continued, 'This is St Joseph's Hospice – in West Whittleham. We have a Mrs Hilda Jones for you. We don't have a mortuary, so we'd be grateful if you could come today.'

'West Whittleham?' Drew spluttered. 'That's thirty miles away. Are you sure it's me you want?'

'There's no mistake. I expect the relatives will contact you shortly. Mrs Jones has only been with us for five days. A very sad cause. She had pancreatic cancer, and it wasn't diagnosed until the very final stages. It's all been very sudden.'

'Could you give me the name of the next of kin?' Drew asked.

'Hang on a minute.' He could hear papers rustling, and some whispering, before the woman came back. 'Mrs Caroline Kennett, from Cullompton. She's the niece. I'll give you her number–' She recited a string of digits. Drew hurriedly wrote them down.

'I'll try and be there before five,' he told her. 'I'll have to contact my partner first.'

Karen made him finish his soup before trying to locate Maggs. His stunned surprise took some time to wear off.

'She came here a couple of weeks ago,' he said. 'Mrs Kennett, that is. Maggs showed her round. She's the woman who witnessed the burial of that body last summer. Or thinks she did. The police didn't seem too sure. She must have decided we'd do for her aunt. What an extraordinary way to get business.'

It was three-thirty before they heard Maggs's bike revving outside. She'd been out when Drew called, and her mother had no idea where she'd gone; all she could do was promise to pass on the message the moment she returned. 'Phew!' sighed Drew. 'We'll just about make it. Where've you been?'

'Shopping,' she said. 'Not that it's any of your business.'

He'd got the van ready, and looked up the route they'd have to take to the hospice. Caroline

Kennett still hadn't made contact, and he'd been hesitant to bother her. Protocol decreed that the first contact should come from the family, but in this instance, he was very unsure. His training at Plant's in that respect had been very thorough. 'What if she changes her mind?' he said. 'We'll be accused of abducting the aunt's body.'

'Nonsense,' Karen had scoffed. 'You've had your instructions from the hospice. If she changes her mind now, you can bill her for your wasted time and petrol.'

Maggs was excited by the whole episode. 'This is more like it!' she crowed. 'A real live call-out. Just like Plant's.'

'Sixty miles, round trip,' Drew reminded her. 'We won't be back until six or later. And then you'll have to stay on a bit, laying her out. The good news is, it doesn't sound as if she had time for any chemotherapy. You know what that does to them.'

'Too right,' she said grimly. Bodies arriving from a hospice were notoriously unpleasant; the combination of terminal cancer and massive doses of chemicals generally led to almost immediate putrefaction. For an undertaker abjuring embalming, this could cause unsavoury problems.

'Off we go, then,' he sang, waving a cheery farewell to Karen and Stephanie.

The route he'd picked out lay through a number of small villages: one of them happened to be Fenniton, where Genevieve lived. 'What a coincidence,' said Maggs, ingenuously.

When they arrived, the hospice receptionist

directed them to a small room at the back of the building, where the body lay on a bench, wrapped in a thin white sheet. 'No need for cremation papers, thank goodness,' said the nurse who'd shown them the way. 'That's always a relief, especially with someone from a distance.'

'Where did she live?' asked Drew curiously. 'Not Cullompton, surely?'

'No, I don't think so,' said the woman vaguely. 'Some small town over your way. Don't you know the family, then? The niece seemed to have a very high regard for you.'

Maggs preened. 'Looks as if we made a good impression.'

In the van again, she remembered something. 'Mrs Kennett said she had an aunt,' she recalled. 'She was going to visit her, and got a taxi to us, before going there for lunch. Didn't say where her auntie lived, though.'

Heading west, into the setting sun, Drew was forced to drive slowly. The dappled shadow of trees lining the country lanes alternated with sudden bursts of blinding sunlight. They followed the same route as before; as they approached Fenniton, Maggs gave a sudden yell. 'There's Stuart!' she shouted. 'Why isn't he at work?'

Drew slowed down. 'Presumably he gets a day off sometimes. Do you want me to stop?'

'Oh, well–' She hesitated. 'Okay.'

The boy looked up in surprise as the vehicle drew up beside him. Maggs leaned out of the window. 'Hiya!' she said.

'Oh – hi!' he managed, as he recognised her.

'What are you up to?'

'We've been on a removal,' she said, importantly. 'We've got a body in the back.'

'Maggs!' Drew reproached her. 'Mind what you say.'

'Oh, Stuart won't be upset – will you?' she breezed. 'He lives on a farm – he's used to death.'

'I need to be, round here,' he said irritably. 'I've just been listening to the woman next door moaning on about her friend dying all of a sudden. You'd think it had never happened to anybody before. *Only seventy-three, and never a day's illness. Then she has to go and die of cancer before we know what's happening.*' He mimicked a tremulous old woman's voice. '*Poor Hilda – she had so much to live for.*' He shook his head. 'I shouldn't mock, I know, but you ought to have heard her.'

'*Hilda?*' repeated Drew and Maggs on a single note. 'Not – Hilda Jones?' added Drew incredulously.

'No idea,' Stuart said, staring. 'She was in a hospice, miles away. Died last night. Cancer of the pancreas, apparently.'

'Well, fancy that,' said Maggs cheerfully. 'Small world, eh?'

Drew didn't say anything. He was congratulating himself on successfully biting back the question: *How's Genevieve?*

Drew phoned Caroline Kennett as soon as he got in. The residual influence of Plant's made him impatient with families who were dilatory in contacting the undertaker, even though he knew quite well that they had innumerable other things to do, as well as coping with grief, shock, denial and bewilderment. A man's voice answered.

'Is that Mr Kennett?'

'Speaking,' came the voice. 'Who's this?'

'My name's Drew Slocombe – from Peaceful Repose Funerals. I'm phoning to tell you that your wife's aunt is now here in our cool room. We've just collected her from the hospice, as requested. Um – under the circumstances, it would be very helpful if you or your wife could call in here on Monday, to make all the necessary arrangements. We'd hope to have the burial by Wednesday at the latest.' He grimaced to himself, knowing that by Wednesday the body would have probably begun to decompose quite noticeably.

'*Wednesday!*' the man repeated. 'Good grief. That's a bit quick, isn't it?'

Drew stifled a sigh. This was going to be a recurrent problem, he realised. People who chose him for their funerals without a full awareness of the implications would have to be told some unpalatable facts, particularly in warm weather. Not for the first time, he wondered why it was that Britain went in for such delayed funerals. Even in America, where embalming was the norm, they left a scant two or three days between the death and the disposal in most cases. The majority of countries across the world managed it in twenty-four hours.

'Not really,' he said patiently. 'Considering she died last night. If it helps, I can take your instructions over the phone.'

'I'll fetch Caroline,' the man said heavily.

'Hello?' came a woman's hesitant voice, a minute later.

'Mrs Kennett,' said Drew. 'Has your husband explained that we have Mrs Jones here now, in North Staverton? I'll need to ask you for a few questions, about the sort of funeral you'd like. And I assume you've been told about registering the death? That has to be done before we can go ahead with the burial. I was just saying to Mr Kennett that we really do need to do it by Wednesday at the latest.'

'We never thought she'd die so quickly,' blurted the woman. 'I can't believe it yet. Poor Uncle George is never going to come to terms with it.'

'She has a husband?'

'Yes, but he's not capable of making any arrangements. I'm having to do everything for him. He's practically senile now, poor old chap. It's got much worse over the past few months.'

'Sad,' Drew sympathised.

'Yes. But poor Aunt Hilda!' she returned to the main subject. 'I was only chatting to her yesterday afternoon. Telling her about your field, and how nice it all was. And she suddenly said she wanted to be buried there. She knew about it already, of course, from the papers. She'd been taking an interest, as it happens. Funny how things come together, isn't it? I told her how I'd seen something from the train, and she said she'd been wondering about that woman, ever since she first read about it.'

Drew politely let her prattle on, not really listening, running through in his head all the things he and Maggs would have to do on

387

Monday. Wondering who'd dig the grave, now Jeffrey had gone.

At last there was a pause. 'So you can come and see us on Monday?' he interposed. 'I can show you where she'll be buried – and you can decide on a coffin. The best thing would be for you to go and register the death first – I'm afraid that'll have to be at the Registrar's office in West Whittleham. I checked at the hospice for you, and they open at ten. The office is in South Street. You need a doctor's certificate, if they haven't provided it already, and then get the death certificate–' Although this had never been part of his work at Plant's, Drew knew the procedure off by heart. The bureaucracy of it offended him at times – forcing confused relatives to travel around the county chasing doctors and registrars – but he also knew that he could help by breaking it down into easy stages.

'Oh, goodness,' the woman bleated. 'It all sounds very time-consuming. Especially as I don't drive.'

'Can't your husband take you?'

'No – he'll be at work. But my son might.' Drew left it at that; there was a limit to how much he could do to assist.

'Let me give you my phone number, and we can talk again tomorrow, if there's a problem,' he offered. 'This is really just to let you know that everything's in hand. I don't want to push you into making any decisions tonight.'

'Thank you,' she said breathily. 'Poor Aunt Hilda! She was so full of life. Such a sharp mind. She had quite a theory about that body in your

388

field. But I told her not to be silly. For two pins, she'd have gone to the police about it months ago, she said. But then she got poorly, and forgot about it.'

This time, Drew *was* listening. But he refrained from appearing too eager. 'That's interesting,' he said lightly. 'I'll look forward to hearing all about it when I see you.'

Sunday passed quietly, with no further contact from Mrs Kennett. Drew left her in peace, assuming she'd sorted out her transport difficulties and knew what she needed to do the following morning. The phone remained silent and a cloudless sky ensured it was the warmest day of the year so far. Drew decided to give their small garden some attention.

Originally, the garden had been part of the field attached to the cottage, and was still separated from it only by a rather unprepossessing chain link fence. The new office, created out of a rickety lean-to, extended beyond the fenced-off area, so there was direct access from the office's back door to the burial ground – essential for carrying coffins to a grave. The garden, however, presented an incongruous image; it had been neglected for ten years or more. Shrubs had burgeoned thickly in one corner – rhododendrons, mainly, but there were also nettles and thistles in profusion. The whole area, measuring something like forty feet by a hundred, needed a complete overhaul, ideally employing a rotovator. Today, though, Drew contented himself with digging out nettles, roots and all, cutting back a straggly and vicious rambling rose, and piling his trophies into a big bonfire. He admitted to himself that he wasn't working primarily for the sake of the garden – but in order to create some thinking time.

He was not inclined to take seriously Mrs Kennett's Aunt Hilda's fanciful theories about the dead woman – but the fact that she had a theory at all was intriguing. It suggested that there might be other people out there, mulling over what they'd read, exchanging ideas, piecing together oddments of information, until they slowly arrived at a complete picture.

The Slocombes lived in an area where people still maintained family and neighbourly connections, meeting at Women's Institutes, in the supermarket, at work and in the pub. They talked over the weekly news, passed on gossip, expressed their entrenched opinions. Murder, and a new way of burying the dead, would obviously feature prominently in these conversations. It was no real surprise that Aunt Hilda thought she knew who the dead woman might have been. As Stuart had told them, her friend lived next door to the Slaters. She would doubtless have seen Gwen last summer, and probably taken note of her height and general appearance. She might even have admired the Egyptian necklace. None of that was in the least unlikely. But it was just one scenario: probably a thousand other individuals nursed their own private theories on the matter too, every bit as plausible.

Drew followed the chain of reasoning again. Genevieve's next-door neighbour was close friends with Caroline Kennett's aunt. Four people. And didn't they say that everyone in the world was connected by just such a chain? Wasn't it only six or seven links before we were all somehow connected – all eight billion of us? If that was true – and surely it couldn't be – then how likely it became that four women, all aged between forty and seventy, living within twenty miles of each other, should be connected. The wild card, the Joker, was the added coincidence of Caroline Kennett being on that particular train at that particular time, and having it stop at that precise point on the line. Now *that*, he decided, was weird. But even that could be explained away. He knew trains did often stop just there, for reasons which he supposed involved a signal or a junction somewhere down the line. In fact, North Staverton had once had its own tiny halt, long ago abandoned as an official stop, but perhaps still in need of a cautious approach.

It was, at least, an intriguing intellectual exercise. It highlighted the realities of human relations, while at the same time warning him against jumping to conclusions.

Maggs confessed to a very similar line of reasoning, when they compared notes on Monday morning. 'I just know there's some sort of connection with this Sarah woman,' she insisted.

'Maybe Mrs Kennett will settle it for us,' he said optimistically.

'I doubt it,' she said. 'If she knew enough to do that, she'd have gone to the police.'

'She hasn't had time. Her auntie only told her on Friday, and then promptly died. Talk about deathbed confessions!'

They waited impatiently for Caroline Kennett to put in an appearance, unable to make any firm preparations for the funeral until they knew what she wanted. He spent a few minutes playing with Stephanie, fitting plastic cups inside each other, hiding things under them, praising her when she quickly picked up the nature of the game. Then he handed her a Marmite sandwich and left her to continue on her own. So long as she thought he was watching with all due approval, she was content to co-operate.

The enforced idleness gave Drew all the opportunity he needed to think afresh about Genevieve. He even permitted himself to talk about her. 'The baby's five days old now,' he remarked, into a long silence. 'I wonder how she's coping.'

'Do you want me to go and find out?' Maggs's reply came so eagerly that he stared at her in surprise.

'You sound keen. Thought you didn't like babies,' he said, before the penny dropped. Her darkened cheeks gave her away, along with the averted gaze. 'It's that Stuart, isn't it,' he teased. 'You want to see him again.'

'What if I do?' she flared. 'He's a nice guy, and he knows things that might help us get this business settled.'

'He seemed pleased to see you too,' Drew said kindly. 'As far as I could tell.' His own illicit and shameful yearnings seemed sordid compared to the fresh young attraction between Maggs and

Stuart; he felt a sort of benign envy.

'So, can I?' she persisted. 'Go and see them again?'

'Not now,' Drew decided. 'Give it a few more days.'

But events superseded Maggs's intentions. At twelve o'clock, they heard a motorbike approaching, and exchanged meaningful glances. Maggs rushed outside, making no pretence at playing hard to get. 'It's him!' she called back to Drew. He'd never heard her so excited.

Stuart came shyly into the office, clutching his crash helmet to his chest. He eyed Stephanie with a momentary surprise, then shrugged and laughed. 'Kids everywhere,' he muttered. 'Can't get away from them.'

'What can we do for you?' Drew asked. 'We were just talking about you.'

Maggs shot him a fierce warning glance, and he said no more, remembering the terror of being teased in front of a new friend or potential lover. He didn't think she'd ever had a boyfriend, and her sudden display of vulnerability touched him. He was just wondering whether he should make an excuse to give them some time together, when he heard a car drawing up outside.

'Looks like Mrs K,' he said. 'You two might have to leave me alone with her for a bit.'

'You can show me my gran's grave – if that's what it is,' said Stuart. 'That's really what I came for.'

Drew orchestrated the next few minutes with some skill. Maggs and Stuart walked up the field, heads close together, while Drew settled Caroline Kennett into the larger of the two office chairs and took her through the details of the funeral, offering her a variety of choices at every juncture. She was obviously out of her depth, and he suggested she bring her son in from the car. It seemed odd that he should sit outside on his own.

'No, no,' she shook her head, 'he says he can't face it. He's always been rather sensitive about this sort of thing. He didn't want even to bring me, to be honest, but there wasn't any option.'

'Did he know Mrs Jones well?'

'Hardly at all. I could never persuade him to go and see her. He found her rather scary when he was little, and never really got over it, I think. She *was* a bit eccentric,' she added.

Which is why she wanted to be buried here, thought Drew ruefully; it was going to be a long time before burial grounds like his were the norm.

'Well,' he pressed on, 'we've decided on a shaped cardboard coffin, carried by me and my assistant, helped by your husband and your son. How many people do you think will attend? Will they mind that there's no church service first?'

Caroline sighed. 'There are five or six friends who might come along. But the distance makes it awkward for them. Uncle George should be here, of course. He should be doing this now, instead of me. But he's just not up to it.'

'No, you said. Poor man,' said Drew with feeling. He paused, contemplating the cruelties of old age and death.

'To be honest, I think George would have

chosen a normal funeral,' she confided. 'But once Aunt Hilda had heard about this place, she couldn't think of anything else. It's my own fault, I suppose. I should never have opened my mouth about coming here.'

Drew raised his eyebrows encouragingly; he had a feeling a few more jigsaw pieces were about to be forthcoming.

Mrs Kennett obligingly continued. 'You see, Hilda's best friend, Vera Mannion, lives next door to some people called Slater. And Mrs Slater had a mother – Gwen something. Last summer, this Gwen was staying with her daughter for a few days, and she got chatting with Vera – well, everybody does, she's a terrible busybody. This Gwen told her she'd been to Egypt recently. She – Vera, that is – made some comment about the woman's lovely thick hair. Really dark grey, it was. Very eye-catching, she said – or something of the sort. "Oh dear," said the woman, "I hope not. I wanted to remain unobtrusive for a while." Well, Vera laughed about that and said she was far too tall and striking for that. And anyway, why should she want such a thing? Then this Gwen apparently got very upset and said there might be people looking for her, and she was staying out of sight as long as she could, because there might be trouble if they found her.'

Drew kept his reaction cool. 'How odd,' he murmured. 'I wonder what she meant by that?'

'Well, Vera asked her, of course – but she wouldn't say any more. She left a day or two afterwards and was never seen again.' She paused for dramatic effect. 'But you can see how she might have jumped to conclusions, reading what was in the paper. A tall, elderly woman with some sort of Egyptian necklace, buried not ten miles away from Gwen's daughter's house. Vera and Aunt Hilda between them decided the body in your field here must definitely be the same woman – this Gwen.'

'So why didn't one of them go to the police?'

'Well, Vera didn't like to. Neither did Auntie Hilda, for that matter. For one thing, she was worried about the effect on Uncle George, if she started getting involved with the police. And Vera hadn't the nerve to go on her own – she thought it would make for bad feeling with the Slaters – which it would, of course. But she kept thinking she should, and last week, they'd almost decided to do it. There was more, you see.' She paused again for dramatic effect. 'She heard Willard Slater telling his mother-in-law, she ought to be dead. Something about her deserving to be punished for what she'd done, she was such a callous bitch.' She whispered the last word. 'That's what he called her. And some other things that Aunt Hilda wouldn't tell me. So, of course, they felt awful about keeping it to themselves – but they just never managed to get up the nerve to tell the police. I mean, you can understand it, can't you? They knew the police would tell the Slaters where they'd got their information–'

'I don't think they would,' Drew argued mildly. 'But I can see your point.'

'I don't know Mr Slater at all, myself. It could all be a silly mistake, from start to finish. And I only made it worse when I told Auntie about what I'd seen from the train. I only hope it wasn't the worry of it that helped kill her. I never should have told her what I saw – that really set her off, and no mistake. But it isn't too late. As soon as this funeral is over and done with, I'm going to tell the police myself.' She clamped her lips together determinedly.

Drew closed his eyes, in shock and fear. *So it's right back to Square One* he thought.

Maggs stood back as Stuart knelt unselfconsciously beside the new grave. 'Funny things, families,' she murmured after a while, sensing that he'd had enough silence, but not sure how to break it.

'Yeah,' he nodded. 'I never knew her, but now she's dead, I feel as if a big hole's been cut in my life. I *wanted* to know her – to talk about travelling and stuff. There's something about Egypt in particular – it must be in the blood. Willard's crazy about the place, though he hasn't been for twenty years. Got loads of books about it all over the place. And the only good talk I ever had with Nathan was about the Pyramids. Sarah'd got him interested – she was always on about mummies and those old gods they had. Even named her dog after some Pharaoh.'

Maggs stood completely still, a hand across her mouth.

He frowned at her. 'What's the matter with you?'

'Nothing.' She was torn between the pleasure of being with him, and the urgent need to run back to the office and tell Drew she'd been right about Sarah. She *had* to be right. The decision was made when she remembered that he still had the Kennett woman with him.

'Why don't we go for a walk, if you've finished here?' she suggested. 'There's a nice bit of woodland down the lane.'

'I'm finished,' he said.

Half an hour later, they returned along the winding lane, in time to see Drew and Mrs Kennett standing beside her car together. They shook hands, and she got in beside the patiently-waiting Jason.

'Drew looks a bit agitated,' Maggs observed. 'Wonder what she's asked him to do?'

Without noticing the pair, Drew went back into the office, and Maggs hurried to catch up with him. Stuart trailed behind her. They all met at the door, Drew with Stephanie perched on his arm.

'Out of the way!' he said impatiently. 'I've got to go out.'

'But I've got something to tell you,' Maggs protested. 'It's important.'

'So is this,' he flung back. Then he looked at Stuart. 'I've got to go and see your uncle and aunt,' he said. 'There's a witness who's convinced that Willard killed Genevieve's mother, and she's talking about going to the police.'

'Wait a minute,' Maggs ordered him. 'If there is good evidence, and somebody else supplies it to the police, that lets you off the hook, doesn't it? And if it doesn't turn out to be anything, there's no harm done.'

'He didn't do it.' Drew stared her in the eye. 'We've got the alibi from the hotel. Genevieve got the whole thing upside down. If the police get hold of Willard's name now, they'll ruin everything.'

'So how are you going to stop them?'

He shook his head in frustration. 'I don't know – I just have to be there. One last time.'

He hurriedly strapped the sleepy Stephanie into her seat in the van, and was driving off before Stuart or Maggs could reply.

CHAPTER NINETEEN

There was a familiar car outside the Slaters' house. Drew hoiked Stephanie hurriedly out of her seat and charged up the path to the side door. His intemperate knocking was answered by Dr Jarvis; the baby's crying was clearly audible. 'Saw your car,' said Drew curtly. 'It looks as if we can all be in at the kill.'

The older man blinked, and blew out his cheeks. 'Steady on, my friend,' he warned. 'You're walking into something of a disaster here. I'm not even sure I should let you in–'

Drew shouldered past him, using Stephanie as a lever. In order to stop him, Doctor Jarvis would be forced to lay hands on the child. 'Too late,' Drew said. 'You already have.'

Willard and Genevieve were standing in the living room. The besmirched sofa was obviously still uncleaned, judging from the smell, although a large blue blanket had been thrown over it. The baby lay on the armchair, red-faced and noisy. Even its bunched fists were red; Drew could see it had worked itself into a paroxysm of enraged misery. Stephanie twitched in alarmed sympathy.

'What's the matter with her?' Drew asked. All his instincts screamed to gather the baby up, do what he could to pacify it, but with his own daughter already ensconced in his arms, there was little he could do.

'Genevieve's taken against it,' said Willard bleakly. 'Says she doesn't want it.'

'More to the point, she's stopped feeding it,' added Doctor Jarvis. 'I've just been phoning the domiciliary midwife, trying to get hold of some formula, bottles and so forth. The poor child's starving. The nephew's gone missing just when we need him.'

'But–' Drew stared around the three faces, wondering once again what sort of madhouse this was. 'But, hasn't there been somebody visiting? Somebody who could have seen this coming?'

Nobody bothered to reply. The baby's wails made conversation difficult. Stephanie wriggled, and Drew decided that her need was less than the baby's. He put her down on the floor and scooped up the little one, all in one rapid movement.

The wails diminished instantly, but did not abate entirely. He felt the universal male helplessness inherent in such a situation. Without a bottle and some substitute milk, there was little he could do to satisfy the suffering infant. But he couldn't endure the noise, and instinctively thrust his little finger into the rigid mouth. With pitiful desperation, it clamped down and began to suck feverishly. It hurt. He could feel the hunger and the fear. But at least the child stopped crying. Relief settled on the room like sunshine flooding through the window. 'Thank Christ for that,' said Genevieve. Drew noticed for the first time that she was still wearing the knitted coat he'd found for her as the baby was being born. Willard looked tired and distracted; Doctor Jarvis was flushed with anxiety.

'What you do with your baby is none of my business,' Drew began. 'I came about the death of Gwen Absolon. I can see this is a bad time, but now I'm here, I might as well say my piece.' He looked at Willard, forcing the man to meet his gaze. 'I've just been told that you were overheard threatening her shortly before she went missing,' he said. 'And that there's a strong chance that the story will be passed to the police, later this week. Whether or not it's true, whether or not you killed your mother-in-law – you'll be questioned, investigated and possibly charged. I came to give you a chance to do something about it.'

'But the tickets!' said Genevieve, indignantly. 'We've got those tickets! The hotel will have a record of our being there that night. And you said there was someone who knows the exact date it all happened–'

'By a strange coincidence, that witness is the same person who's planning to go to the police,' Drew told her. 'I suspect there are quite a few people out there now who think they know who the mystery body is. It would only be a matter of time before they come forward. But yes – your best hope is the Regent Palace Hotel. They've got a full record of your stay there, and there's a chance they'll be able to identify you. But, Genevieve–' He struggled to keep all emotion out of his voice, 'I'd like a truthful answer from you. Just for my own satisfaction. Do you really know who killed your mother?'

Afterwards, he wondered whether she would

ever have answered him. As it was, the doorbell rang and the appearance of a health visitor, laden down with equipment for feeding the baby, interrupted proceedings entirely. She took the hungry infant from Drew's arms, his finger throbbing and swollen. Stephanie began to grizzle.

Doctor Jarvis hovered around the newcomer, assisting her in the task of preparing a feed, muttering about the trouble he'd walked into. 'I'm not even her doctor, you know,' Drew heard him say. 'Just a friend of the family.' They threw questioning glances at Genevieve, who had hardly moved since Drew's arrival.

'Puerperal psychosis,' said the health visitor, quite audibly. Drew wondered if that could indeed be the explanation for the way Genevieve was acting.

But, 'No,' she said loudly, as if in reply to his thought. 'It goes back a lot further than that.' She dropped into the armchair, and rubbed her knuckles across her mouth, echoing her baby's frantic search for nourishment.

'I was twelve,' she said, gazing up at Drew. Slowly he sank onto the floor at her feet, Stephanie on his lap, cuddled against his chest. He rested his chin gently on the top of her soft head, not entirely sure which was protector and which the protected.

'I was the only one who remembered, afterwards, exactly what had happened. My mother and father were fighting. He said she should have aborted the baby, that there was no space in their lives for another one. She said it was his fault in the first place, and how dare he expect her to live with the guilt and trauma of an abortion. He said he didn't think she was capable of feeling guilt. She hit him. She punched the side of his head, while he was driving. The car swerved, just as a huge lorry was coming towards us. It was going downhill, so fast. I still see it in my dreams – like a dragon, rushing at us. It caught the front corner of our car, pulling us along with it.' She hugged her arms around herself, her face white. 'The noise!' she moaned. 'Tearing metal and breaking glass, and my mother screaming, the lorry hooting its horn on and on. Like the end of the world. Then, ages later, complete silence.' She was silent herself for several seconds.

'I had a fractured skull, broken scapula, torn ligaments. I was sitting behind Daddy, you see. Mummy and Brigid were just bruised. I spent a month in hospital. They were afraid I'd be brain damaged if I didn't keep still and let my head mend. My father died. *Nobody* came to visit me.' She fixed Drew with a glittering gaze. 'She never once came to visit me. Can you believe that?'

'She was pregnant, in shock, newly widowed. I advised her not to risk upsetting herself,' said Doctor Jarvis from the kitchen doorway. 'You were all bandaged up, your hair shaved off – they didn't know whether you'd ever fully recover. I told her it would be too painful to see you.'

'Then perhaps all this is your fault,' said Genevieve flatly, with the shadow of a bitter smile.

'Perhaps it is,' he agreed.

When he got back to the van, Drew found Maggs sitting in the passenger seat. 'Stuart had to go to

404

work,' she said, 'so I hitched a ride on his pillion. I didn't know when you might be coming back, and I don't think we should waste any more time.'

Drew sighed, and slowly strapped Stephanie into her seat. 'She's hungry,' he said absently. 'I've got to give her some lunch. I should have brought something with me.'

'Haven't they got anything in the house?'

He glared at her angrily. 'In that house they've got a starving baby, a mentally disturbed woman and two useless men who between them have turned this whole mess into a grotesque tragedy. It didn't seem appropriate to start searching the kitchen for a snack for Stephanie.'

'Okay,' she placated. 'Let's go back, then, quick as we can. Steph doesn't look too desperate to me.'

'Comparatively speaking, she isn't. But after what I've just witnessed, I've got no intention of neglecting her needs – not for a minute.' He was already starting the van as he spoke.

'I've got something to tell you,' she ventured, after a few minutes, 'and I think you ought to listen.'

'Go on, then,' he invited. 'But I don't know how much attention I'll give you. If you only knew what it was like–'

'Sarah Gliddon was *definitely* the same Sarah who was Nathan Slater's girlfriend. No doubt about it. She kept in touch with Gwen after Nathan died – and she was very keen on Egypt. She even named her dog after some old Pharaoh.' She dropped the last remark carelessly, watching him out of the corner of her eye for a reaction. 'It took me at least a minute to see how *that* fitted in,' she added.

It took Drew rather longer than that. In fact, Maggs accused him later of being so uncharacteristically slow-witted he'd never have got there without some help.

'I asked him, while we were on the bike, what sort of dog Sarah had,' she prompted. 'Guess what he said?'

Drew took his eyes off the road for an instant, staring at her in disbelief. 'Surely not a labrador? *What* did the Graingers say theirs was called?'

'Seti. S-E-T-I. Wasn't he one of the Pharaohs? I seem to remember him from a project I did at school. He's one that they still have the mummy of, in a museum in Cairo. I remember being fascinated by the pictures.'

'But–' Drew protested. 'But–'

'They said they had another sad loss last year. Another tragedy. Must have been their daughter. Mustn't it? Maybe they took the dog on when she left home. Drew – don't you think–?'

'I think we've got to give Stephanie some lunch. After that, I don't know *what* I'm going to think.'

Maggs chafed impatiently all afternoon, while Drew pleaded with her to calm down. He could hardly listen to what she was saying; his head was still full of the Slater tragedy. In the end, she decided she'd do best by letting him get it out of his system.

'Gwen ruined Genevieve's life, you know. It was

406

Gwen's fault that Nathan was born with such defects – and that the father was killed. I reckon, subconsciously, that's why she came to me in the first place.' He punched the table lightly, to mark the dawning insight.

'Explain,' invited Maggs.

'To satisfy herself that the woman really was dead. She told herself that she was doing it to ease her conscience – but the idea that someone might have murdered her mother didn't horrify her half as much as it should. Even if it was Willard she'd have forgiven him. It might even have endeared him to her. That's why she wouldn't go to the police, and why she lost interest in the investigation after we'd pretty much ascertained the body was Gwen's. She hated her mother enough to want her dead. It would be easily worth two thousand quid to have it confirmed. She could never forgive her mother, you see.' He shuddered. 'I could feel the hatred. She isn't fit to bring that baby up, and she knows it. Inside, she's still a child herself. She'd do best to give the baby up for adoption. There are thousands of couples who'd give it a loving home.'

Maggs folded her arms on the desk, and rested her chin on them, eyeing him critically. 'It isn't that easy,' she said in a muffled voice. 'Adoption, I mean.'

He met her eye uneasily.

'It all seems very logical, I know,' she said. 'On the one hand you've got people with such messy lives they can't cope with their own baby. They'd forget to feed it, or spend half the time dead

407

drunk, or knock it about. So the nice social workers step in. *We've got this lovely young childless couple in the better part of town. She's got infected tubes – or he's got sluggish sperm – they'd be the perfect parents for the poor little thing.* I know about this, Drew. It happened to me.'

'But it *worked* for you. You get on brilliantly with the people who adopted you.'

She sighed. 'Yes, I do. I did more or less from the start. That's not the point.'

'Of course it's the point,' he told her crossly. 'Don't tell me you'd rather be knocked about, neglected, resented. And worse – much worse than that can happen, you know.'

'You don't understand,' she said regretfully. 'You wouldn't – you're the sort of person the social workers would call the perfect parent.'

He absorbed that without response. 'So – you think Genevieve should keep the baby, do you?'

'I didn't say that. It's not for me to say what anybody should do. I only said, it's not that easy.'

He let her have the last word.

'Can't we talk about Sarah now?' she asked, after a few minutes. 'Have we got Genevieve Slater out of the way for today?'

'All right then,' he sighed. 'Run it past me again.'

She repeated what Stuart had told her about Sarah Gliddon, her dog and the glaring implications. Or some of them – Drew still wasn't quite sure why she wanted to go rushing through the countryside so urgently.

'Nobody's going to *go* anywhere,' he told her. 'They can't possibly know that we've made the connection. We'll have to wait for Karen to get home. And even then–'

'We're going to see them,' she ordered him sternly. 'And see what they've got to say for themselves.'

'You mean, we march in, and demand to know why they never told us their daughter knew Gwen Absolon. That's the only thing we can accuse them of, and that wouldn't make any sense. It's amazing to think that they might have run slap bang into Genevieve, though, when they first came about the dog. She was right here, just the other side of the door. Imagine how that would have changed things.'

'How would it?'

'Well, if she'd realised who they were–' Drew spoke slowly '–she would have wondered what they were doing here. How they knew about this place.'

'They said they saw it in the papers, like everyone else,' Maggs put in impatiently. 'What else?'

'Well, if they'd recognised her – and it's very likely they'd met when Nathan was alive – they'd have known that she knew about Sarah being killed. Because they knew she was Gwen's daughter.'

Maggs interrupted. 'This is all just talk. When can we have some *action*?'

'Simon Gliddon!' Drew remembered, with a jolt. 'I never did manage to speak properly to Simon Gliddon.' He looked up at Maggs, eyes sparkling with certainty. 'Trevor said Simon blamed Gwen for Sarah's death. I was going to try and get to see him in person. But he lives in

Salisbury. Maggs – the person we really want is Simon Gliddon.'

'We're not going to see Simon Gliddon,' she told him, obstinately. 'We're going to see the Graingers.'

It was five o'clock when Maggs and Drew walked along the row of bungalows on the southern side of Bradbourne, having parked fifty yards down the road. The river widened at this point; flanked by gently rolling meadows, it would have been a pleasant spot but for the new dual-carriageway slicing through between the town and the river, removing, in the process, most of the gardens from behind the bungalows. Traffic noise was a constant backdrop, and the road had already brought light industry in its wake, with garages, warehouses and workshops strung along much of its length.

'This must be the one,' said Drew, pausing beside a low wrought-iron gate. The bungalow in question looked much the same as all its neighbours: tiny well-tended front garden, net curtains, no hint of individuality. In the road outside a blue-grey Volvo estate car caught Drew's eye. 'Ah!' he said, as one more cog slipped into place. He was pretty certain it was the car that had hovered in the lane during the interment of Gwen Absolon's remains.

'Do you know what you're going to say?' Maggs asked him nervously.

'Not really. Last time I did anything like this, I almost got my head punched in, and I came away feeling it would have been only what I deserved.

But I *think* the line we take is that we're very much afraid the police are about to arrest the wrong man for Gwen's murder, and from things we've learned, we were wondering whether they might not have something to contribute.' He spoke in a rush, marking each phrase with a hand movement, as if conducting an orchestra 'No accusations – just appeal to their better nature. Give them a chance to have their say.'

'Okay,' she agreed, dubiously.

Mildred Grainger opened the door; bewilderment swamped her face as she recognised her visitors. 'Can we come in?' Drew asked. 'It's about the cemetery. We're sorry to disturb you, but we felt a personal call–'

The woman turned away from them, a hand still firmly grasping the half-open door. 'Hubert!' she called, in a tremulous voice. 'Hubert!'

'What's the matter?' He appeared, holding a newspaper in one hand, wearing carpet slippers.

'See who's here.'

The man's expression changed dramatically. His mouth drooped downwards, in unmistakable suffering. 'Oh,' he said. 'They'd better come in, I suppose.'

Drew felt unclean as he stepped into the spotless house, as if he'd brought something filthy into a carefully-preserved sanctum. 'We're very sorry about this,' he heard himself saying weakly. 'We weren't really sure what to do for the best.' He felt Maggs's disbelieving eyes on his face, but avoided looking at her.

'An unusual way in which to accuse somebody of murder,' said Hubert with dignity.

Maggs could not repress a squeal of surprise.

'Hubert!' his wife reproved him gently. 'Nobody mentioned murder.'

'Why else would they be here?' her husband said. He folded the newspaper slowly, and laid it down on the hall table. 'Come into the living room,' he invited. With courtly manners, he gave them each a comfortable chair, before positioning himself by the mantelpiece and his wife on an upholstered stool beside the window.

'We made a terrible mistake,' he began. 'We realised only moments too late that we'd allowed ourselves to be governed by irrational motives. But it was too late, for all that.' Mildred began to weep into a small cotton handkerchief. 'So we did what we could to make amends.'

'By burying her in my field?' Drew supplied. 'Tucking her in nicely, wrapping her in that pretty sheet, letting her keep her necklace.' Another thought occurred to him: 'And you sent that money to the Council, didn't you? You paid for the funeral?'

The Graingers reached for each other, clasping hands in a tableau of mutual responsibility. Both held their heads high. Drew caught a glimpse of the unbreakable link there must be between them. Regardless of the strength of their marriage, of how much they loved each other – by jointly committing murder, they were bound together forever.

'How did you do it?' Maggs burst in, clearly losing patience with the delicate dance being enacted in front of her. 'Did anybody help you?'

'Maggs!' Drew cautioned her.

'You know about Sarah?' Hubert queried, ignoring the girl's questions. 'I assume you do.'

Drew nodded. 'She was your daughter. She was Nathan Slater's girlfriend, and she believed that Nathan's mother hastened his death.'

'She *knew* she did,' interposed Mildred. 'Nathan had told her about an earlier occasion, when his mother tried to poison him with aspirin. He expected that she'd try it again one day.'

'But that isn't proof,' said Drew. 'What exactly happened?'

'He was in hospital with pneumonia. Sarah visited him that afternoon, and he was getting better. He was going home in the next day or so. Then he died – in the evening. Sarah spoke to a nurse, who mentioned that Nathan's mother had brought him some soup. Sarah was convinced it must have had something in it.'

'But there was no evidence? They didn't do a post-mortem?'

Mildred Grainger shook her head. 'Sarah suspected that the Slaters' doctor was involved, and he would have advised her to use something undetectable. He'd have easily persuaded a colleague to sign the papers for a death cer-tificate. She was never in any doubt in her own mind, though.'

'And did Gwen know of her suspicions?'

Mildred shrugged. 'Nathan came here when they were engaged,' she went on. 'We liked him – he was an unusual person. A strong character. And good company, once you got to know him.'

'But hard work for his mother,' Drew suggested. 'He needed a lot of care. And apparently he could be very demanding.'

'True. But she was going to be free of him, when he married Sarah. That's what we could never understand at the time – why did she bring about his death, just as he was leaving her anyway?'

'Sarah said she was so possessive, she couldn't bear him to be with another woman,' Hubert said. 'And we believed that was the truth. Until–'

Drew interrupted. 'Where does Sarah's death fit into this?' he asked, aware of Maggs stirring impatiently again.

'We believed that Gwen had a hand in it,' Mildred took over. 'You see, ever since Nathan died, Sarah had been trying to get in touch with Gwen, to confront her. But you probably know what Gwen was like – a gypsy, always moving around, never in one place for too long. She always seemed to be one step ahead of her. Then Sarah heard via the college grapevine that Gwen was working as a tour guide, running trips to Egypt. I remember she told us what a coincidence it was – she'd always wanted to see Egypt, and it must have seemed too good a chance to miss. We always knew that Sarah was inclined to see things in black and white terms, as most young people are–' she glanced at Maggs. 'She genuinely deplored the Moslem way of doing things. But the tour leader had a responsibility to ensure that nobody in her group made themselves a nuisance. She should have warned Sarah that she was behaving provocatively. Instead, it sounds to us as if she did nothing at all. We believe she was culpably negligent.'

'But hardly responsible for what happened?' Drew said incredulously. 'The man was a funda-mentalist psychopath!'

'We felt that she carried a lot of the blame,' Hubert said mildly. 'She knew the people there, understood the politics and so forth. She could have stopped Sarah. Instead, she just stood back and let our daughter put herself in a highly dangerous situation.'

'But how did you manage it?' Drew burst out, letting curiosity overwhelm him. 'I don't see how–'

The Graingers exchanged another long look, not even pretending to miss Drew's meaning. Hubert looked steadily at the floor, as he told the story.

'Gwen came here, a few months after the shooting. She wanted to ask us to pacify Simon. He was utterly devastated by Sarah's death, you see. And he blamed Gwen, even more than we did. He made awful threats when she visited him after the funeral. Said he'd get his revenge, that she'd ruined his life, and he'd do the same to her. She was obviously terrified that he meant it.'

Mildred laughed from her seat in the window; Drew heard the hint of cruelty, the brief display of satisfaction. 'She never even imagined that we might be feeling the same as Simon,' she said. 'Wasn't that stupid of her? She came to us, with her hair bleached white, calling herself Wendy something, saying she'd been so frightened of him she'd virtually gone into hiding. Would we do something to help her? Get him off her back.

415

Since he was our son-in-law...'

'Of course, we never suspected that Sarah betrayed her suspicions to Gwen about Nathan's death,' Mildred elucidated. 'But we think she told Simon. She told us, of course. She would always confide in her old Mum.' The flash of pride was pathetic.

'We saw red when she tried to turn us against Simon,' said Hubert, a new grimness on his face. 'We sat her down, and tried to make her understand how much we loathed what she'd done – first to Nathan, then to Sarah. Seti was here, too, poor old boy. He looked at her as if he understood the whole thing. And she smelt of garlic or curry. Seti hated spicy smells. She just carried on, thinking about nothing but herself, how she couldn't go back to Egypt after what had happened, how her family had deserted her. Neither of her daughters wanted anything to do with her, because she'd given all her love to Nathan. We had to listen to all that, for what seemed like hours.'

'Then she said she'd report Simon to the police if he didn't stop making threats,' Mildred added. 'She said such a lot of awful things – but not the one thing that could have brought us over to her side. She never once said she was sorry. *Why* didn't she?' The woman wept, a little storm of frustration and regret.

'But – surely, you didn't just *kill* her?' Maggs asked.

'We wanted her to stop talking,' Mildred replied. 'She was pouring everything out. Hubert has quite a temper, I'm afraid. He smacked her – just a slap across the face to make her stop talking. She didn't like that – flew at him like a cat, scratching and pulling his hair. That's when Seti joined in. He'd disliked her from the minute she arrived, and he was always very protective, you see. He bit her on the leg. Caught the femoral artery – she was quite thin – it wasn't very well covered, and she started bleeding. And she just wouldn't stop. The blood kept coming–'

'You're telling us the *dog* killed her?' Maggs blurted. 'You must be joking.'

'We tried to help her! At first, anyway. We pulled her clothes off, and wrapped her in towels, pressing the wound, like a tourniquet. But she kept on talking, threatening us, saying Sarah had deserved to die. Hubert and I just looked at each other, reading each other's minds. Hubert carried her to the bathroom – she was quite weak by then, she'd lost so much blood – and we put her in a warm bath. Do you know – she wasn't wearing any underclothes! That said it all, for me. She didn't deserve to be treated like a civilised person. Anyway, we held her down in the bath, while she bled to death. Right at the end, she said something, though–'

'When it was too late,' Hubert rumbled sadly.

'What did she say?' Drew hardly dared to ask.

'That she truly hadn't arranged Sarah's death, even though she deserved it. That we ought to be murdering Willard, not her. He was behind it all. He'd suggested Sarah pretend to be in love with Nathan, to cover up their affair. We knew, of course, that Sarah had been his student for a couple of years at college, before she changed to nursing. That's where she met Simon. Gwen said Willard had been sleeping with Sarah all the time she was going with Nathan. So when Gwen found out, she'd wanted Nathan dead, to protect him from realising how he'd been betrayed. She said she knew Sarah would never marry him. She said she loved Nathan, that she was the only person in the world who did. She died smiling at our faces, when we realised what we'd done. And knowing she'd poisoned our image of our only daughter – forever.'

'You *believed* her then?' Maggs blurted. 'About Willard and Sarah?'

'A dying woman wouldn't lie,' maintained Hubert.

'She would,' said Drew. 'This particular dying woman would. You see – she was never any good at taking responsibility for her own actions. It was second nature for her to blame other people. I think she would have done it right to the end.'

Both the Graingers were looking at him, the faintest stirrings of hope in their eyes.

'I really think she lied to you,' Drew spelt it out to them. 'And I think your son-in-law could convince you if you asked him.'

'Simon?' queried Mildred. 'We could never mention it to Simon.'

'Believe me,' Drew persisted. 'I'm sure he could set your mind at rest. He was at college with Sarah – right?' Mildred nodded. 'Well, he'd be very likely to know about it if Willard was seducing female students. In Gwen's day – even Genevieve's – such a thing might have gone unremarked, which is probably why Gwen thought it would make a plausible story. But things are very different now. The authorities are always very watchful for inappropriate relationships of that sort.'

'Right!' Maggs endorsed. 'She made the whole thing up. You can see that, can't you?'

'Even if you're right – we still killed her. We're still murderers,' mumbled Hubert.

'That's true.' Drew clasped his hands together, trying to keep a grip on all the new elements he had to absorb. 'But try not to be too hard on yourselves. That was a vicious thing she did, right at the end – poisoning your minds against your daughter.'

'Especially as she'd already tried to turn us against Simon,' said Hubert slowly. 'It was another attempt at the same sort of thing. You know – I think you're right.' He looked at his wife. 'Don't you think so, dear–'

Mildred nodded hesitantly. 'Perhaps,' she said. 'But – Sarah–'

Drew faced her earnestly. 'Sarah died because she was nothing worse than a rather hot-headed girl, unlucky enough to talk to the wrong person about her views, during a holiday she'd wanted for a long time. Simon went too far when he accused Gwen of deliberately causing his wife's death. Look – there's a man called Trevor Goldsworthy, a friend of Gwen's. If we can find him again, he'll tell you more of the background. Admittedly he was fond of Gwen – but he seems well aware of her failings, too.'

'She did kill Nathan,' Maggs said quietly. 'We

should remember that.'

Hubert Grainger turned a paternal smile on her. 'Why, dear? Because it somehow makes it better that Mildred and I killed her? That's a kind thought, but I'm afraid–'

'Two wrongs don't make a right,' supplied Mildred.

'But we'll probably never know precisely why she killed her own son,' concluded Drew. 'Genevieve and Dr Jarvis both believe it was a selfish wish to escape from the burden of his care. But neither of them mentioned his engagement to Sarah. I suppose your theory could be right – that she was essentially very possessive, and couldn't bear Sarah to have him.'

'The engagement was a secret,' Mildred disclosed. 'He only told his mother about it a few days before he died.'

'There you are then!' Maggs said. 'That clinches it.'

Drew shook his head. 'We'll never really know,' he repeated. 'And after all this time, I don't think it matters too much – do you?'

Nobody answered. For several moments, the four of them were silent. Mildred spoke first.

'You know, I don't think Gwen was sorry to die. I realise it sounds like an excuse, but I really do believe she was glad about it at the end. She didn't suffer, we did our best about that. She was getting old, and life obviously wasn't very much fun any more. And somehow – she seemed to have lost her nerve. She was in such a state that day. Nothing like the old Gwen we'd known years before.'

Hubert joined in. 'She was at the end of her tether.'

Drew couldn't help but agree. He thought of the soulless little bedsit, the estrangement from her family, the damage done to her travel business by the Saqqara shooting. Combined with the guilt and fear that Dr Jarvis had described, and the sad figure of Trevor – apparently her only concerned friend – the picture was of a woman with nowhere to go but down.

'The police thought it was the body of a vagrant,' he said. 'Maybe, when it comes to it, they weren't too far wrong, after all.'

Maggs stirred restlessly, evidently thinking they'd heard the whole story and could now go. But Mildred hadn't finished.

'We put her in one of my dresses,' she said. 'Then we waited a whole day, while we tried to decide what to do with her. The longest Sunday of our lives, it was. The local paper had reported on your field, how you were applying for planning permission for an alternative burial ground, with trees and flowers and everything natural – and we thought it seemed right for her. It didn't make what we'd done seem so bad, somehow, if we gave her a proper burial. She was very light to carry. And there wasn't anybody about. I sat in the car and Hubert carried her up the field. He's strong as an ox, you know. It only took him an hour to dig a grave and lay her in it.'

'Were you scared when the train stopped?' Maggs asked. 'You must have known people could see you.'

The Graingers exchanged bewildered glances.

'There wasn't any train,' Hubert said. 'We waited until past midnight – long after the trains stop running.'

'And it was Sunday the thirteenth, not Saturday the twelfth,' said Drew slowly. 'And there was only one of you.' He stared crazily at Maggs. 'Caroline Kennett didn't see it, after all. Different field, different day.'

Maggs stared back. 'So what did she see?' she asked, one eyebrow raised.

'Someone burying a sheep, or a cow they knew had BSE,' Drew guessed. 'Breaking regulations to save themselves a lot of bother. Happens all the time these days.' So much for coincidence, he muttered to himself.

CHAPTER TWENTY

It was with difficulty that Drew quelled his triumph and prepared himself for the funeral of Vicky Gardner's mother the next day. He had sat with Maggs and Karen late into the previous evening, discussing the death of Gwen Absolon and all its implications. 'The dog did it,' said Karen, unambiguously. 'And the dog is dead. No more to be done.'

'Not true, I'm afraid,' Drew said. 'I'm going to the police as soon as I've done the funeral, and the Graingers are coming with me. They *want* to. They can't go on as they are – especially not now that it's all come out. In one way, of course, they're relieved – at least their daughter has been restored in their eyes, and their initial assessment of Gwen confirmed. But after today, they'll be even more nervous of being caught out. They couldn't stand all the lies and subterfuge any longer.'

'What'll happen to them?'

'They'll plead guilty, with mitigating circumstances. They might even try for a plea of manslaughter. But there's no saying what the sentence will be. They're not all that old – she's barely sixty. They seem to be prepared for the worst.'

'Which is?'

'Six or seven years in prison,' he said glumly.

'And you?' put in Maggs. 'What'll happen to you?'

'I'll be okay,' he said bravely. 'No, really,' he insisted, at their sceptical expressions. 'There's a fair chance that nobody will think to accuse me of anything. I'm the public-spirited citizen, with nagging suspicions, who devoted his own time to investigating an unsolved murder. Nothing like enough evidence to bother the police with, until a series of happy coincidences that led me to the answer.' He grinned. 'Pretty nearly true, when you think about it.'

'So, no mention of the Slaters?' queried Karen.

'Absolutely no mention of the Slaters,' said Drew firmly.

Vicky and Nigel Gardner met him in the waiting room at the crematorium. He shook hands with them, and assured them that everything would go smoothly. Unlike Harold Hankey's funeral, for this one, Drew was to fill the time all on his own. He warned the Gardners that he was intending to include some lengthy spells of silence, to allow the mourners to examine their own thoughts and feelings. A bit risky he knew, but he thought it would be all right.

It was more than all right. Drew spoke for five minutes, initially, about the inevitability of death making no real difference to the sense of shock and outrage every time it happened. He spoke of the ripples spreading out to all who knew the person now gone. He said much that he thought was obvious, and a few things he believed might strike his listeners as original. He spoke of life as a responsibility, to be used with integrity, in the certain knowledge that it could only end in death. He mentioned the need for courage. He held in his mind, throughout the entire twenty minutes, an image of Genevieve and Willard Slater, flanked by Nathan and Sarah and Dr Jarvis. And of Gwen Absolon, dying full of fear and hatred.

He had been warned by Desmond that there was a following cremation, and that any over-running would cause problems. Two minutes before the end of his allotted time, he broke a silence by saying very much the same words as he had done for Harold Hankey. 'And now we say goodbye to Frances for the very last time. As the curtains close around her coffin, we might imagine her going on her last journey, into the peaceful conclusion of her life. Each in his or her own way must let go, and let her make this journey alone.'

Permitting Vicky Gardner a moment of un-restrained weeping, he activated the motorised curtain, as well as the CD player, which quietly filled the air with an innocuous murmur of harp and bell music, subtly suggesting other realms, where all was peace.

Ushering the twenty or thirty people outside was the usual unpredictable affair, some remain-ing sitting just that bit too long, others standing to stare one last time at the closed curtain. Drew allowed himself a moment's self-congratulation at having once again rendered a cremation just about as meaningful as it could ever hope to be.

Outside at last, he stood aside as little groups of

people chatted amongst themselves. Glancing at the far end of the building, where another funeral was preparing to begin, he saw Daphne Plant. Too late, she looked away. Without thinking, he trotted over to her, risking a blatant disruption to the funeral she was obviously about to conduct.

'Not now!' she hissed at him, alarm filling her face and voice.

'This won't take a minute,' he said. 'I just want to tell you I know exactly what you've been doing to try to sabotage my business. And to tell you that if there's a hint of any more trouble I'll go first to the police and then to the papers.'

'Drew!' she snapped. 'Be quiet and listen. This isn't public knowledge yet – but you can be the first to know. I'm selling Plant's to SCI – the American funeral people. I'm signing the papers next week. So I don't care what you do any more. I wash my hands of the whole business.'

He gaped at her. Those three simple letters spelt the enemy, almost the devil, to family-owned British funeral directors. Selling out to them was a cowardly betrayal, or greedy self-interest.

'Then to hell with you,' he said furiously, and turned back to his own almost-concluded funeral.

Driving home, he thought about the implications of what Daphne had told him. It would present the local population with an even starker choice than before. Prices would rise, with funerals ever more slickly packaged. Vulnerable bereaved people would be manipulated into spending more than they wanted to on flamboyant memorials and elaborate coffins. Any-body wanting something different – keeping their dead relative at home for the night before the funeral, or coming in to dress them – would be firmly discouraged. It would be nothing but a conveyor belt.

And Drew could capitalise on this, if he could keep his nerve and face down the mighty power of American finance. He could establish a repu-tation for plain speaking, simplicity, sincerity. He might, if luck was with him, turn Daphne's treachery to his own advantage. He was certainly going to try.

'Plain speaking?' Maggs queried, when he told her the news, along with his thoughts on the subject. 'Is that what I've been listening to for the past six weeks?'

Drew blushed. 'That was a means to an end,' he told her. 'It all came out right, didn't it?'

'Lucky for you,' she sniped. Then she softened. 'Lucky for me as well, actually.'

'How d'you mean?'

'Stuart,' she said simply. 'He's asked me to go out with him. It's brilliant, the way everything's worked out. His Mum's going to take the baby on, without any legal adoption or anything, but just as a sort of long-term foster mother. They'll make sure she knows who her real parents are, when she's old enough. And Stuart's going to be staying around for a while.'

'So something good has come of this,' Drew said. 'Assuming you and he don't fight and cause each other more misery than happiness.'

'Don't worry about that,' she said smugly. 'And I promise never to mention Genevieve in your hearing ever again. She's done enough damage as it is.'

He looked narrowly at her, appalled at the idea that she might know exactly how he'd felt. 'Do you think Karen knew?' he whispered.

'Drew – you're not very good at hiding things,' she said kindly. 'But between us, we'll keep you up to the mark. Now, let's lock up and you can go and be a good husband for a change.'

Karen was in the sitting room, with Stephanie watching the television beside her. She was slowly counting stitches on the everlasting piece of turquoise knitting she'd started so many months ago. She looked up at him and giggled. 'If I'm quick,' she said, 'it might just be ready for the next one.'

This Large Print Book for the partially sighted, who cannot read normal print, is published under the auspices of

THE ULVERSCROFT FOUNDATION